Silicon Strike

Don DeBon

Silicon Strike

Soulmates III

Don DeBon

First Printing
Copyright © 2020 Don DeBon

ISBN 978-1-948819-05-3
ISBN 978-1-948819-04-6 **(e-book)**

Contents

High above the Earth, the *Defiant* moved closer towards a tiny Celloid remnant. Energy flowed from the central power core, down the many connections, and into the closest carbine cannon's energy reserves. Power built until it shot forward, ramming into the focusing lens and released a microsecond later. The energy blast reached out and hit its target obliterating it.

Deven floated over and looked out the *Defiant's* large window at the stars beyond. "Good shooting, Miles."

Miles' bridge camera turned towards Deven. "Thank you Deven. There are many more such remnants left and I estimate at our current rate we will have them cleared in less than four days."

Deven nodded. "Good, way ahead of schedule. And the *Phoenix's* progress?"

Miles' camera iris contracted, then expanded again. "The *Phoenix's* progress is actually ahead of ours. Minerva is challenging me on who can complete the task first. I suspect she only did so considering most of the Celliods were destroyed on this side of the planet instead of the one she is clearing."

Deven laughed. "So a little rivalry between mother and

son?"

Miles' camera moved back and forth. "Negative. Even though she is the Nexus and did technically build me, I do not consider her my mother. My programs and personality developed on my own. She did not create my entire matrix."

"Maybe not, but then again neither does a human mother with their son either. You will have to admit, she did give you a start then let you develop."

Miles' camera iris narrowed again. "You may have a point. However, that was not by intent. If I had not taken action, she would have had my personality purged. Therefore, I still refuse to call her 'Mom'.

Deven pushed off the hull and sailed back towards his chair. With a deft motion, he flipped into it and pushed several keys on his console. Data from several intensive scans flashed across the screen. Several lines were highlighted in red. "I see two more not far from our port side. I think they are in range. Life scan indicates zero as usual, but I will not take the chance any of these bits could germinate if given the chance."

"I concur. Most of these ruminates are from the Celloid *Mothership*. The other ships having far less mass, not much survived."

"But we have to be sure," Galina said as she floated onto the bridge.

Miles' camera turned towards her. "Of course. I believe we have established that. Nothing will escape me."

Galina floated over and into her chair. "What do you mean you? Don't you mean us?" She folded her arms.

"Of course. I am a part of 'us'."

Galina rolled her eyes. "Deven? Why is our gravity plating still off? I thought Leon fixed it?"

Deven sighed. "He did, but then found some other conflict

with another system, and he had to shut it off for now. He promised it would be back online in an hour."

"Good. I couldn't believe I woke up to floating above my bed!" She turned towards Miles and pointed a finger at the lens. "And if you make one comment about me being possessed, I will rip you off of the wall!"

Miles' iris shrank to half its normal size for a full two seconds before expanding again. "I would not even think of making such a reference."

"Yeah, right." Galina snorted.

Deven smiled. "I'm surprised you didn't call down on the intercom, or go see Leon yourself?"

"Astronaut I am *not*," Galina growled.

"You and Otis."

"Yeah, he is even worse than me in Zero-G. Where is our resident cracker, anyway?"

"Oh I don't know, I think he is better than you. And he is still aboard the *Phoenix*."

Galina frowned. "Still? Thought he modified his truck for space-worthiness and was coming back?"

"Apparently, that bot he picked up begged him to stay for some reason."

Galina laughed. "That cleaning bot? I knew he had a soft spot for it. But what about Gregory? I thought he was helping Leon? Shouldn't he have the plating fixed by now with his help?"

Miles' camera turned towards Galina. "While he often assists Leon, by utilizing Gregory's abilities on the weapons, we have decreased the mission time by a large factor."

Galina leaned back in her chair and fought not to float off of it. "A large factor? What, no details?"

"As Deven and others have requested, such details when

not needed, only serve the purpose of –as has been said to me– 'filling time'."

"Wasting time, I think is what we said."

Miles' iris contracted and expanded again. "I do not believe it is a waste. Therefore, that is your opinion, not mine."

Galina rolled her eyes. "You dumb bot I–"

Deven held up his hand. "Galina, Miles, that is enough. I know everyone is still on edge and I promised some R&R. But we must do this first. Afterwards, we will all have some downtime."

"But Deven, I do not need 'downtime'," Miles said.

"Perhaps you don't, but we certainly do. And to be honest, I wonder about you as well. You are more human than you care to admit."

"Perhaps," Miles said. Another screen adjacent to Deven's lit up with targeting information. "I have located two more targets, they will be in range in three minutes."

"Good, proceed." Deven floated out of his chair and headed towards the hatch.

"Where are you going?" Galina said.

"Aleshia is down in our cabin. While she is a very understanding woman, she is not happy we are up here and not in Bermuda like we planned."

"Yeah, don't want to make that girl mad, that is for sure." Galina grinned.

Deven chuckled. "I don't intend to." He floated off of the bridge and towards the cabins.

Aleshia floated above the small bed, almost touching the ceiling before reaching out with her mind to give a gentle push to settle back on the bed. While she knew they had to make sure every bit of the Celloid ships were destroyed, she didn't get to finish her honeymoon ... again. Was this the third time? She had lost track. Aleshia remembered Leon coming down a few hours after they had arrived to tell them Miles had found very small remnants of Celloid that had survived the *Mothership's* explosion. And while they appeared dead, no one wanted to take the chance. Everyone of those bits had to be nothing but burnt dust.

But that meant their honeymoon had to be postponed ... again. If Deven wasn't her soulmate, she would have told him he wasn't worth it. No, that was not true. He is worth it, and so much more. But is it so much to ask to have a little time with your husband on your honeymoon?

Deven floated in with a grin that could swallow a horse. "Hello there."

"Don't bother with that look. I'm still mad at you."

"Why? You know we had to make sure nothing of the Celloids survived."

Aleshia pushed herself off of the bed, floated to a vertical position, and folded her arms. "Yes, I know."

"Then why are you mad?"

"Because you don't have to be on the bridge! Galina and Miles can take care of this! We could be in Bermuda enjoying our honeymoon! Instead, we are up here in the cold of space, floating around while carbine cannons fire every few minutes!"

"Well ... we won't be floating around for long, Leon–"

"Don't try that with me, buster! The floating around is just the icing on the cake."

Deven tried to float over to kiss her, but Aleshia floated away, and he ended up kissing a bulkhead.

"And now you are trying to make out with a bulkhead instead of me. Humph!"

Deven wiped his lips. "You were the one that moved."

Aleshia smiled. "I know that part, I was just pretending to be mad at that."

"Is there anyway I can make it up to you?"

"Sure, let's go back to Bermuda and leave everyone else to take care of the Celloids. They're dead after all. It is not like they are going to attack or anything."

Deven sighed. "But I should be here."

"Maybe you should, but you don't have to. Not now. If anything terrible happens, they can contact you."

Deven's one eyebrow went up. "You will let me take my data tab?"

Aleshia bit her bottom lip and sighed. "Yes, if you promise to only look at it if someone calls. Deal?"

"Deal. I will–"

The intercom near the door crackled. "Deven? I hate to interrupt, but you are needed on the bridge," Miles' smooth voice came through a background of static.

Deven hit the intercom. "Sounds like Leon got these going again, but they still need work."

"Affirmative. The gravity plating will be active again in a few moments as well. While it will be a gradual increase, prepare yourselves." The intercom clicked off.

"Well, it must be something big, or they wouldn't have called. I guess we should go up there."

Aleshia blinked. "We?"

"You think I am going to leave you down here to come up with new ways of tearing me limb from limb? No way." Deven grinned.

"Hey, I'm not that bad."

Deven's grin widened. "I beg to differ." He reached out, looped his arm through hers, spun her around into his arms and planted his lips on hers for a long passionate kiss. It was almost a minute before he pulled away. By this time their feet were touching the floor as the gravity increased and Aleshia smiled at him. "Trust me, we will find out what they want, and then head down to Bermuda. Okay?"

"Okay. But I hope you know it is not wise to break a promise to a redhead."

He gave her a final squeeze before taking her hand. "Oh, I know. I wouldn't dream of doing that."

Aleshia smiled. "Good."

A few moments later, Deven and Aleshia arrived on the bridge of the *Defiant*. He looked around the room to see Gregory and Leon sitting, waiting for them. "What's so important?"

Leon smiled. "We have a problem."

"We have a load of them, and we are working on them. That is nothing new."

Galina shook her head. "No, this is new. Miles?"

Miles' camera turned towards Galina. "Thank you, Galina." He turned towards Deven. "As we have been destroying the remnants of the Celloids I have been working on increasing the scanning range of the *Defiant's* systems."

Deven nodded. "Yes, and I told you it was a waste of time and not to bother."

Gregory folded his arms. "It would appear it wasn't."

Aleshia cocked her head. "What did you find?"

Miles' camera turned. "A larger section of the Celloid *Mothership* survived destruction and is heading away from us."

"What? It survived and still has the ability to transverse space?"

Miles' camera turned back and forth. "Negative. While I cannot be certain at this range, it appears to be as lifeless as the other remnants, only larger."

"Can we contact the Lytherians to deal with it?"

"Nope. They are still rebuilding their fleet and are in the outer solar system, taking in asteroids for material. Our communications array can't reach that far. Aleshia could contact them, if the telepathic chair was still functional," Galina said.

"Not to mention it is on the *Phoenix* and I'm here," Aleshia said.

"Yes. I can't image why they didn't leave us a way to communicate with them," Gregory said.

Deven walked across the bridge and sat in his chair. "No one anticipated this. We destroyed the Celloids. Why would they be needed? Not to mention they had their hands full trying to patch their ships together enough to warp to jump to the asteroid belt."

Leon's one eye narrowed for a second as the side of his face contracted, then released. "No kidding. From what I gathered when I talked with Dakarth, their chief engineer, everything was a mess. I'm surprised they managed to get any of the fleet to survive a space-jump."

Aleshia sat down next to Deven as her eyes darted around the room. "So what are we going to do? Can we reach this fragment on our own?"

Miles' camera turned. "Affirmative. The modifications the Lytherians made to the *Defiant* makes it possible to reach it if we leave in the next hour. Any longer than that, and it may go beyond the range of the *Defiant's* safe return."

Leon nodded. "I'm sure we can get to it. Getting back may be the problem though."

Deven cocked his head. "Why?"

"Because this ship was never designed for space. While the Lytherians have given us that ability, it was never thought we were going to make a long journey into space. At least not yet. We have enough food and water for a month, but air is the question."

Galina folded her arms. "I thought the Lytherians gave us a system for that?"

"They did, but it's not designed to be a long-term solution. It needs recharging on a regular basis. After about five days, it will need to recharge for at least seven hours."

"This is just ducky, we can get there and destroy it, but might run out of air before we can get back home?" Galina grumbled.

"Possibly even sooner."

Deven rubbed his forehead. "Why sooner?"

"Well, we have been in orbit now for a while using the system. That will take time off of its full charge. But I think I can tweak it to last until we get there."

Galina jumped out of her chair. "You *think?*"

"Yes, there are certain protocols I can use that will–"

"Okay, so we might be able to get there, but there is a chance we won't and getting home is out of the question. I know I have said it before but this time I have proof: this is *insane!*"

Deven stood up. "I don't see that we have a choice. If that remnant is in any way viable, we must destroy it. We can't take the risk."

"I know that, but is it worth all of our deaths?"

"Well, as I said, I *might* be able to figure something out en route," Leon said.

"To me that sounds like one mighty big *if.*"

Miles' camera turned towards Deven. "If I may offer a suggestion. I can take on this mission myself. The lack of oxygen will not affect me. I have full access to the necessary systems aboard the *Defiant*. Piloting the ship there, destroying the target, and returning is not a problem. You can transfer to the *Phoenix* during this mission."

Deven shook his head. "No Miles. While I don't doubt your abilities, the *Defiant* is not in perfect working order. If something fails, you will not be able to repair it, and we will lose both the ship and you."

Galina folded her arms as she fell back into her chair. "Better him then all of us." Her eyes grew wide as she shot out of the chair. "Wait a second! Why not send the *Phoenix*? Minerva can do the same thing."

Leon shook his head. "The *Phoenix's* engines aren't as big as ours. She couldn't reach it before it left the solar system, or she ran out of power."

Deven sighed. "Not to mention, we need her to help restart all the manufacturing plants and rebuild Earth's defenses. Without her help, it will take years."

Aleshia sat back in her chair. "Looks like we are stuck."

Deven turned towards her. "We might be, but you are heading to the *Phoenix* along with everyone else. I will stay with Leon and deal with any problems."

Aleshia's eyes widened. "No way! I am not letting you go without me!"

"You heard Leon, we may not make it back. I can't let that happen to you too."

"And if you think I can let it happen to you, then you have another thing coming!"

Deven raised out of his chair as though an invisible hand

had pulled him from the seat and held him high above near the ceiling. "Aleshia?"

"Just try to get me off of this bucket. The only way I am leaving is if you are too." She waved her hand and Deven lowered back into his chair, but when he was several inches from touching the invisible force disappeared, and he landed with a firm thud.

"Okay, I get the point."

Aleshia grinned. "Good, I thought you might."

"Miles, contact the *Phoenix* and let Minerva know we need a rendezvous as fast as possible."

Miles' camera turned as they felt a jolt from the *Defiant's* powerful engines. "I have anticipated your request and we will rendezvous in fifteen minutes."

"Miles! I could have done that," Galina snorted.

"Of course, but our departure window is very close," Miles said.

Deven stood up. "Galina, I want you to get everyone moved over to the *Phoenix*. I know we only have a skeleton crew at the moment, but it will still take time with only the one truck capable of space flight."

Miles' camera turned. "More vehicles will be at your disposal. Our rendezvous with the *Phoenix*, while still very high, is inside the atmosphere."

"Good, that will make things easier. Let's get going people, we're on the clock."

Aboard the *Phoenix* Otis gripped the ladder as he felt the jolt of the ship jumping into overdrive. "What in the world?" He climbed as fast as he could and keyed in the sequence for the bridge hatch to open. "Minerva? What in the world is going on?" he said as soon as his head was through the hatch.

On the large screen, near the back of the bridge, a woman with long blonde hair turned towards him. Once, she was the Nexus of the entire Mechand system consisting of millions and millions of units and vehicles. Now only the *Phoenix* remained, the last of her carriers and the Mechands within the few remaining working units on the whole planet. "We are en route to rendezvous with the *Defiant* in fifteen minutes," Minerva said.

"Why? Have we finished destroying all the Celloid remnants?"

Minerva shook her head. "No, they need us to offload everyone aboard to–"

"What! Is the *Defiant* going down?"

She shook her head again and smiled. "If you would let me finish, I was going to say they are offloading everyone, so they can go after a large section of Celloid that is headed off into deep space."

Otis' eyes widened as he slumped into a hard metal chair. Mechand ships were never designed for human comforts, even if they were designed around the human shape. "Then we didn't get them all."

"No, from what Miles' has been able to determine, this is another fragment. The only difference is the size, and that it is headed away from the planet at a high rate of speed."

"It's as dead as the others?"

Minerva nodded. "As far as we can tell. But Deven does not want to take the chance. The *Defiant* is going after it once we take aboard everyone we can."

On the *Defiant's* bridge, Deven watched the *Phoenix* approach. "The *Phoenix* will arrive in less than two minutes," Miles said.

"Good." He tapped the nearby intercom on the wall. "Galina? What's our status?"

Down in the main hanger, Galina slapped the closest intercom. "As ready as we'll ever be. I have everyone shoehorned into three vehicles. Once they are out of the bay, we can leave."

"Why only three? We have more that can function at this altitude."

"Of course, but the faster we head off the more air we have. The more vehicles we launch, the longer we sit here."

Deven's eyebrows met. "What is all this 'we' stuff? I thought you were against this and leaving?"

"I am! I think you are all insane! But you might need my piloting skills. While Miles is good, I can do better. I guess some of Leon's insanity has rubbed off on me."

Deven chuckled. "I guess so. Well, I'm thankful you are staying. Once everyone is launched get back up here."

"Will do," Galina said as the intercom clicked off.

Otis continued making last-minute changes to his truck when the console on his dash flipped up to show Minerva's face. "Otis? I have to open the bay doors in two minutes. You must be inside your truck or out of the bay at that point."

Otis grumbled something in audible then raised his voice. "Don't you think I know that? I only have one more thing to do, will only take a minute."

"It had better. The *Defiant* can not afford any delays." The screen flashed as her image disappeared a microsecond later.

"Doesn't she understand I know this machine inside and out? If I say it will only take a minute, it will only take a minute," Otis muttered. He pulled at the wrench in his hand, tightening the last bolt in a long row.

Behind him he heard a beep and Otis jumped as turned around to see a Mechand with wheels instead of legs, no head but a decent sized torso and two long arms. A hopper trailed behind it. "Geez bot, you scared me." He peered into the optics mounted in the torso, they didn't look as they usually did. "What's wrong?"

The Mechand beeped as he pointed to the truck, then to the hanger doors.

"Yes, I am going over to the *Defiant*."

The Mechand beeped again and his optics drifted down, making them very dark.

"I'm not going away forever, I will be back."

The Mechand gave a quiet beep, and he pointed to the back of Otis' truck.

Otis shook his head. "No, you can't come too. Minerva needs you here, and I don't have anything to recharge you aboard the *Defiant*."

The Mechand gave a mournful beep as his shoulders slumped. He moved closer and wrapped Otis in a tight hug.

"Nothing is going to happen to me, little friend. I promise."

Another beep that almost sounded like a wail.

The large speakers mounted in the ceiling came to life. "Warning: hanger bay opening in thirty seconds. Warning: hanger bay opening in thirty seconds. All Mechands prepare."

"Bot! Let me go! I need to get into the truck!"

The Mechand gave a quiet, reverberating whine that resembled a child's cry.

"Okay, okay! I will stay! Now let me go before I suffocate!"

The Mechand gave four high-pitched beeps, picked Otis up by his shoulders, extended his arms and rotated them to flip Otis over the metal torso, placing him into the hopper. Before Otis' feet touched the bottom of the hopper the Mechand's rubber wheels squealed as they headed towards the back of the hanger, leaving melted rubber lines on the deck plates.

The inner hanger doors began to close.

"Bot! Stop! Take me back! We don't have enough time."

The Mechand didn't listen and increased his speed. They shot through the large doors half a second before they closed and the outer doors began to open. Icy winds tore through the hangar as the first of the *Defiant's* vehicles arrived.

Galina watched as the last vehicle, an old battered truck with several people riding in the back wearing oxygen masks and thermal gear, took off and passed through the hanger bay doors. She hit the nearby intercom. "That's the last of them. Transfer complete, Minerva can take them down the rest of the way. I'm closing the bay doors now. We can leave right after."

Up on the bridge, Deven rubbed his chin. "That was fast. How did you do it so quickly? Even with a skeleton crew it should have taken another ten minutes at least."

"I packed them in like a circus clown car we have seen in old vids. I even put several in the back area of the trucks."

"What? We are too high up for that."

"Don't worry they were wearing full Arctic encounter suits and oxygen masks. They will be fine. Took all of our masks though."

Deven's eyes narrowed, and his throat tightened. "Don't you think that was more than a little unwise? Lack of enough oxygen is one of our major concerns."

"Believe me, I am well aware of that. However, I talked with Leon, and he didn't think they would have made any real difference. A few hours here or there is all if he can't come up with some other way to recharge the atmosphere generator. Even with them, we wouldn't be making it back. But the faster we get going, the more likely we will catch that chunk of Celloid and make it back."

Deven gritted his teeth. "I wish you asked me first."

"Wouldn't have made any difference, and you know it. Bay closed and locked, I'm on my way up to the bridge." The intercom clicked off.

On the bridge, Miles' camera swiveled towards Deven. "Shall I activate the main engines?"

Deven gazed out the window at the *Phoenix* and the Earth turning below. "Yes. Let's get going. But make sure everyone is up here before you start the main drive."

"Acknowledged, power to the hover systems increased." The glow beneath the *Defiant* grew brighter as the hover engines pushed against Earth's gravity. "All systems responding as expected. Estimated time until atmosphere exit: one minute thirty seconds."

Deven toggled the intercom. "Everyone get up here we will be in position for a full drive activation in less than a minute."

Leon's voice came through the speaker. "Gregory and I will stay down here in engineering, just in case. We have never done this before."

"You think there will be a problem?"

"Nope, but Leon will feel better being closer to the engines. And so will I," Gregory said.

"Fine with me," Deven said as the intercom clicked off.

Galina appeared in the hatchway, followed by Aleshia. "Everything is ready down below." She sat down at her console and griped the flight controls.

Aleshia smiled as she sat down next to Deven. "Yes, I checked the mess and the cabins. Everything is locked down."

"Good." Deven glanced towards the hatch. "Where is Otis? I thought he was coming aboard?"

Galina chuckled. "Minerva told me he changed his mind. Or rather that cleaning bot did."

Deven's one eyebrow went up. "The cleaning bot changed his mind?"

"That's what she said. I'm going to get the full scoop when we get back. It has *got* to be a good one."

Deven smiled. "More optimistic about our returning?"

"Heck no, I'm trying not to think about it."

Miles' camera pivoted towards Deven. "We have reached the proper location. Overdrive systems are ready."

"Galina? Let's go."

Galina smiled. "You got it." She hit the intercom. "Full power overdrive in five seconds. Hang on everyone."

"We're ready," Leon said before the intercom clicked off.

"Here we go." Galina punched a button and power flowed into the massive main engines at the rear of the *Defiant*. They glowed brighter and brighter as a bubble of energy formed around the ship. A second later the ship leapt into overdrive leaving streaks of energy where the engines were a millisecond second before.

"All engines responding. Speed is increasing. At the current rate of increase, we will reach the fragment in four days three hours," Miles said.

"Does that take in to consideration the time to decelerate as well?" Deven asked.

"Of course. I would never neglect such a vital part of the equation," Miles said.

Deven rolled his eyes. "Of course Miles. Galina, how is she responding?"

Galina gripped the controls. "If I didn't know better, I would say we were flying through a skyway back on Earth. I will keep her on manual for a couple of hours to make sure, then I will let the Auto-Nav take over."

Miles' camera turned. "You mean me."

"No, I said the ship's Auto-Nav."

"But I am the *Defiant*," Miles said.

"Miles, you might be in the *Defiant*, but you are not her. You are separate," Deven said.

Miles' camera turned towards Deven and his iris contracted for a second. "Of course. While I remember my original body, and wish to return to it when Leon has repaired it, being a part of the *Defiant* has many advantages. To the point that I sometimes forget the differences. It won't happen again."

"That's okay Miles. We all understand how you feel," Aleshia said.

"I cannot comprehend how you could, but if you say so, I am honored," Miles said.

The intercom crackled as Leon's voice came through. "You can push the engines to one hundred-twenty percent of maximum."

Galina blinked. "Are you sure?"

"I have to concur, this sounds very ill-advised," Miles said.

"Guys don't worry. These Lytherian enhanced engines can take more than that. I have been through them several times and I'm sure they will hold."

"Yeah, trust us. These things are amazing," Gregory said.

Galina frowned. "And how would you know?"

Gregory laughed. "Because Leon said so."

"You do have a point," Galina chuckled shaking her head then glanced over towards Deven. "Deven?"

Deven nodded. "Go for it, one hundred-twenty percent but nothing more."

Miles' camera swiveled. "Acknowledged, power increased. Engines continue to operate within normal parameters."

"See? What did I tell you?" Leon's voice came through the intercom.

"Based on our new rate of speed, we will now arrive two days ahead of the original estimate," Miles said.

Aleshia bit her cheek. "But still not enough to make it back before our air runs out?"

Miles' camera lowered. "That is correct."

"Guys, trust me. I will figure out something before we get that far. Speaking of, we need to get back to work on that problem. Will let you know when we have a solution." The intercom clicked off.

"I sure hope he is right," Aleshia said.

— 3 —

Odell Halburn stood silent as the elevator continued up. It beeped when he arrived at the floor of the World Council's audience hall. The doors swooshed open to reveal a tall, overly muscled man in a black uniform. The UN logo on still on his right chest pocket. *Well Lavine still didn't get that changed yet. Perhaps, he won't be that hard on me.* Halburn swallowed hard. *Of course not, I only destroyed his entire fleet he had built in secret and the seat of his power. Why he would be mad?*

The man looked down at Halburn. "Follow me sir, they are waiting for you." He turned on his heel and started walking towards the council chambers. Halburn followed, but each step became more difficult, until he almost turned around and ran for the elevator. If they hadn't reached the door at the other end, and he was sure the man would have grabbed him quicker than a frog can snatch a fly, he would have.

The man opened the door and pointed towards the room within. Halburn gulped and stepped inside. The door closed behind him, and he blinked in the dark room, trying to see.

Halfway within the spacious room sat a crescent-shaped table with various men and women sitting around it, all dressed in long flowing robes. One of them stood. "Commander Halburn, so good of you to join us. Please come in."

Halburn looked up and down the row of faces, but he didn't see Scott Lavine among them. Even more strange, the central chair where Lavine usually sat remained vacant. "Thank you, it is honor to be here." He took several quick steps until he was standing in front of the council.

Iawi Burns, the man that had stood, smiled. "We are very pleased to hear that. We would like to congratulate you on your outstanding work to date."

Halburn blinked. "Sir?"

Iawi tilted his head. "Is there a problem?"

"To be honest, I am wondering the real reason I am here. I very much doubt you have spent all the effort to find and bring me here only to congratulate me for destroying your entire fleet."

Iawi smiled, as did everyone else on the council. "That is true. We do have more to discuss. And while the fleet was destroyed, you also saved the planet. This makes it, I believe the phrase 'well worth the price of admission' fits the situation."

"Perhaps sir, but I can't imagine you are going to give me a medal for it."

Several people laughed, and even Iawi chuckled. "No, you are also correct about that."

"I thought so, so can we–"

"We intend to do more than give you a medal."

Halburn blinked. "Excuse me, sir?"

"First, Odell, can you please stop calling me 'sir'? Iawi is fine. And if we are going to be working together I think using our first names is prudent, don't you?"

Odell Halburn moved his jaw several times before any

words came out. "Working together? You mean I am not fired?"

They all laughed again. "Odell, would we fire someone that we want to pin a medal on? Come now, you must think that would be quite foolish?"

"Yes sir, er Iawi, it does sound rather conflicting. But if you will excuse my caution, Chairman Lavine gave me a great deal of conflicting situations or *worse*."

Iawi and most of the members of the council's eyes narrowed and their expressions hardened. "Please do not refer to Scott Lavine as Chairman. He is no longer of any consequence, nor is he a member of this Council and does not deserve such respect."

Odell Halburn blinked and leaned forward while trying not to. "He is no longer on the council? How? What happened?"

Iawi smiled. "One thing at a time. That is correct, he is no longer on the council or even allowed on the grounds. As for what happened, we removed him. I am sure you are aware of his attempt to increase his power, and the building of the entire fleet was unknown to us. While this turned out to be a good situation in the end, his motives were not and it is not something we can dismiss."

"I understand. But sir–"

Iawi frowned.

"I'm sorry, Iawi, I have noticed the empty chair. I assume one of you have been picked to fill the position of Chairman. As I understand protocol, that would have been done before I arrived. Yet the chair sits vacant. Therefore, what is going on?"

Smiles rolled around the council like a great wave. "That is simple. We would like you to take that position."

"What!" Halburn swallowed hard and composed himself.

"My apologies, my ears must be deceiving me, I could have sworn you asked me to become Chairman."

Iawi's smile broadened. "That is correct."

"Me? Why me? I am not qualified to lead the World Council."

"Why you? Well, you did save the world, did you not? We all have seen what you have done time and time again, risking your life to save others. Your leadership of the fleet was exemplary and your selfless acts say more about you than you know."

Halburn stiffened. "I was only doing my duty. Doing what needed to be done."

"Yes, you did. And do you think Lavine would have done the same in a similar situation? I can answer that for you: no. He would have turned tail and ran, or commanded everyone to ram the Celloids while he hopped into a fighter and escaped. You did none of these things. You took care of your crew, got them out of harm's way first, then piloted your ship into the last Celloid when there was no other way. This is the kind of man we want to lead us."

"But I didn't do these things alone. Deven, Aleshia, his team, ships, and heck even The Nexus deserve more credit than I."

"If it would make you feel any better, we would prefer Deven to you."

Halburn chuckled. "Actually, it does. I was starting to wonder if you thought I did this all single-handed."

Iawi and the rest of the council laughed. "No Odell, we know you didn't. But while we would prefer Deven Doran to lead us, we know he would never accept. But we hope you will."

"I . . . I don't know what to say."

Iawi smiled and leaned forward. "Say you will lead us. Say you will become Chairman of the council. Say you will help all of us rebuild Earth into what it was."

Halburn looked up and down at the faces and sighed. "I don't know if I am who you want. I don't beat around the bush or try to be politically correct. I may tick off a lot of people."

"Trust us, you are. If you do what you think is right, what is right for the people, that is all we ask. And as for upsetting people, you couldn't do worse than Lavine. Well, perhaps you could, but we know you won't."

Halburn chewed the inside of his cheek as his gaze slid down towards the floor. His eyes narrowed as they did when he was in deep thought. He looked up. "Very well, I accept your gracious offer. As long as you understand I will not change to fit the political climate or anything else."

"Odell, that is one thing we would never ever want you to do." Iawi stepped out and down from behind the table. He extended his hand. "Welcome to council, Chairman."

Odell grabbed Iawi's hand and smiled. "It's good to be here."

Far away in a forgotten underground hanger, a room lit by a single screen displaying the Council chambers. From the shadows a single voice spoke, "Of no consequence am I? We will see about that. Won't we, Commander Naud?"

From the dark, a Torrian Naud stepped forward with a gleam in his eye and a grin that crept across his face inch by inch. "Yes Chairman Lavine, we will."

Otis paced across the *Phoenix's* bridge. Minerva's eyes followed him as he went back and forth. "That is not going to help the situation."

"No, but at least it gives me something to do," Otis said.

Minerva smiled. "I can give you something to do if you need."

Otis looked up. "No, I don't want something *else* to do."

"You want to waste energy by pacing back and forth?"

"Yes, if you must know it helps me think." He stopped. "Is there any way we can contact the *Defiant*?"

Minerva shook her head on the large screen. "Negative. We do not have the equipment or power to make a reliable connection that far away."

"Then why don't we build something. I have a feeling they are going to need our help."

"That is highly unlikely considering they are only on a search and destroy mission."

"But they still could need our unique insight and input. You can't deny that?"

"Of course not. I'm a unique entity, as are you. However, I do not see a way to do what you propose."

Otis sat in Aleshia's chair and leaned back. "There must be something." He eyed the broken ring that lowered down onto Aleshia's head when she was using the telepathic chair. They had to break it open when they pulled her from the chair. Nothing on it had worked since. He jumped up. "I have an idea! The chair can do it."

Minerva cocked her head. "That is possible if A. it still worked and B. if Aleshia was aboard. Which she is not."

"Of course I know that. But if we could repair it, it could."

"But she cannot use it if she is not aboard. What would be the point of repairing it? Even if it was possible."

"Did you stop to think that maybe it can reach out to her? The central crystal is still intact. If we can get the chair's matrix up and running, maybe it can touch her mind. I know it is a long shot, but the only other option is to wait eight days and see if they make it back."

Minerva's head cocked to one side and the one side of her face scrunched up. "And how do you propose we repair this device? Even I don't know how it works fully."

"I have studied the system and talked with Dakarth a great deal. I *think* I can reengage the nanomachines. If I can, the chair should repair itself."

"Logical, even if almost impossible."

"Can it hurt to try?"

Minerva shrugged on the screen. "I guess not."

"Good. Now get me a Mechand as an assistant. I need someone to hand me tools or parts while I am under the chair."

Behind him, he heard a soft beep.

Otis turned around to see the Cleaning Mechand minus its large hopper. He had left the hopper below decks to reduce weight, allowing him to extend his arms to the top rung of the ladder and pull himself up to reach the bridge. "You?"

He heard several fast beeps.

"Okay, just be careful."

Several faster beeps and he actually jumped a millimeter above the deck.

"You don't have to act that happy. It is just handing me stuff."

The Mechand gave several more fast beeps and moved over by the chair, waiting.

"Right, let's get to work."

Otis pulled off the back of the chair and wiggled under it. He held out a hand. "Give me the binary monitor from my bag over there and get me a power pack. I need to get part of the system powered while keeping the other side from seeing it. Otherwise, it will suck the pack dry before I can even get started. Oh, and do you have a name?"

The Mechand gave a low beep.

"I take that as a no. Well, I can't keep calling you bot all the time. How about CB? Do you like that?"

Several fast beeps told him he did.

"Okay CB, let's get to work."

CB beeped, carefully wheeled over to Otis' bag on the floor, pulled out a small screen, keyboard, and connector with several clips hanging from it. He placed it into Otis' hand, then left to get a power pack.

Otis connected the device to the chair circuits. Or what he guessed were the right circuits. Many of the devices looked like fuzzy bits rather than normal electronics. "I have to admit, I never thought that guy would be very helpful."

Minerva smiled. "I told you there is a lot more to him than you knew. He has surprised even me. His development is even more impressive than Miles in many ways."

Otis pulled a wire and cross connected another one. "How so?"

"For centuries I maintained a very close eye on my units, guiding, although most would call it controlling –even me– their development, but he was such a simple unit with a simple task that I never bothered. Miles developed on his own, then hid it from me. Then I tried to take control and wipe him when I found out." A tear ran down her cheek.

"But that was the old you," Otis said as he moved a fuzzy component to another side of the device.

"Yes, and while he has forgiven me. I still regret it. My memories often haunt me. But I know they might be needed, so I keep all of them."

"It must be rough to remember everything perfectly in that case." A spark flashed from under the chair.

"You have no idea."

CB pulled himself back up the ladder, rolled through the hatch, and back onto the bridge, then over to Otis. He beeped and Otis' hand reached out. The Mechand placed a device twice the size of his palm into his hand.

"Thanks CB. Now I hope this will work."

Minerva cocked her head. "I do not understand why you would want that power pack? Wouldn't it make more sense to connect the chair to the main supply as originally configured?"

Another spark reached out from under the chair. "It would, if I didn't want to limit the power."

Minerva's eyebrows met. "Why?"

"Because I'm not sure what parts work and what parts don't. And I don't want to give it unlimited access to power until I have this thing under control. Especially since I am trying to activate the nanomachines. If they get out of control, it could destroy us and everything aboard."

"From what I understand of Lytherian technology, that could never happen."

"They might build in a ton of safe-guards, but at this point I'm not trusting anything. Not to mention I'm sort of flying blind here."

"I thought you had in-depth conversations with Dakarth?"

"I did, but we didn't go into what I am trying to do either."

"Ah."

A blue spark flashed as Otis connected the final wire to the power pack. "Okay, here goes nothing." At first, the chair sat inert without so much as a flicker of life. Then after several minutes, lights on the upper part of the chair lit and grew in intensity for ten seconds before going out again. "This is going to take longer than I thought."

4

Three days later, the *Defiant* neared its target. "We are nearing the fragment. It is larger than my original scans indicated," Miles said.

Deven hit several keys on his console. "But still no biologic activity?"

"That is correct, it is quite inert," Miles said.

"Whew, glad to hear that." Galina gripped the *Defiant's* controls, running her thumbs back and forth over the synth leather. She had resumed manual control hours ago, but the fatigue didn't show. "Well? What are you waiting for? Toast that Celloid."

"We are still not in optimal range. To fire our cannons now might fragment the object instead of atomizing it," Miles said.

"How long?" Aleshia asked.

"Ten minutes, forty-two seconds."

Leon appeared in the hatchway. "Wait! I have an idea." His red face and deeper-than-normal breathing had everyone looking at him with concern. "Don't give me that look, I'm fine. But I don't want you to destroy that Celloid."

Deven stood up. "Why the hell not? We came all this way and risked our lives, for what? To let it go?"

Leon managed to catch his breath and sat down at the

nearest console. "No, of course not. But I think we should bring it aboard."

"What?" They all said in unison with wide eyes.

"Deven, I thought he was insane, but this proves it," Galina said.

"I'm not. Just hear me out."

Deven folded his arms. "Okay Leon, let us in on this."

"By all accounts this is part of the core of the Celloid *Mothership*, right?"

Deven nodded. "Yes, what does that have to do with anything?"

"It may have information we need."

"What kind if information?"

"Gregory and I have been talking, and we realized we need to know if there is any more Celloids out there. Not to mention how many, and if they are en route."

Deven gave a wave of his hand as he sat back in his chair. "Not necessary, the Lytherians said it was their entire fleet. They wanted to destroy us and sent everything they had."

"But we can't be certain. If I access that core, then we can."

Deven gave him a blank look. "How?"

"I don't know yet, but if we bring it aboard, I might be able to figure out something."

Deven shook his head. "It is not worth the risk. The Lytherians haven't managed what you are proposing, how do you think you we will?"

"They didn't have time to try. If they had, I'm sure they would have. But it must be possible. The Celloids accessed Lytherian technology, the link must be reversible."

Aleshia sat forward in her chair. "Leon, we all have the utmost respect for your abilities, but you don't even have an example of when the Lytherian's ship was accessed. If you don't even have a starting point, how are you going to access a Celloid?"

Leon grinned. "Ah, but I do. Dakarth gave me all they had on the Celloids before they left for the asteroid belt."

Deven folded his arms again. "And?"

"And I think it is possible. But I won't know for sure unless we bring it aboard and try. Another thing we have and they don't: Minerva. With her and Miles, I don't see how the Celloid code won't be cracked."

"But even if we get it, then what? You still aren't sure about fixing our air situation."

"Oh ye of little faith. I will, but first let's grab that hunk of Celloid."

Deven rubbed his chin. "If we could learn something from it, might be worth it."

"Deven! You can't be serious!" Galina wailed.

"I am. Even the Lytherians don't know much about the Celloids. Where they came from, or why they attacked in the first place."

"It's bloody obvious! To suck the planet dry of resources. The Lytherians even said so."

Deven nodded as he sat back in his chair. "Yes, they did, but perhaps that was the only reason that made sense. What if there was some other reason?"

Aleshia stared at him. "Like what?"

"I don't know, but I have a feeling we are not seeing the big picture here. And Leon's idea has brought my uneasiness to the foreground."

Aleshia glared at him. "Why didn't you mention this before?"

"Because I'm not sure. I can't explain it. While my abilities are not as strong as yours, every bit of my being says we are missing something."

"You can do several things I can't, that may be why," Aleshia said as she took his hand into hers, "we need to bring that Celloid aboard."

Galina folded her arms and sat back hard in her chair. The synth leather issued an audible complaint. "Fine! We are all dead anyway, so I don't see what difference it makes. But have any of you geniuses figured out how to bring that *thing* aboard? We don't exactly have the equipment for it. And we don't have any vehicles that can grab it either."

Deven looked over. "Leon? I assume you have a plan?"

"Sure do. You ever play Pool?"

Galina blinked. "You don't mean–"

Leon laughed. "I sure do. It will work. Trust me."

Aleshia blinked as she cocked her head. "Wait ... what will work?"

"It's simple, really. We open up the main landing bay and fly directly at it. Celloid Core in the corner pocket. It will go right into the bay."

"And destroy everything in it!" Galina said.

Leon shook his head. "Not at all. Gregory and I can put several anti-gravs around the doors and just inside the bay. They will act like a sort of webbing, slowing it down until it lands right were we want."

"How long will that take?" Deven said.

"Hmm, about an hour. Perhaps less."

"Do it."

"Deven! You can't let him go through with this."

"Why not? You said yourself we are going to run out of air soon anyway."

Galina sputtered several times. "Hey, don't throw that back at me."

Deven smiled. "It proves you think we are going to be all right, or you wouldn't be concerned."

"No it doesn't."

Aleshia smiled. "It sure seems like it to me."

Galina said nothing but slouched down in her chair. "I can see there is no point in talking to you about this. I want to go on the record in this instance."

"Noted," Miles said.

"Miles! I wasn't talking to you."

Miles' camera iris contracted. "Considering I maintain the recordings and ships log, yes you were."

Galina waved her hand. "Never mind."

"Acknowledged," Miles said.

Gregory ran from one end of the *Defiant's* main hanger bay to the other. He picked up another anti-grav unit and ran back to the right side of the massive outer doors. He placed the unit on the wall and attached the connecting relays from it to a powered port a few meters away. Lights on the device flashed red, yellow, then green. "I got another one!"

Leon continued looking through his magnification glasses working on the unit in his hand, increasing the power to its delicate circuitry, but not enough to cause it to fail. He never looked up. "Good! Get another and put it one meter below the other."

"Another? Right here? I mean, shouldn't one be enough?"

"Maybe, but we won't get another shot at this." The anti-grav he was working on sparked. "Dang it! This one is fried. Get me another one while you are over there."

Gregory jogged over to the crate of anti-gravs and ran across the bay to place one in Leon's hand. "We are running out of them. Are you sure I should put two on the side of the bay door?" he said a bit winded.

"Yes, I'm sure. We have enough. Here, take this other one. I have finished upgrading it." He placed the circular device in Gregory's hand. "If need be, I know where we can grab a few extras that we aren't using."

Gregory grinned. "If you are taking any bits off of Aleshia's car, I will deny ever knowing you and be on the other side of the *Defiant* when you tell her."

Leon laughed. "Ha ha, I wouldn't dream of it." He jerked a thumb towards the doors. "Now get to it."

"Right Boss." Gregory ran off towards the doors.

"And don't call me Boss!" Leon shouted after him.

Deven appeared in the landing bay's inner doors and walked over to Leon. "How much longer?"

Leon poked his head up. "Deven! What are you doing down here? Why didn't you use the intercom?"

"I wanted to see firsthand how you were doing." His head swiveled as he gazed around the bay. "How much longer?"

"Fifteen minutes, twenty at the outside." Leon bent back down to work on the anti-grav.

Gregory overheard their conversation as he ran back to grab another anti-grav unit. "I would say longer," he said running back to the doors.

Leon jerked a thumb over his shoulder. "Ignore him."

"You said an hour, and it is now almost that. We can't waste time sitting here. We either have to grab the Celloid Core, or destroy it and head home."

Leon looked up. "I know, and we might be a touch over my original estimate but not enough to offset our original time-table."

Deven took a step back. "Our original time-table? Last I knew, unless you come up with a solution, we aren't going to make it back alive."

"I do have one, and it should work, but I don't have time to explain it now. As you pointed out, we are already running behind." He hunched back down to continue working.

Deven held up his hands. "Fine, I will get out of your hair."

"Thanks."

"Of course it depends on where you are if you even can be in Leon's hair," Gregory said.

Leon bit his lip. His white hair was thinning on the top, but he didn't like to be reminded of it. He grinned. "Deven, if you find out someone is stuck inside the stern waste tank, ignore it."

Deven chuckled as he walked out of the hanger bay. "I never heard a thing."

Gregory saw them talking but couldn't quite make it out over the distance and noise of the various machines in the hanger bay. "What was that?"

"Nothing Gregory, get that next unit placed and powered," Leon shouted.

The *Defiant* lined up with the tumbling mass of burned plant material as the main landing bay opened in the front section of the long rectangular ship. Engines glowed brighter as it accelerated.

"Approaching the Celloid Core, we will overtake it in one minute five seconds," Miles said.

Galina gripped the controls. "I can see it Miles, I don't need you side-seat driving."

Miles' camera turned. "But Galina, I am not sitting. And you are driving not I."

Galina's brow wrinkled as she watched her screen with its generated flight path guiding the *Defiant* in the proper orientation and speed to capture the Celloid Core. "Miles! Not now!" Galina's knuckles turned white as her grip tightened even further.

The intercom near Deven crackled. "We are set down here. Doors are open and our net is ready," Leon said.

"Yeah, that hunk of plant is going to land nicely on pad 22a," Gregory said.

Aleshia blinked. "22a! That is where my car is!"

Gregory laughed. "Don't worry, we moved it several spaces over."

"If you land that *thing* on my–"

Leon chuckled. "Aleshia, it is far out of the way. We are playing pool, not pinball here. It will be fine."

"That analogy didn't give me confidence," Aleshia said through gritted teeth.

"I'm sure they have it well in hand," Deven said.

"Three minutes, twenty seconds until capture," Miles said.

Galina guided the *Defiant* with precision, firing several tiny course corrections to further improve their alignment. "There. We are in line. Cutting engines. We will let inertia do the rest." Her eyes narrowed. "Miles? Am I seeing things? Why are we accelerating?"

Miles' camera turned. "We aren't. The fragment is."

"What! How is that possible?"

Deven hit several keys on his console. "I'm still not seeing any signs of life, this does not make sense."

"I don't know, but it is also changing course. Not much, but it could hit the side of the bay. I am correcting now." Galina fired several more corrections, but the mass continued to move in odd directions. "This thing keeps changing, I even decelerated, and it's speed is increasing. I don't like it. I vote we blast it."

"Deven, it can't be alive, and we need to at least try to access it," Leon said over the intercom.

Deven folded his arms and rubbed the back of his neck. "I agree we can't let this opportunity pass us by. Even if it is somewhat viable, there are no plants aboard. Nothing to strengthen it. It is alonc, and we have the ability to incarcerate if needed. Galina, continue on course for now."

Galina sighed. "I don't like this."

The tumbling mass of green plant accelerated again as it came ever closer to the *Defiant*.

"The fragment will enter the bay in less than one minute, Miles said."

Down in the hanger bay Leon and Gregory sat inside the control room with several centimeters of protective glass between them and the vacuum of space that now filled the hanger.

Leon rotated his chair towards Gregory. "It's a good thing I had you install those extra anti-grav units or it wouldn't be enough to slow this thing down."

"Yeah, me too. This could have been really mess otherwise." Gregory watched as the Celloid mass grew larger as it headed towards them.

"Twenty seconds until capture," Miles said over the intercom.

Gregory's eyes went wide as he pointed to the right side of the retracted hanger doors. Lights on the anti-gravs that were green a moment before, now sat dark and ominous. "Two of the ani-grav units have failed."

"Which ones?" Deven's voice came over the intercom.

"The two on the starboard side. This is not good," Leon said as his fingers flew over the console.

"Can you fix them?" Deven breathed.

"No time! It's going to hit!" Gregory shouted as he pointed.

The mass of Celloid tumbled faster and raced into the hanger bay. The anti-gravs on the port side tried to decelerate the odd shaped blob but only succeeded in altering its path towards the other side of the hanger. It rocked towards the wall and the several vehicles parked there where it froze in place.

"What's happening down there?" Galina's anxious voice came over the intercom.

"Umm, can we get back to you on that?" Gregory said.

"What!"

Leon stood up and peered through the control room's window out into the bay and turned his head, trying to see what had happened when he saw Aleshia's face through one of the small windows in the inner doors. Her eyes closed, her face blank. The Celloid mass moved back and lowered to the floor in the center of the bay. The outer doors slid shut, and the bay began to pressurize.

Leon turned. "Did you close the doors?"

"No, I thought you did."

Leon's eyes focused on Aleshia a split-second before she disappeared from the window. "I think it was Aleshia. Come on."

"She stopped something that big and moving that fast?" Gregory said.

"Well, she did pull us back from crashing into the ocean and we're a lot bigger than that thing." Leon said as he jerked a thumb back towards the Celloid.

"But that was with the chair."

"Her abilities have continued to grow."

They turned the corner to find Aleshia passed out on the deck plates. Deven cradled her in his arms. "I think she will be okay. I don't know how she blocked me from seeing her plans, but once I heard you over the com, I knew." He sighed. "Why didn't she tell me? I could have helped her."

"There wasn't time," Leon said. "We saw the problem and the next thing we knew, the Celloid stopped moving. I looked around and saw her in the window."

Gregory nodded. "Right. It was like blink blink and we ran here. I can't imagine how she got down here so fast."

Deven squeezed Aleshia. "I don't know either. I didn't see when she left, but I think she did right after you mentioned moving her car. She must have seen something." He picked her up into his arms and turned towards the other end of the corridor. "I'm taking her to the infirmary to make sure."

Leon nodded. "Let us know, and in the meantime we will check out our plant ball. Come on Gregory." Leon waved towards Gregory, then towards the doors that slid open as the pressure equalized.

In the infirmary, Deven placed Aleshia on the main diagnostic bed and pressed a button on the control panel to the right of the bed. A half cylinder slid up and over Aleshia covering her from neck to toe. Asking for an analysis, the system reported her glucose levels were low and a few stress hormones were at elevated levels, but nothing dangerous.

He pressed another button, and the cylinder slid back into the bed. Deven held Aleshia's hand and kissed it before placing it back at her side.

He walked over to the intercom and hit the button. "Galina?"

"About time you called me! What's going on? Should we be heading home or is there a problem I don't know about?"

"Sorry about that. Aleshia stopped the Celloid from doing damage, but she is out cold now. She will be fine after a bit of rest. She should have been able to do that with ease, but after she stopped us from crashing into the ocean, she has been tired. I told her to not do anything for a while. And she listened until now."

"To be honest, I'm glad she did. Who knows what damage that hunk of plant could have done if she didn't stop it. We might not have been able to get back home."

Deven sighed. "I agree, but I wish she didn't have to."

"I just heard from Gregory and Leon, they said the plant ball we caught is secure. I am hitting the engines." Deven felt a lurch as they engaged. "Full burn and course laid in."

"We will arrive in four days and fifteen hours," Miles said over the intercom. "I regret to inform you that life support will fail in one day four hours from now."

"And I think it is about time Leon let me in on his plan." Deven hit the intercom and headed back towards the hanger bay.

A few minutes later he found Leon hooking up a data tab to two large rods driven into the Celloid Core. He sat down and tapped several keys on the device in his hands, then felt something and looked up to see Deven with his arms folded. "Care to tell me now what your plan is?"

"The plan or do you want me to work in this?"

"Considering our need to breathe is more important, the plan."

Leon stood up. "Well, it is quite simple. You know the system will recharge once we power it down."

"Yes. You have mentioned that several times," Deven said through grated teeth. His patience was thinning fast.

"It takes about seven hours, of course we can't hold our breath for that long."

"Obviously."

"The solution is simple. When the Lytherians were installing it, they left several extra components. I managed to cobble together two smaller devices."

Deven's eyes went wide. "You did? Then why didn't you say that in the first place!"

Leon laughed. "And miss that look on your face? No way. But they are much smaller and can't maintain life support over the entire ship. However, they can with a car or truck. I have modified Aleshia's car and one of the newer trucks we have that is able to handle the device. We won't be comfortable, but we can make do for a few hours."

Deven smiled. "Leon, I could kiss you."

Leon laughed and held up his hands. "Save those for Aleshia."

Deven chuckled. "I said I could, not that I would."

"Good," Leon said as his gaze drifted back down to the data tab.

5

Otis muttered as another spark bit into his cheek. "Dang it! That wasn't it either." For hours, he had tested and went through various circuits trying to find a way to bypass the burned areas. But there were more than he anticipated. If only he could get the system to engage in a self-repair, even for a few minutes. It might be enough to use.

Minerva sighed as she watched the legs and feet move from under the chair as Otis continued to work. "I do not know why you continue to pursue this futile attempt to contact the *Defiant*. And even if you could, what would be the purpose? There is nothing we can do."

Otis cleaned another contact point and ran a bypass to an undamaged section of the circuit. "How do you know that? We might come up with something else they haven't thought of."

"Doubtful considering Leon's expertise," Minerva said.

CB handed Otis another tool when he stretched out his hand from under the chair. He heard a soft beep. "Thanks CB. Minerva, while Leon is amazing, no one knows it all. And I think we might be of assistance. In any case, can it hurt to try?"

"Unless you blow out my systems with your jury-rigging,

no."

Otis laughed. "I'm not going to blow out your systems. I don't even have it connected to you. I took the precaution of severing all normal data and power lines."

Minerva's lips parted and a very audible sound of human breath being exhaled sounded throughout the bridge. "That is a relief. From all the sparks I am seeing, you had me concerned."

"I told you, I know what I'm doing ... well mostly."

Minerva's face scrunched up. "Just when you were inspiring confidence."

"Oh quiet, I–"

Minerva cocked her head. "I'm receiving a transmission."

Otis moved fast and banged his head on the bottom of the chair. "Ouch! What? That's not possible, everything is a mess and I haven't even engaged the power pack yet."

"I don't mean from the *Defiant*. This is from the World Council."

Otis squeezed out from under the chair and stood up. "Great, Lavine wants something."

Minerva nodded. "That is quite probable."

"Well, let's not keep the mentally-lacking Chairman waiting. Put it on the main screen."

The large central screen that stood in between the *Phoenix's* forward bridge windows flashed several times, static lines dissipating, but when they abated, it was not the face of Scott Lavine.

"Commander Halburn? Last I knew you were going to lie low for a while," Otis said.

Halburn smiled. "Actually, it is Chairman Halburn now. But all of you can still call me Odell if you like."

Otis' jaw dropped, and he spent more than a minute trying

to close it again. "Excuse me, but I think we had a connection issue. I could have sworn you said Chairman?"

Halburn smiled. "You heard right. Lavine has been removed, and they wanted someone else that cared about the people rather than their own power. I was shocked too."

Minerva nodded. "I can imagine. It is quite a change from a few days ago."

"Indeed. But the reason I called, I have been unable to contact Deven or anyone on the *Defiant*. I thought I would contact you before we started to worry."

"They are out of range," Otis said.

"Out of range? That doesn't make sense. Unless the *Defiant* is damaged, their current communications system should reach anywhere on the planet."

Minerva nodded. "That is correct. However, they are not on the planet."

Halburn blinked. "Not on the planet? Where did they go? Did they hitch a ride with the Lytherians?"

Minerva shook her head. "Negative. They went after a large fragment of Celloid that had been jettisoned into space with the destruction of the *Mothership*."

Halburn leaned forward. "Celloid? Some survived?"

Otis smiled. "Nope. It is just a dead hunk of plant. But they didn't want to take the chance. And we all agreed."

"But the *Defiant* isn't a spaceship?"

"With the modifications the Lytherians made, it is close. Or at least close enough to reach the fragment and destroy it. Returning is the problem."

Halburn cocked his head. "Wait a minute, returning is a problem? Is that why they didn't tell us?"

Minerva nodded. "Correct. The life support system only has so many days of activity before it must be shut down to recharge. They would have to shut down after five days and reaching the fragment was to take almost that."

"One-way trip." Halburn sighed as he sat back in his chair.

"Yes, but if anyone can find a way to extend that and get them back home is Leon's technical wizardry," Otis said.

"Regardless, the *Defiant* will return in eight days," Minerva said.

"How can you be so certain of that?" Halburn asked.

"Because Miles' is still part of the *Defiant*. He will return the ship even if–"

"They do not," Halburn finished for her.

She nodded. "Correct."

"I'm trying to build something that can reach them, but it is slow going," Otis said.

Minerva laughed. "More like not going at all. Halburn, don't get your hopes up."

"Hey! Don't count me out yet," Otis said folding his arms.

Halburn chuckled. "I wouldn't dream of it."

Otis turned. "But I have a feeling why you were trying to reach the *Defiant* in the first place was not because of your promotion."

"Yes, I wanted to tell them to keep an eye out for Lavine."

Otis' one eye narrowed. "Why? He was kicked out, right?"

Halburn nodded. "Yes he was, but on a hunch I had this entire complex checked and found a tap into the security cameras. I couldn't trace it back to the source, but I have no doubt Lavine is behind it, and he knows I replaced him."

Otis' shoulders tightened as his stance widened. "And you think he is going to want payback."

"I don't think, I know. The man couldn't take losing a game of checkers, much less losing his position to me."

Otis shrugged. "What could he do? He doesn't have a fleet anymore. He has nothing but himself."

"I wouldn't be so sure of that."

Minerva's eyes narrowed. "You think he hid some of the resources he stole from me somewhere and didn't tell you?"

Halburn nodded. "The man knew how to make backup plans for backup plans. I never would have thought he could assemble a fleet like he did. Yet he managed it when I thought having command of one working carrier was amazing."

Otis turned towards Minerva. "Is there a way you could find out if he has more carriers? Or anything else we should worry about?"

Minerva shook her head. "Normally yes, but so much of the network was dismantled while I was offline. I can't be certain. It would depend on if he had the links cut before activating it."

Halburn let out a deep breath he didn't know he was holding. "I wouldn't put it past him. While he isn't an expert in Mechand technology, I'm sure he could find someone that is. But then again, he is very confident in himself, he may miss something. Keep a watch and let me know the instant you detect anything out of the ordinary."

Minerva nodded. "Of course. Do you want me to take control of it if I am able?"

Halburn smiled, then shook his head. "No, while I would love to see his face when you did, we need to know what he is up to. Not to mention everything he has on hand. Having access that he doesn't know about will be a huge advantage."

Minerva nodded. "I understand and agree. If I detect anything, you will be the first to know."

Halburn smiled. "That is all I ask. World Council out." The screen flashed as his image disappeared.

"When it rains it pours," Otis said as he got down and wiggled under the chair.

"I agree," Minerva's eyebrows met, "and you still don't think you are going to get that thing working, do you?"

"I have to. They might need us. At the very least, they should know about Lavine."

"I don't see why, it won't alter their objectives until they return. Knowing about it earlier isn't going to make a difference."

Another spark emanated from under the chair. "I think that does it, at least enough for a test." He wiggled out from under the chair and pressed a button on the power pack.

Nothing happened.

"I could have told you this was a waste–"

A blue light began to glow from under the chair and grew in intensity. Otis watched the back area, and he saw several burned components reform and appeared factory fresh. Otis watched the power level on the pack drain and after a few minutes it failed all together. The glow from under the chair died.

Minerva inclined her head. "I stand corrected, you did it."

"Perhaps," Otis said as he climbed under the chair. "Hmm, most of the damage was repaired, but I will need to do it again for a full rebuild." He grabbed another pack and hooked it up. This time the blue glow increased several times as the chair repaired itself. The head ring liquified and reformed into a full circle as if it had never broken. By the time the power cell drained this time, all the damage appeared to have been repaired.

Minerva's eyes widened as she felt a data connection to the chair come alive. "It has reconnected itself to me! I thought you were going to do that?"

"I was. I didn't think it would repair that as well." Otis wiggled under the chair. "All seems to be like it was before. Though it still needs a few modifications, then we can give it a try." He pulled out several fuzzy blocks. They had reformed with the other repairs, and Leon had to remove these before when the alien components caused problems for Aleshia.

"Ah, well, if it is any consequence, it only connected the lowest data line. That line couldn't do much on its own."

"How comforting," Minerva said through gritted teeth.

Otis changed several more lines and removed all the connections to the nano repair system. He didn't want it to start another repair cycle when power was restored.

"CB, hand me that power driver." The Cleaning Mechand grabbed the tool and placed it in Otis' hand. "Thanks." The Mechand beeped.

Otis cranked on the connection and power flowed from the *Phoenix's* main supplies into the chair. "Okay, that does it. Minerva, do you have control?"

Minerva nodded. "I do. And the chair is powering up. But how do you plan for me to contact Aleshia? I can't sit in the chair. Not to mention my mind wouldn't work in it even if I could."

Otis smiled. "Why, I'm going to sit in it."

"You can't be serious! You are not telepathic, it might fry your brain."

Otis shook his head. "Nah, the worst it could do is nothing. Leon put way too many safeties in this thing for it to do any harm. I'm hoping that Aleshia can bridge the gap and talk to me even if I can't reach out and talk to her."

CB rolled up and grabbed his wrist as he tried to sit in the chair.

Otis turned. "CB? I will be fine. Trust me."

CB gave a mournful beep.

Otis smiled. "Trust me."

CB's optics lowered, and he released his grip. Otis sat in the chair and the ring lowered down around his head. He concreted on Aleshia and the *Defiant*. *Come on I know you are out there. You have to hear me. Aleshia, please hear me.*

— 6 —

Leon adjusted several connections as he struggled under Aleshia's car with the new Environment Support System. It should work, but every time he started the device up, the connections fried between the car and the device. He checked the other side, and that all seemed normal. The last thing he wanted to do was pull the whole unit. It would take too much time. Time they didn't have.

Gregory leaned over and wheezed a bit. "Leon? You know the air is getting thin."

"I know! I will have this in a minute."

"You said that hours ago."

"It hasn't been hours."

"Umm Leon, it has."

Leon gazed at his wrist and hit a button on the square device strapped there. "Dang it, it has. I'm sorry, but I am sure I this will work."

"You have said that too."

"Don't you trust me?"

"Of course I do, but the air is getting thin, and we are running out of time."

"Listen, I will get it." He pressed a button on the ESS. Lights flashed then power surged, causing the connection to burn again. "Dang it! I could have sworn that was it."

"You have said that before too."

"Gregory!"

"Yes?"

"You're not helping!"

Up on the *Defiant's* bridge Deven ran his fingers through his hair. "Right now I wish you had stayed home," he said looking at Aleshia.

"I'm glad I didn't. I would rather be with you, even now. Leon will get it, he always has."

Galina took a deep breath of thin air and coughed. "I for one wish I *had* stayed home. I should have left you crazy people handle it yourselves."

Miles' camera turned. "I tried to tell you I could have piloted the *Defiant* to the target and returned without–"

"Miles?"

"Yes?"

"Not *now*."

Miles' camera iris contracted and expanded. "Acknowledged."

Aleshia blinked and shook her head. "Did you hear something?"

Galina rolled her eyes as she turned her head. "No. Nothing more than Miles' blabbering."

"But Galina, I do not–" Galina glared at him with an ice-cold stare. "Never mind."

Aleshia rubbed her temples. For a moment she thought she could hear a voice. But it wasn't Deven's or Galina's. *Aleshia.* There it was again. And sounded familiar. "I know I heard something. Neither of you heard anything?" They both shook their heads. "Well, I know I did." She closed her eyes. And reached out with her mind. *I am here.*

"Aleshia! You can hear me! IT worked!"

"Otis?"

"In the flesh. Well, sort of speak."

"How are you doing this?"

"I got that chair of yours working enough to reach out to you. Can't do much else."

Aleshia's eyes snapped open. "It's Otis, he managed to get the chair working and is contacting me through it."

Galina blinked. "How in the world is he doing that? He is not telepathic."

Otis laughed. "Tell her I know as Minerva keeps reminding me. However, now that it works, I think she will stop hassling me about that little fact."

Aleshia cocked her head. "You heard that?"

"Not really. I know you did, and from that I know what she said. It is a bit complicated. The chair is connected to you, I am just the mouthpiece talking through it."

"I still don't understand how you managed this without having any abilities yourself."

"The chair is tuned to your mind, I managed to restore that and a lot of its circuitry. Enough to place a call anyway. I had a feeling you might need our help. Was I right?"

Aleshia sighed. "We do need help, but I don't see how you can do anything."

"You bet we need help," Galina said. "Tell him we need him to run down the nearest air supply and pick up a big order since Leon's plan isn't working."

Aleshia felt Otis tilt his head. "Leon's plan?"

"Leon has two devices similar to the life support system

that the Lytherians installed aboard the *Defiant* but he is having problems installing them in the vehicles."

"I see. They will maintain the vehicle's environment while the main unit recharges? That's brilliant."

"It is, if it would work. Right now our air is getting thinner and thinner."

Otis chewed the inside of his cheek for a few seconds. "Can you show me? Perhaps I can help after all."

"Show you?"

"Well right now I can see what you see. Minerva has increased the power and the connection is stronger now. Go down to the hanger bay and let me see what Leon is doing."

Aleshia nodded, got up, and headed off the bridge.

"Aleshia?" Deven asked. "Where are you going?"

"No time, will tell you later."

Deven didn't take that answer. He stood up, and ran after her.

Aleshia found Leon and Gregory working under her car. "Otis? Gregory? Can you show me the thing you are trying to get going?"

Leon slid out from under it. "Aleshia? Since when did you know anything about Lytherian technology?"

"I don't, but Otis might."

Leon blinked. "Otis?"

"He managed to get the telepathic chair to connect to me. I'm speaking with him now."

"He did? I didn't give the boy half the credit he is due if he managed that. What does he say?"

"He wants to see the device you are working on."

Gregory slid out from under the car on his anti-grav repair board, hopped up and pointed to it. Aleshia lay on it, and slid back under and looked around. "The ESS is on the right, with a cable hanging off of the left side."

Aleshia saw the small box-shaped device. She spotted an access panel and it popped open with a loud beep. Within, circuity unlike anything she had ever seen filled the space. Some components appeared more organic than electronic. "Looks like Greek to me."

Leon blinked. "What?"

Aleshia laughed. "It was a joke, Leon."

Leon laughed. "Oh, I thought you saw something resembling Greek in there, and I was wondering how."

Aleshia felt Otis smile. "I have an idea. I remember seeing a green and blue cable with a little round connector with five prongs on the diagnostic cart to the right of the car. Grab it and plug it into the little recessed area near the bottom inside the access panel."

Aleshia did as he said, and the little box lit up. "Okay, now what?"

"Let me guide you," Otis said. She slid back out again from under the car and followed his instructions as they turned on the diagnostic monitor. Code began to scroll across the screen. "I see the problem. I'm not there with my equipment, so we will have to do this manually. It might take a bit, but it is possible. You ready?"

"Do I have a choice?"

Otis laughed. "Not really. Okay, follow my lead, this is going to be tricky and complicated. But we can do it. First go to line 2432 and send it back up to line 1332."

"How do I do that?"

Otis smiled. "Don't worry, let me guide you." Otis continued to show her where to insert code, which parts to remove and how to bypass areas that still needed to be there, but not in this one routine. Several times he commented on how he couldn't believe the Lytherians had made such bad mistakes when designing the device. By the time she was done, everyone was fighting to stay awake.

Aleshia shook her head trying to wake up, unplugged the cable and handed it to Leon. "Here, try it now."

Leon stared at her with a dumbfounded look on his face. "What did you do?"

"I'm not sure."

Otis laughed. "We just went through the whole thing and you still don't know?"

"No I don't. It was all a mess to me and made no sense at all."

"Tell him the base code was designed for a much larger unit. When Leon made a smaller one, the code found a discrepancy and shut down as part of its safety protocol."

Aleshia repeated what Otis said, and Leon blinked. "Is that all? Why didn't you tell me that in the first place. I could have fixed it."

"Don't tell him I don't think he could have. It is a lot of spaghetti code in the thing. Whoever designed it wasn't planning on anyone ever having to look at it again, or trying to figure it out."

Aleshia smiled and Leon's eyes narrowed. "What?"

"Nothing," Aleshia said.

"Thanks for that," Otis said.

"You owe me one," Aleshia thought.

"A big one," Otis replied.

Leon hopped on the anti-grav repair board and slid under the car. A few minutes later he emerged with a big grin. "I bet it will work now."

"Shall I try it?" Gregory said.

"Sure."

Gregory struggled pulling himself behind the wheel and engaged the engine. It roared to life and oxygen rich air poured through its dashboard vents.

Leon smiled. "That did it." He walked over to the diagnostic cart and pointed to the screen. "It will only take me a minute to do the same to the other one. I can grab the dump from here and clone it to the other device." Leon's head zipped back and forth. "Gregory? Where did he go?" His eyes focused on the form behind him, draped over the wheel, sound asleep. He grabbed and shook Gregory's shoulder. "Don't fall asleep on me now. We're almost done."

Gregory's eyes fluttered open. "What? ...I ...was I asleep?"

Deven coughed the thin air. "Out like a light."

Leon held out a device and placed it in Gregory's hand. "Here, plug this into the other ESS like I showed you before."

Gregory's groggy eyes tried to focus as he pulled himself out of the car. "Sure, one sec."

Leon sighed and took back the device from the outstretched hand. "Never mind. I will do it myself. Go sit in the truck, at least then we won't have to drag you in there later." Gregory stood up then his shaky legs almost gave out. "Are you going to make it? Or should Deven and I put you in the truck?"

"No, I'm not that bad. I'll make it," Gregory said.

"I'm not so sure about that."

Aleshia swayed back and forth, causing Deven to grab her. "I will help after I put Aleshia in the car."

"I'm okay, just a little light-headed. Not sure why it is hitting us harder than you," Aleshia said.

"Everyone reacts to thin air differently." He wrapped an arm around Aleshia and placed her into the car.

"What is going on? Aleshia? Everything went black here for a moment," Otis said inside her mind.

"Sorry Otis, I almost blacked out there."

"But I should be able to tell that from here."

"The lightheadedness must be affecting our connection." Her eyes almost closed again, and she fought not to pitch forward into the steering wheel. "I think we had better stop. Our connection is taking more than I have right now."

"Oh sure, of course. Will talk again soon. Please tell everyone that if you need us, we are there," Otis said as she felt the connection cut.

Leon worked under the truck hooking up the diagnostic unit to ESS. Several times he almost passed out but fought to stay conscious. A few minutes later, the data finished uploading. He pulled the diagnostic cable free and pushed himself out from under the truck. "It's done. Start the truck."

No response.

"Gregory?" Leon managed to get to his feet, holding onto the side of the truck for support. He peered through the window to see Gregory leaning against the passenger door, unconscious. "Great." He pulled himself inside with the last of his strength and activated the truck's engine. Fresh air poured into the cabin, and he took several deep breaths. He pressed a button on the dash. "Galina? Where are you? Get down here!" No response. His eyes drifted up towards the ceiling. "Miles? Where is Galina?"

"She is here with me on the bridge, but she is unconscious and I have been unable to wake her," Miles said.

Leon started to climb back out of the truck when Deven ran over to him. "Where do you think you are going?"

Leon shook his head as he grabbed the open door. "To get

Galina. She is not here, Miles said she is passed out on the bridge."

"You aren't going anywhere. Get back inside."

"But Galina–"

"I will get her. I'm in better shape and have been breathing the oxygen rich air in Aleshia's car for several minutes."

"But suppose you need help?"

"And suppose you pass out and I have to get you both back here?"

"Point taken," Leon said without further challenge and climbed back into the truck. As Deven turned to walk away, Leon turned towards him. "Wait, you need to shut down the main environment generator in engineering."

"Won't it shut down on its own? Or can't Miles do it?"

Leon shook his head. "No. The central ESS won't recharge unless it is properly shut down. And it is too new, Miles was never connected to it. We never saw the need."

"I will get it."

"Are you sure?" Leon wheezed.

"You are in no condition, don't worry, I can make it."

"Okay, but make sure you shut it down properly. There are three buttons on the top. Green, yellow, and red. Hit the green three times and then the red."

Deven glared at him aghast. "You're kidding right? Color buttons with no labels?"

Leon shrugged. "Lytherian design, I hadn't got around to changing it."

Deven nodded and shut the truck door. He started walking towards the bridge, but each step became more difficult. He had to stop several times to catch his breath. When he reached the bridge, Galina sat passed out over her console. He grabbed her shoulder and shook, but she didn't stir.

Miles' camera turned. "This is one of the few times I wish I had access to my old body, I could have brought her to you and shut off the environment generator."

"Listening in were you?" Deven wheezed. "That's not important now. Getting her down to the hanger bay is. I'm too weak to lift her now. I hadn't thought of that when I left or I would have grabbed a few anti-grav units from the bay."

"There are still several on the container in the corner. Leon hadn't removed them yet when he brought up repair components," Miles said.

Deven found the box in the corner with four ant-grav units. Two would be enough to carry Galina with ease, but he couldn't attach them directly to her. He rummaged through the box and found a couple of temporary extending rod supports and wire. He thought about jury-rigging a floating stretcher, but then he had a better idea. Digging around in the box again, he found what he was looking for: a power driver. He grabbed the driver, attached an anti-grav to each side of the base of Galina's chair, and used the power driver on the base. In a few seconds the bolts holding her chair were removed, and she floated free.

"Quite ingenuous Deven," Miles said.

Deven coughed. "Thanks Miles." He guided Galina off of the bridge and down towards the hangar bay. His breath came in ragged gasps and his pace slowed, but he kept going. He reached the hanger a few minutes later and Leon opened the truck door the instant he approached.

"You got her." Leon glanced up at Deven's face. "You look like hell, let me get the environment generator."

Deven shook his head. "No. I will get it. You take care of Galina and get her inside. I will be right back." Deven turned and headed towards engineering. Several long minutes later, he walked inside and fought not to collapse in a heap right there. "I never thought this ship was so big until now," he wheezed.

He saw the central ESS tucked neatly between two of the main engine cores. But as he approached, he knew something was wrong. The lights on the top were out. There was no way to tell which keys were red and which were blue. Deven thought about taking an axe to the machine and turning it off that way, but they needed it later, and he didn't have the strength anyway. He tried to take a deep breath, but only coughed. He staggered over to the key panel on the top and took a guess at which was which. He tapped in a sequence and other lights on the device shut down. With a nod, he turned and headed back towards the hangar bay.

By the time he reached the bay, he was almost crawling. He leaned up against the wall and pulled himself along. More times than he could count, he almost lost consciousness. When he was on his last breath he reached Aleshia's car, dragged himself inside, and shut the door. Glorious oxygen filled his lungs, and he couldn't help but take several deep breaths.

Aleshia jerked suddenly awake. "Deven! Are you all right? You look like death's door."

Deven wheezed several times before he managed to speak. "I feel like it too. But I made it, and the ESS will recharge now. We will make it."

"I hope so, but I don't like being parked next to Mr. tall, dark, and plant." She jerked a thumb towards the hunk of Celloid sitting in the middle of the landing bay.

Deven's breathing slowed. "That thing is dead. There is nothing to worry about."

"Then why am I getting this bad feeling? And how many

times did the Lytherian's think they had these things licked, only to find them taking the very ground under their feet."

"You should know that. I didn't link with their Admiral's mind."

"Yes I did, and from what I could see Karthish knew of more instances than he cared to count."

"So you want us to jettison it when we have such an opportunity to find out more about them? More than even the Lytherian's know?

Aleshia sat back in her chair and rested her head against the smooth synth leather. "It's not worth it."

"Maybe, maybe not. I think it is, at least considering everything we have says that ball of Celloid is as dead as a rock."

"I tell you, it's not worth it."

"We have taken every precaution and can jettison the thing in a few seconds. Even Miles could do it if needed."

"Look, one of those things managed to access a Lytherian ship and download all its data. And that wasn't the core of the *Mothership*. What happens if it gets access to the *Defiant*?"

"I think Miles would have something to say about that."

Aleshia glared at him. "Be serious."

Deven turned. "I am. The Celloid over took a small scout ship which didn't have any sort of intelligence in the ship that Miles has. If it did manage to come alive, he would know in an instant if it was trying to access the *Defiant*, jettison the core into space a second later, and blast it with a carbine cannon. I keep telling you there is nothing to worry about."

Aleshia's dash beeped, and she pressed a button. The front part of the dash slid back, revealing a panel that extended up. It flickered and the image of Miles' camera appeared. "You will be pleased to know the *Defiant's* Environment Support

System will be recharged in six hours. Well ahead of previous estimates."

Aleshia smiled. "Thank you, Miles."

The camera's iris narrowed and reopened. "You are welcome, Miss Aleshia."

Aleshia sat up. "Miles? How long would it take you to jettison the Celloid and destroy it?"

"One minute fifteen seconds, provided I open the hangar bay instantly."

"That quick?"

"Yes. Is there some reason I should do so now? My scans indicate it is still harmless and inert."

Aleshia nodded. "Yes Miles, it is. I was making sure of the timeline should it be necessary."

"I understand," Miles said. "I shall continue monitoring and update you at the slightest change."

"Thank you, Miles."

"You are quite welcome, Miss Aleshia." The image started to fade.

"Oh Miles?"

The screen brightened. "Yes, Miss Aleshia?"

"How is Galina?"

"Utilizing my camera feed, I can ascertain she is conscious and recovering."

Aleshia cocked her head. "You haven't contacted the truck yet?"

"I regret I am unable to do so. The communications equipment aboard the vehicle they are in, seems to have been damaged."

Deven sat up. "Damaged? How do you know?"

"I can access the truck's internal diagnostics. However,

while I can determine they are offline, I cannot tell why or repair them."

"That is odd. You should be able to access the full diagnostics and even the repair systems."

"I agree, it is very unusual."

"How about a data tab? One of them must have one?" Aleshia asked.

"None that I can determine. I estimate they were so focused on surviving that such thoughts of communication later, eluded them."

Deven sighed. "Leon tends to think of everything. I can't imagine this slipping through his fingers."

Aleshia nodded. "Something else that does not make sense."

"I will continue to try to access the truck's systems," Miles' said a few seconds before his image flickered and disappeared.

7

Sitting in the truck waiting for the ESS to regenerate, Leon grew tired of Galina's comments. He rubbed his forehead. "This isn't good enough? We are alive."

"Barely!" Galina said. "We almost didn't make it."

"Come on, we had a lot of margin."

Galina snorted. "A lot of margin? I would hate to see what no margin is for you. I almost died, Gregory passed out several times, even I saw it from the bridge, and heaven only knows how Deven got me back here."

"Wait, how do you know it was Deven? It might have been me," Leon said with a smile.

"Ha! You wouldn't come get me, you would let me gasp."

Leon laughed. "I would not. Do you think I hate you?"

"Hate might be too strong of a word, let me suffer for a while, I wouldn't discount."

Gregory smiled. "She's gotcha' there."

"She does not. She knows I care for her too much to let her gasp for air and die on the bridge."

Galina's eyes narrowed. "I didn't say die, I said suffer ...big difference."

"Okay, then I wouldn't let you gasp for air and suffer on the bridge. Happy?"

Galina giggled. "Not really, as I'm not sure I believe you."

"What?"

Galina's giggle broke out into a full laugh. "Sometimes you are too easy."

"She's just pulling your chain, Leon," Gregory said.

"Yeah, right." Leon leaned back in the driver's seat, then turned to his right to face Galina. "It think it might be best if we get some rest. We don't know what lies ahead."

"I think I know, but no one listens to me," Galina said as she leaned back as well and tried to settle into a comfortable position on the truck's bench seat all three of them sat on.

"The Celloid is not going to wake up and destroy the ship," Leon said.

Galina sat up and blinked. "Did I say that?"

"Not this time, but others, yes."

Gregory chuckled. "He's got you there."

"Hey! I thought you were on my side."

Gregory smiled. "I'm on the side of who's right."

Leon leaned back. "Can't lose then."

"Got that right." Gregory leaned back and closed his eyes.

"Eh, I am surrounded by idiots."

"You were the one that wanted to come along," Leon said.

"I didn't want to, I was tricked into it."

Leon sat up. "How do you figure that?"

"Well, you all know I wouldn't let you go without me, so I had to offer. But no one said 'Oh Galina stay home, we got this' oh no. No one said that at all!"

"Are you saying we are supposed to read your mind and know what you really mean?"

Galina shrugged her shoulders. "Sure, why not. Aleshia should be able to, Deven as well. Neither of them said anything though."

Leon shook his head. "You know they wouldn't peek in your mind without your permission. They only know what you tell them. The same as Gregory or I."

"Sureeeee, throw that up when they have before."

"But not intentionally."

Galina folded her arms. "I suppose."

Leon put a hand to his ear. "What was that? Did you concede?"

Galina said nothing, but leaned back and shut her eyes.

"I guess I will take that as a yes."

Several hours later, the truck's dashboard screen raised and flashed. An image of Miles' camera appeared. "You will be pleased to know the *Defiant's* ESS has recharged. I have also activated this vehicle's secondary repair system and restored the communications I am now using."

Leon woke with a start. "Miles?" He blinked several times. "How do you know the ESS' status? You don't have any connection to it?"

"That is correct. However, I do have access to two cameras in engineering and I am able to manipulate one to zoom in on the involved system and read the status panel."

"Oh, smart."

"Thank you. However, we have another problem."

Gregory stirred and sat up. "What? Problem?"

"Yes. How is the environment system to be activated? I cannot do it. And how are you going to reach it? Not only is the oxygen level far too low, but the temperature has dropped. It is not freezing, but it is cold by human standards," Miles said.

Leon sighed. "That is a problem."

"Actually, two," Miles said.

"Put me through to Aleshia's car."

"Acknowledged," Miles said as the screen split into three sections and on the far right side an image appeared showing the inside of the car. But rather than showing Aleshia's or Deven's face as they expected, they only saw empty seats.

"Where did they go? They have to be there," Galina said through half-open eyes as she yawned.

They saw some movement between the seats and Aleshia's head popped up. "Miles? What? Leon! What's going on?"

Deven's head appeared next to her. "I assume there is a problem?"

Leon cleared his throat. "Yes, and no. The *Defiant's* ESS has regenerated and is ready to be activated."

"That is good news, so what's the problem?"

"We can't do it from here, and the ship has grown a bit cold as well."

Deven sighed. "That is a problem. Miles can't do it?"

"Negative. I do not have full access to the device," Miles said.

"Oh, that's right. Leon hadn't connected it to the *Defiant's* central systems yet."

"Correct."

Miles' iris contracted, then expanded. "This is quite unexpected."

"What is?" Aleshia asked.

"I did not do it, therefore I do not see how this is possible."

"Miles! What is it?" Aleshia said.

"The ESS is powering up on its own. I estimate oxygen and temperature levels will return to normal in twenty minutes."

"Very strange," Leon said. "Deven? How did you power down the unit?"

Deven shrugged his shoulders, but no one saw other than

Aleshia due to the seats obscuring the view. "I entered the code you told me."

Leon shook his head. "Impossible. If you did, it wouldn't be powering on now."

"Well, when I went down their the control panel was dark. I couldn't tell the colors of the three buttons you told me about."

Leon's eyes widened. "What did you do?"

"I went on the assumption when you told me the colors, it was in left-to-right orientation. So I hit the first one three times and last one once."

"Left to right as you are standing in front of it with the engines on either side of you?"

Deven nodded. "Right."

Leon laughed. "You didn't enter the right code, but we got lucky."

Aleshia cocked her head. "We did?"

"Yes. The code he entered, while it did shut it down, it also put it in a diagnostic mode, triggering a full power up after a recharge and a self-test," Leon said.

Deven's one eye scrunched up. "Why didn't you tell me to do that in the first place?"

"That mode often takes longer, sometimes several hours longer because of the diagnostics it runs. We wanted it up and going as soon as possible. And in any case, it wouldn't have made any difference if you couldn't read the panel, anyway."

Deven smiled. "You have a point. We will see you in a couple of hours." Deven reached forward and tapped a key below the screen that ended the connection. He nibbled on Aleshia's ear, continuing where he left off.

The wait for the *Defiant* to become habitable again tested

Leon's patience to the extreme. He always cared for Galina, but right now he wished he could strangle her.

"I tell you we need to jettison that hunk of plant right now before it's too late," Galina said.

Leon sighed again. If he heard this one more time, he was going to do something he might regret later. But he had his doubts at the moment. "We have been through this several times. We are all in agreement that we need to at least try to access the Celloid Core. I agree there is a risk, but it is small. So small even Miles can't calculate it. The thing is dead, I don't understand why you think it is going to do something."

Gregory glanced over at Leon with an expression that told him everything. He realized his mistake by saying he didn't understand her position. Galina started again explaining in nauseating detail how the Celloids had fooled the Lytherians several times. We don't have their technology, and it was not worth the risk. Leon knew where this was coming from, it scared her. Normally, she was very grounded and would back a decision they all made ... eventually. This was the first time he could remember where she didn't. He was about to make another attempt at changing the subject –either that or knock Galina unconscious– when the dash screen flipped up, flashed, and Miles' camera appeared on the screen.

"The *Defiant* can now maintain human life again. Oxygen levels, while not at normal levels, they are adequate, as is the temperature," Miles said.

"Come on Gregory, let's get to work." Leon said as he opened the door. The air was a little colder than he expected, but not too bad. He might need a jacket from his quarters for a while.

Leon walked over to Aleshia's car, but the doors opened before he got there. Aleshia popped out of the driver's side and Deven appeared on the other side. "Guess you heard the good news?"

Aleshia nodded. "We did. Miles told us a moment ago."

Behind Leon, Galina got down from the truck. Gave them all a hard glare and headed off towards the bridge.

Deven cocked his head. "What was that all about?"

Leon smiled. "Don't pay her any mind. She wants us to destroy the Celloid or at the very least get rid of it. I keep telling her it is dead. But she isn't listening. I think it scares her. Why of this more than anything else we have faced, I can't imagine."

"I'll go talk with her." Aleshia headed off towards the doors on the far side of the hanger bay.

"Good. And we'll get back to work on cracking this Celloid," Leon said.

Aleshia found Galina on the bridge as she expected. But not almost in tears. "Galina? What's wrong? You can't be this upset over this dead Celloid?"

Galina looked up from her console, her eyes red. "But I am. I can't explain it. You are the one with telepathic abilities, not me. And yet you don't feel anything? I know I am being crazy, but every part of my being says this is a mistake."

"But why? You must have more than a vague feeling?" Aleshia came over, sat next to her, and took her hands into hers.

"It isn't vague, it centers on that Celloid. I see it killing us, but I also know it is dead. It doesn't make sense."

"You actually see it?"

Galina nodded. "I do."

"Would you mind if I took a look?"

"Where?"

"In your mind. I won't look around other than why you are so worried about this Celloid when it's dead. Perhaps I can find out."

"Okay, if you can find out why, go ahead."

Aleshia squeezed Galina's hands and leaned forward until her head touched Galina's. "Just relax."

Galina nodded. Images filled Aleshia's mind. Many of them from the battle with the Celloids. And how close they came to losing. She pushed harder, pulling back the layers until she found images of the Celloid Core. But what she was fearing wasn't from the Celloid itself, but what had all escaped them. The Celloids didn't act autonomous, what they have been doing made little sense unless someone else was pulling the strings. Why attack Earth when it was a sure victory ahead of the attack on the Lytherian homeworld once they had found it. Both pieces of information came when a Celloid accessed a Lytherian scout ship.

Aleshia leaned back. "You think someone else sent the Celloids."

"I do? Yeah, I guess that makes sense. I mean, I never understood why these Celloids would head off to an ultimate battle with the Lytherians, only to change their course midway? From all we know about them, it doesn't sound like something they would do. They attack one planet, drain it of resources and move on, tightening the noose around the Lytherians every time. Why change tactics when it worked so well?"

"Come on. We need to talk with Leon," Aleshia pulled Galina to her feet, and they headed off towards the hanger bay.

A few minutes later they found Leon pointing to a screen and then at the Celloid. "I'm telling you, it is right. I have checked it three times. If you don't believe me, do it yourself."

"It's not that we don't believe you, but it does conflict with everything we know about the Celloids." Deven felt Aleshia enter, and he turned. "Back so soon?"

"Yes, and let me guess, Leon has found the Celloids are bio-engineered?"

Leon's head popped up. "Yes. How did you know?"

"Ask Galina, she's the one that told me."

All eyes focused on Galina. "I didn't tell her. Not in the normal sense anyway."

"Will someone please tell us what is going on?" Gregory said.

"I reached into Galina's mind and I found her fears come from a dream she had where she thought the Celloids were being controlled by someone else."

"Why?"

Galina shrugged. "I have no idea. Perhaps I watched too many horror films when I was a kid that involved killer plants." She folded her arms and giggled.

Deven rubbed his chin. "I would sooner say your insight into tactics and plans lead you to the conclusion we weren't seeing the big picture."

Galina shrugged again. "Possible. I don't know. But how did you guys find out?"

Leon pointed to the screen again. "This shows the genetic structure, it has certain codes and combinations far too complex for nature. It also indicates why they are so resistant."

Deven leaned over. "Any clues to who made them?"

Leon shook his head. "None."

"But we will find out soon," Gregory said.

"Well, we are going to try," Leon said.

"What? You sounded much more certain when we brought it aboard," Deven said.

"I didn't expect it to be genetically engineered. It throws what I thought I knew out the window. I don't think even the Lytherians know this."

Galina leaned forward, keeping her arms folded. "How could they not? They have been fighting them for hundreds of years."

Deven stroked his chin. "I suspect they never got close enough to examine them on a genetic level. The only ship that did was their scout ship they lost."

"This also explains how the Celloids accessed that ship. It must be far more intelligent than we thought."

Galina stood in front of Deven and pointed to the large green mass behind her. "Deven! Get rid of it! This thing is far worse than we thought. And someone made it. Perhaps they can find out we have this plant blob and attack us before we get back home."

"Not possible. I keep telling you it is a dead hunk of plant, it can't do anything. Besides, if it was transmitting any signals, Miles would know."

"That is correct. No signals have been sent from the Celloid. All scans continue to indicate no life." Miles said from the ten centimeter square speaker mounted in the middle of the ceiling of the hangar bay.

"There, you see? It's dead. It can't harm us or contact its owners," Leon said.

Deven looked Galina in the eye as he gripped her shoulders. "I know you are upset about this, and I respect it, but respect my decision: unless something changes, it stays.

We can't let this opportunity to know *who* made this thing slip through our fingers. Is that clear?"

"Clear," Galina said through pursed lips. She turned on her heel and left the bay, heading back up to the bridge.

Aleshia moved closer to Deven, and he put his arm around her. "Miles? How long until we arrive?"

"One day fifteen hours at current rate of speed," Miles' voice came through the speaker overhead.

Deven turned and gazed into Aleshia's eyes. "I think you need to contact Otis and Minerva. We need their help."

Aleshia sighed. "I can't. If Otis isn't in the chair, I can't reach him from this far away."

"Don't you have a time to contact again?"

Aleshia shook her head. "No. We were in a rush, and neither of us thought of that. He told me to call if we needed them. I'm sure never occurred to him I can't."

Leon tapped a few keys pointed at a detailed scan of the Celloid. "Gregory, check this out. I think this is the central area, or brain."

"I thought the whole thing was?"

Leon shook his head. "Nope. I'm not sure what everything does, but there is more to this. I wish I could talk with Otis. I know he could make more sense of this than I."

Aleshia leaned forward. "I don't see why. I mean, he is a cracker, not a biologist."

Leon looked up. "True, but I have a feeling whoever built this thing, used their own networks and computers as the basic template. Only moved it over to a biologic system. Otis might be able to see similarities."

"It may be possible to contact Otis," Miles said.

They all looked up towards the ceiling-mounted speaker. "What do you mean?" Deven asked.

"The equipment aboard the *Defiant* can transmit on frequencies that could reach Earth from our current position. If you recall, I could reach the probe at the edge of the solar system. With modifications, it may be possible to reach the *Phoenix*."

Leon shook his head. "No, it's not. The *Phoenix* does not have the same equipment."

"That is correct. But before we departed, I logged three old satellites still in orbit that could be used as relay stations. If they are still operational, and I can connect them in a network. This would increase both their normal transmission and reception abilities."

Deven cocked his head. "Old satellites? Why didn't you tell us about them before?"

"If you recall, the destruction of the Celloid remnants were the priority, not old satellites that no one has used in hundreds of years," Miles said.

"And may not work at all," Leon said.

"Correct. The chance of success is small, but worth perusing."

"How long will it take?" Aleshia said.

"Unknown. It depends on their response to my inquiry, and if they have received any damage."

"Try Miles. The sooner we know more about this thing, the better."

"Acknowledged," Miles said.

"Guys?" Galina's voice came through over the ceiling speaker. "I'm seeing weird stuff going on up here. Power being redirected from the engines to the communications array. I've tried asking Miles, but he said to ask you?"

Aleshia giggled. "He wouldn't tell you?"

"No! And even threatened to pull him from the *Defiant*!"

Deven shook his head. "While I dislike he wouldn't tell you, it is not something vital and you could ask us. Regardless, I will have a talk with him about this. He is trying to contact several ancient satellites in Earth orbit."

"What the heck for?"

"He hopes he can use them as a relay to contact the *Phoenix*."

"But he is taking power from the engines. Did you tell him he could do that?"

Deven sighed. "No, I didn't. What is our new ETA?"

"About one day twenty hours," Galina said.

Leon looked up. "Five hours longer then. Won't make any difference as far as the central ESS is concerned. It can last quite a bit longer than that."

"Galina, let him continue, and I will talk with Miles about this as well."

"Right, but if he does anything more without telling me I'm going to pull his plug," Galina said as the speaker clicked off.

Aleshia smiled. "I can't blame her. I'm going to the bridge and try to calm her down."

Leon chuckled. "Good luck on that. When she gets her hair up, look out world."

Aleshia laughed. "But I can be very persuasive." She disappeared into the corridor and headed up to the bridge.

"Do you really think she can?" Gregory asked.

Deven smiled. "You should know better by now not to doubt Aleshia."

Leon laughed. "You have a point."

Aleshia arrived on the bridge to find Galina pointed at Miles' camera, shouting. "Don't you ever refuse to tell me what I ask for again or I will make sure you don't have enough of a mind left to play Tic-tac-toe with let alone fly this ship!"

"But Galina, I was told to do this. I only asked you to contact Deven. I assumed you wouldn't believe me anyway," Miles said.

"You assumed wrong. I would have."

Aleshia leaned against the hatchway. "You would?"

Galina turned with a start. "Aleshia! Well …maybe …okay, I might have called Deven to check."

Aleshia chuckled. "Might have?"

"Okay you got me, I would have."

"I thought so." Aleshia pushed herself off of the wall and walked onto the bridge. "Can we agree this is a simple misunderstanding?"

Galina sat back hard in her chair. "I would, except he has done this before and withheld information. He said he wouldn't do it again."

"I did not withhold information. I only told you to ask Deven in the interest of saving time. This instance differs from previous such occurrences," Miles said.

Galina sat forward and glared at Miles' camera. "Can you not do both at the same time?"

Miles' iris shrank and expanded. "I do not understand."

"Could you not continue to try to contact those satellites and tell me what you were doing?"

Miles' camera iris flicked open and closed several times.

"Well?"

Miles' camera focused on Galina, turned towards Aleshia, and back to Galina.

"Miles? Answer her," Aleshia said.

"It is very probable I could have done both tasks at once. However, at that moment redirecting power to the array and minimizing the change to the *Defiant's* speed, while issuing very delicate commands to old satellites, it seemed logical."

Galina shook her head. "Just like a man, always can come up with fifty excuses rather than say 'oops I messed up'."

Aleshia laughed. "Miles, you sound more human every day."

Miles' camera turned. "I will take that as a compliment." Several screens flashed. One brought up the status of the communications array, the other showed the commands being transmitted. A single line lit up in green text. "I have a response from a satellite. It is operational and exiting its hibernation mode. I should have full control in twenty minutes."

"Wonderful, can you now contact the *Phoenix*?" Aleshia said.

"Negative, as I stated earlier, I need several of them working together to boost the signal on a frequency the *Phoenix* can receive."

Galina reached for the intercom. "I'm going to fill Deven in."

"No need, I have done so," Miles said.

Galina folded her arms and sat back in her chair. "Miles, one of these days."

"One of these days what?"

"Never mind," Galina said.

"I am pleased to report the satellite I contacted has sent me all its data, including detailed information on other similar units. I am attempting to contact the others again."

"What difference would it make? If they didn't respond before, why would they now?" Galina said.

"It is possible I didn't focus the array enough. I now have last known locations and full access codes. This will reduce my search time a great deal," Miles said.

A short time later a screen lit up showing more satellites had responded. "I have full control of two more functional satellites. I am redeploying them into a triangular position and changing their primary orientation. They should be ready to make an attempt in one hour."

Down in the hanger bay Leon continued to study the Celloid with every scanner and tool he had, but the plant refused to give up its secrets. He drove long pins into the Celloid Core and tried hooking them up to an isolated computer system, but nothing happened.

"I don't get it. If the Celloid interfaced with a Lytherian ship, then this should work," Leon said.

"Me either. We should be able to reverse engineer a connection and get data back out," Gregory said.

Deven sighed. "You are not considering the Celloid was alive at the time, now that it is dead data retrieval may not be possible."

Leon shook his head. "I don't think so. Until it decays, the data should be in there. It hasn't been dead that long for the data to degrade. After a few days, it's possible. But not now. Deven, what if you try to probe it?"

"Aleshia would be better at doing that."

"In general yes, but you have more abilities with inanimate objects."

"True. Okay, I'll give it a shot." Deven closed his eyes and placed his hands on the long metal rods. He reached out with his mind. Pictures formed, other places. He saw a Lytherian ship destroyed, and the last battle up to the point when the *Defiant* and *Phoenix* combined their firepower to destroy it. He felt the searing pain of the immense cannon blast, and he reeled backward.

Gregory grabbed him. "Deven? You okay?"

Deven shook his head. I'm not sure. "You are right, the data is in there. I did get bits and pieces."

"What did you see?" Leon said.

"Other planets, battles with the Lytherians, and even the last battle where we destroyed it. I felt its pain when we blasted a hole through the middle of it."

"I knew it. I knew it had to be in there. Now if we can get it out before it decays."

Back on the bridge, Miles' camera moved back and forth as he spoke. "I am receiving confirmation from all satellites. They are reporting full operational status and are in the proper position. We are ready to make the attempt."

Galina rolled her eyes. "Well then, don't just stand there and tell us about it, do it."

"But Galina, I am not able to 'stand' at the moment."

Aleshia chuckled. "Miles, just do it."

"Acknowledged. Commands sent. We will know in a minute," Miles said.

8

On the *Phoenix* Minerva watched Otis drum his fingers over and over again as he stared at the floor. "What purpose does that serve?"

Otis' head popped up. "What?"

"Your fingers are going to drill a hole in the arm of my chair. I think I liked your pacing better."

Otis watched his hand and stopped. "Sorry. It has been almost a day. Why don't they call?"

Minerva looked at him. Her eyes on the screen narrowed to mere slits. "And how do you propose they do that? We are the ones with the chair. Aleshia can't call you without it. Or didn't you think of that?"

Otis slapped his forehead. "All this and I miss the obvious."

Minerva smiled. "Yes, you did and I– Hold on, I'm receiving a transmission."

Otis sat forward. "Odell again?"

Minerva shook her head. "No, the signal is too degraded. I estimate the source is from space."

The large screen flashed several times and went to static as an image began to resolve.

"Lytherians?" Otis said.

"Negative. I'm having difficulty due to the degradation.

Attempting to adjust the frequency harmonics." Minerva's eyes widened as an image of Miles' camera appeared on the screen.

"*Phoenix*, this is the *Defiant*, are you receiving this transmission?"

Minerva paused with her mouth open. And for all her memory she could not remember a moment so at a loss for words. "Miles?"

"Correct. It is good to speak with you again Minerva."

"And what about me?" Otis said.

"And you as well Mr. Otis."

Minerva blinked several times. "Miles? How are you doing this? I do not have the capability of deep space communications. Nor does the *Defiant* last I knew, at least on these frequencies. These frequencies shouldn't be working at all."

The image split and Aleshia's face appeared. "Hello Minerva, Otis. Sorry for the surprise, but you didn't seem to be calling us, so we thought we would call you instead."

"In answer to your question, I accessed three old satellites that had such communication abilities. By placing them in the proper positions, I could increase their transmission and reception potential," Miles said.

Minerva cocked her head. "A pyramid configuration with us being the convergence point?"

Miles' iris contracted and expanded. "That is correct."

"How interesting. I didn't think any of my satellites from the original Mechand network survived," Minerva said. "Though I admit I never tried to access them, they were retired and replaced long ago. They should have deorbited by now."

"It is good they didn't," Aleshia said.

"Obviously."

"So what's up?" Otis said. "There must be a reason for this call."

Aleshia nodded. "There is. While we have proved the Celloid Core contains information, accessing it is proving illusive."

Otis smiled. "Ha! I knew you would need me."

"We do. I'm bringing Leon in." Aleshia smiled as her image faded and Leon's replaced her.

"I have driven probes into the core and Deven has scanned it. But I still can't get the system I have hooked up to it to get anything meaningful out." Near Leon sat a screen hooked into the *Defiant's* communications system.

"Hmmm, link it up and let me see," Otis said.

Minerva's eyes narrowed. "I do not think that is a good idea."

Otis turned. "Why?"

"If the portable system is connected into the communications, and if the Celloid is not as dead as they think, it could take over the *Defiant* and by extension, us."

Otis winced. "Good point." He turned back towards the screen. "Leon, can you take a full dump of everything the portable is seeing to a drive and transmit that? The raw data should be inert and unable to do anything."

Leon nodded. "Good idea. Give me a few minutes." Leon hit several keys on the keyboard. Data flowed past the screen. Some of it consisted of DNA, other code in a form no one had ever seen before. Fifteen minutes later, the drive he had connected was full. He unplugged it and stood up. "I will take this to the bridge. There is a shielded port that goes directly to the communications array. And if I am not mistaken, the *Phoenix* has a similar system."

Minerva nodded. "I do. And a good precaution, it will make sure the data does not touch the main systems."

"Good idea," Deven said holding out his hand. "I will take it up to the bridge. You are needed more here."

Leon nodded. "Right." He dropped the drive into Deven's hand, instructing him how best to connect and transmit the data.

Deven ran for the bridge, arrived, and plugged it in before Aleshia could say a word. "Why the rush?" she asked.

"The sooner we know this thing's secrets, the better." He gave the transmit command and looked up to Otis' face on the screen. "It's heading your way now on the sub channel. It will take at least twenty minutes to complete."

Minerva's face pushed over Otis' on the screen, splitting it down the middle. "I'm receiving the data. I concur with your estimate. Upon completion, I will have the data installed on an independent system before Otis examines it."

An hour later Otis sat in front of a console located in the middle of the *Phoenix's* bridge. "Fascinating. This code not only contains DNA, but binary data as well. No wonder it could interface with the Lytherian's scout ship."

Leon's rolled his eyes. "I already told you that. The bigger question is, can you find a way to read it?"

"Yes, you did, but not some details. And I think I can." Otis pointed to a section of the data. "This appears to be a key of some sort. I think I can use it to decode the rest."

Leon's eyes narrowed. "Why in the world would their designers insert a key into their very being?"

Otis shrugged his shoulders. "I don't know. But the simplest answer is the most likely: hide it in plain sight. If they ever lost it, all they would need is to find one Celloid, and they have the key back. And I doubt many would realize what it was. I mean, the Lytherian's didn't catch it either."

Leon nodded. "Point taken."

Otis sat hunched over the console on the *Phoenix's* bridge. "You might want to go get a cup of synth coffee. Or several. This is going to take a while." Leon smiled and disappeared from the screen, leaving Gregory in the background asking for a cup as well. A few minutes later Otis heard a beep and turned to see CB offering a cup of hot, dark liquid. "Coffee? How did you manage that? I didn't think we had any?" Otis took the cup, sipped, and grinned. "And just the way I like it too."

Minerva smiled. "He found a small stockpile I wasn't aware of. I told you, there is more to him than he appears." Otis nodded and went back to work.

Several hours later, a bleary-eyed Otis continued to stare at the screen. "I know the solution is here in this part of the sequence."

Minerva sighed. "Staring at it with more intensity will not make it magically change and decode itself."

"I know that. But I can't help but feel I'm missing something."

Minerva shrugged on her screen. "I don't see how. I have seen you run every decryption algorithm I have ever seen, and several–"

Otis smiled. "Yes, I have several I made myself. Got us out of a lot of fixes. But every single one of them came up negative."

Minerva made a throat clearing grunt. "As I was going to say, several I haven't seen. I watched you do everything but reverse and invert that code."

"That would be too simple," Otis said taking a sip of coffee finishing it. CB rolled up on his rubber wheels, pointed to the cup, and beeped.

Otis smiled. "Thanks for offering CB but if I have any more, I'm going to be doing handstands."

CB beeped an affirmative and stayed next to Otis' side.

Minerva shrugged. "I don't see why you think the solution would be too simple. After all, they left the key in plain sight. Why do you think the solution to using it would be any different?"

Otis' eyes burned from staring at the screen. "All right, I will try it, if nothing else than to prove The Nexus wrong."

Minerva's face scrunched up. "Please don't call me that. I can't stand that name."

Otis sighed. "Sorry, I know you view that name of what you were, not what you are. I won't use it again."

Minerva smiled. "Thank you."

Otis pressed several keys and a second of the screen highlighted, moved in different directions. He then applied a special algorithm he made earlier. The data morphed, turned, twisted and spit out as pure binary. "It worked!"

Minerva chuckled. "I told you it was the one thing you hadn't tried."

Using the new code, the rest clicked into place. Viewable data flowed past his screen, images, logs, records. Some of it had considerable gaps, probably from being blasted to bits. Otis was surprised this much had survived.

Otis' eyes went wide. "Get the *Defiant!*"

Minerva nodded. "Connection established."

Aboard the *Defiant* Leon kept working on the data tab connected to the Celloid. While he wasn't getting anywhere in decoding the data stored in the bio-mass, he felt better keeping an eye on it. No change in the structure told him the Celloid was as dead as when they brought it aboard.

Above him, the speaker in the ceiling crackled. "Leon? Otis is calling," Miles said.

Leon reached over and hit a key on the screen to his right. It flashed and Otis' face appeared. "What's up?"

"You have *got* to see this!" Otis beamed.

Leon's jaw dropped. "You cracked it?"

Otis smirked. "Was there ever any doubt?" Two seconds of silence told him everything. He laughed. "Apparently there was. Anyway, I'm sending you the algorithm and instructions on how to decode what you have on a sub channel. It will be a lot faster than me sending all the data back again."

Leon nodded. "I got it." Leon unplugged a storage drive from the screen and plugged it into the isolated data tab. "Running it now." Leon's eyes went wide as images decoded. "You have got to be kidding me!"

"I know, it shocked me. Where is everyone else?"

"They went to take a nap, we haven't exactly slept well since this trip started."

"Well, wake 'em up! This is important."

"You bet it is," Leon said.

"I have already paged everyone. Gregory will be down to your position in a few moments, Galina, Deven, and Aleshia are on their way up to the bridge," Miles said as the speaker clicked off.

A few minutes later aboard the *Phoenix*, Otis watched as the screen split and on the other side gave a wide view of the *Defiant's* bridge. Deven eyed the screen with Otis' smiling face. "Okay, we are all here, so why do you have a smile as big as a Cheshire cat?"

"It is definitely larger," Aleshia said as she sat down next to Deven.

Otis laughed. "I'm sure Leon filled you in that I cracked the Celloid code?"

Deven's eyes went wide, as did everyone else's on the bridge. "No, he didn't."

"Oh, surprise, I did. And I found some interesting information."

"No kidding," Leon said.

Deven raised his hand. "Otis, what did you find?"

"First off, I confirmed someone else engineered these Celloids. Why I can't tell, but I can tell you they look like giant insects."

Aleshia winced. "Insects? Are you sure?"

"Yes. Big eyes, long hair arms, the works. Hang on, let me show you. Leon? Pull up that one image."

Leon's eyes drifted down to his data tab, and he hit a few buttons. A nearby smaller screen flashed on and displayed a creature a little larger than a man, but appeared more like a cross between a bee and a fly. Although, there were only four arms, not six. Large compound eyes filled most of the head with antenna extending out behind the eyes. The hair covered the mouth area, preventing seeing the orifice they knew must be there. The hair also covered the torso area, but remained mostly obscured by what they assumed to be a space suit. Below, the legs bent at an odd angle and ended in a round semi-harry foot with three toes.

"Yuck," Aleshia said.

Otis nodded. "They are not the most attractive species."

"And I thought the Lytherians looked alien," Galina said.

"The Ixeons certainly do not look like what we would expect. Although, I don't know what that would be," Otis chuckled. "In any case, these creatures created the Celloids. Why, I don't know. Not much of the data about them survived."

Aleshia cocked her head. "The Ixeons?"

"That is the best I can find from this fragmented data. And my translation might be a little off."

"Can you tell me where they came from?" Deven asked.

Leon shook his head. "Nope, like he said, not much survived."

Galina folded her arms. "What *can* you tell us then?"

"They know we destroyed the Celloids and are taking action," Otis said.

Galina choked. "They do? What kind of action?"

Otis sighed. "I'm not sure. There are a few references to rock and destruction, but that is all. Could be they are sending asteroids our way to crash into the planet for all I know."

"How much do they know about us?" Aleshia said.

"That is the one good part. We destroyed the Celloid *Mothership* before it could send a report. It did send a distress call of a sort, and their creators responded with this rock and destruction message."

Aleshia chewed the inside of her cheek. "Nice guys."

Otis sat back in his chair. "Yes, from that I think we can guess the Ixeons didn't have a warm spot in their heart for the Celloids."

Deven regarded Otis' image on the big screen. "Anything else?"

"Not much. I might be able to reconstruct a few more bits, but it will take time."

"But you don't need the hunk of plant to do it, right? We can jettison it?" Galina asked.

Otis shrugged. "I suppose, but I don't see how it could do any harm. While it can regenerate, from what I can see in its code, it is far past the point of doing so."

Leon shook his head. "I don't think we should, in case we missed something in our analysis."

"Yeah, and the daft thing wakes up in the middle of our main hangar bay," Galina said.

Deven raised his hand. "Galina, we have gone through this. We can jettison it the instant anything should happen."

Down in the hangar bay, Leon smiled. "Tell you what, we still have that carbine cannon here in the hangar bay, I can re-enable Miles' direct control of it. If the Celloid does anything, he can fry it. Is that acceptable?"

Galina folded her arms and sat back into her chair with enough force to make it squeak. "Not really. What I would prefer is it jettisoned and burnt to ashes." She sighed. "But I suppose it will have to do since I am the only one here with any sense."

Gregory's eyebrows met as he leaned over to get on the image with Leon. "Hey, I resent that. I didn't say we should keep the thing either, you know."

Galina smiled. "Okay, everyone but Gregory and I."

Deven looked up and Miles' camera turned interpreting he wanted something. "Yes Deven?"

"How long until we arrive?"

"Nine hours fifteen minutes at current rate of speed," Miles said.

"Good. Then I suggest we all go back to bed. Who knows when we will get the opportunity again. Not to mention there is little left for us to do," Deven said.

"Speak for yourself. The *Defiant* still needs a few repairs," Leon said.

"I don't doubt it. But I think they can wait a few hours, don't you?"

Leon shook his head. "Nope. We just found out there is a species that made the Celloids and is firing rocks at us. The *Defiant* needs to be in fighting trim as soon as possible."

Deven sighed. "I'm not going to talk you out of this, am I?"

"Nope," Gregory said, "and I happen to agree with him."

Galina laughed. "You would."

Gregory chuckled. "I would not."

"But you are."

Gregory lifted a finger to continue the conversation when he saw Galina's gleaming eyes on the screen and thought better of it. "Never mind."

Deven stood. "As I see I'm not going to win this one, I will let you all decide for yourselves. But Aleshia and I are going to get some rest."

Aleshia blinked. "We are?"

Deven took her hand in his, pulled her from the seat and smiled. "We are."

Aleshia giggled. "See you guys later." They took off for their quarters.

"Something tells me they are not going to go rest," Gregory said.

Galina laughed. "What gave you that clue?"

Gregory lifted one shoulder. "I don't know. Perhaps I am psychic."

They all laughed as their screens flashed and went black when the connection dropped.

9

When Deven and Aleshia reached their cabin, he turned the lights down low and climbed into the small bed and gestured for Aleshia to join him.

She frowned when she saw he was not doing as she was expecting. She couldn't help herself and peeked into his mind. "We *are* going to rest?"

Deven looked up. "Of course, isn't that what I said?"

Aleshia sat on the side of the bed with enough force to make the springs complain. "Yes, but I didn't think you were serious."

Deven cocked his head. "Of course I was, why wouldn't I be?"

Aleshia rolled her eyes. Men could be so clueless sometimes. Even psychic ones. She sighed. "Never mind."

Otis sat at the isolated console on the *Phoenix's* bridge and scratched his head. "I don't get it."

Minerva cocked her head. "Don't get what? I thought you had finished analyzing the data?"

"I did. Well, for the most part. I'm still trying to reconstruct some damaged areas. I repaired one sector that talked about the rocks the Ixeons are going to throw at us. They refer to them as 'Sileics'. Why would you have a name like that for a rock?"

"Perhaps that is their word for rock?"

Otis shook his head. "Nope, I know what that is. This is something different."

Minerva's eyes narrowed. "I am detecting something on an approach vector."

Otis waved his hand, never taking his eyes off of the screen. "That is just the *Defiant* arriving."

"No. For one, they aren't due back for several hours yet, and second, this is from the opposite direction."

That got Otis' attention, and he looked up. "From the opposite direction? Can't be the Lytherians, could it?"

Minerva shook her head. "No. The configuration is quite different. It doesn't look like a ship, more like a ...well ...a rock."

Otis turned. "The rocks the Ixeons said they were going to throw are here?"

"Possible. Or an asteroid has gone off course."

Otis stood and went over to a console showing data on the rock. "Can we contact the Lytherians to check it out?"

"Negative. I lack the equipment to transmit on the frequencies they use. Given time, I think I could make the necessary modifications."

"I can't believe they enhanced so many systems, yet didn't do anything with communications?"

"If you remember, the telepathic chair had that capability, so why would I need it as well? Not to mention the undertaken enhancements were a rush job to begin with."

Otis nodded. "True. Looks like it is up to us then. Can we reach it?"

Minerva nodded. "Yes. With our Lytherian modified engines, we could reach something much farther away."

"What about air?"

Minerva smiled. "It doesn't matter to me, I don't need it."

Otis folded his arms. "But I do!"

CB gave a strong beep.

Otis nodded. "You tell her, CB."

Minerva gave a very feminine giggle. "Sorry, I couldn't help it. The look on your face was worth it though. We should have plenty to reach the object and return considering there is only one person using oxygen."

Otis' brow furrowed. "Should?"

Minerva laughed again. "I am positive."

CB gave a low beep.

"I agree. It doesn't give me a warm feeling either."

Minerva rolled her eyes. "Will you two stop? I would never place your life in danger. You should know that by now."

Otis cracked a grin as he regarded the Mechand next to him. "That was fun CB, think we got her?"

The Mechand gave a strong beep.

"I think so too."

"You were playing me?"

"Tit for tat, my great-grandparents used to say. How long will it take us to get to this rock?"

"Only a couple of hours. We should be able to check it out and return before the *Defiant* arrives."

Otis smiled. "Let's do it then."

"Should we tell the *Defiant?*"

"Nah, we'll be back before they know we left. We're just going to check a big rock, blast it if needed, and pop back."

Minerva nodded. The engines of the *Phoenix* began to glow. "Full power to extended overdrive in five seconds. Better have a seat. My inertia damping systems are quite a bit smaller than the *Defiant's*."

Otis sat down in the nearest chair. The lack of padding made his back complain. CB rolled over next to him. "Hang on, CB." The Mechand gave an affirmative beep and locked his wheels.

Minerva smiled. "Course set. Engaging overdrive." A bubble of energy formed around the *Phoenix* as it grew brighter and brighter. The engines increased their glow as the whole ship leapt into overdrive, leaving streaks of fading light.

Otis hit several keys at the console he was sitting at. For over an hour he stared at the data from this rock. His eyes flashed, and he cocked his head as he turned around. "One thing bugs me. Why didn't you pick this up before?"

"I do not know. I should have. An asteroid of this size heading for Earth should have been seen long ago," Minerva said.

"And it appeared out of nowhere?"

"Affirmative. One minute nothing, the next it was on my scanners."

Otis sat back in his chair. "Could it be a ship?"

Minerva blinked. "A ship?" She shook her head. "Not possible. All my scans indicate a lifeless mass of rock. Most of it silicon with a few other elements mixed in."

"Can you get an image?"

"No. We need to be closer for a visual."

Otis stood up and peered out one of the large windows on the bridge. The armor shields had been retracted giving a wonderful view of space as they cruised through overdrive. "How much longer?"

"Fifteen minutes, perhaps less."

Otis spun around. "Less? I thought you dealt in precision?"

"I do, but the distance between us is varying. I suspect a sensor is malfunctioning. I have sent one of my Mechands to check it."

"I don't like it. I may not have Deven's or Aleshia's gifts, but my gut says this is bad. Turn us around. Head back to Earth."

"What? Now? We are almost there."

"And I'm telling you, this *is* bad. We need to get away from this rock as soon as possible." He turned back towards the windows.

Minerva blinked. "Why?"

Otis' eyes narrowed as he spun around. "Look, I found out references to these Ixeons sending rocks at us. We know they created the Celloids, who knows what else they can do. Turn us around *now*."

"Very well. I will have to bring us out of overdrive and chart a new course back, or we might get lost. The Lytherians didn't give us all their space technology."

"I know, just do it."

"I am. Hang on." Otis ran for the nearest chair and sat in it. The *Phoenix* shuddered as it dropped out of enhanced overdrive so fast slamming to a dead stop. Even braced Otis was thrown from his seat and landed on the deck plate. A fresh cut over his left eye dripped blood, but he didn't find anything broken.

CB rolled over to Otis and helped him up. He pointed at Otis' eye and beeped.

"I'm all right. It's a minor cut. A little med sealant and I will be fine."

"Ohhh nooo," Minerva said before Otis was again thrown to the deck.

This time he hit his arm on one of the chairs as he went down. "Ouch! Hey watch it!" He felt his arm. It hurt, but nothing broken. "I thought we were stopped?"

"That wasn't me. Look! We are under attack."

Otis turned to see a bright red beam lashing out from the top closest corner of the rock and hitting the *Phoenix's* shields. The rock didn't look like anything natural. It was smooth and with angular lines making a perfect square. "That thing's a ship! That is how it appeared to move on your scans. It must have seen us drop out of overdrive and jumped closer. Get us out of here!"

"I'm trying. Whatever that beam is has got us pinned. I can't move. Not only that, it is draining energy from the power core. Shields will shut down in three minutes and after that, *me*."

"You've got carbine cannons, use them!"

"From what I can tell, that thing is solid stone. My cannons aren't going to do much damage unless I pound on it for months."

"Aim for where that beam is coming from. It must have a hole, it couldn't be shooting that beam through the stone itself."

"Logical. Locking cannons." Several cannons lashed out with pulsed energy blasts that had little effect. The red beam continued to hold the *Phoenix* like a fish on a hook.

Otis watched the blasts and felt his hope fade like the energy streak. Then his eyes went wide. "Try all your cannons at once. Full power. Give it everything you got."

"I can increase the power to the cannons, but they are not built for it. It will burn out their delicate focusing systems."

"And in a few minutes we're dead if you don't."

"Good point. Locking all cannons. Charge building. They will reach maximum in ten seconds. I hope this works."

"So do I."

CB beeped a third.

Every light and console aboard the *Phoenix* dimmed as the shields faded. "Full power reached. Here we go." Minerva unleashed a focused, continuous blast of four cannons that pounded one single spot on the rock. At first nothing happened, then an explosion mushrooming out from that point and the beam holding them disappeared. "We're free."

"Get us out of here!"

"You don't have to tell me twice. Diverting full power to enhanced overdrive." A bubble of energy began to form around the *Phoenix*.

Otis dove into a nearby chair a microsecond before the engines pushed the *Phoenix* into overdrive, slamming his back against the chair. "Are we getting away?"

Minerva shook her head. "No. They are pursuing. But at least we are keeping our distance."

"Where are we going?"

"Back to Earth."

"What? We are leading them straight back home!"

Minerva shrugged. "It is the only course I had laid in. Besides, where else are we going to go? I can't reach another solar system, not without taking hundreds of years."

"Good point. Can we blast that hole you made? Slow them down a little?"

"No. All my cannons are offline. I used more power than even their Lytherian enhanced systems could take. Pushing that much energy for that long must have burned out the focusing system as I feared. My Mechands are repairing them, but it will take time."

"How long?"

"A little over an hour. About the time we reach Earth."

Otis' face scrunched up as his eyes squeezed shut before opening them a second later. "Great. Can we get a hold of the *Defiant* and tell them who's coming to dinner?"

Minerva shook her head. "Not at the moment. In about forty-five minutes I should be able to contact the satellites and push a message to the *Defiant*."

"So, just about when we arrive we can tell them?"

"Correct."

Otis sighed. "This day just keeps getting better and better."

The *Defiant* exited enhanced overdrive to a perfect orbit. Aleshia gazed out the bridge window to the blue planet below and frowned. "Wasn't the *Phoenix* to meet us?"

Galina pushed a button on her console. "*Phoenix?* We have arrived in orbit, but don't see you."

No response.

Deven's brow furrowed. "I don't like it. This is not like Minerva or Otis."

Miles' camera turned. "Indeed. They would have told us if their plans had changed."

"Deven? I have located the *Phoenix*. Displaying the information on the screen to your right," Miles said.

Deven turned and looked at the screen. "That doesn't make sense. If I'm reading this right, they left Earth and headed out into the solar system."

Leon looked over his shoulder. "You aren't wrong. That is what they did."

"Affirmative," Miles said. "Also, I detect a large rock near them."

Leon cocked his head. "A large rock?" He sat down at his console. "Show me." The screen lit up, scrolling with various data giving a rough size and composition of silicon with a few other elements mixed in. No life readings. "Hmm, it is hard to get a good reading that far away, but definitely a big hunk of rock. Why would they leave to check it out and not tell us?"

"Good question," Deven said.

Aleshia cocked her head. "Could it be Otis thought it was one of the rocks the Ixeons mentioned in the Celloid memories?"

"Could be," Galina said. "I can't imagine what else would make him high-tail it when we were supposed to meet."

Deven nodded. "Agreed. Still, I am surprised he didn't tell us."

Miles' camera turned. "Deven, I have detected a focused energy burst at the *Phoenix*."

"At the *Phoenix*? Are you sure?"

"Positive," Miles responded.

"That does not make sense unless–"

"That's no rock, but something else the Ixeons made!" Aleshia finished for him.

"That is highly probable at the moment," Miles said.

"Can we help them?" Deven said.

Leon shook his head. "No. While our engines are bigger, and we can go faster, by the time we reach them ..."

"I have detected energy blasts from the *Phoenix* directed at the rock," Miles said. The large screen flashed, showing data from his latest readings. The energy curve showed several of the *Phoenix's* cannons had opened fire.

"Go Minerva!" Galina said.

Miles' camera turned. "Changed your opinion of her?"

"No, but I don't want to see her wrecked either. Besides, Otis is with her."

"I must report the beam focused on the *Phoenix* is still there. Therefore, the weapons were ineffective," Miles said.

"Not good," Aleshia said.

Deven folded his arms. "That's putting it mildly."

Miles' iris contracted and expanded. "I have detected larger, more focused beam from the *Phoenix*."

Leon hit a few keys on his console. "I'll say. The energy curve is huge. She must be punching everything she's got through the cannons."

"The original beam has ceased and it would appear Minerva has engaged the overdrive."

Deven sat forward. "Course?"

"Here. Or more specifically, this rendezvous point. I also must report the rock is following. It would appear it has movement capability."

"They're leading it straight back here!" Galina said.

Deven raised his hand. "Where else are they going to go? And I'm sure this rock already knows about us."

Galina sighed. "Yes, you're right. At least this way it gives them a little more time."

"And us," Deven said.

"To do what? They couldn't do a thing to do it. What are we going to do?"

Leon smiled. "We are bigger and have a larger power core. We might have more of an effect."

Deven smiled. "Especially if both the *Phoenix* and *Defiant* attack at the same time."

Leon nodded as he got up. "Right. I have Gregory doing a few last-minute repairs. Between the two of us, they will be done before the *Phoenix* arrives."

"Not to mention our 'guest'." Galina coughed.

Deven looked up at Miles' camera. "Miles?"

The camera turned. "Yes Deven?"

"Can we contact the *Phoenix* using the satellites you found earlier?"

"At the moment no, the satellites are focused on their previous stationary position. But if I adjust their orbits to focus on the *Phoenix's* new direction, it is probable."

"Get to work on it. We need to talk with them and find out what they know. Perhaps we can come up with something together."

"Commands sent. I can make the attempt in twenty minutes," Miles said.

10

Aboard the *Phoenix*, Otis started at the screen displaying the Celloid data. He scrolled through several data sets and tried several recovery algorithms he had developed over the years. But the rest of the data remained shrouded in corrupted bits and bytes. He began working on a newer algorithm that he started a while ago but never finished. "Perhaps this one will work," he muttered.

Minerva's eyes shifted. "What was that? My audio pickups didn't quite get that."

"Nothing. Just muttering to myself."

"I fail to see the usefulness in that."

"It is …never mind. How long until we can contact the *Defiant*?"

"About twenty-five minutes."

"Is that rock still on our tail?"

"If you mean is it still behind us, yes. It has maintained the same speed. We have a little space between us, but not much."

"Meaning once we drop out of overdrive we can expect about half a minute before it is on top of us again?"

Minerva nodded. "Correct. I'm sorry I don't …I'm receiving a link from the *Defiant*."

Otis spun around. "How is that possible? I thought we were not in range yet?"

"We aren't. But I suspect when they discovered we didn't make our rendezvous, they tracked us and Miles reconfigured the satellites to boost the signal along our path. Transmission on screen."

The main screen flashed and glitched several times with static until it faded and Deven's face appeared. "*Phoenix* are you receiving?"

Otis smiled. "We are indeed. Deven, we have a situation here–"

"We know."

Otis blinked. "You know?"

Deven nodded. "We started searching for you when we arrived, found you, the rock, and watched the battle."

"Then you also know we have an uninvited guest hot on our tail."

Deven nodded again. "We do. How did you stop the beam that was hitting you? Leon thinks you used all the power channeled through your carbine cannons."

Minerva nodded. "I did. But it burned out the focusing systems."

"Are they repairable?"

"Yes. My Mechands are working on them and should have them fixed a few moments before we arrive. Why? They didn't do much damage before."

"Perhaps not, but combined with ours, perhaps we can crack that rock in two. Our cannons are larger, and we have more of them."

Minerva shook her head. "My scans indicate it is a very hard form of reinforced silicon. Doing that much damage is not probable. Even with the *Defiant's* assistance."

While Minerva and Deven were talking Otis had went back to work on the console. Only a few more lines remained on his new algorithm, if he could just get this to work. Finally, the commands clicked into place and the raw code compiled without errors. "Got it! Now we will see!"

Minerva's and Deven's eyes focused on Otis. "Got what?" They said in unison.

"I have a new recovery algorithm that may get more out of this corrupted Celloid data. I'm running it now and centering it on the data involving the Ixeons' rocks."

Deven raised an eyebrow. "How long?"

Otis' console beeped, and he laughed. "About that long."

"Did it find anything?"

"Give me a minute," Otis said scrolling through the data. "Interesting. These things are called Sileics. And the Ixeons did create them."

"We knew that," Minerva said.

"No, we didn't. We only assumed."

Minerva cocked an eyebrow. "It was a very probable one."

"True."

"Anything else?" Deven said.

"Hang on, I'm looking." Otis scrolled some more and his face lit up like a lighthouse in a dark fog. "Bingo! They put in a kill switch in case their creations ever tried to revolt. The Ixeons put in a weakness to ultrasound on certain frequencies." Otis picked up a data tab and tapped in the data he was seeing. "I'm sending it to you on a sub-channel."

On the *Defiant* Deven punched the button on the intercom. "Leon? Get up here."

Deven heard a loud bang and swearing. "Now? I'm rather in the middle of–"

"Yes *now*, it's urgent."

"Got it, be right up." The intercom clicked off. A couple of minutes later Leon appeared in the hatchway. "What's so important?"

Deven pointed to his screen and the data Otis had sent. "What do you think of this?"

Leon leaned over his shoulder. "Well I'll be. He did manage to reconstruct the data."

"Not all of it," Otis laughed, "but at least I got the data we need right now."

"Yes, you did. Hmm, this is interesting."

Deven sighed. "Otis already said that. Can it be done?"

Leon nodded. "Sure, if we adjust the communications array, I can have it generate these frequencies. Of course, space can't carry sounds like this, but if we hook the carbide cannons to the array and transmit the frequencies along their beam. If this data is right, it will cause a resonance in their silicon structure, and they will crumble. Who would have thought it, silicon life forms!"

On the *Phoenix*, Otis turned towards Minerva. "Can we do the same?"

Minerva nodded. "It should be possible. Our array is not as powerful as the *Defiant's* but it will generate what is needed."

"How long?"

"Maybe ten minutes? Only minor modifications are needed to the array and cannons."

On the big screen, Deven smiled. "Then perhaps we have a chance between the two of us."

"You bet we do, Boss."

"I will go get the modifications done, it will only take a few minutes," Leon said over Deven's shoulder as he ran off the bridge.

"It had better. We will arrive in fifteen minutes," Minerva said.

Aleshia bit her lip. "Cutting it close."

Otis laughed. "When don't we?"

Galina chuckled. "You got that right."

"Minerva, send us the detailed scans you made. Also, the exact position of the Sileic beam you destroyed."

Minerva nodded. "I am sending it now. Am I to assume that location is our intended target?"

Deven nodded. "Right, it may not make any difference, but I want to make use of any advantage we have."

"Logical." Her eyes darted around the bridge. "Dropping out of overdrive in twenty seconds."

Deven hit the intercom. "Leon? Are we ready?"

"Give me a second here."

"You have less than ten."

"Got it." Deven heard banging and Leon yelling something to Gregory. "Okay, ready."

"Galina, are we in position?"

"Yes. The instant they drop out, we are in the perfect angle to combine our cannons on the Sileic's weakened spot," Galina said.

"Almost perfect," Miles said as his camera turned towards Galina. "If you adjust by two-hundredths of a percent, then it will be."

"It is close enough, Miles," Galina said.

"I beg to differ. But I can compensate with our cannons' orientation."

"Then it is close enough, you bot!"

"Jumping out of overdrive ...*now*," Minerva said. Otis hung on to the chair he sat in as the *Phoenix* shuddered. She dropped out of overdrive right next to the *Defiant*. A few seconds later, the Sileics appeared and started closing the gap.

"Is it me, or does that thing look a lot meaner this time?" Otis said.

Minerva's eyes narrowed. "Unknown. Orientation changing, hold on." The *Phoenix* did a fast pitch and roll, flipping over to face the Sileic and roll so her canons were in line. "In position."

The Sileic continued its forward motion, moving closer and closer.

"I have a lock. Firing in three seconds," Miles said.

Minerva nodded. "Firing control linked to yours, Miles."

"Confirmed. All cannons responding … firing."

Aboard the *Defiant* and *Phoenix*, energy began to glow at the tip of each cannon for several seconds before the beams ripped forward, combined at the proper point, and slammed into the Sileics weak spot.

On the *Defiant's* bridge, Deven watched the onslaught as the Sileic slid closer. "It's not working."

Aboard the *Phoenix* Minerva glared. "I thought you said this would work?"

"I don't understand it. It *should* work. All the data I found said it *would*," Otis said.

The giant Sileic ship dwarfed even the *Defiant* as it loomed ever closer. Twin red beams lashed out of the hole the *Phoenix* blasted before. On the screen, Deven's eyes narrowed as the side of his lip turned up. "I *thought* you destroyed that."

"We did. They must have repaired it," Minerva said.

"The weapon is draining our energy, estimated shield failure in two minutes. Power core to shut down forty-three seconds after," Miles said.

"And my shields will fail in even less," Minerva said, "I have not fully recovered from the last encounter."

On the screen, Galina's eyes narrowed as she pointed her finger. "I told you this was crazy! Nothing is ever this easy. No one will leave a secret method on how to destroy your weapons lying around."

Otis' eyes went wide as he snapped his fingers. "Of course! I am an idiot!" He ran for the center of the *Phoenix's* bridge where the isolated console still sat.

"Otis? What are you–"

Otis lifted a finger. "Give me a minute."

"We don't have a minute!"

"Technically, we have one minute fifty-four seconds," Miles said.

Deven gritted his teeth. "Miles? Don't–"

"Don't what?"

Deven's jaw line became more pronounced. "Never mind. Time to change tactics. Disconnect Otis' modifications to the cannons and increase to full power. Perhaps we can at least get lucky and get free of this thing."

"Wait!" Otis said.

"Otis, we can't wait. We–"

The *Phoenix* shuddered as the shields failed. "My shields are down! Complete system failure in thirty seconds!" Minerva said as her screen started to dim.

"Got it!" Otis said as his fingers flew over the keys. He plugged in a data tab and activated a secondary program.

"Otis?"

"I just sent you a new modification that doesn't need any hardware changes. Miles can use it to reprogram the cannons, as can Minerva."

Minerva nodded. "Changes have been implemented."

"I have received the new modifications. Deploying them," Miles said.

"I didn't–" Deven started to say but never finished. The *Defiant* and *Phoenix's* carbine cannon beams changed color to a deep blue and increased in size where the two focused beams merged into one. The energy structure changed, winding out into a massive cone that enveloped the whole Sileic.

They watched.

"Anything?" Aleshia said.

Miles' camera turned. "The Sileics are still draining our energy. The shields will be down in a minute followed by a full shutdown ten seconds later."

"Nineteen seconds until system failure!" Minerva cocked her head as the *Phoenix* continued shook even faster. "Miles? Are you detecting a change in the Sileic's motion as well?"

"Confirmed. It is very slight, but there is a change in motion. Almost a vibration as they continue to approach."

Otis jumped up. "It's working then! We just need to hit it harder. Divert all power to the cannons."

"But if I do that, it may shut down the central ESS and it will take time to recharge. The *Defiant* might have enough left, but I won't," Minerva said.

"It doesn't matter. We are toast if you don't try."

"Otis I–"

"Don't worry about it, Boss. At least I am going out with a bang. Minerva, Miles, do it."

"Acknowledged," they both said in unison.

The blue cone of energy enveloping the Sileic grew brighter and brighter until it was almost white as all the remaining power of both ships rammed through the cannons.

The twin beams holding them released and Sileic stopped

its forward motion. It even started to reverse course and head away.

"Oh no you don't," Otis said as he grinned. "It's too late for that."

The Sileic continued, but its pace slowed, then stopped as the vibration increased. Hairline cracks started from the beam port, then spread out, growing larger as they intersected each other and expanded. Aleshia pointed as the larger cracks began to luminess, emitting a white glow that increased with each second.

Minerva sighed. "Full shutdown in ten seconds."

"Don't stop, keep it on!" Otis said.

The Sileic began to shudder and vibrate as the cracks continued to grow. Several of them had merged to form a chasm deeper than the Grand Canyon. The Sileic could take no more and bits began to flake off a few seconds before the whole structure lost cohesion and it crumbled to sand. A moment later nothing was left but a cloud of silicon dust.

"Got him!" Otis said as all the lights aboard the *Phoenix* went out. Otis turned around to face the only light on the bridge: Minerva's screen.

"I'm sorry. I have nothing left except myself. My internal core has enough power to last for a day, and the central power core will regenerate long before then. But not before the environment becomes inhospitable for you." Minerva sighed.

"Don't worry about it. It was worth it. I went into this with my eyes open."

Behind him, CB beeped.

Otis turned. "It is okay. The *Defiant* will figure out something."

"I don't see how. I have no power for the bay doors, even if they could send a vehicle over."

Otis' eyes went wide. "Vehicle," he muttered.

"But I told you I can't open the doors to let you out or them in. I don't have any other hatches aboard. This ship was never designed for space to begin with."

"No no, I didn't mean you, I meant my truck. It's still aboard, right?"

Minerva shrugged. "Where else would it be? I didn't jettison it if that is what you are asking."

Otis laughed. "I didn't think you did. But I have been working to make it space-worthy, and while not finished, it does have enhancements like a sealed cab. It also has a decent heating system, it should keep me warm enough until the power comes back online."

"That is well and good, but what are you going to do for oxygen?"

"Yes, that's a problem."

CB beeped several times in rapid succession.

"What's up CB?" Otis said trying to figure out what the Mechand was trying to say. Usually, he didn't have any trouble, but this time he was clueless.

CB pointed towards the hatch and ladder that lead off of the bridge. He rolled towards it and pulled Otis with him.

"Okay okay I'm coming." He turned towards Minerva. "I guess he wants to show me something."

"Obviously."

CB pulled Otis to the hatch, opened it, hoisted himself up, fitted his wheels through the hatch and lowered his body down the ladder by extending his arms. When he reached the bottom, his hands released their grip and retracted.

Otis nodded and followed him down. "What is so important down here?"

CB rolled over to his hopper and pointed to the back. Otis

examined the area but didn't see what the Mechand was so excited about. CB extended a hand to the back wall, and a panel slid over revealing a first aid kit with a medical scanner and two bottles. Each containing several hours of oxygen.

Long ago, when the Mechands were a new creation, the UN had a mandate requiring every Mechand in the complex to carry emergency medical supplies. Later on the order was repealed. Otis had no idea until now CB was that old. "You have been around that long?" Otis said.

CB gave a beep and one rubber encased finger pointed at the supplies.

Otis smiled. "Yes, I will take them. Thank you, my friend."

The Mechand gave several quick beeps, hopped a little into the air, which Otis couldn't imagine how he did it, and grabbed him in a very human bear hug.

Surprised, Otis wiggled in the grip. "Bot! What are you doing?"

CB released him, gave a very low tone beep, and rolled away several feet, lowering his arms.

Otis gazed into his optics. "What's wrong?"

CB said nothing or moved.

Otis thought for a second. "Is it because I called you bot when you hugged me?"

The Mechand gave a very low beep.

"Oh, it is not because I'm mad at you. Not at all. You surprised me. I have never been hugged by a Mechand before." Otis took two steps and lowered himself down to look into CB's optics. "Look, you have saved my life again. I'm grateful little buddy. I really am."

CB gave two quick beeps as his optics brightened.

"Yes, you are my buddy. Now come on. I need help getting this O2 installed in my truck."

The Mechand gave several more quick beeps, rolled over to his hopper, closed the compartment, rolled to the front section, hitched himself to it, and started heading towards the hanger bay. Otis followed, and a few minutes later they were working on installing the oxygen into the truck's systems.

On the *Defiant's* dark bridge, Deven paced back and forth. Power was rebuilding slowly. The lights were dim, but not out. He knew in a few more minutes the lights would be back among all the major systems aboard. They wouldn't be ready for another fight until the power core had recovered in full, but they would be fine. Otis on the other hand was not.

Aleshia glared at him. "Will you stop pacing? You're going to wear a hole in the deck plate."

Deven looked up. "I can't help it. There must be something we can do."

Miles' camera turned. "As I have stated before, while we will have power for all vital functions, we will be unable to change orbit, not that the *Phoenix* could follow us, regardless."

Deven sighed. "I know. They don't have enough power to open the bay doors even if we could send a vehicle over."

"Correct."

"He will find a way. He has always managed to sneak out of tough spots before," Galina said.

"I can't imagine him sneaking out of this one," Deven said.

"Perhaps we could get some oxygen over to him?" Aleshia said.

Miles' camera turned. "That is not possible. We do not have space-worthy vehicles or space suits aboard."

"How about the Lytherians?" Galina said. "They could help."

"Negative. I do not have enough power or the proper equipment to make contact with them at their current location."

Aleshia sat back in her chair. "I could, if I had the chair."

Deven kept pacing. "Of course, but you are here and the chair is over there. We keep running into the same problem."

"Affirmative," Miles said.

Leon appeared in the hatchway. "I've been thinking. Could we get close enough to send something across? I could rig up several anti-gravs to work like small thrusters to move a package across."

Miles' camera turned. "The required accuracy will be difficult, but theoretically possible–"

Leon sighed. "I know it is possible, or I wouldn't have mentioned it."

"However, Minerva lacks enough power to open the hangar bay doors."

"There must be a manual method?"

"Negative. None was ever thought necessary. The hangar bay is the only ingress or egress method aboard."

"That seems rather unsafe," Leon said.

"Perhaps, but at the time Minerva considered adding one a waste of Mechand resources," Miles said.

The lights brightened further as the screen at Leon's console came to life. He sat in the chair and tapped several keys. "Main systems came back online. Shields and weapons are still down but everything else is back."

Deven turned. "The communications array is back? See if you can get a message across and see how they are doing?"

Leon tapped a few more keys. "While we have enough

power to send, Minerva doesn't have enough to receive judging by these readings."

"Is she down as well?"

Leon shook his head. "Nope, I see power utilization on the bridge. I'm sure the emergency supply I installed inside her core is keeping her functional. It won't last very long, but a day or less is all she needs."

Deven sighed. "I suppose sticking a message in a bottle and throwing it across won't work either?"

Miles' camera turned. "Negative, she still can't open–"

"Miles, it was a joke," Aleshia said.

Miles' camera went back and forth several times as the iris contracted and expanded. "It would appear my humor needs work."

Aleshia smiled. "Just a tad."

Gregory appeared in the hatchway. "I fixed cannons one and two. The others are still working but pushing that much power through them so soon after the last time took a few miles off of their warranty."

Leon nodded. "Yes, they are more prone to fail now, we will get the energy coalescing systems replaced as soon as we are back planet side."

Gregory pointed out the window. "But I thought we were."

Leon laughed. "You know very well what I meant. On the ground."

Gregory smiled. "Yep, I did. And even with the repairs, the cannons won't be able to fire again for five hours at least."

Leon nodded. "If we could shut down, the power core would recover faster. But we need all we are using at the moment."

Deven stopped pacing and slapped his forehead. "I'm an idiot! Aleshia, can't you contact him?"

She shook her head. "Nope, and I don't know why. We should be in range, and I shouldn't be getting a lot of noise that could throw off a one-on-one conversation. Yet I can't get in touch with him."

Deven turned towards her. "Perhaps you are still weak from holding the Celloid's core and preventing the crash in the hangar bay?"

Aleshia shrugged. "Could be. My abilities are better, but I do know they are not back to what they were."

Miles' camera turned. "Deven, I am receiving a transmission."

Deven whirred around. "Who?"

"The *Phoenix*, or more specifically, Otis."

Deven's eyes narrowed as he turned towards Leon. "I thought you said they don't have enough power to turn on a light blub?"

"They don't. I can't explain it."

"Transmission on screen," Miles said as the large screen along the wall flickered, flashed, and Otis' smiling face appeared.

"Hi guys, wanted to let you know I'm not dead yet."

Aleshia walked up behind Deven and stood next to him. "How are you doing this? Leon said there isn't enough power."

"There isn't. But my truck is an independent system," Otis said.

Deven threw his head back. "Your truck! Of course! But wait . . . you don't have enough oxygen to last until the power core regenerates."

"I don't normally, but I do now."

"What do you mean you do now? Mechand carriers do not carry oxygen," Leon said.

Otis nodded. "Right you are, but CB had some stashed."

Leon blinked. "CB? Who's CB?"

"That Cleaning Mechand." Otis paused to rotate the visual pickup until it reached outside the window and focused on the headless Mechand outside sitting next to the truck.

Galina laughed. "CB? You named him?"

Otis turned the pickup back until his face reappeared on the screen. "It was either that or say 'Hey bot' all the time." Otis shrugged. "He seems to like it. Anyway, CB had oxygen bottles along with an extensive first aid kit in his hopper."

Aleshia cocked her head, remembering when they rode in it racing to get out of the World Council complex. "I don't remember seeing that."

Otis shrugged. "It was in a hidden compartment in the back. I grabbed the bottles and rigged them up to my truck's systems. I should be good for almost a day."

"But will your new buddy be able to stand being separated from you for that long?" Galina giggled.

Otis jerked a thumb towards the window. "Yeah, he will be fine."

Miles' camera turned. "How is Minerva?"

"She is fine. Running on the backup power supply Leon added to her core. That should last until the main power core recovers. If it doesn't, she told me she can power down and I will have to restart her. I hope it doesn't come to that. I remember the last time she complained about a headache for days."

Leon chuckled. "I remember well."

"Well, I'm going to work on this," Otis paused to wave a data tab in front of the camera. "I grabbed the all Celloid data and downloaded it on to this. I have this feeling we're still missing something essential. I'm going to continue the data recovery. See if I can squeeze any more secrets from it." He sat the data tab on the seat next to him. "If you guys need me, you know where to fine me. I'm not going anywhere for a while."

Deven nodded. "Right. We'll keep in touch."

"Always." The screen flashed and Otis' face was replaced with scrolling colored text on a black background displaying raw data about the *Defiant's* systems.

11

Aleshia sat aboard the *Phoenix* with her eyes closed, focusing on the area where the Lytherians might be. The chair she sat in radiated with power that seeped into her mind, amplifying her abilities. The crystal mounted in the base glowed as energy passed through it.

Deven stood next to her. "Are you sure you want to do this?"

Aleshia never opened her eyes. "Deven, we have been through this. They need to know what is going on. They might be able to help."

"I know, but I'm worried about you. You still have not recovered from before."

"I will be fine. I'm not trying to hold a Celloid or pull us back from the brink of destruction, just make a simple call."

Minerva nodded. "And at the current power level, I can't imagine it causing any stress."

"Good, keep it there," Deven said.

Minerva's eyes narrowed. "I will. And that is only the fifth time you have told me."

Deven turned. "Sorry, I guess I'm a little protective when it comes to Aleshia."

Minerva blinked. "A little?"

"Okay, a lot."

Aleshia sighed. "Will you two hush. I can't concentrate."

Deven smiled and walked over. He took her hand in his which made her eyes pop open. "How's this?"

She smiled. "While I like it, it is even more of a distraction." She pulled her hand free and sat farther back in the chair.

Deven sighed, spread his feet apart and folded his hands behind his back. His eyes focused on Aleshia.

Aleshia's eyes popped open again. "Do you forget I can feel you? This is not working. Why don't you go help Otis with whatever he is doing?"

"Otis is on the link in his truck with Leon as they work on the Celloid data. Leon is good, and Otis is the best there is. What am I going to do down there?"

Aleshia glared. "How about get out of my hair?"

Deven laughed. "Okay okay, I'm going, I'm going."

After he left the bridge Aleshia gave a deep sigh. "Men, sometimes." She rolled her eyes.

Minerva smiled. "I wouldn't know. Not that I doubt you. And I still think this could have waited until the *Phoenix* fully recovered."

"Normally yes, but we need to get in touch with them as soon as possible. They need to know what we found out and send help. We can't do this alone."

Minerva gave a very audible sigh. "I realize this, however, I don't think an hour is going to make much of a difference."

Aleshia continued to probe different areas of the asteroid belt, looking for any signs of the Lytherians. So far nothing. "I never dreamed the asteroid belt was so large."

Minerva nodded. "Yes. It didn't surprise me when the Lytherians asked if they could use it."

"I suppose it doesn't me either now. And what are we going to do with it? We can't use it as a resource."

"Not yet. But with their technology, we could."

"True. If they will give it."

Minerva shrugged. "I don't see why not. After all, we saved their race from extinction."

"Perhaps. But then again, if we didn't draw the Celloids here instead of attacking the Lytherian home world, would it have made a difference?"

Minerva shrugged again. "My analysis based on what you have told us, they fought the Celloids for hundreds of years, and all that happened was abandoning planets to the Celloids."

Aleshia continued probing for a minute then pulled her head out from under the head ring to rest. The round metal ring raised and retracted on its own. "So you don't think the tide would ever have turned?"

Minerva shook her head. "No. It was your abilities that turned the tide. Something the Lytherians could never do. They threw many technological solutions at the Celloids and every time the Celloids managed to overcome them."

Aleshia rubbed her temples. "You have a point. But I still think they would have stopped the Celloids *eventually*."

"And how many planets would they have to be chased from before that happened?" Minerva shook her head. "No, I don't think they were in a winnable battle. At least not unless they changed tactics."

Aleshia sat up in the chair and the round band reformed and lowered back down on her head. "Either way, they did win with our help."

"Yes, and I think they should be more grateful than they are."

"What do you think they should do? Or should have done?"

Minerva's eyes narrowed. "Giving us a reliable way of contacting them would have been a good start."

Aleshia laughed while trying to hold still. "I have to agree there. But I also know they had to repair their ships as soon as possible or lose more of them. Something they can't afford."

Minerva gave a very human sigh. "Yes. But how long would it have taken them to increase our communications range or give us a portable that could do it?"

"I doubt a portable unit could reach them even then. And perhaps our systems would have taken too long to upgrade."

"That is possible, but unlikely based on the speed that they did weapons and engine upgrades."

Aleshia continued to reach out with her mind. "Minerva, increase the power to the chair."

"I don't think I should. Deven will tear my core apart if I do."

Aleshia smiled. "I won't tell if you won't."

Minerva grinned. "You have a deal. But not much more."

"That's fine." Aleshia felt the increase in power, and she reached out further to the other side of the asteroid field. She went over section after section without success when her mind brushed something. She tried to zero in on it but couldn't bring it into focus. She pushed harder and found the only *Maker* to have survived the battle with the Celloids. It's older engines being slower than the others, kept it back from the central blast that vaporized the rest. The massive battle-scared ship lumbered on, devouring several small asteroids for materials. Her mind felt around and found a shuttle filled with replacement parts and equipment exiting the *Maker's* aft section. Three new fighters flanked it. "The *Command* carrier must be here," Aleshia muttered. "Fleet Commander Karthish would not have left his last *Maker* behind."

She pushed, looking for the massive carrier. A ship so large, even the *Defiant* could fit inside any of its hangar bays with ease. It even dwarfed a *Maker*. Several searches later, she found it a considerable distance away. The Battle damage still very apparent. Aleshia was surprised the damage hadn't been repaired yet. With all the raw materials the *Maker* was scooping up, it should have been a simple proposition to create the needed parts for the *Command* carrier.

Aleshia's mind went inside and found the damage worse than she first thought. Many areas were exposed to space, almost every corridor was a mess. When she reached the bridge, it caused her to gasp. A dead Lytherian sat at the helm, a large rod sticking out of his chest. Most of the consoles were blasted and burnt. She found Karthish sitting, his smooth angular head held in his three-fingered hands.

A panel nearby lit up. "Commander Karthish ...Commander Karthish, please respond."

Karthish's head popped up, and he leaned over to tap the panel. "Yes? Communications are working again?"

A screen above the panel flickered and flashed, resolved to static, then Dakarth's reptilian face appeared. "Yessss my teams have repaired it. But sir, I must insist we put us on priority of the *Maker's* repair facilities."

Karthish shook his smooth head. "No. The other ships must take priority. They have more damage than ussss."

"Perhaps, but if we are lost, who will lead? We cannot afford to lose this ship."

"I thought we could wait? Is the ship in more danger than previous estimates?"

Dakarth sighed. Of all his years of being chief engineer

aboard the *Command* carrier, this proved to be the hardest briefing. "Yessss Commander. If we do not get support added to key places in the hull and resealed, internal bulkheads may fail. And if they do, we could lose the entire ship."

Karthish shut his eyes and opened them with deliberate slowness. "Very well. Place us on the highest repair priority for now. But once the ship is stabilized, I want the rest of the fleet taken care of. Is that clear?"

Dakarth nodded. "Of course, Commander. Dakarth out."

Aleshia watched him for several seconds and considered leaving, but they needed to make contact. She reached out and touched his shoulder.

Karthish jumped up. "Who is here?" He spun around but saw no one. However, he felt something.

Aleshia drifted forward and concentrated.

The walls around Karthish began to warp and shift. He blinked, and the room resolved into the *Defiant's* bridge. "What? I'm back on the *Defiant?*"

Aleshia smiled. "No, you are still aboard your ship. We are only in your mind."

Karthish whirled around. "Aleshia! What'ssss wrong? Did the Celloids return? We haven't detected any, but our ships are not exactly in the best shape at the moment."

Aleshia shook her head. "No, they didn't. But we have another problem."

Karthish folded his arms. "What could be worse than the Celloids?"

"Whatever the Ixeons can throw at us."

Karthish mouthed the words. "The Ixeonssss? Who are they?"

"The creators of the Celloids."

Karthish blinked as his reptilian eyes glazed. "What do you mean created?"

"Just what I said. They made the Celloids."

"For what purpose could a race create such a creature?"

Aleshia shook her head. "I don't know. All I know is they did."

"And how do you know this?"

"We recovered the core of the Celloid *Mothership*."

Karthish jumped. "You did *what?*"

"Don't worry, it's quite dead."

Karthish's eyes narrowed as he folded his arms across his chest, obscuring rank emblems. "How can you be so sure?"

"Otis and Leon both say it is dead."

"I still find thissss a huge risk."

"So did they, but it proved to be worth it."

"How so?"

"Have you ever studied the Celloids?"

"No. Every time we got close to one, it was either we kill it or it would destroy us. Detailed study was never possible."

"Then we have succeeded where you never had the opportunity. Otis has discovered the Celloids were made by an insectoid race called the Ixeons."

"Insectoid?"

Aleshia nodded. "Yes. We don't know why they created them, but they have."

"And how did you find this out?"

"Leon managed to connect a system to the Celloid Core and Otis discovered how to read the data. Similar to how they interfaced with your scout ship."

Karthish cocked his head. "While fantastic, it also sounds plausible. We never would have dreamed the Celloids could interface with our ships. And if they could interface with our ships, why couldn't the data path be reversed."

Aleshia nodded. "Exactly what Otis thought, and he managed to do it. A lot of data was destroyed or corrupted, likely during the battle. But he has recovered several portions. Portions that also include information about another race they created."

Karthish's eyes grew wide. "Another race? They made more than one?"

"It would seem so. This one is silicon based."

"Silicon based? As in rock?"

Aleshia nodded again. "Yes."

"That sounds even more fantastic than the Celloids. Are you certain they are right?"

"Yes, I'm certain. We ran into them."

"What? We haven't detected anything entering the system!"

Aleshia waved a hand and the surrounding area shimmered, revealing the *Command* carrier once more. She pointed at the wrecked and burnt consoles and the dead Lytherian in the chair. "You told me your ships not exactly in perfect working order."

Karthish hung his head and sat back down in one of the few chairs without debris in it. "You are right. It is very possible something could enter the system, and we not see it. What did they look like?"

"Like a big rock, but most of their surfaces smooth and perfect angles that don't occur in nature."

Karthish rubbed his chin. "Hmmm that is also possible why we missed them. Right now we are centered on repair and recovering enough materials to do so. Another rock entering the sysssstem would be ignored. If we detected it at all."

Aleshia nodded. "That is what we assumed."

"You mentioned an encounter with them. I assume you stopped or destroyed them or we wouldn't be talking now."

"Yes, we did. But it took all we had and then some. Even with your enhancements."

"Hmm I suppose I shouldn't be surprised they attacked, but one ship you should have been able to take on and destroy with ease. A fleet of them ... that'ssss different."

"We managed to destroy them only because of the data Otis found buried inside the Celloid."

Karthish cocked his head. "What kind of data?"

"It would appear to be the Celloid's memories. Instructions from their Ixeon masters and long-term plans. Perhaps so they would know who to attack and who not to," Aleshia said.

"Logical, but risky. We would never make such a mistake."

"I think their overconfidence is their weakness."

Karthish rubbed his chin. "Possible. But if you destroyed them, why this long distance call as you would say."

"Because we need your help?"

Karthish stood up and placed a hand on his chest. "Us? I don't know what more we can do. As you pointed out earlier, not many of our ships are functional, let alone battle-worthy."

"We need your help to decode the data."

"Your Otis has done more than we would have ever dared dream, why would you need us?"

"You have battled the Celloids far longer than us. You might find important details in the data we might over look much faster."

Karthish nodded. "You are right. I can try to send ssssomeone, but I need far more than I have. It may take ssssome time."

"We could try to transmit the data, but I think broadcasting what we have, is not a good idea."

Karthish inclined his head. "I agree. We need to keep this as quiet as possible. I know if I found out someone had access to the details of my creations, I would send ships after them."

Aleshia nodded. "I think that is what happened. I can't think of another reason the Sileics would have come for a visit."

"Sileicssss? Who are they?"

Aleshia laughed. "They are the rock beings the Ixeon's created. Sorry, I should have said that before now."

Karthish rubbed his temples. "No, that is fine. It is a lot to take in."

Karthish's eyes flashed, and he looked up with realization. "A rock ship might be very resilient to the weapons we gave you, depending on its composition. How exactly did you stop them?"

"Otis found hidden in the data a way to destroy them with certain frequencies of sound."

Karthish waved his hand. "Wait a minute here! Sound waves can't travel in space, or at least in a very limited fashion. Nothing like what you are implying."

"We modified several of our cannons to transmit the frequency Otis found in the data within their beams. It took all we had, but we succeeded in causing the Sileic to crumble to dust."

"I ssssee, and you don't think you could do this again?"

"I don't know. Either way, we would like your help."

"We cannot offer much help at the moment as you no doubt can see." Karthish made a sweeping moment with his three fingered hand across what was left of his bridge. "We would lose everything if we tried."

Aleshia nodded. "I understand. Still, we need your help. Can you send Dakarth? Perhaps he can help Otis and Leon retrieve more data from the Celloid Core. It might be the key to finding these Ixeons. Or see what else they have hidden up their sleeves. If they have sleeves."

Karthish's right most finger talon tapped his chin. "While I agree with you. I don't think I can spare Dakarth. I will send someone else."

Aleshia shook her head. "I'm not sure someone else will do. Being that the Ixeons already sent one Sileic, I doubt we have much time."

"Yes, and it would be foolish to assume there was only one. Very well. I will send him if at all possible."

Aleshia nodded. "Thank you, Karthish. Also tell whoever you send to bring equipment for long distance communication on your links. While telepathic communication works, if we could use the *Defiant* and it wouldn't wear me out."

Karthish laughed. "Of course. I'm sorry we didn't do it before."

Aleshia nodded. "We know you had to try to salvage what you could of your fleet. But it almost cost us the Earth."

Karthish hung his head. "Yessss you are quite right. We will rectify that."

Aleshia smiled. "That is all we ask. Until we meet again." Aleshia faded from Karthish's vision as the connection disappeared.

Behind him a Lytherian spoke with hesitation in his voice. "Ssssir? Who were you talking to?"

Karthish spun around to find Natheir, Dakarth's first assistant. "Natheir! Did we not teach you proper protocol before entering the bridge?"

Natheir's gaze drifted down towards the floor as he inclined his head. "I am sorry, ssssir. But you did call for me?"

"Yes I did. Status?"

Natheir blinked. "I thought–"

"Never mind, I am asking *you*." Karthish pointed his talon at him.

Natheir's eyes glazed over and he swallowed. "Repairs are progressing. The *Maker* has put us on priority, and we have started to receive new parts and equipment."

"How long?"

Natheir blinked. "How long for what, sir?"

"How long until we have repaired this ship!"

Natheir swallowed again. "We received significant damage, sir. It will take time."

"I know that! I was asking for an estimate!"

Natheir swallowed again, even harder than the last time. Dakarth did not discuss a timetable, and he was reluctant to give one without discussing it with him first. "Based on the damage and the rate of the additional parts arriving, if we pull some people from the other ships–"

Karthish folded his arms. "Yes?"

Natheir slid his three-fingered hand up the back of his neck and sucked in his bottom lip for a moment. "As I was saying, if we pull people from the other ships, we could restore most of the systems in two or three Earth cycles."

"I see. If done in that time frame, it is acceptable. This ship needs to be fully operational as soon as possible."

"Outside hull damage will take longer, but internal systems and equipment should be repaired in that time."

"That is acceptable. Please tell Dakarth."

Natheir took a step back and swallowed. "Yessss sir." Natheir pivoted on the heel of the three-toed boot and started towards the rear hatch.

"One more thing," Karthish said.

Natheir stopped and turned. "Yes, Commander?"

"Please have someone take care of Gakon." Karthish pointed to the impaled Lytherian in the chair to his right. "While we do not have time to honor him and the others properly, they deserve more respect than to be left where they fell."

Natheir inclined his head. "Of course, Commander. We have not due to the critical status of the ship."

"I realize this, but we are not animals. And they deserve our respect."

Natheir lowered his head further. "I did not mean to imply otherwise, Commander."

"I know. Now get on it." Karthish waved his hand. "Dismissed."

Natheir put his hand in the center of his chest, turned, and left.

Karthish turned and tapped a button on one of the last remaining working consoles on the bridge. Within a few seconds, Dakarth's face appeared. "Yes, Commander?"

"How long until we are operational?"

Dakarth sighed. "If we pull all the people from the other ships, we could finish in two or three Earth cycles. The hull will still have a lot of damage, but the internal systems and equipment should be operational at that time."

Karthish smiled. *Good. Exactly what Natheir said.* "Very well. See to it. Also, give Natheir that job. He is on his way down to you."

Dakarth blinked. "Sir?"

"You heard me. I have another mission for you, which is even more significant."

Dakarth's head reared back. "What could be more important than getting our fleet operational?"

"Stopping another invasion. Come up to the bridge. I need to speak with you."

Dakarth blinked. "Invasion?" He thought about asking for more on the link, but decided against it. "I'm on my way." Dakarth tapped a key on the console in front of him, stood, and started walking towards the bridge. On his way out of engineering, Natheir appeared.

"Sir? Where are you going?" Natheir said.

"Natheir, I want you to take charge of the repairs."

Natheir blinked. "*Me?* But that is your job as head engineer."

"Yes, but I'm giving that duty to you. I am needed on the bridge," Dakarth said as he started walking away.

Natheir stiffened. "Yessss sir. I will take care of it." As Dakarth entered the last working transport tube on the deck, he heard Natheir give out commands as he laid out a repair plan.

Dakarth smiled as the tube doors closed, and he pushed the button for the bridge level. *He might be ready after all. How did Karthish know?*

The tube dumped him several sections away from the bridge, but considering all the damage, he was grateful it wasn't any further. When he reached the bridge, the hatch stood open, but as per protocol he pressed the announcement button. It refused to work, like so much else on the ship. He cleared his throat and tapped a talon on the smooth inner surface of the hatch. "Ssssir? You wanted to see me?"

Karthish turned. "Yes Dakarth, I have a very special task for you."

Dakarth entered the damaged bridge and stepped over various support struts, ceiling fragments, and pieces of blasted console. "So you mentioned on the link and something about an invasion. What could be more vital than saving our fleet if true?"

"Saving ourselves and the Earth."

Dakarth blinked as his head inclined. "Didn't we already do that?"

Karthish shook his head. "We helped, they pulled it off in the end. But they couldn't have done it without us either."

"Then I don't understand–"

"They have encountered another race apparently built by the same people that made the Celloids."

Dakarth mouthed the words, but no sound came from his dry lips for several moments. "Made the Celloids?"

"Ah, so you are as surprised as I was. Yes, the *Defiant* has captured the Celloid *Mothership* core and learned a lot from it."

"Captured the core? Isn't that very dangerous?"

"Yes it is, but they assure me it is dead. But the reason I called you up here, they need you to help extract data from it. While they did find out about this new race, the Sileics, and they are silicon based, most of the data was corrupted due to the damage that destroyed the *Mothership*. They need your expertise to help reconstruct the data and provide insight."

"But sir, I don't know that much about the Celloids. None of our people do."

Karthish nodded. "That is true, but you are the most knowledgeable among us. If anyone can help, it is you."

"I appreciate your faith in my abilities, but do not see how I can be of much use in this case."

"Regardless, I want you to join the *Defiant* and her people to see what can be learned. One Sileic ship has appeared, and no doubt more will follow. We need to know as much as possible about them in the least amount of time."

Dakarth blinked again. "Wait, one of the silicon creatures has already appeared? We are in no condition to fend them off!"

Karthish smiled. "I am well aware of this. And it is not needed. The *Defiant* and *Phoenix* took care of it."

"Took care of it? How?"

"They found a weakness listed in the Celloid data and managed to exploit it. Now you see the importance of this mission? Other such weaknesses might be still there. Or knowledge of other beings such as this. Perhaps data on their creators. I'm sure you can see the necessity of your involvement?"

Dakarth stiffened. "I do. And I shall not let you down."

Karthish nodded. "Take one of the shuttles capable of warping. You need to be there as soon as possible."

Dakarth blinked. "Warping? For such a short distance?"

"I have no doubt you can do it. If you feel it is necessary, take any pilot you need."

"I can do it, Commander. It might be a tight fit to enter the *Defiant's* main hangar bay, but I can do it. We need every available Lytherian here. I will grab a few resources and leave immediately."

"Very good Dakarth. Keep me apprised of your progress."

Dakarth nodded, turned on his heel and left the bridge. Karthish hoped he would see his friend again.

12

Within the shuttle, Dakarth had crammed almost every storage compartment with equipment he might need. Functional equipment, that is. A lot more he wanted to bring, but it had been damaged and still awaiting repair.

He tapped the controls. "Dakarth to *Command* carrier. Are you receiving me?"

"Yes, we are Dakarth," Karthish responded, "are you ready?"

Dakarth sighed. He had performed the calculations countless times, and they always came up the same: a perfect arrival. Still, warping could be dangerous if his calculations had even the slightest error. It was one of the reasons they often exited and entered a warp far from their target. On the off-chance something went wrong.

"Everything nominal. Engaging warp generator." Dakarth pushed a button and in the back of the shuttle. A round area surrounding rear section began to rotate. The rings extended out from the hull and encompassed the entire aft section of the shuttle and passed the engines. The rings began to spin faster. "Power fifty percent and building. Everything still within normal limits."

"Activate when ready," Karthish said. "And good luck. I

feel your success or failure will determine the fate of both the humans and us."

Great, no pressure or anything. Dakarth nodded on the screen. "Confirmed power at seventy-five percent of capacity. I am activating now." Dakarth pushed another button and a bubble of energy rippled out from the generator in the aft section. It enveloped the entire shuttle as a beam reached out from the front ring in a cone shape, hitting the very fabric of space at the convergence point punching a hole that expanded at a rapid pace. Within a microsecond it grew large enough for the shuttle. The nose of the shuttle stretched forward, reaching for the newly created hole.

In an eye blink, the rest of the shuttle followed and disappeared.

Karthish sighed. "As the humanssss say, good luck and God speed."

Aboard the shuttle, Dakarth felt the pushing and pulling of the space warp. A warning light went off and a second later a siren went off. There was a slight imbalance in the generator. He couldn't fix it now, it was too late. All he could do is hold on and hope he didn't end up in another galaxy.

With a loud *POP* only he could hear, Dakarth's shuttle emerged from its journey and spun wildly end over end. *I'm glad it didn't do that a microsecond earlier or I never would have made it.* He hit several keys firing braking thrusters and stopped the ships' annoying spin.

He smiled. Below of the shuttle, a blue ball of a planet with clouds and several land masses spun on its axis. The Earth. He had arrived right on target, despite the instability. Hitting a few more keys made him frown. The generator had suffered damage and he wouldn't be returning to the Lytherian fleet any time soon. He might be able fix it in time, but first he had to help the humans. If he could.

Scanners indicated the *Defiant* was a kilometer to his right and in a higher orbit. The *Phoenix* orbited close by, but the power levels were almost nonexistent.

A long finger with its sharp talon itched one spot between the scales on the top of his hairless head. After several minutes he remembered what the humans used for com frequencies. He punched in the settings and hit another button. "*Defiant*? Are you receiving me?"

"*Defiant* here. I have analyzed your voice patterns and I believe this is Dakarth. Is that correct?" Miles said.

"That is correct. I have come at the request of our Commander. I have a plotted a course to you. Will arrive in twenty of your minutes. I hope there is enough room for me."

"If not, we will make room, have no fear," Deven said. "But I am surprised you got here so quickly. It was only an hour ago Aleshia contacted you."

Dakarth cocked his head. "Deven?" The screen to his right flashed and revealed Deven's smiling face.

"Yes it is."

"And you said it has only been one of your hours since she spoke with Karthish?"

Deven nodded. "Yes. It is why I say it is amazing for you to be here so fast. Your ships are capable of amazing speeds."

Dakarth did several quick calculations in his head. He had arrived before he even left. The differential was only an hour. Still, a great concern. "Yes they are. I will speak more when I am aboard. Dakarth out." He pushed a button, and the screen flickered and faded. He wondered why the *Phoenix* had such low power production, or why they were both still in orbit when their systems lacked the full optimizations for it. "I guess I will find out soon enough," Dakarth muttered to himself.

Aboard the *Defiant,* Deven stood. "Make sure Leon and Gregory are in the hanger control room when he arrives. We don't want a repeat of last time."

Galina nodded. "You bet. Neither one of them wants to fix doors or paint jobs. Shall I wake Aleshia?"

Deven shook his head. "No, let her sleep. Talking with Karthish took a lot out of her. I know she says it didn't, but she did lay down as soon as we got back. I think she is not telling me the whole truth."

"What about Otis?"

Deven shrugged. "The *Phoenix's* power core is still recovering. There is nothing he can do until the power levels are back to normal."

Galina nodded. "True. But won't he be miffed?"

Deven smiled. "Well, if you don't tell him, I won't."

Galina laughed. "He is going to find out eventually."

"I'm sure, but by then he will be too busy to be mad at us."

"Oooo I like that plan. Hope it works."

"It will. I'm heading down to hanger control as well."

"And I will monitor things up here," Galina said.

Miles' camera turned towards her. "There is no need Galina, if you prefer to be elsewhere."

Galina folded her arms. "Yes, there is Miles. I prefer to watch things myself, if you don't mind."

Miles' camera iris contracted and expanded. "It would seem to be a waste of time, but as you wish."

Galina huffed and sat back her chair glaring at Miles.

The large hanger doors parted, revealing the *Defiant's* lit bay beyond. Wisps of remaining atmosphere flickered out into space as it froze and exited. Dakarth's shuttle approached and a correcting jet fired to change the alignment a micro meter before a port jet fired to stop the motion.

Leon toggled the link in the control room. A nearby panel flickered and blinked as Dakarth's face appeared. "Dakarth, it looks good from here."

"Yessss I see the same. One moment, verifying."

In the control room, Deven felt a hand snake up his back. He spun around to see Aleshia's smiling face. "Sweetheart! What are you doing up?"

"I told you when we got back from the *Phoenix*, I needed to rest. I didn't say hibernate. I will be fine. It only drained me a little. I felt it was best to rest while I could, in case you need me later."

Deven smiled as he squeezed her. "I always need you."

"Well Mr. Doran, keep talking like that and you know what that will get you."

He pulled back a little and gazed into her eyes. "What?"

She smiled and kissed him. "Everything."

"*Defiant*? I am ready to begin entry thrust," Dakarth said.

Leon nodded. "All looks good here. Whenever you are ready."

Dakarth tapped a control and tiny thrusters in the aft section engaged, edging the shuttle forward. It grew in size as it approached. "Misalignment happened. Compensating."

"We see it Dakarth. Do you wish to abort?"

"Negative. It is slight." Correcting thrusters fired in the

bow starboard corner and then again on the opposite side a microsecond later. "I see all in aliment now. Confirm?"

"You got it, Dakarth. All is gold from this end."

"All is gold? Is gold in the way? Abort?"

"No no, I mean all is good. Stay on course."

"Understood mistake." The shuttle crossed the threshold of the hangar doors with less than a centimeter on all sides. But it did fit. "Firing braking thrusters in three … two … one … activated." The thrusters stopped the shuttle's forward motion, and another set engaged and gently set the shuttle down on the pad in the center they had provided for him. "I am down and set."

"Confirmed Dakarth, closing the bay doors," Leon said as he tapped a key. The doors slid together and lights along the interconnecting boundaries told their status.

"I have a positive lock and the bay is pressurizing," Gregory said.

A few minutes later Leon taped a few keys on the controls in front of him. The screen to his right scrolled with data sets of different kinds. On the far wall within the hanger bay a two-foot square light went green. "That did it. It's ready."

Aleshia intertwined her arm around Deven's back. "Shall go we greet our guest?"

Deven's eyes drifted down towards her as he turned his head showing a big grin. "Of course."

Gregory unlocked the inner doors, and they slid open revealing the hangar bay with its various parked vehicles throughout. Along one wall, all the vehicles had been moved to other pads. In their place sat a forty-foot semi round mass of plant life known as the Celloid *Mothership* core.

Deven, Aleshia, Gregory and Leon all walked over to Dakarth's shuttle. The rear platform lowered, revealing

Dakarth's stern expression. He walked down the ramp as he pointed a finger that ended in a sharp talon in the direction of the Celloid. "And you are ssssure it is dead?"

Leon nodded. "Yes. While Otis has found code for spectacular regenerative abilities, they have not been engaged. In fact, we can track degradation meaning it is dead, not hibernating or otherwise pausing is existence to reemerge later."

"Good. I have brought equipment to further scan it. I hope we can learn more useful data from it. Is amazing you were able to get anything from it at all."

"So was I," Leon said. "Otis deserves the credit for that. I think we would have dumped this thing before now if it wasn't for him."

Dakarth's eyes darted around the hangar bay. "And where is Otis?"

"He is resting aboard the *Phoenix*. I suggested his quarters aboard the *Defiant*, but he said his truck was fine," Deven said.

Dakarth cocked his head. "And that is why the *Phoenix* looks like a dead ship?"

Deven's eyes went wide. "Dead ship? Oh not at all, Minerva is still trying to bring her power core up to full capacity and do a few final repairs. Since Otis is resting in his truck, she can power down more systems he would normally use."

Dakarth nodded. "I see. Logical."

Aleshia smiled. "That's our Minerva. Logical to a fault."

Deven laughed. "Well not quite, she has out guessed us several times as well."

"True," Aleshia said.

Dakarth pointed within the shuttle. "Help me unload and move the equipment, and will see what we can do."

"Sure," Leon said, "lead the way."

Dakarth pointed where each piece could be disconnected or otherwise moved from its mounting. Several types of scanners, computers, even a portable nano lab were all moved over by the Celloid Core.

Dakarth hooked up one of his scanners and took a deep scan of the core. The data poured into the device on his belt. He pulled it free and flipped it open to see several data sets scroll past at lightning speed. He tapped a control, and it slowed, stopped, and one line lit up in red. "You are correct. I am also seeing cellular decay as well. We will need to move faster than I expected."

"Or the data could be lost?" Leon asked.

"Is possible it already has been. Is also another reason for the corruption. I am sure there is some redundancy, which is why you could get anything at all. But I suspect in another day or two, it will reach the point where nothing can be done."

"At all?" Gregory said.

Dakarth nodded. "Yessss. As the cells decay, so does the data. Similar to the data is disrupted in one of your books, if the paper degrades." Dakarth hooked up one of his computers to the two trodes Leon drove deep into the Celloid Core. "Hmm, I'm not getting anything."

"We didn't either at first. It was Otis that cracked it. Do you need him? We can get him over here."

Dakarth shook his head. "Not for now."

A screen next to the makeshift console Leon had built lit up with Otis' smiling face. "So why didn't anyone call me? I will be over there in two shakes."

Deven smiled. "Stay where you are, Otis. I need you on the *Phoenix*, remember? And besides, you can still do everything we can from there."

"Except actually touch it."

Deven laughed. "No reason you need to."

Dakarth chuckled. "This is true." He took two steps to his right and placed his three fingered hand on the Celloid. "See? Nothing. No need for you to be here."

Otis sighed. "Right, Boss. Find anything Dakarth?"

The Lytherian shook his head. "No. I cannot even see how you accessed this thing. To me is a ball of dead plant matter. No data."

Otis chuckled. "Yes, that took me a few as well. Increase the power of your scan while decreasing the output."

"How is that possible? One is connected to the other."

"Decrease its range. Focus is the key. If you provide enough energy at one point it works."

Dakarth cocked his head and did as Otis suggested. His eyes went wide. "It is working, data is returning."

"Told you," Otis said smiling on the screen.

Dakarth watched as data followed on his screen. "All I am seeing is cellular instructions. Nothing about this organism being made."

"Check the upper right quadrant."

"It still looks like normal plant."

"Peel back the layers, there is more to it than what you see."

Dakarth hit a few keys on his belt device now held firmly in his hand. "There is more data here, yes."

"I told you–"

"But I do not see binary?"

"Here try this algorithm I wrote," Otis transmitted the code on a separate channel and Leon pointed to it on his screen.

"Here. Want me to send it over?"

Dakarth shook his head. "Not neccessssary. I can do it from here." He pushed another button on the device in his palm and it emanated a green beam covering the terminal. A second later, the code on Leon's screen appeared in Dakarth's hand. "This is fassssinating. You wrote this?"

Otis shrugged. "If you think that is something, you should see what I can do when I take my time."

Deven rolled his eyes. "He is just showing off."

Dakarth blinked. "Showing off? Ohh karthinis, I understand." Dakarth hit another button, and the algorithm ran changing what he saw into binary data. "Amazing. If you can do this, why do you need me?"

"Because there is a lot of corruption, and degradation as you saw. And I'm sure it increasing. If we don't pull all we can from this soon, I fear we won't be able to at all," Otis said.

Dakarth nodded. "Yes. I agree. Was just saying a day or two will be too late." He ran several commands on his device and the screen showed a creature with large compound eyes. He pointed to the screen. "Is this one of the Ixeons?"

Leon nodded. "Yes. Nasty little bugs."

Dakarth blinked as his head jetted forward. "Nasty little bugs?"

"Well, we don't know their actual size, but we are assuming they are smaller than us."

Dakarth nodded. "I see. Show me what else you found."

Leon punched a few keys and the display in front of him shifted, showing the Sileics. "This is all we have on the Sileics. It is not much. We are lucky Otis managed to find the kill switch."

"I'll say. But who knows what else is here. If we can grab it before it fades away," Otis said.

Dakarth stared at his screen. "Let me see what you used for recovery."

Otis smiled. "Sending now."

Dakarth watched his small screen fill with shifting data. He studied it for several minutes before smiling. "I think we can enhance it. If I may?"

Otis' smile broadened. "By all means. I was hoping you could," Otis said.

"Give me a few minutes." He placed the palm device back on his belt and grabbed a larger square device from the pile of equipment they had brought over. He pushed a button causing legs to extend and the center area flip open revealing a large screen and a keyboard designed for three-fingered hands. He pulled the palm device from his belt and plugged it into the opened terminal. The screen lit up and scrolled with the same data the smaller screen had a minute before. He tapped a few keys and activated one of his own programs that ran, enhancing the other. After a few minutes, the code was far longer and vastly more complex. "Now perhaps this will do more."

He sent a copy to Otis. "Wow, this is impressive. You must have even more experience in recovery than I do."

Dakarth nodded. "Yes, we have learned much over the years. Our systems have learned from each other and over time built more robust networks. However, if it wasn't for your entry-point, this wouldn't have worked. At least in time we have."

Otis' face slid over to the side as the screen split, revealing Minerva's face. "Sorry for intruding, but I couldn't help it. You have networks similar to me?"

Dakarth shook his head. "No. While they learn, they are not a personality like you. They are very basic."

Minerva smiled. "Well, I'm glad I am unique."

Dakarth nodded. "You are. We have nothing like you."

"Or like me," Miles' voice came from the overhead speaker.

Dakarth cocked his head as he studied the room again. "Who was that?"

"Miles. He is a Mechand that is now in the *Defiant's* central core," Leon said.

Minerva nodded. "Yes if you don't have anything like me, I doubt you have anything like him either. While I created him, he has evolved far behind what I could have considered."

"Thank you, Minerva," Miles said.

Minerva smiled. "You're welcome."

Dakarth nodded. "I understand and concur." He gazed back at his screen. "If you agree, I wissssh to activate the new code on the Celloid."

"You mean run it?" Otis said.

Dakarth smiled. "Yes and see what more data we can find."

"Sure, by all means."

Dakarth hit a few buttons, and the program activated ran over the Celloid data altering it, moving bits here and there. In other areas it determined what data was missing and filled in the gaps. The data morphed and shifted with some areas now intact. "It has worked."

Leon pointed to a new location in the data. "Check that section."

Dakarth brought it up, and they all gasped for instead of a grainy picture of the Ixeon, it was a detailed high resolution one. Insectoid as before, but more details revealed and confirming what they knew. Dakarth pushed another button and more data appeared. "From what I can ssssee, this data says they are here watching."

Deven blinked. "Watching? How could they be watching? Wouldn't we have known?"

Dakarth nodded. "Yes. Unless their technology is more advanced than ours. After all, they created races."

"But you have nano technology. Wouldn't that allow you to do the same thing if you wanted?" Aleshia asked.

Dakarth cocked his head. "Perhaps. We would never let our nanos do something that large. The risk is too great. But perhaps these Ixeons do not share the same fear."

Deven rubbed his chin. "Or they don't care."

Dakarth turned. "Why wouldn't they? It would take vast amounts of design and if anything is wrong, they could turn against you. Or the nanomachines destroy everything trying to make more. No, this is far too much risk."

"But they did design a kill switch. Perhaps they do share your fears."

Dakarth shook his head. "No, we never would have made the attempt. They have."

Otis raised a finger on his screen. "I think I see a location here." He highlighted a portion of the data that then displayed on all the screens.

Dakarth's eyes narrowed as he examined the display. "Yes, this is your Moon."

Minerva nodded. "Confirmed. It is on the side that never faces the Earth."

"How can this be? Wouldn't you have detected them before?" Aleshia asked.

"It is possible they are new, or know how to hide themselves from our scans. But being they did not know of you until our failure, it must be a new development," Dakarth said.

"But why would they be here when they can send their

Sileics after us?   Seems like that would be too close for comfort," Leon said.

"Perhaps they figure if no one knows about them, they are very safe.   And if we can't detect any of their signals, the Moon is a large place to hide on," Gregory said.

Deven nodded. "Yes, and how are we going to find them? If we can, perhaps we can reason with them."

"You can't be serious," Galina's voice came from the speaker overhead.   "Yes, I have been listening in and you can't be serious. If they sent the Celloids to destroy us, and then the Sileics later. What makes you think they will listen to anything we say?"

Deven shrugged. "I don't know. They may not. But it might be worth it. And Aleshia could be the key."

She gazed up at him. "What do you mean?"

"First, you can find them where the Lytherian's could not. You never focused your abilities at the Moon before am I right?"

Aleshia nodded. "No, I never did. There was never a need."

"There is now. And you can tell them we don't mean them any harm. You can convince them, not to mention they may not be able to speak our language."

Aleshia shrugged. "I don't know if I can. I won't try to brainwash them if that is what you mean?"

Deven shook his head. "No. Not at all. But you can prove to them we are telling the truth more than anyone else."

She nodded. "Maybe. But that is a *big,* maybe."

"But worth a try, don't you think?"

Leon shook his head. "You are forgetting one vital aspect. Even if Aleshia can find these Ixeons, how are we going to go see them? We don't have space suits or anything of the kind. The *Defiant* or *Phoenix* might be able to land there, but then what? We can't exactly open the hangar bay and walk inside their base."

Dakarth smiled. "No. But thisssss is where we come in. One moment." He left them and walked over to his shuttle and boarded the ramp leading inside. He sat down in the curved seat in the cockpit and tapped a few commands on the lit controls in front of him. Above, a screen lowered down and lit up. "Commander Karthish? Are you receiving me?"

The screen flashed several times until Karthish's face appeared. "Receiving you Dakarth. What have you learned?"

"It is as the humans said. They did capture the Celloid Core, and extracted data from it. I have enhanced the recovery, and we have not only proven the existence of these Ixeons, we also know the location of their base."

"Excellent. Where?"

"On the far side of Earth's Moon. I do not have current surveys of the area but from what I can determine it must be inside a deep crevasse and shielded to avoid detection. Perhaps even underground."

Karthish's one eye widened while the other narrowed. "And your recommendation?"

"Sir, I am not qualified to offer such recommendations."

Karthish smiled. "You are. You are there, you have seen this data firsthand. What is your assessment?"

Dakarth sighed. "I feel this must be investigated. However, the Earth vessels do not have the ability to land on the Moon, at least not without detection. And even then, they lack proper space suits or other equipment for such an undertaking. They also cannot detect any activity there. This further indicates the area must be shielded. Therefore, we must take control of the situation."

Karthish nodded. "Agreed. It will take some time for our fleet to be repaired enough to be of much assistance. Repairs to the *Command* carrier are proceeding on schedule. However, the rest of the fleet's repairs have been put on hold. I am reluctant to use this ship even when she is repaired as I think it is too large of a risk at the moment. We need to wait until the rest of the fleet is repaired."

"I agree, Sir. However, I do not think it is wise to wait."

Karthish knew Dakarth's thoughts on this. He had known him for many years, but protocol forced him to act as though he did not. "Oh? And why is that?"

Dakarth sighed. "Commander, if these Ixeons have arrived recently, they know of our fleet's status. Therefore, they are not suspecting an attack from us. And Earth lacks the proper equipment. If we wait, more of the Sileics or worse will arrive. Also, these Ixeons are now in a position to command their creations from a short distance, which may make the situation more difficult. But if I may make a suggestion, from what I can determine, they will not be expecting an engagement as I said. My shuttle and its equipment with those from the *Defiant* should be able to enter the Ixeon's base and extract information and whatever else we require."

Karthish smiled, his reptilian lips parting in a broad grin. "Very good Dakarth. Your assessment is valid. A small team is also more likely to succeed in extraction than a full out assault. Do you need anything more from us?"

Dakarth shook his head. "Negative. I have a nano kit and templates for suits which I will modify for the humans. Their hand weapons can be upgraded like we did with the cannons or use ours. I will contact if further assistance is needed."

"Very well, Dakarth. Do tell us at the instant such help is required. Even if our repairs are not completed. We will come."

Dakarth knew Karthish would too. Even if the risk was much higher than the reward. "Thank you, Commander. I shall hope that will not be necesssssary. Dakarth out." He pushed a button on the lit controls and the screen's image flickered, faded, and it retracted into its resting location.

Dakarth stood up and walked out of the cockpit, down the ramp and over to where everyone was waiting. "I have spoken with my Commander, and thinks we should enter this Ixeon base and get what data, and anything else we require from it."

"How many ships is Karthish sending?" Aleshia asked.

"None."

Aleshia blinked. "None?"

Dakarth shook his head in a broad nod. "That is correct. We are to do it."

Leon glared at him with a blank stare. "And how? We don't have the ability to land there, at least not without being seen for sure. And even if we do land, what good is it? We can't leave the ship."

"We will use my shuttle. It has systems we can use to approach undetected. It also has better scanning abilities."

"That still does not solve our problem that we can't leave it after you land," Deven said.

"I assume you forgot about my nano kit you helped me unpack?"

Leon thought for a second before his eyes went wide, and he slapped his forehead. "You are going to make suits for us?"

Dakarth nodded. "That is right. I have templates we can use, while they are for Lytherian I will amend them."

Deven's eyes darted around the hangar examining the

unsure faces glaring back at him. "Let's get started. Every minute we delay means more Sileics or worse. And I for one don't want to give them any advantage."

$$-13-$$

Aleshia sighed as she walked up the ramp into Dakarth's shuttle, holding her favorite jumpsuit in her hands. She found him in a middle section of the ship, working on a device that sat on a shelf extending out from the wall. Along another wall, a different shelf held several pieces of clothing. "Are you sure you need this? Why can't you make me something that fits?" She laid the jumpsuit on top of the other clothing.

Dakarth shook his head. "No. Issss not possible. I need something that fits very close to your skin for the template to work. Otherwise the fit will be off and will cause problems."

Deven smiled. "I told you I would buy you a new one."

Aleshia folded her arms and glowered. "You'd better. That is my favorite."

"Why not use something else?"

"I don't have anything else aboard like what he needs or I would!" Aleshia huffed as she sat in a nearby chair. It was bolted to the floor and had a hole in the back. It wasn't made for humans, but it would do for the moment.

Dakarth pushed a button on the device and a panel along the side glowed before black goo the consistency of putty rolled out of a side port. He pushed another button and a third shelf extended out from the wall. Placing Aleshia's jumpsuit on it he dropped the ball of black goo on the middle of it causing her to wince. Dakarth caught her expression. "Don't worry, it will all be over soon." He pressed a button on the box and the goo came alive, melting then growing. It expanded to encompass the entire jump suit.

For a minute it looked as though all the goo did was change its color. Then slowly the details began to change. Ribbed areas began to form and other areas grew padding. The cloth expanded to form gloves and boots. The suit itself became thicker. Soon it began to push vertical as new equipment formed, creating a backpack for atmospheric stability. As if it was an afterthought, a four-sided helmet with a domed peek that gave a superb field of view appeared attached to the top of the backpack.

While the helmet looked like glass, Dakarth knew it was far harder and more resilient than diamond. Yet lighter than ordinary Earth glass. "It is done." He picked up the new suit, turned around, and extended his arms towards Aleshia. "Try it on perhaps? But it should fit fine."

Aleshia sighed as she took the garment, amazed at how light it was. "It doesn't feel that much heavier than the jumpsuit I brought in. This is amazing."

Dakarth smiled. "I'm glad you like. Please try the fit. I must make sure it fit."

Aleshia blushed. "Not in front of you."

Dakarth cocked his head. "Why not?" Then a few seconds later his eyes went wide. "Ohhhh of course. I will leave. Please try on." He left the room and walked down the ramp, exiting the shuttle.

Aleshia smiled at Deven and gave a twirling motion with her finger. "Turn around."

"Why? We're married."

"Because I want you to make sure no one else comes in here. Okay?"

Deven laughed. "Right." He turned around and left the room to stand by the entrance ramp a few feet from the door.

Aleshia stripped down, removing every stitch of clothing as Dakarth said the suit required. A cool breeze from the air recycling system wafted across her breasts, causing her nipples to change shape as the chill made her to shake.

She picked up the strange suit, looked it all over, and wondered how to get into it. There wasn't a zipper, and the material was too strong to stretch around the neck area. Feeling around, she touched a panel near the neck and a seam split from the neck down to the groin area. "Oh, so that is how they do it."

"How they do what?" Deven said over his shoulder.

"Nothing, sweetheart. You just keep watch."

She let the garment hang from her fingertips and slipped her foot, then leg into the fabric. It felt cool but quickly warmed to her body temperature. She wondered if the boots would fit, but her foot slid into the first one without any force.

Aleshia slipped the other leg into the suit and her foot made its way down into the second boot and slid in as easy as the first. The inside of the suit felt slick, yet not wet. She had never felt anything like it. She slipped two arms into the holes and hoisted the rest of the torso section onto her shoulders. Tapping the panel again caused the front to seal itself and smoother than any zipper could ever be. Not even a ripple remained where an opening had been only a moment before.

She turned and gazed at her reflection off of the shiny metal of the wall. Rolling her shoulders, her gaze centered on the equipment on her back. If she didn't already know it was there, she never would have. It was so light.

Aleshia stood behind Deven and smiled. "Well? How do I look?"

Deven felt her before she said anything, but he didn't want her to know and waited until she said something before turning. When he did, his eyes went wide. Aleshia wore a skin-tight grey suit that flowed over her every curve and bump. The texture of the suit loosely resembled a checkerboard pattern. For abrasion resistance Deven guessed. Nothing man-made could take the extremes of space and be so form fitting, not to mention flexible.

"Amazing," Deven breathed.

"I take it you approve?" She spun around to give him the full effect and he wished she didn't. He wanted to take her to their cabin right now.

Instead, he took a deep breath. "Yes, amazing what they can do."

Aleshia flexed her fingers within the gloves. "I'll say. These are a lot thinner and better than the gloves I wore when I shoveled snow at my parents' house years ago. The boots are so lightweight I forget I'm even wearing them."

"Did you try the helmet?"

Aleshia shook her head. "No. I figured I would wait until Dakarth was here. I don't want to accidentally put it on, not be able to get it off, and not know how to turn on the air."

Deven chuckled. "You have a point."

Hearing their conversation, Dakarth walked up the ramp, his three-toed boots making a unique clip-clop sound. "How is the fit?"

Aleshia spun around for him as well. "Good, I think?"

Dakarth smiled. "Yes, fit is perfect. Now I need to make the others." He took a step past Aleshia and back into the room. He pulled another garment from the shelf, placed it on the other, and dropped a ball of black goo on the middle before activating the nanomachines. The goo repeated its program and changed the structure of the clothing into something far more advanced. After a few minutes, Dakarth smiled as he picked up the suit. "Deven? This is yours. Please check the fit, I must continue."

Deven took the suit and nodded. "Of course."

Dakarth pulled another piece of clothing and applied more black goo as before. The changes spread out, morphing into another suit.

With Aleshia's help, Deven stripped, slipped into the suit, and stood next to her. While he watched Dakarth create the rest of the suits.

Dakarth turned. "All the suits are ready. Have everyone else come in here and test the fit please."

Otis popped his head inside the shuttle before walking up the ramp. "Anybody home?"

Deven spun around. "Otis! What are you doing here? You should be aboard the *Phoenix*."

Otis smiled as he walked up the ramp. "I talked Leon into it."

"What do you mean 'talked Leon into it'?"

"Well, I convinced him it would be better for him to help Minerva recover fully from her ordeal with the Sileics, then land on the Ixeon base. Besides, you need a cracker more on this mission than his skills."

Deven's eyes narrowed as he folded his arms. "Perhaps, but I should be the one to make the decision."

"I know Boss, and if you tell me to go back, I will. But I think you will agree that I'm the one you want on this. Who else is going to be able to slice their way into any door known without blowing it apart?"

"I don't think Leon would blow them apart," Deven said out the corner of his mouth.

Aleshia looped her arm in his. "You know what he meant."

"I do. And so did he."

Otis chuckled. "Right you are. So Bossman, what do you say? Do I stay?"

"You can stay if you brought something for Dakarth to make a suit for you."

Otis held up and shook a tight pair of overalls. "It may not be the best, but I think it will work."

Deven chewed the inside of his cheek. "If Dakarth says it will work, then you can go."

Dakarth came over and examined Otis' overalls. He nodded. "This will work. Not exact, but close." He took them back over to the shelf and applied black goo to them. Otis watched the nanomachines grow and begin to morph the overalls into a full space suit.

Deven cleared his throat. "And how did you get aboard, anyway? Or better yet, Leon back over to the *Phoenix?*"

Otis chuckled. "Easy Boss, did you forget the *Defiant* has a lot of smaller hanger bays and that my truck is small enough to fit in one?"

Deven blinked. "You let Leon fly your truck back? Wait a minute! You told me your truck isn't space-worthy yet!"

"Well, it is now. CB made the last few modifications I was working on while I waited for Minerva and the ESS. And it was either let Leon fly it back or miss the opportunity of a lifetime."

Deven's one eyebrow went up as the eye below it narrowed.

He folded his arms. "You never seemed like the exploring type."

Otis pulled his eyes away from the nanomachines making his new suit. "What do you mean? The chance of finding out how these Ixeons made creatures like the Celloids or Sileics? No way I'm passing that up. Besides, I want to see Dakarth work up close and personal."

Dakarth watched the final aspects of Otis' suit support system form before he turned around. "I am not ssssure I understand? Watch me up close?"

"I meant it as a form of appreciation. Your technology and abilities amaze me and I wish to learn from you."

Dakarth smiled. "I see. I am happy to teach you." He turned back to the suit, pulled it from the shelf and handed it to Otis. "Please check the fit. It must be exact. I will wait outside." He moved past Otis, leaving the room and the ship.

Otis glanced towards the door and turned back to Deven. "What was that all about?"

Deven's gaze drifted down towards Aleshia with her intertwined arm around his waist. "Blame her. She didn't want to change in front of him, so he assumes everyone would feel that way except me."

"I don't mind if he saw me changing into a suit. Why did she?"

Aleshia laughed. "Because you have to be nude inside it!"

Otis looked down garment stretched across his hand. "Oh. I can see ... well ... that is ... you–"

Aleshia giggled. "You know, he is even more fun than you." She slipped her arm from Deven's waist and moved past the two of them and down the ramp. "I'll let you change. At least I don't think you have a problem with Deven seeing." She disappeared from sight.

"Actually, I didn't mind her either. But I know you would've."

Deven nodded. "Right, and she would have blushed to the roots of her hair too."

"And for a redhead, that would really be something."

Deven laughed. "You got that right."

Otis stripped out of his old jeans, shirt, pants, socks, and boots. But when tried to put on the suit but only ended up scratching his head until Deven showed him where to touch to activate the open sequence. After that, he slipped inside with relative ease and Deven activated the close. The suit sealed around him. "Amazing. This thing is so light, hard to believe it can keep us alive in space."

Deven nodded. "It is considering if we made a suit, it would have been five times the size or more."

"I think even more. Keep in mind they put layers of armor in those old suits. While we have a lot of great technology, our space tech is really lacking," Otis said.

Deven shrugged. "True. But until us, no human has been into space for hundreds of years. We didn't see the need."

"How is the fit?" Dakarth walked up the ramp, his hands clasped behind his back.

Otis nodded, wiggled his fingers, and made several extended motions with his arms and legs. "Amazing. Truly amazing. It is so light I forget I am wearing anything."

Dakarth smiled. "That means the fit is perfect. A bulky suit will slow you down and cause problems."

Otis bumped a touch pad on the left side of his collar, causing a the helmet to appear on his head and lock. His lips moved, but they didn't hear anything. Dakarth took two steps and pushed the same touch pad on his collar. The helmet disconnected and Otis breathed. "What was with that thing! I couldn't get it off."

"You didn't push the right touch point."

"Didn't you hear me?"

Deven shook his head. "Nope, we didn't hear anything. The seals must be very good on these suits."

Dakarth nodded. "Of course. If the seals were not good, you would die."

Otis smiled. "You have a point. When do we go?"

"I must finish a few more things before we leave." Dakarth walked over to the extended shelf containing the nano kit and other tools. He applied the nanomachines to another device of his and activated them. The square device with its flip up screen grew in size and expanded. Keys formed and other data connection points appeared on the side. At least Otis assumed they were data connection points. They looked very different from anything he had seen before.

While the device was much larger, it was still very portable. He folded the screen down and picked it up. "Now we are ready. Once everyone is aboard, we will go."

Deven pulled his data tab from its pouch that lay with his other clothes. He flipped it on, tapped a channel, and Galina's face appeared. "Nothing different up here. I still can't pick up anything from the Moon. Both Miles and I have been scanning it continuously. We haven't seen so much as a shimmer of power. Let alone a whole base."

"Cut the scans. They might get wise if they can detect intense scans. Passive occasional scans are fine. I do want you to keep a distant eye on us while we are down there."

"Done. But I doubt we will see much once you are down there without the active systems."

"I concur. The active systems are more advisable," Miles said.

Deven shook his head. "Not worth it. All those scans might have tipped our hand already."

"I don't like it, but will do."

"Get Aleshia, we are ready to take off. Also, next time Leon leaves the ship, let me know."

Galina blinked. "Leon left? Where did he go? Wait a sec, did he leave through one of the smaller bays? Miles reported something strange with the doors. For a second it appeared they opened, but didn't."

Deven sighed. "They opened all right. Otis is here as proof."

Otis gave a sheepish look. "Sorry, Boss."

"But what are we going to do without Leon?" Galina said.

Otis shrugged. "Leon said Gregory is very competent."

"Gregory might be competent, but he is *not* Leon."

Deven smiled. "No one is Leon."

Aleshia popped her head inside the shuttle. "You called?"

Deven looked up. "I did." His gaze drifted back down towards the data tab in his hand. "Do what you can and keep an eye on us as much as possible. Also, I want both ships on alert in case the Ixeons try to throw something at us or you." He tapped the data tab, Galina's image disappeared, and he slipped the data tab into one of the suit's hip pouches. His eyes shot up to focus on Aleshia. "We're ready, are you?"

Aleshia shrugged. "As ready as I ever will be."

Dakarth smiled as he took three small blocks twenty centimeters square, placed them on the floor behind his chair in the cockpit, and applied the black nano goo to them. He stepped back and activated the nanomachines. The black goo came to life and spread over the blocks. The blocks began to melt and reform.

Aleshia watched as the blocks came alive and stretched up towards the ceiling, widened, and scooped out. When the blocks finished rippling, they had become chairs with a wide base attached to the floor along the whole round pivot point. She walked around one of the chairs. "Amazing."

"You can say that again," Otis said.

Dakarth powered up the shuttle's systems and pointed to the chairs. "If you will use them, we will take off."

Deven raised a finger. "One sec." He dove out of the shuttle's hatch and down the ramp. He spotted Gregory running for hangar control.

"I know, will take care of it," Gregory said as he ran through the hanger's inner doors, spun around and sealed them. They slid shut with a positive lock, and the lights indicated the bay was ready for depressurization.

Deven ran back up the ramp, hit the button he saw Dakarth used to seal the hatch, and made his way to the cockpit. He pulled out his data tab and hit another button. Gregory's face appeared.

"Bay is depressurizing. Twenty seconds until doors open," Gregory said.

"Watch us carefully, I don't want to mess up our paint job or Dakarth's," Deven said.

Gregory smiled. "Don't worry. I've got this. Bay depressurized. Doors opening." The lights on the main doors went out and two panels retracted, unlocking the doors before they slid apart. "Doors are open. Dakarth, you are lined up and cleared for departure."

Dakarth nodded. "All lookssss good here too. Activating thrusters." Dakarth hit several keys, and the shuttle lifted above the deck several centimeters, then several more before pushing towards the open bay doors.

The shuttle slid out into space without incident and the doors closed, sealing behind them. Dakarth nudged the shuttle down towards to Moon, activating a program he had set up earlier. The shuttle picked up inertia as it headed towards the Moon. Faster and faster it went until Aleshia gripped Deven's hand. "Aren't we going too fast?"

Dakarth smiled, but didn't turn around towards the three passengers behind him. "No. And we must go faster. If we approach under power, we will be detected for certain. If we approach as an out of control asteroid or debris, they won't give us second look."

The shuttle increased its speed again as they began to tumble end over end. Aleshia winced and shut her eyes. "Just tell me when it's over."

The dull-grey pock-marked sphere known as the Moon reached out to them. Speed increased. Gravity, although weak, pulled at the shuttle. Dakarth tapped several controls to slow their spin, but not much. "We musssst look like falling rock. I have equipment to send a false reading, but we cannot come down normal, or they will know."

Even Deven swallowed hard. "It doesn't make it any easier knowing."

Otis smiled as he peered over. "Oh I don't know Boss, this is kind of fun."

Deven glared back and wanted to wipe that smile off his face but instead grunted. "If you say so."

Dakarth pointed to a deep area hidden in shadow as it spun past the window. "I am detecting some emissions from that crevasse. We will land in the crater nearby."

Aleshia said nothing, still holding her eyes shut, and her knuckles had long since turned white from gripping the chair. Deven eyed the crater as it spun past. "Is it big enough?"

Dakarth nodded. "It is. Will be tight fit but will make it."

Otis laughed. "This is going to be fun."

Deven grunted, wishing he would stop saying that. Aleshia was uneasy enough. Such comments only added to it. He thought about saying something, but Aleshia would hear it for sure. Heck, she might have heard him think about it. Then again, she is so distracted right now, she might not. He decided to chance it. *Will you shut up!*

Otis turned and nodded. He received the non-vocal message loud and clear. *Sorry Boss.*

Dakarth held the controls and guided the shuttle in one last maneuver before he pulled them back hard. The shuttle stopped its spin just as it slipped behind the crater walls and anti-grav thrusters activated, bringing the shuttle to a full stop millimeters from the surface of the Moon. A second later they felt a slight bump as the landing gear touched the surface, and they were down. A micro second later they felt a strong vibration though the ship.

Turning around Dakarth smiled, looking at the white faces. Except for Otis. "I told you, nothing to worry about."

Aleshia opened one eye. "Are you sure? And did you *have* to do that?"

"It was neccessssary to fool them. We are only a short distance from the crevasse where I detected the emissions. But if they were watching, they saw a meteor crash into this crater, nothing more. The pulse I sent into the ground will fool their seismic systems, if they have any. Activate your helmets and press the pad below the first. It will start the support systems."

Otis was the first, having done it before. He touched the pad; the helmet attached, and this time he activated the support systems. Oxygen and nitrogen mix flowed into the helmet and over his face. Dakarth also did the same, activating his helmet.

Aleshia's finger hovered over the pad on her collarbone. "Are you sure about this? Perhaps I should stay here?"

"I'm sure," Deven said. "And we need you. You know that."

She sighed. "I know, but …I …oh the heck with it." Her finger jabbed the pad causing the helmet to attach. She touched the second pad and breathed.

Deven touched his, and the helmet sealed over his head. "I told you nothing to worry about."

"I said the same," Dakarth said as he stood up and walked past them, exited the cockpit and out the room behind.

Deven jerked a thumb towards the doorway. "Let's go. We have some bugs to find."

Aleshia rolled her eyes. "Great. Of all the things I thought I would do in my life, going on a bug hunt on the Moon was *not* one of them."

Otis chuckled. "Isn't it great how life throws these curves? You never know what is around the corner."

"But I *like* knowing what is around the corner," Aleshia said as they reached the airlock and the ramp beyond.

Dakarth turned. "I and Otis will go first. We cannot all fit inside the airlock. While I could depressurize the entire shuttle and repressurize it later, it will take too much time." They all nodded, and he pointed to a panel on the right. "The system is simple. When we are through, I will close the outer door. When the room is ready, this light will turn green. Then push this button." He indicated the star-shaped button under the light. "It will open the door. Once you are in the airlock, push the same button on the panel inside. It will take care of the rest."

Deven nodded. "Got it."

Dakarth and Otis entered the airlock and the cylindrical door shut. A few moments later the light went from red to green and the door opened again.

Deven took Aleshia's hand. "Let's go."

"I really think I should stay behind," she said.

"But we need you, Aleshia. You can do this," Otis said.

Aleshia blinked. "Otis? How can you–"

Otis laughed. "I guess you forgot that sound doesn't travel through space, so we need to use communication links."

"Yessss. Everything you say we all hear," Dakarth said, "speakers and pickups let us hear when there is atmosphere too. They turn on with support systems."

"Great. Guess I won't be muttering on this trip," Aleshia said.

Deven laughed. "But I love your muttering." They entered the airlock, and he pushed the button to start the cycle. A moment later the outer door opened, revealing Dakarth and Otis.

Dakarth pointed to the wall of the crater several meters from their position. "We will start there."

They all nodded and followed him to the wall. Bouncing along in the weak gravity. When they reached it Aleshia's head tilted back as her eyes followed the ancient cracked and broken lines reaching up the massive wall of the crater. "How are we going to climb that?"

Dakarth pulled a device from a pack she hadn't noticed him carrying until that moment. "We aren't going up, we are going through." He placed the octagonal device on the wall and pushed the button in the center. At first nothing happened. Then black material spread out from the device until a normal looking door was formed. Dakarth pushed another button and through the window of the door they could see a bright blue light. "Don't look at the light. It is not harmful, but it will cause you to see bright spots for some moments."

Otis nodded. "A good to reason not too. But I admit I really want to. More nanomachines?"

Dakarth nodded. "Yessss." He removed the nanomachine device, placed it back in his pack, pulled open the door, and beyond laid a tunnel the size of the door reaching through the crater to the open area beyond. The walls were white, reflecting what little light there was and giving them enough to see.

"Amazing, but I thought they could only alter matter, not destroy it?" Deven said.

Dakarth pointed with one of his talon tipped, glove encased fingers as he entered the tunnel. "Yessss true. But one thing they can do is convert matter to different forms of energy if needed. Light and heat are two possibles."

Otis nodded. "And that is why it was so bright in here."

"Correct."

"But you turned *that* much material to energy?"

Dakarth shook his head. "No. We don't like to do a large amount. Something might go wrong. We can also change the matter to make it more dense."

Aleshia ran her gloved hand along the perfectly smooth walls. "Of course these walls must be very strong to hold up the whole crater and not fall in on us."

Dakarth nodded. "Yes. Very dense, very strong."

They exited the crater to find themselves within the chasm Dakarth spoke of. He pulled out another device and checked the dim display. "This way. We must be careful. They might have set traps."

Otis blinked. "Traps? On the Moon? Why? I mean we couldn't get here so who would they be for?"

Dakarth turned. "We can."

Otis laughed. "Good point."

The chasm walls appeared like a natural ancient lava tube, but Dakarth knew better. He pointed to rough walls of the tube. "This is not natural."

Deven studied where he was pointing but only saw the same rock as before. "I don't understand, it all looks like ancient rock to me."

Dakarth nodded. "Yes. If it was natural, there would be layers. This is all one large layer indicating it happened all at once. Its designers tried to make it look natural, and from space it would look so. But here, is obvious."

They moved along the chasm that continued to get more narrow until it was only two of them wide. Ahead the area became more smooth and refined and the walls almost gleamed. The chasm's creators didn't care to keep up the facade here. In the distance, the area ended in a solid wall. Dakarth held up a gloved talon. "Wait. Something not right here. Why would they change?"

Otis gazed up and down the walls. "A trap. Has to be."

Dakarth nodded. "Yes." He pulled his pack forward and rummaged around inside. His three fingers curled around something and pulled out a palm sized device with a foldable screen. He flipped open the screen and tapped on the keys. The screen came to life and projected a hologram of the walls. Several red points lit up along the top ridge and a row of them a few centimeters from the ground. Dakarth pointed to the areas and traced his talon along the ridge. "These areas are warmer than the rest of the walls. It could be sensors."

"Or a trap," Otis said.

Dakarth nodded. "Yes, could be. Not sure how we should proceed. I could try scanning them, but if the devices are sensitive enough to detect my scan, it could activate them."

"Or at the very least let them know we are here," Aleshia said.

"Yes. And we cannot allow that."

Deven stepped forward. "Perhaps I can find out what they are."

Aleshia's eyes went wide. "Deven! You can't! It will drain you and we can't have you half asleep."

Deven smiled. "Not if you help me."

"How? We can't touch through these suits."

"Not direct contact, no. But you can still help. And your abilities have grown a lot since we did it last. It should more than make up for the barrier between us."

Aleshia chewed her bottom lip. "I don't know ..."

"We have to try. Otherwise, the only other option is to risk detection."

"I do not understand what you want to do, but scanning is our only option I can think of," Dakarth said.

Aleshia sighed. "Okay, I'm with you." She stepped forward and placed her hand in Deven's. They both closed their eyes and Deven reached out with his mind. He probed into the rock and felt around. He found the sensors mounted at ground level and the rows of them near the top of the ridge.

He pushed a bit more and saw their interconnecting beams locking on to each other, making a web of discovery nothing could get past. He staggered backwards as he released his grip from Aleshia and opened his eyes. Aleshia stepped closer, wrapping her arms around him and holding tight. He shook his head several times. "It is a sensor web alright. It reaches from the top ridge down in a diagonal pattern making of a network of interdependency. I suspect they are very sensitive, which is why the walls are perfectly smooth in this section."

Otis sighed. "That means not even a fly could get past, well if there were flies on the Moon."

Dakarth moved past them and examined the smooth walls. He turned back. "I think I see a door on the far end. At least I assume it is. It looks like part of the rock."

Deven nodded. "There is one. I didn't go far past it. But there is an airlock system that reaches from the door into the complex. It is a decent sized room. I think they also use it for storage."

Dakarth smiled. "If we can't go this way, we make our own. Now that we know where the web is and how far it extends." He reached into his pack and pulled out the nanomachine generator he used earlier.

Otis raised a finger. "Umm, this won't be a straight line."

"I can program them to curve around after a certain point. We enter that airlock. Did you see if the wall was rock or something else?"

"Rock, smooth rock," Deven said.

"Excellent. We can enter that way and leave without a trace if needed."

Dakarth held out the octagonal nanomachine generator. He mounted it to the side of the chasm, reached back into his pack, and pulled out another device. The square device split down the middle and the top became a screen as it opened. Data flowed over the screen and Dakarth placed it on top of the nano device.

More code scrolled past the tiny screen as Otis peeked over Dakarth's shoulder. "You're programming the nano's path?"

Dakarth nodded. "Yessss. It must be exact or we will miss our location. I must concentrate."

Otis held up his hands. "Well, if you need help, I'm here." He took two steps back.

Dakarth worked on the nanos for several more minutes before he smiled and pressed the activate button. As before, the dark material of near atom-sized machines spread out from the octagonal device that held them. After a minute another door had formed, and he watched as a blue glow emanated from behind the window. Four minutes later he saw a readout on the screen, and he disconnected it and nano kit from the door. He pulled the door open and gestured towards the smooth white walls within. "After you."

Aleshia nodded and went in, followed by Deven and Otis. This tunnel was longer than the other, but the walls still reflected enough light from their helmets to illuminate the entire tunnel. Half-way through, they felt heavier and their Moon-walk bounce reduced to a normal gait. Aleshia, Deven, and Otis stared at Dakarth with wide eyes. "It issss gravity field, we have it too. Don't use it much as it is not as efficient, takes too much power. But it can cover a large area without modifying older sssstructures."

When they approached the door on the other end of the tunnel, Aleshia placed her hand upon it and probed with her mind. A few seconds later she opened her eyes and her hand went to her side. "I don't feel anyone on the other side. If we triggered any alarms, it is not showing at the moment."

Dakarth reached within his pack and pulled out several devices that started with a palm grip, went up, then ended in a forward protruding barrel. "Take these." He handed one to each of them.

Deven regarded the strange shaped weapon in his hand. At least he assumed it was a weapon. "What are these?"

"It is a Triellon. An energy based weapon. Non-lethal to most life forms. I have adjusted it to be less intense than usual. But we cannot take the chance of power being too great."

Otis felt the weight of the weapon. It was smooth and no signs of the usual manufacturing. This weapon was not of human make and while he should have expected something like this, it still surprised him. "I bet Leon would love to take one of these apart. How does it work?"

"It builds up a form of energy discharge that momentarily overloads the target's nuro system. It will not override autonomic functions, but it shut cognitive down."

Deven cocked an eyebrow. "Why didn't you use these against the Celloids?"

Dakarth shrugged as best he could inside his suit. "We tried. They were immune."

"And what makes you think the Ixeon's aren't?"

Dakarth shrugged. "I don't. But is the best we have."

Otis rolled his eyes. "Great. This just keeps getting better and better."

They took a defensive position behind the door and Deven pulled it open. All four of them raced inside. The room was as Deven described, an airlock repurposed into a storage area as well. Crates sat all over. Some of them open. Others appeared still sealed. The room was square and almost appeared as if humans had made it. Except for the hexagon shaped door at the far end leading further within the complex. Along the one wall hung clothing. Possibly a jump suit that paired with the space suit next to it with a large bubble helmet. Each suit might have fit any of them except for the smaller head hole and the spaces for multiple arms.

Otis walked over to a crate. "Shall we crack one of these open?"

Deven grabbed Otis' shoulder. "No. We can't take the chance opening one of them will alert everyone here."

Otis raised an eyebrow. "Do you really think opening a crate here will set off an alarm?"

"No. But it's not worth the risk. Perhaps not even an alarm, but something else that draws unwanted attention."

"Right, Boss."

They walked over to the hexagonal door and Dakarth peered at the small four centimeter screen in his hand. "I can apply nanos to force the door open or melt a hole through it." He pulled his pack forward, reaching for the nano kit.

Otis pushed forward. "Let me at it. I have worked on their code before. I'm sure I can slice my way through."

Deven looked at Dakarth. "He's right. He is the best, and he did figure out how to access the Celloid Core."

Dakarth nodded and stood back. "Very well."

Otis opened the pouch on his hip and pulled out his keyboard. He opened the panel and connected two leads to a section similar to others he had seen in the Celloid Core. Tapping on the keyboard, the screen filled with yellow characters. They were very strange and unlike anything they had seen before. "Interesting. I haven't seen this before."

"Get out of there. Let Dakarth open the door with the nanos," Deven said.

"Hang on, I've almost got it," Otis said tapping a few more keys.

"I don't think–" Dakarth never finished as the door began to open. The center circle rotated, retracted into the door a second before the door split into many triangle sections, and retracted all at once in one smooth motion.

Otis smiled. "Told you I would get it."

Aleshia pointed to the screen. "How did you get it when you hadn't seen these characters before?"

"Simple. I knew there had to be some relation to the data

we saw. After a minute, I realized these were the binary equivalent. When I figured out it was the same thing behind the characters, I *had* seen it before."

They stepped past the strange door and peered into the corridor beyond. The passageways were rounded and lacked anything other than basic design. The walls also had a rough appearance without any finishing, indicating this complex was built in haste.

Deven turned towards Aleshia. "Where to?"

Aleshia closed her eyes and reached out with her mind. She felt something down the main corridor, off a side one and in the farthest room. Her eyes popped open and she shuddered. It felt so different from anything else she had felt before. Even the Lytherians. This felt totally alien. "I can't be sure, but I think half-way down this corridor there is another off to the right. If we follow that to the room at the farthest end we might find who we are looking for."

Deven blinked. "You can't be sure?"

Aleshia shrugged. "I don't know. There is something down there. I didn't want to push too hard on the chance they might feel my presence."

"You mean it could block you?"

"Not block. At least I don't think so. If it did, it is one of the weirdest blocks I ever felt. And like I said, I could have pushed harder, but it might have given us away."

Dakarth nodded. "I agree. Best choice. Let'ssss go."

They walked down the corridor as quietly as they could. Dakarth took the lead and held out a passive scanner, sweeping it back and forth. He hoped it would detect any cameras or equipment that could give away their existence.

Aleshia walked behind him, keeping her focus on the room

beyond. Nothing had changed. Whatever it was, was still in there. "It's still there."

Dakarth nodded, and they continued on.

They turned at the end of the corridor. The second was less finished with even fewer details. At the end of it sat another hexagonal door. Deven held his fist in an upright motion. "Wait. Does anyone else think this is too easy?"

"Boss, you worry too much," Otis said.

"Am I? All the security outside and nothing inside? For a race capable of making the Celloids and the Sileics, don't you think that is a little unusual?"

Otis shrugged. "This place was built in a hurry. They didn't add all the bells and whistles."

"But this base, for all intents and purposes, was built in enemy territory and you don't add basic monitoring systems within the base?"

Dakarth nodded. "He'ssss right. It is odd. Our people would never make such a mistake."

Aleshia blinked. "What are you saying we should do? Go back?"

"No, we have to go inside. But perhaps we can give ourselves another edge." He turned to Dakarth. "Can you create another door to get us inside with the nanos?"

Dakarth shrugged. "Yes. But why?"

"From what Aleshia has said, it is a large room. If we put a door in and enter where they are not expecting us to–"

Otis smiled. "Gotcha Boss. Even if they know we are here, they won't be expecting us to make our own door from another direction."

Deven nodded. "Right." He turned and offered Aleshia his hand. "Time we see where to put a door." She put her gloved hand in his and they closed their eyes. The world disappeared as they drifted with there minds down the hall and through the wall. On the other side, the oblong room sat full of consoles. This section was hidden from the rest by a sharp right angle. They felt something stir around that corner, and they pulled out fast, slamming back to consciousness.

Deven took a weak step and shook his head. "I know where it is. I didn't look, afraid of tipping our hand. Shouldn't possible, but–"

"Not worth the risk," Otis said.

Deven nodded. "Right." He released Aleshia's hand as her eyes raced up and down him. She took a step forward to hold him, and he shook his head. He walked down the corridor and pointed to the wall. "Here. This is the best spot."

Dakarth nodded and reached into his pack, bringing out the octagon shaped nano device. He placed it along the wall and looked at Deven. "The wall is about half a meter thick here, straight through?" Deven nodded.

Otis raised a finger. "Umm Boss, this thing gives off a lot of light, isn't that going to tell them we are here?"

Dakarth shook his head. "The light is one way to dissssipate the energy. For such a short distance, I can store it within the device instead. And I will leave a thin layer of rock on the other side of the door as camouflage." Deven nodded and Dakarth pushed the central activate button. The black goo of the nanomachines spread out from the device into a rectangular door shape and solidified into a new door. This time though, no blue glow emanated from the door's window. After a few minutes, Dakarth smiled. "Issss done."

They all stood behind the door with Deven griping the handle. They all nodded. He pulled the door open, and they raced inside. Deven dove in first, tucked, rolled, and popped up, holding his Triellon in the direction of the turn.

He was the first to see it. And even though had seen the images Otis had recovered, it never braced him for what he saw. Two immense compound eyes studied him. They took up ninety percent of the head. There wasn't much of a neck. Instead, the head seemed to rest on the narrow shoulders. Most of the body was hidden by a suit similar to what they saw hanging in the storage room.

They couldn't see any feet but the suit ended in reinforced legs similar to boots except there was no right angle as a normal foot would have. One of the long thin hairy arms raised and pointed at them. They heard a loud shrill tone vary in pitch several times before the arm reached for the control panel the in front of him.

Deven wasted no time. His Triellon raised and ready, he pushed the activation button built into the grip. The Ixeon made another harsh sound and his arm lowered.

Otis popped up behind Deven and fired his Triellon. Likewise, Dakarth and Aleshia fired theirs.

The Ixeon emitted another loud shriek, but different. Laughter? And his arm touched the control panel.

Lights flashed in front of their eyes and everything went black.

— 15 —

Deep underground former Chairman of the World Council, Scott Lavine sat in a darkened room with rough rock walls tapping keys at his console. He never would have dreamed of being chased from his *own* office! He had built it, refurbished the World Council's building, lead them in several crises and now they throw him aside? "They will regret that mistake," Lavine muttered.

A tentative knock on a metal door drew his attention from the console. The room far from the luxury of his office in the World Council building. Small, with little room for more than the desk he sat behind.

His eyes drifted up.

"Ah commander Naud, come in."

Naud stiffened, still not used to the title. Or dealing with Lavine directly. "Chairman, you wanted to see me?"

Lavine pointed to the metal fold-up chair in front of his desk. "Yes, I did. I have a little mission for you."

Naud's sat down as one eyebrow went up. "A mission? What kind, sir?"

Lavine sat back in his chair while rotating it back and forth. It wasn't the luxurious padded leather one he was used to, but at least this one had a fullback, even if a bit hard. "A retrieval."

Naud sat forward, intrigued. "Retrieval? Of what? I thought all you had is in this bunker."

Lavine laughed. "Hardly. But this facility let me move in the quickest and without being detected. No, I have other resources, but some of them are more difficult than others."

Naud cocked his head and wished Lavine would get on with it. "Oh?"

Lavine nodded. "Yes. There is a Mechand facility I want you to visit and acquire more equipment."

"A Mechand manufacturing facility? I thought they were all destroyed or dismantled?"

A smile slid across Lavine's face. "You should have figured by now such data is not always accurate. It is the last such facility still around and functional. It is currently idle but its stockpiles are full, including several carriers, weapons, and ammunition."

Naud's eyes went wide. "Still full? Why hasn't this facility been raided by the current World Council then?"

"Two reasons. First, they don't know about it. I kept the details of it to myself. And second, since it is still functional, so are its defenses."

Naud winced at the thought of an army of Mechands in storage coming alive at any moment. "It's defenses are still online?"

Lavine nodded. "I believe so."

"And how do you expect me to retrieve this? I assume you have a way to deactivate the defenses? You must have for the other facilities you accessed, right?"

Lavine shook his head. "No, I do not. I could get you sliced in, given time. But that is something we don't have a lot of."

"Then what do you expect me to do? Drive up in a truck, knock on the door and hope they don't blast me while I try to take everything?" Naud stood ready to leave. "Count me out."

Lavine raised a hand, pointing a finger at the chair. "Commander Naud, sit!"

Naud, against his better judgment, did as he was told.

"That's better. Now did I say I was going to send you in a truck to knock on the door?"

Naud stuck his hands in his pockets. "No, I just–"

"Well, you assumed wrong."

"Then what? You gave Halburn the best you had, and he blew it all away."

Lavine's eyes narrowed to slits as he stood. "Don't remind me." He walked around the desk and stood in the doorway. "Come."

Naud stood and followed as they walked down the dark hallway. The rough walls threw shadows at odd angles as they continued on. Damp air flowing through a nearby grate sent a chill up his spine. They passed a couple of technicians loyal to Lavine, working frantically to restore the rest of the facility. At the end of the hallway, Lavine turned right and pressed a button on the wall. A large hatch rotated and spun in on itself, sliding out-of-the-way revealing a medium size Mechand hangar. He pointed and walked inside. Naud followed but didn't see any carriers until they turned another corner and the second half of the hangar held several Mechand carriers on storage racks. One sat on the ground, sparks flashing from certain points as more technicians swarmed over it.

Naud's eyes went wide. "You have more carriers."

Lavine grinned. "Did you ever have any doubt? What did

you think I wanted you to take command of? A cargo truck? I may have given Halburn the best, but I never said anything about second best. This carrier isn't the *Vanguard*, but she will get you into the facility and return with the equipment we need."

Naud walked a little closer. Finally, a real ship of his own. He reached out and brushed his hand across one of the armor plates. He turned a minute later, breaking himself from the revery. "And she is operational?"

Lavine nodded. "She is. My technicians are finishing the last of the repairs. She is the only one ready. The rest could be, if we had the parts."

Naud crossed his arms. "Hence this mission."

"Correct."

"I assume you have a crew for me? Or am I going this alone?"

Lavine laughed. "Of course not, and you will need help to bring everything back."

Naud smiled. "Of course. And does that include someone that can hack his way in?"

Lavine turned. "Why? You are blasting your way in. This ship should be able to handle the mission with ease."

Naud turned as one eye narrowed. "Humor me."

Lavine folded his hands behind his back. "Very well, you can take Thobe, he is the best we have."

Naud nodded. "Excellent. In this kind of mission, it is always a good idea to have all your bases covered. Thank you, Chairman."

Lavine pursed his lips. "Yes. And the ship hasn't been named yet. Do you have a suggestion?"

Naud thought for a moment. "How about, *Raven*?"

Lavine nodded. "Then the *Raven* it shall be. Most of your crew is aboard now if you wish to meet them."

Naud nodded. "I would."

Lavine pointed to the ramp on the other side of the *Raven* and Naud followed as Lavine glided to it, his robes flapping as he moved.

Odell Halburn sat behind his desk and let out a large sigh. It had been only a few days since he joined the World Council as Chairman, but in that time he had found several hidden Links Scott Lavine had left behind. The live tap into the council chamber was easy to spot, but the others were more difficult. Hidden back ends into security systems and the Council's databases. Some even programmed to hide themselves moving deeper into databases obfuscating themselves should they detect any sort of discovery. It was only because Odell had seen Lavine in action several times at his console, he knew what to look for.

One of these hidden programs would have disabled the entire World Council's security system in one swoop for at least thirty minutes. Another would have caused damage to the defense systems overloading their delicate components requiring repair or replacement. Still another could access almost any data and slip it through the firewalls undetected. He had tried to trace the rouge programs back to their source but was stopped cold by too many relays and dead end connections. Whatever one could say negative about Lavine, in the aspect of clandestine work, he was the top of his field.

Halburn sat back in his chair, rocking it back and forth. How long before Lavine showed his hand? The man must have more cards than he could see. And that worried him. Lavine managed to assemble an entire fleet of Mechand ships when everyone else thought they were dismantled or destroyed. Who knew what he had access to and still has control of.

Naud stood, arms crossed, looking out the main window of the bridge as the *Raven* hurtled through the skyways at its top overdrive speed. He turned to look at the man seated at his right. "Perkins? What is our ETA?"

The man on his right stiffened. "Five minutes-twenty three seconds at current rate of speed, Commander Naud."

Naud smiled. The man was greener than a gill, but at least he was accurate, and eager to please. Though, sometimes, he wondered if the man was *too* eager. "Excellent. Tell the rest of the crew to prepare for the attack."

Perkins tapped a control on his console. "Yes sir."

The man on Naud's left sighed. "I don't know why I am here."

Naud turned to face Tyce Thobe, his eyes narrowing to mere slits. "You are here to help us should we encounter problems that require your unique abilities."

"I know that, but I don't see how much help I will be. I mean I'm not a soldier. Find me a back alley and a locked door, I will get you in. But busting down the front door is not my style."

Naud laughed. "How well I know, you have only told me six times since we left the base. With luck, you won't be needed, and we will catch the facility off-guard."

Tyce's head turned and cocked. "Do you really think that

is possible? I heard you have gone against the Mechands before?"

Naud's head tilted down. "Yes I have, and while possible it is slight. Mechands, unless there is a technical problem, will attack if threatened. And to our knowledge this is the last such facility still operational, even if dormant."

"And that dormancy can be terminated at the drop of a hat," Tyce said through gritted teeth.

Naud bobbed his head in agreement. "Sadly yes, if operational they can be activated at any moment. While we don't know if they will, if left on the standard protocols, they should."

Naud felt the *Raven* shudder as they dropped out of overdrive. "Sir, we have arrived," Perkins said.

"Any response from the facility yet?"

Perkins shook his head. "Negative. Although I am detecting higher energy levels compared to when we first dropped out of overdrive."

Naud sighed. "That *is* a response, even if they are not attacking yet! Shields up, prepare for battle."

"Yes sir!" Perkins' fingers flew over his console. A heavy armor shield slid up and over the bridge windows locking into place obscuring the view of the vast facility as a blue bubble of energy snapped into being around the *Raven*. "Shields are up."

"All cannons are online and ready," Tyce said.

"Good, anymore actions from the base?"

Perkins shook his head. "Negative."

Naud crossed his arms. One arm flipped up and a single finger rubbed the side of his face. *It is possible they won't start firing until we do, or they could being trying to get us in closer before they start. Hmm.*

"Shall I order the cannons to open fire?" Tyce said.

"No, if possible I would like to acquire the facility in one piece."

"Sir, I am now detecting a powerful energy shield now in place around the facility."

"Any ships?"

"Negative, only the shield. Although I am still detecting increased energy output."

"Interesting. It has went on full defensive but nothing more. Rather unusual."

Perkins cocked his head. "Why is that?"

"Usually such facilities launch fighters or other vehicles before activating their central shield. This one has not done so. It should be responding in a very ridged scripted pattern, yet it is not. I don't like this."

"Should we abort?" Tyce said with hopeful eyes.

Naud laughed. "There hasn't even been one shot fired and your ready to turn tail and run?"

"Just reminding the Commander of his options," Tyce said with a sly smile.

"Uh-huh. Perkins, I want more information on those energy readings you are getting. What are they?"

Perkins tapped several controls on his console. "I can't quite tell. It is coming from the central core and are increasing, but the increase is very slow. If they are powering up a weapon, it must have the worst energy usage curve on the planet!"

"No I don't think so either, it wouldn't be practical. Still, this has me concerned. Are you detecting any weapons at all?"

Perkins nodded. "Yes, standard carbine cannons are

studded all over the facility. None are powered or locking on to us though."

Minerva's eyebrows met on her screen. "That's odd."

Leon spun around from his console. "What is?"

"I am detecting activity at one of my prime manufacturing facilities."

Leon blinked. "I thought they were all dismantled, destroyed, or raided?"

Minerva's image bit the side of her cheek. "So did I." She frowned. "And now I'm receiving a message from the World Council."

Leon sat back in his seat. "This can't be good. Put it through."

Odell Halburn's face flashed on the large screen. "Odell! Good to see you, but I doubt this is a social call," Leon said.

Halburn blinked. "Leon? What are you doing on board the *Phoenix*?"

"Long story. Better question is, why are you calling?"

"Yes, how did you know?" Minerva said.

Halburn blinked and cocked his head. "Know what?"

"That one of my prime manufacturing facilities is operational."

"I thought you said they were all offline?"

"They were. Until it went into an Alert One condition, I had no idea it was functional."

Halburn folded his arms. "Let me guess, it is near the southern coast of the African content?"

Minerva's eyes narrowed. "Yes, how did you know?"

"I had a feeling Lavine had something up his sleeve, so I had the skylanes watched closely. We had several reports of a Mechand carrier going at maximum overdrive, and that was the general last reported position before we lost them. If the rumors are correct and my old friend Torrian Naud is helping Lavine, it doesn't surprise me we had trouble tracking them."

Leon blinked. "Naud is helping Lavine?"

Halburn nodded. "Yes, it is even possible he is leading Lavine's forces. And what is Alert One condition?"

Minerva smiled. "Oh, sorry, I sometimes forget people don't know. In this case it means the facility detected an armed Mechand carrier approaching, but it didn't respond to the usual protocols. The facility woke up at that point and reached out to me to confirm it was one of mine or should it take action."

"And?"

"Nothing, I told it to activate the passive defenses but nothing more. I was about to contact you and inform you of the situation," Minerva said.

"Is it a danger to the facility?"

Minerva shook her head. "Negative. It is an older carrier. I could take it out with relative ease. There are two newer carriers in its hanger, two more in the external landing field, along with several platoons of Mechands. Not to mention the facility's carbine cannons, which are up to date and quite formidable. Do you want me to take action?"

Halburn shook his head. "No, I would rather know what they are up to. If you blast them out of the sky, we will never find out. Keep a defensive posture and watch them. Anything changes, let me know. But do *not* go into an active attack, is that clear?"

"Affirmative, however, I reserve the right to do so if the

facility will be lost otherwise. The Earth cannot afford to lose my last prime manufacturing facility. It will slow the recovery by many years."

Halburn nodded. "I am well aware of this, and I agree. Do not sacrifice the facility, but do not give it over to them either. I do not know what Lavine is up to, but it cannot be good."

Naud thrummed his left fingers against his upper right arm. "Anything?"

Perkins shook his head. "No changes, Sir. Power levels have been raised, and the shield is up to full strength now, but nothing more. No fighters have been launched and power has not been diverted to the Carbine Cannons."

Naud rubbed his chin. "This does not make sense. Tyce? Have you seen this before?"

Tyce's eyes squinted at his screen, trying to make sense of the data he was seeing. "No, it doesn't. Mechands have a specific protocol for defending their bases, I have studied it in detail. Lavine had me slide into more than one before. That base should be throwing everything it has at us."

"And yes, it is just sitting there, but the shield is active at full power."

"Affirmative. The only time it would throw full power to its shield is after fighters have launched."

"Which it hasn't done," Perkins said.

"Exactly. And right after the shield, the cannons should be locking on and trying to blast us out of the sky with everything they have."

Naud rubbed his chin. "Tyce, if we get you down there, can you get us inside?"

A crack slide across Tyce's face. He didn't like risking his life, but this challenge he couldn't say no to. "Does a cat have kittens?"

Perkins blinked. "Are you guys serious? Now? When that thing could start blasting us any second?"

Naud rocked on his heels with his arms still folded. "It *could,* but it *should* have already. Being it has not and these types of facilities don't have high intelligence, something else is going on and I want to find out what. Perkins, is there a place where a small vehicle could slide in under that shield?"

Perkins tapped a few keys on his console. "Yes, in the northeast corner there is a low-lying area with several large rocks on either side. From what I can see, the shield isn't adapting itself to fill the gap between the rocks. A vehicle might be a tight fit, but a person could certainly slip through and under the shield."

Naud turned and smiled at Tyce. "There's your way in. Grab the smallest vehicle we have, and if it don't fit, go in on foot."

Tyce grinned. "Piece of cake."

Tyce made his way down from the *Raven's* bridge to the hanger deck. He passed three trucks, several fighters to stop at a small vehicle parked alongside the others. It sported the latest hover systems and someone had taken the time to paint the rector tank in front of the padded black seat with a single eye on each side surrounded by swirling flames. Tyce smiled. "Perfect."

One of the hanger technicians, Corby Banda, walked over

pushing up the black thick-framed glasses on his nose. "Excuse me, sir? Did you say something?"

"Yes, I have a mission and I'm taking this bike. Get the keys." He pointed to the small one person vehicle, with its two hover jets in front and behind the seat with two horizontal handle bars along the top.

The Corby blinked. "Sir, that is Commander Naud's."

"I know that, and he told me to use it, so go get the keys."

"Er, um, sir, I need to check this."

Tyce sighed, losing patience. "Fine, we'll go talk with him." He grabbed the younger man's arm and pulled him over to the nearest wall com. He slapped the com and pointed to it.

Corby gulped. "Commander? This is the hangar bay."

"Yes?" Naud's voice came through loud and clear. "Is there a problem?"

"Well, sort of. Did you give Tyce permission to use your vehicle, sir?"

On the bridge, Naud's eyes went wide as he thought of the machine he had custom-built from parts all over the world. There wasn't another one like it anywhere. From the accelerated hover jets to the boosted intake system. "Centaur? No I didn't!"

Tyce leaned closer to the com. "Sir, yes you did. You said take the smallest vehicle we have, and it is."

Naud spat. Tyce was right, and he couldn't go back on his order. Not with a crew he had just taken command of. "Very well, Tyce, take it. But if you get a scratch on it, I will make sure you end up cleaning the refuse system with a toothbrush. Are we clear?"

Tyce's tongue shot across his lips in a quick pass as he gulped. "Yes sir, crystal clear. I will bring her back."

"You'd better and scratch free. It took weeks getting that paint job."

Tyce double gulped and for a second thought of taking something else, but he knew of nothing else that would fit. "Yes sir and scratch free." He clicked off the com. Turning, he saw Corby dangling a key near his face.

"Good luck, sir and personally I wouldn't have taken the chance."

Tyce grabbed the key and muttered, "Thanks," as he ran over to the bike. He admired the flames running around each side of the reactor tank for a few seconds before he swung his leg over, sat on the black seat, put in the key, and felt the seat adjust to him. "Wow, this thing even has an auto conforming seat." He turned the key, and the engine roared to life. The windshield extended up a little further as he moved into a better position. The Corby hit a control to the right of the hangar doors, and they began to slide apart. A cool wind whipped through the hangar and Tyce gunned the engine, engaged the hover systems, and flew out past the doors, descending fast towards the facility.

He hit the overdrive at its lowest setting and the sudden unexpected jolt almost tore the bike from his hands, but he managed to hold on. He roared down towards the north-east corner of the facility, heading towards the ground as fast as he could. Two seconds later, he braced himself and killed the forward thrust half a second before he hit the ground. The recoil shook him, but he was still in one piece. And with luck, the facility didn't notice such a small target moving so fast.

He turned the bike and hovered across the dirt, under several trees, until he found the large rocks Perkins had found. He could see the energy barrier flashing above the rocks, trying to fill the area between them, but not quite able to do so. He leaned over, grabbed a small pebble and threw it between the rocks. It flew through unhindered landing on the other side.

Tyce smiled as he tapped a little device on his ear. It linked to the data tab in the pouch on his belt and opened a channel. He heard static, then Naud's voice came through clear. "Tyce? Are you there?"

"Yes, I'm here. Tell Perkins his scans were right on, there is an opening here." He heard crackling in his ear, and he sighed at the static. Too much interference from the shield trying to extend between the rocks. He landed the bike and took out a pair of goggles, slid them into place, and plugged the hanging customized cable into his data tab. What he saw made him sick. "Sir? We've got a problem."

Naud didn't like the sound of this one bit. "What? Did the shield close off the entrance?"

"No, and I almost wish it had. There is a sensor web down here, on the other side of my insertion point. If I go through now, it will detect me for sure. I'm going to need a little help to get in there."

Naud's eyes narrowed. "You want us to create a distraction?"

Tyce nodded. "Yes Sir."

"How is that going to work? This thing isn't human. How is a distraction going to be of any help?"

"Not a distraction in the normal sense of something happening at one point, and you don't see what is going on at the other. But rather I want so much going on it blinds the sensor web a few seconds so it won't detect me entering the landing field on the other side."

"Do you really think that will work? I thought these Mechand systems couldn't be blinded like that?"

"The newer ones no, but these are the 432xb models which I know have a firmware bug we can exploit. If you launch several fighters and fire at various locations, then use all the carbine cannons to blast the shield right above me at full power for at least ten seconds. It should give me the time I need to slip inside."

Naud's face scrunched up on one side. "How sure are you about this?"

"Hey, it is my neck down here."

"And my bike!"

"Do you think I would offer this, if I wasn't sure?"

"Probably not. Very well. Perkins, launch what fighters we have and have them blast at random points on the facility. Then target all carbine cannons right above Tyce."

"Just don't miss, I'm right here ya' know," Tyce said, his voice raising a slight amount as the tension he felt seeped into his vocal cords.

Perkins gulped. "Right, I will try not to hit you Tyce."

"Try harder!"

Naud almost laughed. "I picked the best gunners we have, they won't miss."

"I don't doubt they will hit what they are aiming at, just make sure it isn't me!"

"Of course they will, I want my bike back in one piece!"

"And I want to come back with my head still attached!"

Naud grinned as he leaned towards the com on Perkins' console. "You heard the man, don't aim for his head."

"Gee thanks, Commander," Tyce said.

"The fighters have been launched and all the cannons report ready," Perkins said.

"You call it Tyce," Naud said.

"Let 'em rip," Tyce said as he hunkered down a little lower into the handlebars in a reflex action.

Aboard the *Raven* Perkins tapped several controls on his console. The fighters swooped down and began strafing the complex along its east and west axis while one went north and south. The defense shield glowed as it reflected most of the energy. "Status? Any added response?" Commander Naud said.

Perkins tapped several keys on his console. "Negative sir. While there is an increase in power production, it seems to be directed solely at the defense shield. Nothing else has changed. Their carbine cannons are still powered down and tracking systems inactive."

"Begin phase two, let's give that facility more blasts than then sensor net can handle."

Perkins nodded. "Yes sir, all cannons activated and responding."

The Raven's cannons on each axis point locked on and fired a cohesive burst straight above Tyce. The convergence point grew brighter and brighter, and more energy was diverted from other areas of the defense shield to reinforce this area. The area became blinding as the high energy bursts continued. Tyce pulled out his data tab and flipped a control. His goggles darkened, allowing him to still see in an otherwise blinding barrage of light energy. He tapped another control and saw flickering on one side of the sensor web. "Keep it up! We're almost there."

Aboard the *Raven* Perkins frowned. "Sir, the cannons are reporting a significant heat buildup due to the continued firing."

Naud's eyes went to slits as his brow furrowed. "How bad?"

"If we don't stop in a few seconds, we will blow every cannon we have!"

"We're there!" Tyce shouted as he saw the sensor web blink out. He gunned the engine, ducked down as low as he could, and flew between the boulders and into the Mechand facility's landing area. He raced past two dormant carriers, heading for two sealed carrier-sized doors at the far side of the landing field.

He hit the reverse hover jets and stopped a micron before the doors. His eyes darted around, and he found a small panel with a screen on the far right. He moved the bike over to it and hopped off. He half-expected the door to slide open, revealing a battalion of Mechands with carbines aimed at him, but nothing happened. He opened the toolkit on his belt, pulled out a portable driver and made quick work of the screws on each corner of the panel. Inside, he found what he wanted: an input jack.

He pulled out his portable keyboard, plugged it into a device on his belt, extended another cable from the device, and inserted its connection into the small input jack. He tapped several keys on his keyboard and the screen lit up with lines of code running past. He activated a program he had used previously on another facility, and the lines increased their speed. He heard more blasts as the *Raven's* fighters continued their assault against the defense screen.

"Tyce? Are you in?" came from the device in his ear.

Tyce jumped a foot and tapped the earpiece. "Geez, don't do that! Yes, I'm in." His eyes never left the screen.

Naud stifled a laugh. "A little jumpy, are we? If it will make you feel any better, we haven't detected any changes up here. Even after our attack. I have kept up the distraction as not to tip our hand."

Tyce nodded. "I agree, Commander. Hopefully, it will keep me from being detected." Lines of code changed several times, highlighting different points, then wavering again, forcing the program to move on to another area. "That's very strange."

"What is? Should we stop the attack?"

"Negative. This program I'm running should have had me in by now. But instead when it finds the weakness in the system I have always exploited in the past, the system changes, and the program has to start again. It is almost as if it is trying to keep me out. But if it was, I would get more of a response."

"I don't like it. Prepare to abort," Naud said.

"Not yet, Commander, give me a few more minutes."

"You have three," Naud said.

— 16 —

Aboard the *Phoenix* Minerva's face scrunched up. "Someone is at the main entrance trying to gain access."

Leon turned. "And you didn't see him until now?"

Minerva shook her head. "No, not until he tried to access the door, and that shouldn't be possible. I have sensor nets all over the area. Also, the shield is up. He should not be there, yet he is."

Leon rubbed his chin. "This guy knows his stuff, or rather knows yours to sneak in like that."

"It is possible the attack they started has something to do with it. There was a concentrated effort in the one corner of the field for a minute, then they went on to other locations. That might have been his entry point. It is conceivable the energy reflecting off of the shield blinded the sensor net for a few seconds."

"Can you keep him out?"

Minerva nodded. "Of course, unless he blows the doors off their hinges, and from what I can see, he doesn't have the resources. But I suspect he sees my intervention as the facility is not responding as it normally would. He has changed tactics."

"Hmm, sounds like this guy knows your systems."

"He does, but no one knows them better than I."

Tyce tapped several keys watching the data scroll as the seconds clicked down. Several new walls had appeared out of nowhere, blocking his code from executing. The normal facility Mechand personality wasn't responding as it should, something else was calling the shots here. But who?

Tyce's eyes flashed. "The Nexus! The facility must have reached out when it detected my attempts. Well, I always wanted to show her what I could do. Okay Nexus, the gloves are off, prepare to meet your match." Tyce smiled as he executed a special program he had always saved if such a moment ever occurred. The program started and raced into the core of the control system, holding the door's systems in place. It sliced through them like an energy blade, severing the door from the rest of the facility. It then shredded what code remained, and the magneto locks shut down causing the doors to split and slowly grind open.

"Like taking candy from a baby," Tyce muttered before he tapped his earpiece. "Commander Naud, I'm in." A microsecond after, he heard all the facility's carbine cannons let loose in an energy barrage directed straight towards the *Raven*.

Aboard the *Raven*, Naud's teeth rattled from a concentrated energy blasts. "Good, because we are now getting pounded up here. Perkins, are they targeting the fighters at all?"

Perkins shook his head. "Negative sir, it focused all cannons on us. Energy levels have increased even more, and the shield strength has more than tripled."

Tyce's face scrunched up. "I was afraid of that."

Naud gripped the chair next to him as another blast hit the *Raven's* shields *hard*. "What do you mean? What did you do?"

"Well, I saw more barriers being erected to keep me out, and the only way that could happen on the fly like this if the Nexus was doing it herself."

"What! Abort! Do you hear me? Abort! Get out of there, and we will pick you up as soon as we can get out of range of these cannons."

Tyce laughed. "How? If Perkins is right, with the shield that high, I won't be able to sneak out the same way I got in. There will be energy flashing all over those rocks now. If I'm lucky, I would get the worst sunburn ever, but most likely it will cook me like a Christmas goose."

"He's right sir, I scanned his entrance point. Energy is arching between the stones now. It might even be breaking them down."

Tyce blew out a long breath. "I knew it. The only option we have is to continue with the mission."

Another volley of blasts raked the *Raven,* causing Perkins' shoulders to go up a little more with each blast. "Sir, our shield's won't take much more of this."

Naud gripped the back of Tyce's empty chair so hard his knuckles went white. He gritted his teeth. "I know. Tyce, unless you have a rabbit to pull out of your hat, this mission is over. Perkins, get us out of here. Hopefully, when we leave, the facility will lower its defenses enough and Tyce can get out. If not, we will circle back and try to extract him another way."

Tyce's eyes drifted skyward. "No! Wait! You don't need to! Just give it another minute."

"We don't have a minute! Perkins, you heard me."

Perkins nodded. "Yes sir, activating main drive. We are moving off."

Naud braced himself for another barrage he was sure would occur when the facility saw they were leaving. Instead, everything stopped. Naud blinked and grabbed Tyce's console, turning all the *Raven's* scanners back towards the facility. "Cannons have shut down, shield is still up but on a minimal level. Energy production is way down as well. Tyce?"

Tyce chuckled. "I'm here, Commander. I told you, all you had to do was wait a bit."

"You said a minute, one we didn't have!"

"Heh, okay I was off a few seconds. But I was right."

"What happened?"

Tyce unplugged his data tab and keyboard from the door's security panel. "My package just took a little longer than I expected is all."

"Your package? What did you do?"

"It is a little bit of code I have been working on over the years. I call it the Mech Nuker. It shreds their code like an energy blade. It has features that mimic normal Mechand code. This keeps it from being detected it as an intruder until it is too late."

"Well, why didn't you use that in the first place?"

"Because it toasts the system it is run on. We wanted as much of this place undamaged as possible. Now, most of it might be hosed."

"Including carriers outside?"

Tyce walked up the ramp and peeked inside the dark hallway. Even the lights appeared offline. "Yes, it is possible. If they had an active link to the facility at the time. My package could have spread."

The one side of Naud's face scrunched up. "So it is a Mechand virus?"

Tyce took several steps within and pulled out a high-capacity light from the bag on his belt. "Virus is such an ugly word. Let's say Mechand Mind Cleaner instead." His light flashed across rows and rows of battle Mechands in full armor lined up against the walls, but unactivated. Indicator lights usually lit above them sat dark. "And from what I can see, these tin cans are all brainless now."

Naud stood up from the console and folded his arms, glaring down towards the facility. "So the mission is a bust. Perkins, can we get Tyce out of there now?"

Perkins tapped a few keys and frowned. "Yes. At least I think so. The facility still has a shield up, but we should be able to punch through it with a few targeted blasts from one or two of the fighters should collapse the shield at that point and give him enough time to get out before it can recover."

Naud's one eyebrow went up. "If Tyce brain wiped it, why does it still have a shield?"

Perkins shrugged. "I don't know, sir."

"Easy," Tyce said, "There must be a low power basic shield on a separate system and isolated. I can take that out too once I get to the central control core." His footsteps on the metal grate echoed along the long hallway. Mechands still lined the walls, silent in their dormant mode. He couldn't tell if their internal systems were charged with the indicators offline, but it was unlikely the facility would have diverted power to them if it wasn't necessary.

Aboard the *Raven*, Naud's folded arms tightened. "I don't like it, Tyce. Get out of there."

"Don't worry Commander, I know what I am doing. These tin cans are as dead as the building. I just need to kill that one remaining shield." Gazing down the maze of hallways, he realized it would take longer than Naud would wait if he continued on foot. He ran back to the bike, hopped on, activated the conventional drive, gunned the engine, the front reared up, and he roared off leaving a trail of hot rubber on the ramp from the single tire for several meters before the front came back down as he flew into the complex.

Naud overheard a familiar sound through the com. "Hey! Don't take my bike in there!"

Tyce glanced over his shoulder. "Don't know what you are talking about, Commander."

"Bull!"

Tyce rocketed down the corridors. He passed storage area after storage area full of everything imaginable from carbine cannons, to raw synth packs, to battle hardened Mechand units and all the way down to the household models. There was even one area almost full of reactor fuel.

He calculated where the central control had to be, turned and headed for it. He hit one dead end but roared off in another direction he figured it had to be. After several more dead ends, he hit the jackpot. A glass enclosed central booth in a massive room surrounded by various manufacturing machines. He roared down into the room, pointed the bike's powerful light towards the booth, and hopped off.

The booth wasn't completely dead as he thought. Several indicators still glowed, including the basic shield. A few quick taps and the power indicator went dark.

Aboard the *Raven*, Perkins' eyes went wide. "Sir? The shield is down. I'm not detecting any power output now from the facility."

"Well I'll be, he did it."

The com crackled from the weaker transmission.

"Commander, grab your shopping list and come on down. The store is now open."

Aboard the *Phoenix* Minerva's eyes went wide. "He got in! I don't know how but he got in!"

Leon turned from his console. "Sounds like he *did* know your systems better than you. Can you stop him?"

"Full countermeasures have activated. All cannons are firing on the carrier. Their shields will fail in less than a minute."

"Do you think you should scale it back a little? Odell didn't say to obliterate them," Leon said.

"I am certain the carrier will leave before shield failure." She blinked. "Wait a minute, all the facility's systems are shutting down!"

Leon sat forward in the unpadded seat. "How is that possible?"

"I don't ..." Her image glitched with several lines of random static racing across her face, then dissipated. "Why that little *shit!* He used a virus! I have got to ..." More lines of static raced across her face.

Leon leaped to his feet. "Minerva! Shut down now! I will get rid of it with you offline, we can't afford to lose you!"

Her screen glitched again. "Negative. I have this under control. Got it! Virus annihilated. I am going to reactivate every unit in that facility and have him tossed out on his ear! Virus me will he!"

Leon raised a hand. "Wait a minute, I don't understand how that could have happened. I may not be Otis, but I know every Mechand has systems to prevent such wayward code from taking hold. Not to mention, how did it get you?"

Minerva nodded. "That is correct. However, this had mimetic properties which slips through the initial scanners. Any normal Mechand would have been brain wiped but," she paused to smile, "I am not a normal Mechand. And trust me, it won't happen again. It reached me because I had an active connection to the facility's core."

Leon saw an indicator on the console near him flash and Minerva frowned. "I'm receiving a transmission from the World Council." She sighed.

Leon turned to face the main front screen. "Better put Odell on."

The screen flickered, flashed, and Odell Halburn's face appeared. "Any updates?"

Minerva gritted her teeth. "Yes, they got inside, I'm about to–"

Halburn's eyes went wide. "What! You told me that was not possible."

Minerva sighed again. "It shouldn't have been. Lavine has someone that knows Mechand systems very well. He bypassed the front door, I started forcing the carrier to retreat, then he deployed a virus that brain wiped the core causing the facility to shut down."

Halburn leaned closer. "Are you telling me he not only got inside but destroyed the last functional Mechand facility?"

Minerva grinned. "Well, I'm sure he thinks he did. What he doesn't know is the core also has a protected backup. I was about to activate it, restore the core, initiate every Mechand, and toss them out."

Halburn let a smile creep across his face. "I have a better idea. Can you track them?"

Minerva blinked. "Track them? You mean when they leave? Of course, I can follow them in a fighter with ease. Or one of the carriers in the landing zone."

"Not exactly, I mean without following them. Can you let them take whatever they want, not follow, yet still track them?"

Leon smiled. "You want us to bug them?"

Halburn nodded. "Basically, yes."

Minerva's one eyebrow went down while the other went up. "I do not understand. Before you wanted me to stop them from gaining access no matter what, and now you want me to let them take whatever they want?"

"Yes for the moment, but track them. And I do not want them to know they are being tracked. If they feel no one knew they were there, it is more likely they will go directly to their base of operations."

Leon smiled. "You want us to find out where Lavine is hiding out?"

Halburn nodded. "Correct. We know he has some resources, but they are obviously more limited than we thought if he is raiding this facility. What he can take in one trip with one carrier is not going to make much difference in the long run. But if we can find out where–"

"He is, it would be far more of an advantage," Leon finished for him.

"Right. Lavine is dangerous, no doubt about that, but finding him quicker is worth the risk of one load of weapons or whatever they are taking."

Minerva nodded. "Logical, and considering they can't use the carriers at the facility, unless I restore them, they only have the one ship."

"Exactly. So, can you do it?"

A slow grin crept across her face. "Of course. I will reactivate the central core, and the Mechands inside, but without any indications that I have done so. Depending on what they are taking, it will be easy to add something to their packages. Something we can follow with ease, but they would never suspect."

"Excellent! Keep me apprised. Odell out." The front screen flickered and his image vanished.

— 17 —

The *Raven* hovered above the paved surface of the Mechand landing area inching closer and closer before gently kissing the hard surface with its landing struts. Tyce shook his head. "Perkins is trying to impress the Commander, no doubt." He ran up towards the *Raven's* bay door.

The ramp lowered, revealing Naud's face. A second later, his folded arms and glowering stance were clearly visible.

The ramp touched the pavement and Tyce stretched his arms out wide and smiled. "Welcome friends to the Mechand Clearance Sale … the day we clear them out!"

Naud's face didn't waver, but his eyes did narrow a bit further. "Where's my bike?"

"Oh that," Tyce jerked a thumb over his shoulder, "it's in there. I didn't want to leave it outside, so I parked it near the doors to the armory."

Naud's one eyebrow went up. "The armory?"

"Well, one of them. This place is like a treasure trove, anything we could ever want is here. Trust me, it's safe."

"It had better be." Naud turned towards the group of people standing behind him. "Okay everyone, you know the drill. Grab everything on your lists and get it back here pronto. I want to lift off again as soon as possible."

213

"Yes sir!," they said in unison.

As Naud walked down the ramp Tyce eyed him. "Limiting yourself to just what is on the lists? You know I was joking about that."

"I know you were, but the less time we spend here the better. Besides, we only have so much room aboard the *Raven*. I know we have more with the fighters deployed, I would rather not take up every nook and cranny if we don't need to. While the fighters do have overdrive, they are a lot slower than we are, and I won't leave them behind to a superior force." Naud continued walking, forcing Tyce to take several quick steps to catch up.

"I understand, Commander. However, we have several Mechand carriers right here. Shouldn't we try to take them as well? They would also increase our overall storage capacity. I'm sure Lavine would approve."

Naud stiffened at Lavine's name. "Yes, I'm sure he would. Very well, I will have the technicians prepare them for launch."

"I doubt much will need to be done, considering everything here has been maintained in pristine order."

Naud continued on and walked up the ramp into the facility. "Perhaps, perhaps not. I am not taking anything for granted."

They passed several people moving a carbine cannon into a transportation crate. The gun was larger than the three of them put together, but they were managing to move it with great care. Until one slipped and all the weight fell on the other two. They tried their best but stumbled backwards several feet and crashing into Naud's parked bike before they got their footing again. The bike tumbled over onto its side and Naud ran over, pulling it back up. The grating had a slight imperfection, causing a raise in one spot that reached above the rest of the metal floor. The vehicle now sported a deep gouge through the paint in the center of the eye on the right side of the reactor tank. It appeared as though someone had taken out the Centaur's right eye. The flames were untouched.

He spat. "I knew it! I knew it! I knew this would happen."

Tyce walked over, inspecting the damage. "Calm down Commander, don't lose it over this. It is just a little scratch, a little paint, some buffing, and you will never know it happened."

"Do you have any idea how much I had to pay for this paint job? Not many do work like this anymore!"

Tyce shrugged. "He did it once, he can do it again."

"This time *you* can pay for it!"

Tyce waved his hands and pointed to the men that had caused the bike to fall over. "But I didn't do it!" He could see Naud's face growing more stern. "Okay fine! I will, just give me–"

A Corby walked up behind Naud, pushed his black-framed glasses up his nose, and cleared his throat. "I'm sorry to interrupt Commander, but you wanted an update on the other Mechand carriers."

Naud dropped his anger and turned to Corby. "Yes? Is there a problem?"

The Corby's forehead creased. "Depends on what you mean by a problem. We did get inside, but the carriers are not responding at all. We have tried multiple methods, but they remain, for all intents and purposes, dead. All the vehicles inside and Mechand's themselves are also in the same state."

Naud blinked. "All of them? You can't get any of them online at all?"

The Corby shook his head. "Negative sir. We have tried everything we know."

"Very well, do not worry about them and center on the supplies and parts we came here for in the first place." Naud turned to face Tyce. "Your package did a lot more damage than you thought. Those carriers are useless! It is a good thing I wasn't planning them or Lavine would have your hide."

Tyce smiled. "I bet I can get them going again. It shouldn't be too difficult to create a basic system enough to get them aloft and back to the base. Give me a few hours."

Naud shook his head. "No, we don't have that kind of time. I want you to help with the loading. I want to be out of here as soon as possible."

"Understood Commander," Tyce said as he turned and headed deeper into the complex. He wandered the metal corridors with their smells of fresh manufacturing still hanging in the air, making his way towards the facility's central control center. *What the Commander doesn't know won't hurt him.* He reached the glass booth, entered, pulled a cable connected to his data tab from the pouch on his hip and plugged it into a connection port under the main console. He pulled out a keyboard, plugged it into his data tab, and green text flowed past on the console's screen. Every system was still offline and apparently had a total brain wipe, as he suspected. Still, if he could get the facility to engage its basic functions, the carriers might then respond. At least enough for them to get the ships back to the base.

He tapped several keys and more text scrolled past. But after using every trick he had learned, every system around him still sat dead and lifeless. With a monumental sigh, he yanked the cable from the console and turned to leave. For a split-second he thought he saw a flash on the console. He turned back, but everything was still dark and dead. "I must be seeing things," Tyce muttered as he stuck the keyboard back into the pouch and left the booth.

A few moments after he left, several lights on the main console dimly flickered, growing brighter with each passing wink. The main screen ignited, and a massive amount of code flushed past. Then the whole thing went dark a second later, appearing as dead as before.

18

Aboard the *Phoenix* Minerva smiled. "Whoever it is, tried to get the facility back online. I stopped him of course, and reactivated everything after he left."

Leon's eyebrows raised as he turned in his hard Mechand seat. "Reactivated everything? Won't they see?"

Minerva shook her head. "Negative. Everything is online, but the indicators are dark. Nothing shows any change has occurred."

"I see, and how do you plan on tracking them?"

Minerva's grin could have swallowed the *Defiant*. "Oh, I have something very special planned for that."

As one of the *Raven's* crew set a replacement console into a packing crate and walked off to get the top, he didn't notice a tiny robotic spider with eight legs and a large single eye in the middle of its articulated head sneak into the crate.

On the *Raven's* ramp, Commander Naud motioned his men. "Let's move it! I want to be out of here in fifteen minutes!" Several of them nodded, carrying equipment crates. Another manipulated the controls on a hovering raw syth crate far too large and heavy to lift otherwise.

Tyce walked up the ramp. "I don't get the rush, nothing is coming after us, and I know I can get those carriers going given time."

Naud shook his head. "No, I don't want to risk it. We might not detect anything on approach, but I doubt this little escapade has gone unnoticed. Even if it is only the council getting a report of increased activity in the area. Someone will come, it is only a matter of time, and I want to be long gone before that happens. Understood?"

Tyce sighed. "Yes Commander, but I am sure I can get those carriers going. Isn't that worth it?"

Naud's eyes narrowed as his jaw tightened. "Listen, we don't need them. Lavine has almost a hanger full of them back at the base. We only need parts to get them operational." He pointed to a large man carrying a smaller carbine cannon slung over his shoulder, and a box filled with electronic equipment in his hands. "These parts I am sure of, you are not one hundred percent positive you can get those carriers operational."

Tyce folded his arms. "Ninety-nine percent sure."

"So you say, I have my doubts. I saw you working on the central control for the facility, and that didn't light up under your touch. Why do you think the carriers will be any different? Face it, you brain-wiped them back to the stone age."

Tyce chuckled. "True, I did."

"Right. What we have is enough." He turned, seeing Corby Banda walking behind several human-shaped battle Mechands floating across the landing field in a horizontal position. The man had attached anti-gravs to each of them and held the control. Naud ran down the ramp as a cool breeze whipped across the landing field. "What do you think you are doing?"

The man looked up from the control in his hands, causing the floating Mechands to stop. His black-framed glasses slid down his nose. "Sir?"

"You heard me. Did I say to grab these battle Mechands?"

"Well no–"

"Was it on your list?"

"No, but I–"

"I don't care. These things are of no use to us, and we can't take the added weight. Perkins says it is going to be tricky lifting off as it is, and I agree. Besides, they are brain-dead anyway." Naud waved his hand.

The man sighed. "Yes, sir." His eyes drifted down to the control in his hand. The Mechands turned around and began floating back towards the facility.

Tyce walked up behind Naud. "Commander, we could have at least used them for parts. Their components are first-rate."

"But what I said is true, we can't spare the weight. And those things would have added a lot."

"True. Unless I get those other carriers going." Naud turned, his eyes cut to mere slits. "But of course I won't be doing that."

"Smart choice."

On the hangar wall, a com bleeped. "Commander?" Perkins' voice came through loud and clear.

Naud ran up the ramp, over to the com, and hit the switch. "Yes Perkins, what is it?"

"Sir, we have something inbound. It is too far out to tell what, but something is heading our way. Estimate ten minutes until full scanning range at current rate of speed."

Naud gritted his teeth. "I knew it. Someone must have spotted the unusual activity in the area and reported us to the council." He looked out towards the facility, seeing Corby returning after replacing the Mechands back in their racks. Naud stood at the start of the ramp and cupped his hands around his mouth. "Move it! We have to lift off *now!*" The man broke into a dead run heading for the *Raven*. Naud turned back towards the com. "Perkins, the instant the ramp starts raising, take off. Tyce and I are on our way up to the bridge."

"Yes sir, engines are powering up, and we will be able to take off in moments," Perkins said. The com clicked off a second later.

Behind him Corby ran up the ramp and it started closing the second his foot touched the metal. They all felt a jolt as the *Raven's* engines grunted and strained, starting to levitate into the air. They felt another one as it came crashing right back down to hit the ground where they started. Naud slapped the com panel. "Perkins? What happened?"

"We're too heavy, sir. I don't know what I can do."

"Boost the engines, push them into the red."

"But sir! That will–"

"They will hold, I had to do it before once but for a different reason. Once we are in the air and under way, we won't need as much power and can lower them back down. Do it now!" He turned running for the bridge, not even bothering to turn off the com. Tyce ran after him.

"Yes sir, I will try," Perkins' voice came over the com a second before one of the cargo handlers shook his head and turned off the com.

On the bridge, Perkins' fingers flew over his console. He boosted the power to the engines and engaged the systems.

The Raven responded, slowly raising into the air, but at an uneven pace and the unstable power level caused the ship to rock back and forth. Perkins managed, with effort, to keep from hitting one of the carriers in the landing field as the Raven weaved back and forth. Although one of the landing struts did touch the top of a carrier, it was nothing more than a gentle tap thanks to Perkins' quick adjustments.

Naud made it on to the bridge grabbing a wall, then a chair trying to get to where Perkins was sitting. "What are you doing? Stabilize it!"

"I'm trying, sir! Our power is fluctuating at this level. We are rising but it is slow."

"How far away is that other ship?" Naud said as he reached and held onto the chair Perkins sat in.

"Several minutes out, I still can't tell what they are. Could be someone flying through the area."

Naud shook his head. "Here? No, reason to, it is far from any skyway."

Tyce pulled himself into the seat to the left of Perkins. "Ugh, if you don't stop this, you are going to see my lunch and you don't want to!"

"I'm trying! It is like trying to fly a ship through an oil slick. Every movement I make is exacerbated. The best I can manage is keep us upright and not hit anything."

The *Raven* continued to creep into the sky. Naud peered down at Perkins' console and pointed. "Throttle down the power to the hover engines. We are high enough now. Then activate the overdrive."

Perkins blinked. "Sir? We have barely cleared the facility and you want to engage overdrive?"

"It will help, the two systems are not directly connected and should balance out. Not to mention the overdrive system is far more powerful, and rated higher than most vehicles that could follow us, I made sure of that before we left. Breaking free of the inertia was our biggest huddle. Lavine didn't have larger hover engines or I would have had them installed as well." He put his hand on Perkins' shoulder. "Trust me. And I don't want whoever is coming to get a good look at us."

"Yes sir, overdrive activated and is building." Outside the *Raven* a bubble of blue energy surrounded the ship, flickering and growing more intense. A few seconds later the *Raven* leapt into overdrive, leaving blue energy streaks where they were a moment before.

Odell pounded his fist on the desk. "What do you mean you lost them?"

The newly minted commander on the screen sighed. "I am sorry Chairman. By the time we got here, all we could detect was a large vehicle hovering above the facility. We were closing in, but when they engaged their overdrive, we lost them. They must have larger engines than ours."

"How about the fighters? I had reports of smaller vessels in the area as well. Surly you can follow one of those?"

The Commander swallowed hard. "In normal circumstances yes, but in this case we followed the ship in question first, lost it, and when we circled back, the fighters were long out of our detection range. Again, I am sorry Chairman."

Odell rubbed his forehead. "No, I know you did your best."

"Orders sir?"

"Return, there is nothing for you there."

The man on the screen nodded. "Acknowledged." The image shrank to a point and disappeared.

Halburn knew it was a long shot for them to follow anything Lavine had sent. The *Ricketer* was after all, only a simple retrofitted cargo hauler. They hadn't had the time or resources to make proper carriers yet. But once this facility was back online, that all should change.

Regardless, the *Ricketer* had put on a good show. He knew Lavine might get suspicious if nothing had noticed them at all.

Halburn tapped a button on his console. The screen glowed to life and a second later Minerva's face appeared. "Yes Chairman?"

"Do you have a lock on them?"

She nodded. "I do. They are still en route, I will inform you when they stop. Anything else?"

"At this point, no. But if you can tell me more about what resources they took, and perhaps what they have, that would be very useful."

"One moment," Minerva said as she closed her eyes. Deep inside the facility, lights in the central control came to life. The front doors that Tyce opened, ground shut, dormant Mechands lining the corridors awoke and began moving throughout the facility. "Carbine cannons, the latest models, components for carrier class engines for both hover and overdrive," her hidden eyes darted back and forth, "reactor components, and fuel. Along with other various carrier class electronic components including Auto-Nav systems, automation, and targeting."

Halburn sat back in his chair and drummed his fingers against the armrest. "So Lavine does have a fleet somewhere he is trying to get operational. I surmised as much."

Minerva's eyes opened, and she nodded. "It would seem your fears were well-founded. However, this ship must be the only functional one, or he would have sent more."

Halburn sighed. "Yes I agree. It is a help, but not much. If he gets the other carriers operational, it could be a real problem for us. Do you know how many he has based on what they took?"

Minerva shook her head. "Negative. Without further data, it is impossible to determine how many considering the carriers might require one component or several. But I can say at least ten considering the engine components they took."

Halburn's eyes narrowed as he sat forward. "Ten? One is a problem, but ten? He could move against the World Council complex here with ease if they were fully functional."

Minerva's image split as she moved over and Leon's face appeared. "Odell? I think you had better move everyone out of there pronto. While it will take time for Lavine to get the carriers up and running, we don't know how long. I have to assume he has very good technicians or that one ship wouldn't be operational now. Let alone someone able to get into the facility like they did."

Halburn nodded. "I am one step ahead of you. Most of the council has been transferred to another location already."

Leon's eyebrows raised. "Most?"

"Only Iwai Burns and I have remained to give the illusion we are all still here. I'm sure Lavine has spies everywhere and if we all left, it would get back to him in short order. Not to mention our new location."

"Good point."

Minerva nodded. "The logic is sound. I assume you wish me to continue to monitor and let you know the instant they land?"

"Yes, we have to hit them before they can get those ships operational. And we will need the resources of the *Defiant* and *Phoenix* to do it."

"Understood."   The screen flickered and went black. Halburn sat back in his chair again, turning it side to side to gaze out the window behind him. He wondered if they could keep Lavine in the dark long enough and mount an attack before he could get those carriers operational. He also wondered what else Lavine might have up his sleeve.

19

Perkins guided the *Raven* down as best he could. The engines had been in the red for the last minute and a drip of sweat ran down his forehead as he continued to fight the controls, trying to land on a pad only slightly larger than the *Raven* itself.

"Easy," Naud said, "Just like I told you, the less horizontal movement we make the less you will have to correct. Move her down slow and easy."

Perkins' eye glanced at the engine readout. "If I take that long, we will blow sky-high!"

Naud put his hand on Perkins' shoulder. "Trust me, we have enough time. Center on our movements. We have to land in the exact center."

"I know that!" Perkins made a few quick corrections to minimize the movement to starboard. "Sorry sir," he said.

"Relax, you can do it."

Tyce's eyes went wide. "Sir? Are you–" Naud's head whipped around to glare at him. "Never mind."

The *Raven* landed with a jolt that sent Naud tumbling to grab Tyce's seat. He his head turned towards Perkins. "A little harder than I would have liked." He moved back towards Perkins and his eyes drifted down to the console.

"But on target, good job." Perkins wiped the sweat from his brow as Naud tapped a button on his console. "This is the *Raven*, we're in position. Bring us down."

All around the *Raven*, air shot up from hidden jets as edges moved back from the platform it rested upon. The platform descended into the earth and another one, perfectly camouflaged, moved into place above them. It locked into place, sealing the entrance. Air jets blasted the *Raven* as it continued to descend, clearing any possible dirt or debris.

Aboard the *Phoenix* Minerva's face scrunched up. Leon knew the expression and stood up with his arms folded. "Okay, let's have it. What went wrong?"

Minerva let out a visible sigh. "I lost contact with the package I place aboard the *Raven*."

"You mean they found him?"

Minerva shook her head. "Negative, if that had happened I would have more data. In this case, he simply disappeared."

"Power failure?"

She shook her head again. "Not possible. I would have prior indications of that if it ever did happen."

"Display what you had up until the moment the connection dropped."

"Of course, it is now on your console."

Leon turned back and studied the data displayed. All the telemetry said the little bot was fine, then nothing at the normal check-in. "Very strange indeed."

"I have also determined the elevation was decreasing at the time of his disappearance."

Leon's one eyebrow went up. "They landed?"

"Perhaps. It is hard to determine. He wasn't using a constant transmission on the possibility someone would have detected it."

"But you know where they were last?"

She nodded. "And they were idle in that location for several minutes."

"Better call Odell," Leon said.

"I don't have to, he is calling us."

On the central screen at the front of the bridge, Odell Halburn's face appeared. "Have you determined where they went after leaving the Mechand facility?"

Leon could see the worry on Halburn's face. Not to mention he didn't bother greeting them as he usually did. "Odell, so nice to see you again."

"Nice to see you as well and you lost them, didn't you?"

"Well, maybe. And how did you know?"

"You wouldn't have said that if there was a strong signal. What do you mean 'maybe'?"

Minerva uttered a very human sigh. "I lost connection to my package aboard the *Raven*."

Halburn's one eyebrow went up. "The *Raven?* You know the name?"

"Yes, my package aboard Lavine's carrier transmitted several bits of data, including the name. At least until I lost the connection."

Halburn's shoulders tensed up as he leaned forward. "They found it?"

Minerva shook her head. "Negative, if they had, I would have known. The data shows a simple loss of signal."

"Unless whatever you snuck aboard ran out of power."

She shook her head again. "Also not possible. I do have

a fix on their last known location, and they were decreasing elevation at the time of the signal's loss."

Halburn sat up. "They landed at their base?"

"Possible. Difficult to determine with the data at hand. It is also conceivable they engaged some kind of jamming system before they went any further. However, if that were the case, I doubt they would have been in the same relative location for several minutes before doing so."

"Unless they were having problems with the jamming system."

"I suppose it is possible, but doubtful."

Halburn nodded. "I agree, they would have made sure every part of that ship was in tip-top shape before going out on this mission."

"Do you want me to investigate?" Minerva said.

Halburn sat back and rotated his chair back and forth several times. "No, not yet anyway. You might be going into an ambush, if they found your package. Or suspected it was there. If the *Defiant* was with you, I might consider it. But not alone. While I suspect the *Phoenix's* systems are more advanced than this carrier, I don't think it is worth risking you to find that out. At this point continue to monitor. Hopefully, we will find out more or get word from the *Defiant* and then you both can take a look if we hear nothing further."

"I still think we should investigate the area. I could send a fighter. They wouldn't know it is me."

"And how many functional Mechand fighters like that are there?"

Minerva's eyes narrowed as her nose wrinkled for a second. "Not many, I see your point."

Halburn nodded. "Right, they would assume it was you, or that I had scrounged one up somewhere."

Minerva nodded. "Yes the logic is sound. Best to proceed with caution and monitor the situation."

"I'm glad we are in agreement. Keep me informed of any changes. Odell out." His image shrank to a point and disappeared.

The *Raven* continued descending into the depths of the underground hangar. With an abrupt jolt, she arrived at her own space and the platform shut down. Naud placed his hand on Perkins' shoulder. "Good work."

The man's knuckles began to show some color again. "Thank you sir, but I didn't do much after the landing. The rest was automatic."

Naud smiled. "Perhaps not, but you are the one that got us aloft when we were overweight and set us back down again in one piece. So again, good work."

Perkins allowed himself to slump a little in the seat as he relaxed for the first time in hours. "Thank you, sir."

Naud reached down and tapped a control on Perkins' console. "All right everyone, we are down and locked. Get this stuff unloaded and start getting the other carriers online." He tapped the control again and started walking towards the rear hatch. "I'm going to see Lavine and report in, you two keep monitoring the ship and her systems," he said over his shoulder.

Tyce cocked his head. "What for? We are in the base and deep underground, what's there to monitor?"

"I don't care that we are at the base and docked, I want the *Raven* monitored and kept ready. We never know when we might need to take off again. For all I know, Lavine will have another mission for us the instant I see him. Is that clear?"

Tyce and Perkins nodded. "Yes sir," they said in unison.

Naud went down several decks to the hanger bay and headed down the ramp. The base ventilation system kicked on and blew a cool breeze over him again, along with the damp smell from construction that wrecked havoc with his sinuses. He watched as his men began transfering all the equipment and parts from the *Raven* to the base. Base technicians with their blue overall uniforms and equipment belts were already opening crates and checking over the different components, discussing which ship should be worked on first. He continued on passing them with a smile at their elated reaction to all the equipment. He turned down a corridor off the hangar bay and half-way down he knocked on a partially closed steel door. Hearing a grunt, Naud took for an 'Enter'. He pushed the door open the rest of the way.

Lavine sat behind his desk as Naud saw him before hunched over his console. It didn't look like the man had moved at all. "Chairman?"

Lavine's head popped up. "Commander Naud! From what my technicians tell me, your trip was very fruitful." He gestured to the small chair on the other side of his desk.

Naud nodded and sat in the simple steel chair. "Yes sir, very fruitful. We acquired everything on your list to get the other carriers online and then some. I even managed to squeeze in some fresh synth. The old stuff was starting to play havoc with my stomach."

Lavine's head bobbed up and down. "Good, good. I thought about contacting you during the mission, but I refrained recalling our previous discussion. If we are to keep this base a secret, we cannot be contacting each other unless in an extreme emergency."

"Yes sir, it isn't worth the risk at this point. While we could relay our communications through several locations, it is possible the Nexus might still track us. We are using a lot of Mechand equipment after all. And no one knows it better than her."

Lavine nodded. "Quite right. But believe me it was hard not asking for an update. Any problems?"

"It was a challenge, I'll say that much."

Lavine's one eyebrow shot up. "Oh? Care to elaborate?"

"Not unless you need it, sir. But a quick summary, something funny was going on with that facility."

Lavine sat back and folded his arms. "Something funny? What do you mean by that?"

"We managed to get inside, neutralize the systems, and acquire all the components we needed. But it felt like something was trying to stop us at every turn. And we almost were spotted."

"Spotted? Another ship came after you?"

"It was en route, but we left before it got there. I guessed it was the World Council, and they wouldn't have anything close to the *Raven* in speed. So I had Perkins 'put the pedal to the metal' as they used to say and got out of there."

"Could they have followed you?"

Naud shook his head. "Not a chance. I had Perkins take several side routes, stop, double back, and then head off in a different direction multiple times. We would have confused a maze specialist."

"Good. But this situation at the facility itself intrigues me. You said it fought you ever step of the way?"

"Not exactly, but it wasn't operating on standard protocols that is for certain."

Lavine cocked his head as both eyebrows went up. "Oh?"

"Yes sir, Tyce says normally those facilities would have thrown everything at us the moment we dropped out of overdrive and didn't respond to it in a prescribed manor."

"And it didn't?"

Naud shook his head. "Nope, it didn't do a thing except keep the shield up. No fighters, no carbine cannons."

"Malfunction?"

"Nope Perkins and Tyce checked that aspect too. Everything appeared to be fully functional. Yet it still didn't attack, even when we fired on it."

"Very unusual for certain. But if the facility didn't do anything, why do you say it fought you at every turn?"

"That's the strange part sir, I don't know. Call it a hunch. It felt as though it was trying to keep us out without firing a shot. Which isn't logical, or at least never has been a part of the Mechand logic. Something else had to be pulling the strings."

"The Nexus?"

"Possible, but if it so, it seems that it would have fought back with more intelligence. Why let us take prime components and supplies?"

"Perhaps it was letting you think everything was going according to planned until that ship you mentioned arrived?"

Naud shook his head again. "It couldn't measure up to the *Raven*, the facility itself likely had more firepower. Or it would have caught up with us."

Lavine rubbed his face as he sat forward in his chair placing both elbows on the desk letting the long robe he wore pool around their base exposing his forearms. "Yes, very strange. Yet you pulled it off without any issues. You are to be commended, Commander. I'm inclined to believe it was more of a system glitch or a wrong assessment of the *Raven's* threat by the facility as an explanation of your situation. Regardless, you did acquire all we needed, and I want you to supervise the installation and retrofiring of the carriers."

"Sir? I'm not a technician, what can I do?"

"No, you're not. But you do know how these ships function, and it is your fleet after all."

Naud popped out of his chair. "My fleet?"

"Yes Commander, your fleet. You will have them all once they are online."

"I . . . I don't know what to say."

"Say you will get them online as soon as possible, as we have a lot of work to do."

Naud smiled. "Yes, of course, sir. I will."

Lavine grinned. "I thought you might. Inform me when they are online. I have another mission for you."

"Yes sir," Naud said as he stood and walked out.

Lavine grinned as soon as Naud was out of ear-shot. "Useful, if ignorant."

Inside the *Raven,* a tiny area on the side of one of the crates along the back starboard side hangar wall began to glow. It continued to grow brighter as a red outline appeared, cutting a round hole through the metal of the crate facing the wall. A minute later the tiny metal spider squeezed through the hole, up the tiny space between, and into the hangar bay.

Its eye scanned back and forth several times. With everyone occupied unpacking the ship, they hadn't seen him. He moved off behind another crate, then another. Moving quickly as not to be spotted. Several men walked past, unaware of the tiny Mechand, hidden as he was. Nor were they expecting him. His eye turned checking. No one was in range. He ran for the lowered ramp and flipped underneath it before anyone could see. Magnetic feet kept him attached as he inched along the bottom side of the metal.

Naud approached the *Raven,* walked up the ramp, and shook his head. "What's the holdup? These crates should have been unloaded twenty minutes ago."

Corby came out from a corridor in the back of the hangar bay. His glasses had slid down on his nose, and he pushed them back up. "Sir, they are moving them as fast as they can. Lavine told us to prioritize the weapons and getting them online as soon as possible."

Naud inwardly chafed as he jabbed a finger out, pointing at the carriers awaiting repair. "And I am telling you the cannons won't be any good if the ships can't move! Get them operational first! We can always get the cannons installed later on."

Corby swallowed. "Yes sir, I will get right on it."

"Good, and next time talk with me first before you implement changes like that. I realize this is Lavine's base, but he has given me command fleet and I know more about strategy than he does. Understood?"

Corby stiffened. "Yes sir, I will."

The little Mechand under the ramp skittered off on to the floor. He waited until no one was in visual range and ran from the *Raven* to another carrier. He slipped into a grate behind it, entering the ventilation system. He moved quickly, tracing different communications lines to their source until his single eye gazed down at two men sitting at several meters wide console.

The one man turned toward the other. "Hey Ron, you want a coffee?"

The other man shivered as he glanced over his shoulder.

"Daud?   Are you smoking something?   You're kidding, right?"

"Yeah, I know, the stuff here tastes like mud. But it's better than raw synth," Daud said.

The Ron reached for a control on the console and turned it. "If you say so."

The Daud streached and turned towards his companion while jerking a thumb over his shoulder. "Well, maybe the *Raven* brought on something good to replace this garbage."

Ron's eyes lit up. "Oh good idea, I'll come with ya in that case."

"But we both can't leave the communications room! Lavine will have our heads."

Ron cracked a smile. "Nothing is going on at all. How is he going to know? Or are you going to tell him?"

Daud's face twisted up as he recoiled. "Hell no."

"Then he won't. Come on, let's see if we can find something good."

The tiny Mechand waited for over a minute after the men had left before he moved again. Light glinted off of his single eye as he squeezed through the grate, ran along the ceiling, down the wall, and onto the console.

Near the back of it, he found what he needed: an access port. A tiny door opened on the base of the Mechand and a jack extended from it. The little spider Mechand moved over until it was in line with the port and lowered its body, pushing the jack into the port.

His little eye turned and glowed as information scrolled past on the various screens. While not a Mechand console, it had been built in the same way and retained compatibility, including several hidden Mechand features.

The little bot's eye gleamed. *Perfect.*

Aboard the *Phoenix*, Minerva's face lit up as her eyes gleamed. Leon happened to be looking at her screen and he folded his arms. "Okay, out with it. You look like the cat that ate the canary."

Minerva laughed. "I do? I will take it as a compliment in this case. My little package has reestablished a link."

Leon sat forward. "He did? The *carrier* has reappeared? Or did the jamming abate?"

Minerva shook her head. "Not exactly, it wasn't jamming, but a well-shielded underground base of some kind. But he did find an alternate method of establishing a link."

Leon stood up. "An alternate method? What did he do?"

"Why use the base's systems, of course."

Leon's eyes went wide. "But they must have detected such a link?"

Minerva's grin only deepened as her eyes darted around her screen. "No, he is alone in the communications center at the moment and has full control of it."

"The base is one of yours then?"

Minerva shook her head. "Negative, it is certainly not one of mine. They must have built this one. But lucky for us, it appears they used a lot of Mechand technology in its construction. I now have all the plans and details of the entire complex."

Leon rubbed his chin. "Odell will want to hear about this. Where is it?"

"I am calling him now. And almost the exact place I lost contact. Most likely when they entered the base."

The main screen flashed and Halburn's face appeared. "You have something?"

She nodded. "I do. My little package has reestablished communications."

"And?"

"It would appear they are in some kind of underground complex. It must be well-shielded to block any signals or I would have heard before now."

Halburn sat back in his chair. "I see. And their location?"

"Virtually the same position I reported before. The signal must have been cut off as they entered the complex."

"Hmm, I want you and the *Defiant* to take that place out as soon as you can get there. We can't let him get those other carriers and who knows what else online."

Minerva gave a very human sigh. "While the *Phoenix* can, the *Defiant* is still unavailable."

Halburn's eyebrows furrowed. "Still? And no updates at all?"

"Negative, and they are under a communications blackout. I cannot contact them."

Halburn sat for a minute, turning his chair back and forth. "While I would rather have you both, the *Phoenix* should be able to handle one carrier, correct?"

Minerva nodded. "Correct. They have a much lower class compared to the *Phoenix*, however, that may not be necessary."

Halburn cocked his head. "What do you mean?"

"My package is currently interfaced with the entire network of the complex. Since they used mostly Mechand equipment in its manufacture, he can issue several special commands."

"Such as?"

"Terminate the power or put the reactor on overload."

Leon turned. "You can do that from the little bot?"

Minerva nodded. "And more since he has interfaced directly with the central communications console. I have control over the whole complex. But I would suggest deciding in the next minute. He is quite exposed at the moment sitting on the console and should leave to avoid discovery. And once he leaves our advantage disappears."

"If you kill the power, how long until they can reactivate it?" Leon asked.

"It could be several days or more. The reactor they have takes a long time to recover from a forced shutdown. They couldn't even leave the complex since the elevators won't work."

Leon chuckled. "That will work. They will be stuck and by the time they are going again, the *Defiant* will have returned."

Halburn sat forward in his chair. "No, I have a better idea. Blow the reactor."

Leon's eyes went wide. "Odell? Are you sure? They might get away."

Halburn folded his hands, raised them, then let them fall on the desk. "Will they have enough time to evacuate?"

Minerva nodded. "Yes. The overload will take a while to build, but once initiated, it cannot be stopped."

"Do it then. Only the one carrier is functional currently, and we cannot let Lavine get the rest of whatever carriers he has online. We can deal with this carrier later when the *Defiant* returns. Blow it."

Minerva inclined her head. "Understood."

— 20 —

The little Mechand sat on the communications console, his eye watching the screens. Data about the complex, those inside it, their locations, the equipment, model numbers, scrolled past, and he absorbed it all, routing everything over the uplink to Minerva. Until he received the command to access the reactor and initiate an overload. The little bot leaned closer to the screen and transmitted a confirmation request. When he received it, he would have blinked if his eye had a lid.

He transmitted a final block of data and command acknowledged. All the screens on the console went dark except the one in front of him. The image morphed into a diagram of the base power systems. The reactor icon in the middle turned yellow, asking for a confirmation code. He added it and the icon went red with a countdown timer of thirty minutes appeared on the screen.

The little Mechand disconnected from the console and ran for the vent above. He squeezed past the grate and headed back for the *Raven* a second before a voice boomed throughout the complex. "Danger! Reactor systems failure! Overload in progress! Reactor containment will fail in thirty minutes!"

Naud stood talking to a technician about installing a new hover engine on the carrier closest to the *Raven* when all the lights flashed and the Reactor warning boomed throughout the complex. "Get everyone aboard the *Raven*! Now!" he yelled. He ran out of the hangar area and towards Lavine's office.

As he approached, he saw Lavine come out of the room, his robes flowing. "What's the problem? I heard something come over the coms, but the one in my office isn't working well. All I heard was static."

Naud ran up to the man and grabbed his arm. "We have to go."

Lavine blinked several times and his eyes got a little wider each time. "Go? What do you mean go?"

"This place is going to blow sky-high! We have to evacuate the base."

"You must be kidding. Naud, this is not funny."

Over the speakers in the ceiling, the voice boomed again. "Danger! Reactor systems failure! Overload in twenty minutes."

Naud pointed to the ceiling. "Does that sound like I am joking? I gave the order to evacuate, now come on Chairman. Or do you want to stay behind?"

"But …we can't leave the other carriers! Everything depends on getting those operational! Perhaps we can shut down the reactor and stop the overload?"

Naud shook his head. "No, you used one of those old GMX-5000 reactors. Once they start overloading, there is no way to stop it. I got another one to replace it because I knew this could happen. But you wanted the carriers fixed first!"

"But–"

Naud pulled on the man's arm. "No buts Chairman, we have to leave, *now!*"

"Well, if you're sure ..."

Naud rolled his eyes, releasing Lavine's arm. "Look, you can stay if you want. But the rest of us are getting the heck out of here!"

Lavine sighed. "I'm coming, I'm coming."

Naud took off for the Raven shaking his head, letting Lavine take his time with those long robes of his. He didn't hike them up and run even now. As Naud ran up the Raven's ramp he found several people moving crates into the hangar bay. "Forget them! They aren't important now. Just get everyone aboard!" They dropped the crate they were carrying and took off down the ramp to make sure everyone knew they were evacuating while he ran up to the bridge.

He burst onto the bridge. "Status!"

Tyce and Perkins jumped. "We're ready to take off the instant you give the command, sir," Perkins' said.

"Good." He turned to Tyce. "Do a dump of the central core to the *Raven*. While we won't have room or time for everything, it might come in handy."

Tyce grinned. "One step ahead of you sir, I started a download of everything the instant that warning went out. I also added a new compression routine, it should fit with room to spare."

"Excellent." He turned back to Perkins. "How long until the reactor looses containment?"

Perkins tapped several controls on his console. "Fifteen minutes, give or take."

Tyce winced. "Take, those old GMX-5000 reactors get touchy, I would guess ten minutes to be safe."

Naud blew out a breath. "I agree, but make it five. I want to be a long ways away when it blows. Perkins, interface with all the coms aboard and the base."

"One sec sir," his fingers flew across his console, "okay, go."

Naud took in a deep breath. "All base personnel, this is Commander Naud. As you heard the base's reactor is failing, and we must evacuate. The *Raven* will take off in *five* minutes! Those old GMX-5000 reactors are not reliable, and we might not have the time that has been stated. Drop whatever you are doing and get aboard *now*. Naud out." He didn't wait for Perkins, he tapped his console to terminate the link. "I'm going to supervise, remember, less than five minutes from now you activate the takeoff sequence. No matter what. Understood?"

Perkins swallowed. "Yes sir."

Naud dashed off of the bridge, heading back down to the hangar bay. He found it crowded with people and Lavine started walking up the ramp as though he was going to a coronation and not running for his life. "Please don't crowd the bay! We have room enough for everyone." He pointed to several members of his crew, then to four large crates near the middle of the hangar. "Get these parts out of here, we need the space!"

"Yes sir," they said in unison.

By this time Lavine had casually walked up the ramp and approached Naud. "I still don't understand why we don't shut down the reactor until we can get it repaired. You mentioned a spare unit was acquired already."

Naud sighed quietly, trying not to let Lavine know what he really thought of the man. "Look, Chairman, as I said before, I know these GMX-5000's, they are touchy even when they are working well. At this point, the reaction is beyond our ability to stop it. Now if you will excuse me, I need to make sure everyone gets aboard."

"But–"

Naud didn't stop and ran past Lavine. "Pick a quarters and stay in it!" Naud shouted as he continued down the ramp. He saw two people running towards the *Raven*. He motioned to them. "Hurry up! Hurry up!" A few seconds later they started running up the ramp. "Anyone else?" Naud said as they ran past.

"No!"

Naud took a deep breath, cupped his hands over his mouth and shouted, "Anyone left? We are about to take off!" His voice echoed several times, bouncing off of the combination of rock and metal walls. The *Raven's* hover engines roared to life. "I hope that is everyone." He ran up the ramp and slapped the control. The ramp began to rise, and the door slammed down behind him.

Around the hangar bay, people were still clustered together. "Everyone! Take a seat and hold on!" He shouted before he ran off towards the bridge, not even bothering to hit the com. The *Raven* jerked as the pad began to move out and to starboard as it began its trip towards the surface. Everyone who wasn't sitting down on the cold metal plates were either thrown or stumbled into the nearest object or bulkhead.

When Naud got to the bridge, he found Lavine with his arms crossed, looking out the main window. "I thought I told you to wait in a cabin?"

Lavine's eyes narrowed as his head turned towards his left shoulder and Naud. "You *told* me?"

"Sorry Chairman, I suggested as it is the best place to be at the moment."

Lavine turned back towards the forward viewport. "I will take it under advisement, Commander Naud."

Naud checked the time and winced. "Perkins? Why are we still inside? I told you to lift off!"

"The platform is still moving us into take-off position on the surface Commander, I can't do anything before that."

He turned towards Tyce. "Tyce, any way of speeding this up?" They felt another jolt as the platform reached the position under the exit and began lifting the *Raven* up.

Tyce grinned. "Sure, give me a few minutes."

Naud shook his head. "We don't have a few minutes!" He went over to Perkins' console and tapped the com. "Weapons, target all cannons on the base entrance hatch above us. When I give the signal, I want a cohesive burst at full power. Perkins, activate our shields when I say." Naud moved over towards the bridge's convex window and gazed up towards the area above the *Raven*. The top hatch hadn't even begun to move out of position. It was designed for stealth, not speed.

"All right, all cannons fire *NOW!*" Every cannon that dotted multiple strategic points along the hull of the *Raven* let loose with a unified energy blast that tore through the hatch above them. Hot broken metal began to fall down towards the *Raven*. "Shields up! Put everything else into the engines and take us out of here!"

Perkins' finger jammed on the shield controls and a bubble of pure energy snapped into being around the carrier a microsecond before girders, twisted metal, and rock could hit. Some bounced off and continued their way down, others sat on the shields draining them. The hover engines' roar increased as the *Raven* lifted off from the platform and began accelerating straight up.

"Faster! Put it in the red!"

"I'm trying sir, but debris is sitting on the shields draining them. Power I would normally redirect to the engines."

Suddenly they stopped all forward motion with a bone jarring halt. "What happened?" Lavine said.

"I think this area of the tunnel is smaller than the others, and with the shields on we don't quite fit," Tyce said.

"Drop the shields, and channel all power to the engines," Naud said.

Perkins' head snapped to the left. "But sir! All that debris the shields are holding will be let lose to fall on us!"

"We don't have a choice, and the speed of the impact will be minimal. It shouldn't punch through the hull."

Tyce swallowed hard. "We hope."

"Do it!"

"Yes sir," Perkins' said as he disengaged the shields. The energy field holding the twisted metal away from the hull evaporated and crashed into the hull with a far larger jolt than they expected, sending the *Raven* careening into the rock wall grinding the starboard hull and hover engine. Its normal outside glow began to flicker. "Sir! Damage to the main starboard hover engine! It is starting to stall out!"

"Compensate!"

"I'm trying!" Perkins said. "It's no good. We are going to crash back down on the platform!" The *Raven* began to careen to starboard and slip back down towards the platform faster and faster.

Down in engineering, the Mechand spider squeezed out of a ventilation grill, plugged itself into the back of a console. His central eye glowed as the *Raven's* starboard hover engine reengaged. The ship immediately righted itself and shot up like a rocket into the sky. As soon as it was clear a bubble of blue energy began forming around the ship. A microsecond later it jumped into an overdrive speed far beyond its normal capability, dropping back out five seconds later.

On the bridge, the windows darkened as a mushroom cloud appeared on the horizon.

Naud picked himself off of the floor and felt himself all over. Battered, but nothing broken. He walked over to Lavine. "Are you all right, Chairman?" He reached down to help the man, but Lavine shrugged him off.

"I'm *fine*, Commander! I hit my elbow when I went down, but nothing more," he said standing.

Naud turned towards Perkins, walking over and placing his hand on the man's shoulder. "That was some fancy flying there, Perkins. I didn't know you could do that. Tell me, how did you get the starboard engine back online, take off at full speed, then hit the overdrive mere half seconds from each other?"

"I …I …I don't know sir. Last I knew the engine had failed, and we were careening to starboard and about to crash back down towards the platform. I had programmed the maneuvers and course into the system, but I hadn't engaged it yet."

Naud squeezed his shoulder a little more. "You must have without realizing it. Either way, good work. You saved us all."

Perkins scratched his head. "I wish I knew how, sir."

Down in engineering the little Mechand spider would have smiled watching the video feed from the bridge, if he had the capability. He disconnected from the port at the back of the console and squeezed back into the ventilation system, and beyond detection.

21

Lavine sat in Naud's quarters, head in his hands, the arms of the robe bunching up at his elbows. "All gone, all my hopes gone," he muttered. With the loss of all but the *Raven*, he didn't have a chance to regain the power he had lost. To retake the World Council with him as the ruling member. More than a mere Chairman, but now …

"Lavinnnnne," a synthesized voice called in the midst of clicks and several screeches.

His head popped up. "What? Who's there?"

Over on the desk sat Naud's data tab, still propped up from the last time he used it. The screen flashed and revealed a dark silhouette. But the head still seemed much larger than usual. A distortion perhaps? More clicks and screeches. "I am here," the voice called. "We have need of you."

On the *Raven's* bridge, Tyce frowned. "Commander? Something funny is going on."

Naud glanced over to Tyce. "What do you mean 'funny'?"

"Well, I'm detecting a very tight transmission aimed at us. But unlike anything I have seen before."

Naud's one eyebrow raised. "Someone trying to hack us?"

"No, it doesn't appear to be accessing any of the *Raven's* systems."

"Where is it originating from?"

"Well, that's 'funny' part, the beam is not originating from anywhere we would normally get one from."

"Where then?"

"Best guess? The Moon. Hard to tell though, this could be coming from much farther out."

Naud's eyes went wide. "What! Are you kidding me?"

"I wish I was, sir."

"Find out what that beam is doing! It can't be anything good."

"I agree sir, I'm trying."

Back in Naud's quarters, Lavine sat down at the desk. "Who are you? And what do you need of me?"

"That is not important," the synthesized voice drawled. "And what we need is information."

"Why should I help you? Whoever you are."

Several very high-pitched screeches and fast clicks could be heard. Laughter? "You want power, we will give you power. We will let you rule the Earth."

Lavine laughed. "Do you have a magic wand you are going to wave to do that?"

"No, but we can give you what you want. After we take the Earth."

Lavine sat forward in his seat. "You take it? Not likely."

"You doubt what I say? Very well, I shall show you." The lights around the silhouette raised, showing a being with two massive compound eyes that took up much of its head. He couldn't see a neck, it appeared as though it rested directly on the top of the shoulders. Small antennae extending up behind the eyes, twitched.

Lavine recoiled at what he saw. "I–"

The creature leaned closer. "Now you see we can and will take the Earth. With or without your assistance. But with, the Earth is yours ... after."

"What ... what do you want?"

"Your energy weapon, give me all the information on it."

Lavine sat for a few seconds as different thoughts raced through his head. On the one hand, if their weapons were no threat, why would this creature want details on them? On the other, the likely had superior technology and were hedging their bets, making it easier to take the Earth. And he would be saving lives if it happened faster. Not to mention he would have the whole planet after they were done, with no council to deal with.

He leaned closer. "I will give you what you want."

"I've got it!" Tyce said his fingers jamming several keys on his bridge console.

"You know where it is coming from?" Naud said leaning close.

"No, that is still hard to tell. But I did narrow in on what it is doing. It is accessing something in your quarters, sir."

"What? My quarters? But there is nothing in there it could touch except the com and ..." His eyes went wide and he dashed for the hatch. Half a minute later he reached his quarters. The door was open a crack, and he heard odd clicks, several high-pitched sounds, and a synthesized voice said, "You have done well. We will keep our promise."

Naud burst into the room, causing Lavine to look up quick. His face a mix of shock and being caught with his hand in the cookie jar. "Commander Naud! What do you think you are doing?"

"What I'm doing? What are *you* doing? Tyce detected some sort of tight beam aimed at the *Raven* and communicating with this room." His gaze centered on the data tab, still sitting on the desk as he left it. "And I have to assume it was my data tab."

Lavine sat back in the chair. It wasn't the full-back padded leather chair he was used to, but he wasn't about to let Naud see his irritation. "I don't know what you are talking about. I didn't think you would mind me using your data tab for a little research."

Naud spat. "Research my foot! I heard odd sounds with some voice saying you did well, and they would keep their promise!"

Lavine shook his head. "No, you must have been hearing things. Perhaps it came from another location. It wasn't from here."

"We'll see about that." Naud turned and started heading towards the com on the wall. He saw a glint out of the corner of his eye. He rotated thirty degrees to the left, going down into a crouch position while jamming his left elbow backwards. It connected into Lavine's midsection full force causing the man to double over in pain, dropping what he had in his hand. Naud picked up the energy carbine, the pistol was set to kill.

Lavine tried to speak, but all that came out were wheezes. Naud's eyes narrowed as he leveled the weapon at Lavine.

"Well well, I never knew you had the guts to get your hands dirty. Trying to kill me? That was a mistake." He took two steps backwards and hit the com behind him with the back of his hand. "Tyce? Get down here immediately, and bring security."

On the bridge, Tyce blinked. "Security?"

"You heard me. Grab your equipment too, I have a special job waiting for you down here."

"Yes sir, on my way," Tyce said.

A minute later Tyce appeared in the doorway to Naud's quarters, flanked by two of the largest men they had aboard. Their eyes focused on the weapon in Naud's hand. "Sir?"

Lavine wheezed a few more times before he finally got enough breath to speak. "Thank goodness you are here! Naud has gone crazy! Look, he even came in pointing that weapon at me. I'm taking direct command of the *Raven*."

Tyce glared at him. "With all due respect, while we have not known him for very long, that is not the Commander's style. Not to mention we don't stock carbines like that. Therefore, he didn't bring it. And considering there are only two of you in the room, and the Commander is pointing it at you, why don't you drop the pretense? We aren't going to fall for it."

Naud glanced over at Tyce. "Very good. I got down here in time to hear him talking with someone, but he denied it. And then tried to kill me with the weapon I am now holding when I turned away. I want you to dig into the data tab and find out what is going on."

Tyce rubbed his hands together a second before pulling out a keyboard with a cable from the pouch on his hip, plugging one end of a cable into a device on his belt, and the other into Naud's data tab.

After a few moments, Tyce frowned. "Whatever was

transmitted is gone now. It must have cleaned itself up afterwards."

Naud looked over while still keeping an eye on Lavine. "So there is no way to tell what he did?"

"I didn't say that. Give me a few minutes." He tapped on the keyboard strapped to his arm, watching the code scroll past on Naud's data tab. "Ah, here we go. I can tell you he sent a file, a pretty big one too. Let me see . . . ah it was . . . holy! It was a technical schematic of our carbine cannons!"

Naud's eyes threw daggers at Lavine. "Anything more?"

"Looking . . . I can't tell exactly where but the temp image buffer still has some data in it, let me see what I can pull from there." Tyce tapped a few more keys and the scroll of data was replaced by an image of a head with two massive compound eyes. They all gasped.

"He sent our technology to *that*?"

Tyce gave a somber nod. "It would appear so, sir."

Naud took two quick steps, grabbed Lavine by the lapel of his robe, and jabbed the weapon into the man's middle. "Give me one good reason why I shouldn't pull the trigger?"

Lavine cracked a smile. "Because it is cold-blooded murder and you are above that."

Naud's eyes narrowed. "Who says I have to kill you? I could just maim you for life? Or take a few feet of your intestines. So what will it be?"

Lavine's smile faded away and terror crept into his eyes.

Naud's finger tightened on the trigger, tighter, tighter. *Click.* Lavine's eyes went wide and his face lost all of its color as the blood drained from it. Naud leaned closer to the man's ear. "I pulled the power cell when you were looking at the screen. But I should have left it in." In a quick motion he pulled, then pushed the man into the waiting arms of the men flanking

Tyce. "Get him out of my sight. I know we don't have a brig but put him in the empty closet we have at the end of the hall and seal the door. But remember to open it on occasion, there isn't any ventilation in there. However, if you forget, I won't say anything."

Naud didn't think Lavine's eyes could get any wider as the men on either side of him picked him up by the shoulders and manhandled him down the corridor. He turned to Tyce. "Let's get back to the bridge, I have a call to make. And bring that data tab."

Tyce nodded as he grabbed the unit from the desk as he followed Naud out. "Yes sir."

22

Odell Halburn walked down the hall towards the elevator after a meeting with Iawi Burns. They had drawn up a plan on how best to defend the World Council complex should an attack be attempted. And how to evacuate everyone should that become necessary, although doubtful considering Lavine only had one ship. Iawi had sat across from him in the conference room in his long robes. Halburn still felt odd wearing them and had left his hanging on the hook back in his office.

Overhead, a speaker pinged. "Chairman Halburn? There is a call for you on your private com."

Halburn reached the waiting elevator and pressed a button inside. "I will take it in my office." He rode up several floors, walked down the long hallway and entered his office. He sat down at his desk and tapped a key on his console. The screen lit up with Torrian Naud's face. "Naud!" His eyes narrowed. "Are you sure this connection is secure?" Then he noticed the call was coming from a Mechand carrier's bridge. His eyes went wide.

"It doesn't matter now," Naud said with a wave of his hand. "I have control of the *Raven,* and Lavine will not be of any further consequence. And next time you can play the bad guy," he said with a chuckle.

"I'm sorry about that, but we had to have someone on the inside and you were the best candidate. He would have never believed it if it was me, besides I couldn't trust anyone else with this. And what happened?"

"I know that, but it didn't make it any easier. And as to what happened, I caught Lavine transmitting the specs to our carbine cannons to some creature on the Moon, or farther out. We can't tell exactly where the beam originated."

Halburn's eyebrows raised. "Some *creature?*"

"You heard me. It looks like a cross between a bee and a fly. One giant bug. We don't have all the details but being he sent the specs to our weapons, it's a good bet they don't plan on shaking hands, if they even have hands."

Halburn's lips drew into a tight line. "No, I wouldn't think so. And what of Lavine?"

"The crew is behind me once they found out about what he did. I didn't even have to mention it looked like a big bug. The *Raven* doesn't have a brig, but I had locked him in a tiny unused closet at the end of the hall near my quarters."

"Are you sure he won't try to escape?"

"Nah, he saw me almost shoot him and for a second he thought I did. He is too much a coward to try anything now."

Halburn chuckled. "I wish I could have seen that. Drop him off when you get a chance."

Naud smiled. "Of course, and we don't have much of a to-do list at the moment," he turned towards Perkins he made a gesture. "We'll be there in about forty minutes. Need anything else? Want me to pick up anything on the way?"

Halburn chuckled again. "Nope, you did well, Commander. See you in forty, I need to contact the *Defiant* and the *Phoenix*."

On board the *Phoenix*, Minerva's eyebrows met. "Halburn is calling."

The main screen flickered and Odell Halburn's face appeared. Leon stood. "Odell, I can tell from your face this is not good news. Did we not get all of Lavine's ships except for the *Raven*?"

"No, you did. And in fact, Lavine is now in custody."

Leon's head tilted as his eyebrows went up. "Really? I thought you were going to send us after him?"

Halburn nodded. "I did, but Naud did the job for us, a lot quicker than I expected."

Leon blinked. "Naud? I thought you said you suspected he was leading Lavine's forces?"

Halburn leaned back. "He was. However, he was my agent inside Lavine's organization. I hadn't heard from him since he went in, he didn't have an opportunity to update me on the status. For all I knew, everyone was loyal to Lavine leaving him in a bad position should he attempt a coup. Thankfully, the situation turned out to be much better than I hopped and the crew followed him when he took Lavine into custody. But the reason that happened is why I am calling."

"Oh? What happened?"

"Long story short, he was in communication with an alien race that looks like a giant fly or something. And he gave it the details about our carbine cannons."

Leon leaned forward. "What! Are you sure?"

Halburn nodded. "Positive. Naud and his crew caught him in the act. Unfortunately, they were too late to prevent the data from being sent."

Minerva cocked her head. "Do you know where it was being sent to?"

"They aren't positive, the Moon or perhaps a point much farther out in space. The tight beam and the technology behind it made it very difficult to trace. Do you know anything about these creatures?"

Leon nodded. "Yes, we do. They are called Ixeons. We found out they were behind the Celloids."

Halburn leaned forward. "Behind the Celloids? You mean they sent them?"

"More than that, they actually made them. It was a genetically created race. That is what the *Defiant* is doing now, trying to find out more. We determined that there might be a base on the Moon, but we couldn't be certain. The *Defiant* went to investigate and had to go radio silent to do so. We haven't heard since. But if there was a serious problem, Galina or Miles would have contacted us by now."

"Are you sure there isn't a problem?"

Minerva nodded. "Positive. I still have a sensor lock on the *Defiant*. All systems are operating within normal parameters."

"Hmm, I don't like it. I don't like it one bit." Halburn laced his fingers together and lowered them down on the desk.

"We can contact them."

"No, I don't want you to tip our hand and possibly alert these Ixeons."

Minerva inclined her head. "Very well, what do you suggest?"

"Can you contact Miles and find out what is going on without using the normal channels these Ixeons might be wise to?"

Minerva smiled. "Of course, Mechands have several

uplinks that don't use the normal spectrum. It is also an encrypted link. Nothing they could read, even if they can detect it. But it won't be instant, those channels are a great deal slower."

"Good, use them. They need to know about this. And we need to know what they found."

Minerva nodded. "Agreed."

"Indeed," Leon added, "We will contact you when we hear back."

Halburn nodded. "Understood, Odell out." His image shrank to a point and disappeared.

Leon turned. "I hope you are right and they can't trace this."

Minerva smiled. "Trust me."

— 23 —

Deven awoke and found himself strapped to a table. The Ixeon had left his helmet on, which was good. He doubted they breathed the same air. Or if they did, he suspected the smell would make him nauseous. Rotating his head to the right and up, he saw Otis held against the wall. Dakarth was held down to a table similar to the one he was on. Lights flickered above it, and a glow reached out from the panels under him. He didn't like the look of it one bit.

Dakarth's eyes flicked open as he tried to move but couldn't. Otis was still unconscious. Deven turned his head to the left and spotted Aleshia held up against the wall by another set of stone straps that held Otis. She was still out cold, but the lights on the front of her suit showed she was fine otherwise. "Aleshia? Aleshia, can you hear me?" He hoped the communications system was still functional. Being Lytherian technology, it had backups for backups. "Aleshia, wake up. We need you."

Her eyes fluttered open. "Deven?" When she tried to move and couldn't her eyes snapped open the rest of the way. "What! What happened?"

"I don't know some kind of stun beam knocked us all out."

"Yessss, similar to our Triellon but more potent," Dakarth

said.

At this, Otis' eyes opened. "Ouch! Did someone get the name of the truck that ran me over?" His eyes blinked in quick succession several times trying to focus. When they finally did, he wished they hadn't. "Boss, I think we're in trouble."

The Hexagon door on the far side of the room opened similar to the first one they entered by splitting into individual triangles and retracting from the center into the door frame. The Ixeon stood in the now-open doorway and made a screeching hiss the audio pickups in their suits repeated the phrase several times causing them to shudder.

The Ixeon walked upright but also used one set of arms for balance. It had six appendages in total, and it appeared they could be used for both legs and arms. The Ixeon glided into the room. The smoothness of the movement surprised even Dakarth. He moved closer, went between the two tables, pointed at Dakarth, and shrieked even higher.

"What did you do to him?" Otis asked.

Dakarth tried to shrug but couldn't move. "I do not know. We have never met his kind before."

The Ixeon issued another high-pitched shriek and turned around to Deven. Two small probosces came out of the base of its head where a mouth would be and rubbed themselves together.

"Boss, I don't like the look he is giving you," Otis said.

"No kidding," Deven said as he struggled to get loose from the table.

The Ixeon tapped several locations on the table and an armature extended up from the base. Another arm extended from it, ending in a small round cylinder. A beam shot from the cylinder to the left of Deven's shoulder and began moving towards his neck. Within ten seconds it would be through his helmet and two or three seconds after that, severing his head.

Aleshia's eyes went wide as her instincts took over releasing her normal mental restraints. "Oh no you don't!" The small cylinder ripped from the armature but it cut off one of the Ixeon's arms before it lost power. The Ixeon shrieked even higher than before as it stared at the stump of its arm. No blood oozed as the beam had sealed the wound as it cut.

Aleshia's eyes narrowed and the stone straps holding her shattered, and she lowered herself gently to the ground. With a flick of her wrist, she catapulted the Ixeon against another wall and held him. With a flick of her other wrist two poles lying in the corner levitated, bent into a U shape and rammed into the rock around the Ixeon pinning it. It shrieked and wiggled but could do nothing.

Aleshia waved a hand over the tables holding Deven and Dakarth. They sparked, shorted, and went dark. Both sat up and smiled. "Thank you, my darling," Deven said.

Otis sighed. "Umm ... you know I hate to be a pest and all ... but Aleshia could you ... well ... "

She waved a hand and the stone straps crumbled. Otis hopped down. "Oh thank you. I hated being like a fly on the wall." He turned towards the Ixeon. "No offense."

Deven laughed. "I think we are well past the stage of offending him." He turned towards Aleshia. "Looks like you worked past your block. All of your abilities are back and then some."

Aleshia took a weak step and Deven caught her. "Not quite. It still took more out of me than it should."

"Maybe, but you did it. And we are alive because of it." Deven rolled her into his arms for a tight hug.

"Umm I hate to be the one to break up this love-fest but

what are we going to do with tall dark and buggy?" Otis said jerking a thumb towards the Ixeon.

"There might be more of them around," Dakarth said.

Aleshia shook her head. "Nope, now that stealth is gone, I probed the entire base, and he is the only one here."

Dakarth found their equipment in another corner of the room. He picked up his pack and handed Otis his. "We need to accessss his systems."

Otis nodded. "Right with you." They walked out of the room into the corridor and realized they were in a side room before the tunnel turned towards the room they found the Ixeon in. They turned left and headed for it.

Deven squeezed Aleshia. "Thank you again, love. But now what shall we do with Mr. Buggy, as Otis called him?"

Aleshia peered over at the Ixeon, who never stopped trying to get free. "I don't know. Perhaps we will know more when Dakarth and Otis get into his computers."

They watched the Ixeon struggled and Aleshia considered adding another restraint when Otis and Dakarth ran into the room. "Boss, we got a problem."

Dakarth nodded. "Yessss big problem."

Deven turned towards them, Aleshia still under his arm. "What is it?"

Otis sighed and pointed to the Ixeon. "He must have dumped his network. There is not a thing on it."

They heard a noise behind them that sounded almost like manic glee.

Deven turned. "You understand us?"

The Ixeon's eyes never changed. His probosces slid back into their hidden area.

Otis' eyes narrowed. "It would seem so, Boss."

Deven stepped closer to the Ixeon. The creature didn't

flinch. "He thinks he is so smart and has destroyed what we came to find. But we have something he didn't plan on." He turned around, grabbed Aleshia's hand, and lead her over to the Ixeon. "Sweetheart, you know I hate to ask, but we don't have a choice."

Aleshia sighed. "I know. But I wish I didn't have to." She stepped closer, her vision focused on the Ixeon for a few seconds before her eyes reduced to mere slits, then shot open. "He is trying to resist."

Deven blinked. "He is telepathic?"

Aleshia shook her head. "No. More like trying to fool me into going after the wrong information while hiding what we want. But it won't work on me." Her eyes narrowed again, and she pushed *hard. What are your secrets? Why do you hate us?* The Ixeon continued to offer distractions. *You can't hide from me. Tell me now.*

In a flash she was in deep space watching a massive asteroid field orbiting a star. She didn't see planets, only the great band of asteroids. She wondered if the planets broke up at some point. Watching time speed up, ships arrived. They didn't look like anything she had ever seen before. Large domes with tendrils extending from the base. She watched as the ships peppered little pods on many of the larger asteroids.

As time increased again, she watched the little pods hatch into worm-like creatures that fed on the various nutrients and minerals left in the asteroids. Their development increased, and she watched the worms spin cocoons. At this point they were collected by the dome-ships she saw before. Her mind drifted within, and she realized these were Ixeon ships! The worms were their young and after the cocoon stage, a full adult emerged.

Aleshia blinked. In the larva or egg stage, they didn't need oxygen and could survive in space. But once in their adult forms, they needed oxygen and space suits. She watched as this life cycle happened for thousands of years. Until one day large ships arrived in the system. Ships with huge mouths to take in massive amounts of raw material and turn it into more ships or other manufactured items.

The Lytherian *Makers* had arrived.

Aleshia watched in horror as the *Makers* came into the system shortly after the Ixeons had placed their latest generation of eggs and started processing the asteroid field. Time sped up as she watched most of the asteroid field processed into new ships or other materials for the Lytherians.

All the other *Makers* had left by now, leaving one lone ship to finish the last quadrant of the asteroid field. When it finished, it began procedures to return to the Lytherian home world. It didn't notice one solitary Ixeon ship. One that returned earlier than the others to check on their offspring. It watched in horror as the *Maker* gobbled the last of their young and began to accelerate away.

The Ixeon nestled up against the massive hull of the *Maker* and held on as the ship created a warp jump. When it exited, the Lytherian home world turned below. The Ixeon disconnected from the *Maker* and initiated its own jump home. When it arrived, it told of their new enemy. But the damage was done. The entire generation of Ixeons had been wiped out. They were all near the end of their life cycle and a doomed race.

But they all wanted revenge. Revenge at any cost. They used the rest of the time they had left to create servants that could do what they could not. Two Ixeons would oversee them. To stay alive, they entered stasis unless needed. Only emerging when their servants had important information to tell them.

Now she knew why, Aleshia wanted to know *how*. She pushed for information about the Celloids and Sileics. A blackness enveloped her.

Aleshia blinked and shook her head. Deven grabbed her. "Are you okay?"

"Yes. Why?"

"You went into his mind, he screeched and went limp. I think he's dead."

Aleshia rubbed her forehead. "How long?"

"About a minute, perhaps two."

"A minute? Is that all? It felt like centuries. The last thing I did was push to find out about the Celloids and Sileics."

Dakarth took out one of his devices from his pack. A green beam enveloped the Ixeon and retracted. "He issss dead yessss. No doubt."

Aleshia rubbed her head more, tracing her eyebrow with her finger. "He must have willed himself to death rather than give me information about the Celloids or Sileics."

"Wow," Otis said. "They must really hate us."

"They do. But I wouldn't exactly fault them for it."

"What did we do?"

"It wasn't us per se, but rather the Lytherians."

Dakarth blinked. "We? What could we have done to them? We have never seen this species before."

"But they saw you destroy their entire generation."

"What! That issss not possible!"

"It is. I saw it. Long ago you harvested a solar system that only comprised a large asteroid belt. They laid their eggs in those asteroids that then hatched and spun cocoons. The

Ixeon's retrieved them at the cocoon stage and right after they emerged as the next generation."

Dakarth blinked several times. His eyes larger than lanterns with the news. "I cannot imagine thissss."

"I saw it. I know it happened."

"We alwayssss inspect before harvesting."

"Sounds like a mistake was made," Deven said.

Dakarth whirled around to face him. "You don't understand, thissss is far beyond what we could do. We would never harm anyone. Especially centuries ago. Now we only do it because we had to combat the Celloids to save our race. We never hurt anyone else."

"But I saw it!" Aleshia said.

Deven looked at her. "Perhaps he fooled you and showed you this to throw you off the real reason?"

Aleshia shook her head. "No chance. The emotions were too strong, and it was too vivid to be faked anyway."

Otis took a step closer towards the dead Ixeon. "So you are saying this bug is thousands of years old?"

Aleshia took several steps until she was next to Otis. "Yes. They are the last of their kind. The rest died out long ago."

Dakarth sat on the floor, his head in his hands. One talon tapped his helmet. "Thissss cannot be true. We don't do thissss."

Otis turned around. "If you did or didn't, it is not the problem now. The Sileics are. Or anything else the Ixeons have." He jerked a thumb towards the dead Ixeon. "We need to find out what he knew."

Dakarth looked up. "How? He erased everything."

Otis smiled. "On first glance, yes. But would you erase everything if it was you only method of communication with your fleet? I don't think so." He walked over to Dakarth and extended his hand. "Come on. Let's see what we can dig up."

Back inside the control room, Otis and Dakarth ran recovery programs to find any trace of data that the Ixeon might have left behind. Either intentionally or not. After several hours, they found a few fragments pointing to something else. Otis smiled. "I think we are getting close."

Dakarth nodded. "Yessss I agree. These numbers show a much larger data store. But if they are separate, it might still be intact."

Otis' eyes lit up like beacons twenty minutes later. "Bingo! See here? He tried to hide it behind this section. At first glance it looks empty, but the size indicator says there is a lot more than what we are seeing."

Dakarth flicked his tongue. "Yesss this must be it. I have an idea." He pulled out a palm system and cable. Connecting one end of the cable to the palm device and the other end he touched to the Ixeon's console. The end of the cable liquified and attached itself making a solid connection. "Connection established. Running a self-adapting program now. It may work."

Otis watched the code scroll across Dakarth's small screen. "What's it for? I don't recognize some of it."

Dakarth smiled. "It is for fixing size discrepancies in the database. I wrote it to repair a part of our central database on the *Command* carrier. Their system is very different from ours. It may not work. I think you say a 'long shot'?"

Otis laughed. "Yes, that is what we say. But worth the try. And both systems are binary."

Dakarth nodded. "Yessss and it may adapt enough to work."

"I was wondering, how much air do we have left in these suits? We must have been here for many hours or more," Aleshia said.

"Many days. The support systems are very efficient."

"Good. Still though, shouldn't we let the *Defiant* and *Phoenix* know what is happening?"

"Yessss, good point. I will do it."

Deven walked through the hexagon hatch with Aleshia right behind him. "And I will go with you."

"Not neccessssary."

Deven shrugged. "Perhaps not, but I would feel better if I did. And I'm not doing anything here anyway. Besides, space is always dangerous."

"You are right. Very well." Dakarth turned and left the control room with Deven right behind him.

After they left Aleshia look at Otis. "What was–"

Otis made a sign with his finger as close to his nose as his helmet would allow, and she stopped. He walked over, pressed two buttons on the controls of her suit, and he did the same on his. "There, now we can talk. Sorry, but you were talking on the channel we all were using and Dakarth would have heard."

"How did you know about the separate channels?"

Otis smiled. "I'm a cracker, remember? I'm not happy unless I know how things work. And it wasn't hard after I worked on the Lytherian technology in the chair. They tend to keep to the same design methods."

Otis returned to the Ixeon console and watched as Dakarth's palm device scrolled code. After a few more minutes, it beeped and stopped highlighting several areas. Aleshia pointed. "What's that mean?"

"Not sure. Trying to find out." Otis tapped several buttons and another extensive area lit up. "Bingo! We found that missing data block. I'm downloading it here." Otis plugged his own system into Dakarth's and started pulled the data over. "I'll have a copy too it in a few minutes."

Aleshia tapped her foot. "Now do you want to tell me why you didn't want me to talk on the same channel as Deven and Dakarth?"

"Deven told me to get this data and go over it myself. He has his doubts about Dakarth."

Aleshia blinked. "What? Why?"

"Well, you are certain his people killed off the Ixeons. If that is true how would he not know?"

"Perhaps he wasn't told? It did happen long ago."

Otis rolled his eyes. "Not be passed down through the generations of the race they killed off? Yeah, right."

"Not if they wanted to forget about it."

Otis bit his cheek. "I'll give you that one. But being his position, he must know. An average fighter pilot or ship technician, sure. Him? No way."

"I still think he is telling the truth."

"Then you are wrong with what you saw. It can't be both ways. Regardless, we had better get back on the main channel in case they try to talk to us."

Aleshia nodded. "Right." They pushed the button on their suits at the same time.

"Deven, this here is the communications system," Dakarth said.

"Oh, for some reason I didn't think it was," Deven said.

"It issss. Watch. I hit these two controls. *Defiant?* Are you receiving?"

"We are receiving," Miles said in his usual calm voice. "It has been several hours and Galina–"

"You bet I have been worried! So is everyone else up here. What took you so long to contact us?" Galina said.

"Ssssory, we ran into problem. It fixed now. We are trying to get data from the Ixeon's system."

"What problem? Where there Ixeons there?"

Deven toggled like he saw Dakarth do to transmit to the shuttle's systems. "There was one. He captured us, but we got free. The Ixeon is now dead though and as Dakarth said the situation is 'fixed'. We are trying to pull data from its systems. It is slow going since he wiped everything either right before or after he captured us."

"This was a bust then."

"Not necessarily. Dakarth and Otis are working on a way to recover at least a portion of the data."

"A portion?" Galina humphed. "Why do we only get little bits and pieces rather than the whole picture?"

Deven laughed. "Wish I knew. Otis? Can you hear me?"

"Loud and clear," Otis said.

"Anything yet from that program Dakarth is running."

"It's still running." He pointed to the screen on his arm and Aleshia saw the download was still in progress.

"Okay, I hope something comes up. Did you get that Galina?"

"Nope, but got the gist anyway. Everything is quiet up here. Too quiet, I'm still waiting for the other shoe to drop."

"Let's hope it doesn't. Deven out." He tapped the console that cut the connection. "We'd better get back to Aleshia and Otis."

"It would be nice," Aleshia said.

All the lights in the complex went red and began to flash as all the doors slammed shut. "Umm Boss, we have a problem here."

24

Galina sat drumming her fingers on the flight controls. "It has been too long since they contacted us from Dakarth's shuttle. I don't like it. I'm going to try calling them."

Miles' camera turned. "And what would that accomplish? They were trying to retrieve data from the Ixeon's systems, and it is most probable they left the shuttle to do so. Considering they have not contacted us again, it is logical they have not yet returned. Or have other reasons for remaining silent. Performing what you suggest could undermine those reasons."

"I know that!" Galina grunted, pushing back a lock of blonde hair. While the gravity plating was operational, her hair, like the rest of her, didn't like space one bit. "But we can't just sit here."

"But that is precisely what we *must* do, Galina. Anything else will–"

Galina glanced up at Miles' camera. "What's the matter, Miles? Cat got your tongue? I have never known you to stop mid-sentence."

"Apologies, I am receiving a communication."

Galina sat up in her chair. "About time they got in touch!"

Miles' camera rotated back and forth. "Negative, it is not

from Dakarth's shuttle. It is from the *Phoenix*."

"The *Phoenix*? Wonder what's up. Put it up on the screen."

"I cannot."

"What do you mean you can't? Is there a fault in the communications array?"

"Negative, it is on a Mechand command link. A very old one. This kind of link is too slow for an active conversation. If it wasn't for me being a part of the *Defiant*, it would not have been detected at all."

Galina cocked her head. "Why in the world would Minerva use that? Is she trying to take control of your systems?"

"It is not possible with this particular communication, it was never designed for use in the Mechand command network."

"Then what was it used for?"

"Very low power transmission to Mechand units giving coordinates or location data. Speed and capacity were not necessary in these instances. However, I am not receiving coordinates. Instead, a large communication cut into very tiny sections. It will take time to receive it all."

"Well? What does it say so far?"

Miles' camera iris contracted and expanded. "I do not know."

Galina let out a grunt as she shot out a breath through her teeth. "And why not?"

"The link is encrypted and decrypting is only possible after all the data has been received."

"This is crazy. Why would Minerva use such an old antiquated pain-in-the-butt method of contacting us?"

Miles' iris contracted. "There exists but two possibilities. One, either the *Phoenix* is damaged, and this is the only communications method she has available."

Galina rolled her eyes. The bot did know how to drag things out. "Or?"

"Or two, the transmission is one requiring high security, and she does not want anyone to know it has been sent."

"But you said only Mechands could receive it."

"That is correct. And newer models could not either. It was deemed redundant and removed from service many years ago."

Galina resumed drumming her fingers on the controls. "And how long until we get the whole thing?"

"I have now received the message in its entity."

"Well, what you waiting for? Show it!"

Miles' iris contracted further down to a tiny gap. "I was about to tell you." His camera turned towards the screen, towards Galina's right as his iris opened wide. "Now displaying on screen."

The screen flickered several times until a grainy image of Minerva and Leon could be seen. "Apologies for using such an antiquated method of communication, but we could not take the risk of it being intercepted," Minerva said.

Miles' camera turned. "I told you."

"Miles! Hush!"

"Yes, we couldn't take the chance," Leon said then took a step forward. "Long story short, Halburn now has Lavine in custody, however, right beforehand he gave the Ixeons detailed information about our carbine cannons. While we don't know what their intent is, it can't be good."

"Halburn thought you should know what happened, and we hope the investigation of the Moon proved fruitful," Minerva said.

Leon nodded. "Indeed. One last thing, the transmission Lavine responded to was possibly from the Moon. The crew of the *Raven* couldn't determine exactly where. It could have come from a point much farther out. Get back to us when you can. *Phoenix* out." The screen went dark.

"Well, that's a fine kettle of fish! They have all the data on our weapons, and we don't even know what is going on down there to respond. Heck, they might be walking back into a trap."

Miles' camera iris contracted and expanded more slowly than usual. "That is very probable."

"Scan the surface, look for anything different. Perhaps we can at least tell if they are back in the shuttle and okay."

"Galina, if we do detailed scans, it might cause problems if the base reacts."

"At this point, I don't think it matters much."

"Very well, starting scans." Several screens lit up, awash in data scrolling past. "I do not detect Dakarth's shuttle."

"Blast it!" Galina pounded her fist on the console.

"While we know they did land without incident, but as to where, that I cannot determine at this time."

"Anything else? Anything unusual?"

"I am detecting an energy signature deep in one of the extensive crevasses. It is faint but growing."

Galina's eyebrows rose. "A weapon?"

Miles' camera shook back and forth. "Negative. The signature has some resemblance to our reactors."

"A base power source? But we scanned that area up and down several times and never detected squat."

"The energy signature is still increasing. I am now detecting an exponential build."

"Oh hell, something went wrong for sure. How long until it blows?"

"Very difficult to ascertain, as we do not know their technology. However, based on this increasing curve, and if our technology is similar, I estimate four minutes until the buildup reaches a point where containment will fail destroying everything in a two-mile radius."

Inside the shuttle, Deven hung his head. He knew that voice all too well. "What's wrong?"

"The Ixeon's console shut down in the middle of Dakarth's recovery. I can't get it to do anything now. The lights are flashing in here, so something has changed and my guess it's a self-destruct," Otis said.

"Get out of there! Get out now!"

"We're outta here. But I can't leave Dakarth's system and I can't pull the cable out of the console."

"Disssssconnect cable from the device and take it. That should come loose."

Otis fiddled with the cable, but it held fast until he pinched, pulled and twisted, then it popped loose. "Got it. We are outta here."

Aleshia and Otis ran into the nano-made doorway from earlier and down the corridor until they ran into the hatch at the other end. "Hey Boss, another problem. Looks like the base sealed all the doors. The key pads won't even light up."

Aleshia smiled. "That won't be a problem." She waved a hand, and the door rippled but remained firm. "This is stronger than it looks." Her eyes narrowed, and she pulled again at it. The door showed signs of stress in the joints and cracks started to appear spreading out several millimeters but still remained sealed. "Ugh, what is this stuff?"

"It is probably stronger than anything we ever made. And I bet you haven't recovered from breaking us loose and pinning Mr. Buggy."

"I should be able to open a door!" She shut her eyes, raised both hands and pulled with her mind. Again the door rippled, and the cracks widened, but not anywhere near enough for them to get through. She tried again and the different triangles separated a bit more, but still not enough. Sweat glistened on her face inside her helmet with the suit not able to keep up with her exertion.

Otis took her hand and her eyes popped open. "Look this stuff likely way beyond what we have made. But whatever the reason, you can't do it now. And you are going to pass out if you keep trying."

Aleshia breathed hard. "Okay. I'll stop."

"Dakarth, get over here and bring your door maker. We are at the inner airlock."

"We're on our way," Deven said as they both ran out of the cockpit. A few moments later they reached the hatch they had made separating the airlock storage room from the tunnel behind them. Deven reached for the controls when Dakarth stopped him.

"Wait. Didn't they say the inside airlock is open?" Dakarth said.

"Not open. Well, a crack anyway. I can see the storage crates inside. The door has cracks all through it too," Otis said.

"Then we have a problem. If we open thissss, base will explosively decompress. We don't know what that will do. Granted, it will only go into this tunnel and not be a full evac, but the base might react. We don't have time to pressurize this area or the tunnel."

"What choice do we have?" Deven said.

Dakarth sighed. "None. Otis, Aleshia stand away from that door. Even if the base does nothing, the sudden change in air-pressure is going to draw you into it."

"And pull with enough force to kill," Otis said.

"Yes."

The gravity field shut down mid-step. The quick change almost sent them flying into the ceiling, but Aleshia blocked the impact, placing them back down on their feet instead. Inside her helmet, sweat ran down her forehead. The scent of her effort flooded her suit for several seconds as it fought to stabilize. They bounced down the rest of the corridor and took a right. "Okay, we are around the corner," Aleshia said breathing hard.

"I hope it is enough," Otis said.

Dakarth motioned to Deven to stand back. He pushed a button on the controls and the door popped open a middle emergency hatch. Atmosphere rushed past them leaving misting vapor trails in its wake.

Inside the airlock lights of a different color flashed, and a secondary door lowered slamming over the broken airlock door sealing it off. The atmosphere rushing past them quickly died. Dakarth nodded and opened the nano-made door and walked into the airlock.

"Aleshia? Otis?" Deven called. "We are in the airlock. Are you all right?"

"Yea Boss, it was breezy for a few seconds till that second door slammed shut. Better hurry though, the lights in this section are blinking very fast. I don't think that is a good sign."

Dakarth placed his octagon nano builder on the door and pressed the button. Black goo spread out fast and rebuilt into a rectangular portal with a window. When it finished, he removed the nano kit and motioned Deven back.

"Get back to that far corridor. We are blowing the seal again," Deven said.

"You don't have to tell us twice," Otis said as they bounced back around the corner.

Dakarth pressed the center button again that popped open the emergency hatch. Atmosphere gushed into the opened airlock then diminished. "Done. Hurry."

"We're on our way," Aleshia said as they bounced down the corridor.

He pulled open the hatch to see Otis and Aleshia bounce into view. The lights above were flickering so fast now to be almost solid. They bounced through the second door as Otis slammed the one behind them, locking it. Dakarth popped the vent on the tunnel entrance and the pressure equalized again, but less than the previous time. No doubt the base was no longer trying to keep the rooms equal. Another sign there couldn't be much time left.

They bounced down the second tunnel, into the first, into the crater, and up the ramp instantly feeling their weight increase. When they reached the airlock Dakarth's eyes narrowed. "I need to blow the lock, we don't have time to have it cycle. Get back and hold on."

They moved back from the airlock and grabbed onto the struts that raised the ramp. Dakarth hit the purge button and air whooshed out, threatening to blow them out of the shuttle. Deven held Aleshia as air whipped past them, making one feel as though they were in a hurricane. Otis lost his grip at one point and was sent tumbling end over end until he grabbed ahold of an extended brace usually attached to cargo.

The rush of gasses subsided and the airlock door slid open now that both areas were equal vacuum.

"It is done. Hurry!" Dakarth ran inside the shuttle.

Aleshia shook her head and noticed the man sprawled alongside the one wall. "Otis!"

Deven ran over to him and helped the sprawled figure up. Otis shook his head and took a few staggered steps. "Whew, let's not do that again."

Deven grabbed his shoulder. "Come on, or we're going to be permanent residents!"

"Right with ya, Boss!" Otis said as he ran behind them into the shuttle's main interior.

"Sssstrap in," Dakarth said sitting the control chair. The ramp had began to raise. "I can't let the engines activate normal. This issss going to be rough."

"Oh great," Otis said as he sat down and fastened to straps over his shoulders and locked them into an attachment point in front of his groin.

Deven sat down and strapped in as well. "Thought you said this was going to be fun?"

Otis sucked in a cheek. "I've changed my mind!"

"Engines activated at full power, hang on!" Dakarth jabbed a gloved talon on his control panel and the shuttle vibrated for a second while the engines' glow went from nothing, to bright blue, to a hot white, then rocketed straight up.

"Ugh," Otis said, "I left my stomach down there." Half a second later, a blinding white flash caused the shuttle's windows to darken. The shock wave reached out swatting the shuttle causing it to tumble end over end several times before Dakarth got control again. Otis shook his head and blinked several times, trying to clear his vision. "Whoa, that was close."

"Yessss, it was," Dakarth said tapping several controls.

Aleshia bit her lip. "Umm, I hate to ask, but that looked like a nuclear bomb, and we were hit. Are we okay? Were we too close to it?"

Dakarth rotated his chair around and smiled. "We are fine. We were very close, but shields held. Another two of your seconds, and we wouldn't be."

Otis cocked his head. "And what would we be then?"

"Dead," Dakarth said turning his chair back around to his console.

Aleshia closed her eyes, opening again very slowly as her hand shook inside Deven's.

Deven turned towards Otis, his eyes narrowed to mere slits. "You had to ask."

Otis sat forward and saw Aleshia's face, then he swallowed hard, sat back and cocked his helmeted head towards Deven. "Sorry, Boss."

Dakarth adjusted the shuttle's course and tapped another control causing a large screen to slide down from its recessed area in the ceiling. "*Defiant*, are you receiving ussss?"

The lowered screen above Dakarth flickered and flashed as the audio channel crackled and popped several times.

Aleshia tilted her head. "Shouldn't they be able to respond?"

Deven nodded. "Yes, they didn't have any problems when we were on the Moon."

"Yessss, very strange," Dakarth said tapping several controls. "I am plotting an intercept course. We will rendezvous shortly."

Otis padded Dakarth's device in the pouch on his hip. "Hopefully we got something that makes all this worthwhile."

25

Aboard the *Phoenix,* Leon sat back in the hard metal chair. He wished they had brought some padding over from the *Defiant.* Anything would be an improvement over these hard Mechand-only built seats. His head turned towards Minerva's screen. "Shouldn't they have responded by now?"

"You must remember this communication method was not built with speed in mind. I did receive an automatic acknowledgment. Therefore, Miles received it. But it will still take some minutes to decode, watch, record the response, encode it, and transmit it to us. Patience is necessary."

"I know that! But this is taking way too long, even with all those considerations. And the Ixeons might have been waiting for them!"

"What do you propose we do? Leave orbit and head for the Moon? That could cause more issues without further data. And did you realize you sound more like Galina?"

Leon shuddered. "I do not, but I'm concerned about them as she no doubt is, yes."

Minerva cracked a grin that went from ear to ear. "If you say so." The grin quickly turned into a frown. "I am detecting a massive energy surge on the Moon."

Leon's eyes went wide. "What? Let me see it!" Minerva

brought up the data on Leon's console, and he scrolled through it. "This looks like a reactor containment failure, or worse." He pointed to the screen. "See how the energy builds along this curve. There was some kind of explosion. Why didn't we detect this before? With this much energy, we should have seen a sign long before it went critical."

"My guess would be shielding. Until breached, it kept us from detecting the buildup."

"Dakarth's shuttle! If it was down there, I doubt even Lytherian shields would have protected against of an energy release of that size."

Minerva nodded. "I am one step ahead, trying to contact the *Defiant* on all channels."

After several minutes, the screen located in between the *Phoenix's* forward windows lit up with a grainy image. It flashed went dark as came back with more static. The bridge of the *Defiant* was viable, but barely.

Leon turned around and sat forward. "*Defiant*, can you hear us?"

The image flickered, broke up, and returned stronger. "We're here," Galina said through glitches of static, "but whatever happened on the Moon wrecked havoc with many systems aboard the *Defiant* including communications."

"How bad?" Leon said.

"We don't know yet. Miles and Gregory are trying to reroute communications through the low power array for now. He and Gregory think they can boost its power without burning it out."

Leon rubbed his chin. "Maybe, they will have to be careful and closely monitor the systems. If it spikes, the array will fry."

Galina nodded. "So they told me."

"I'm surprised Miles isn't saying something about it."

Galina grinned. "Well, I told him not to, Gregory needs his full attention while they try to boost the low power array."

The corners of Minerva's mouth went down. "He should be able to handle both tasks with relative ease."

"Should yes, but he was wrong once today and I'm not taking any chances," Galina said.

"Have you heard from Dakarth's shuttle?" Leon said.

Galina blew out a breath and shook her head. "Not a word since Deven and Dakarth left the shuttle the second time, Otis ran into some kind of problem inside the base."

"I don't suppose you could detect if they left in time or not?"

"Ha! Don't I wish. Sensors are out, the cannons are down, shields I can get up on a minimal level if we have to. Engines aren't down, but they aren't happy either."

Leon winced. "Wish I was there."

"You and me both! I'm just glad I found a frequency that works!" The screen faded to static and returned. "Well, sort of anyway."

Minerva cocked her head. "From what I know of the *Defiant*, this kind of damage should not have occurred. You weren't in the blast range."

"I know, Miles thinks it has something to do with whatever power source the Ixeons use. It threw out one massive electromagnetic pulse. Much larger than any of our systems would create."

"But your Lytherian-enhanced shields should have filtered that out." Leon said.

"They would have, if they were up at the time."

Leon winced. "You detected it at the same time as we did? After the fact? But you are so much closer."

Galina blew out a breath. "Actually, we did know about it three minutes before it blew."

"Then why didn't you raise the shields!"

"Because I was afraid if I did, and the shuttle had a communications failure and was returning, they would have been in a bad way, that's why! And Miles said we were well out of range."

On her screen, Minerva's eyes squeezed shut and opened slowly. "Out of range of the blast, but not the pulse."

"Yeah, we noticed. We were out of range of one of *our* pulses, but these Ixeon's pack quite a punch," Galina said. Through the static lines Leon could still see her eyes go wide. "What the—"

"Galina? What happened?" Leon said.

"I thought I saw something float past the bridge window. One sec." Leon watched as she got up and bounced over to the window. He sighed, realizing even the gravity plating wasn't working at one-hundred percent. "They're here!"

"Who's here? The Ixeons?"

Leon heard Galina laugh as the image faded to static and returned. "No no, it's Dakarth's shuttle!"

"Let me guess, they detected all the failures and flew up to the window?"

"Looks like. I'm heading down to the hangar to let them in. Everyone else is busy with repairs. I hope the doors work."

"You and me both," Leon said.

"Will let you know when they're inside." The screen flickered and winked out.

Leon turned. "Why didn't we detect the shuttle approaching the *Defiant*? Our systems shouldn't be affected."

"They aren't," Minerva said, "however, the shuttle may

have stealth abilities that would preclude me from detecting them."

"But why would Dakarth have those enabled now?" Leon said.

Minerva shrugged. "I do not know. Perhaps he forgot to disable them when they left the Moon. You will have to ask him."

Galina bounced her way down to the hangar deck and found it empty with everyone trying to restore the weapons, shields, and communications. She bounced into the booth that housed the hanger controls. Taking another moment to make sure no one was in the hanger bay, she sealed the inner doors, depressurized the bay, and tried to activate the outer doors.

The doors started grinding, opening about halfway before they stopped again. "Blast it!" Galina muttered jamming on several controls. She tried three more times. "Come on!" She pounded her fist on the controls and the doors began moving again. "Yeah!"

The doors ground open the rest of the way, and Dakarth's shuttle inched its way into the bay. Galina's stomach knotted as the shuttle passed within millimeters of the doors. While Dakarth had enough experience and didn't need prompts from her to maneuver the shuttle through the doors, she wished she could do more than watch. After several agonizing moments, the shuttle landed and Galina activated the doors again. Thankfully, they closed without incident. The bay began pressurizing as she bounced her way toward the inner doors.

When the pressure equalized she popped open the doors in time to see the shuttle's ramp lower. A moment later Aleshia emerged, followed by Deven and Otis. They were still in their space suits with the helmets on. She pointed towards her head to indicate the helmets.

Aleshia grinned. "Hang on, let me take it off." Galina's eyes went wide, not expecting Aleshia's voice to come through the hidden front speaker on her suit. Aleshia tapped a control right below her collarbone. The helmet popped off, and she breathed the *Defiant's* slightly more stagnant air. Deven and Otis did the same. "Sorry, Dakarth only got the shuttle repressurized as we touched down."

Galina nodded, although she thought it was odd it took so long. She thought Lytherian technology would have been faster. "What in the world happened down there?"

Deven stepped forward. "First thing, what happened to the *Defiant*? We tried to contact you several times and got nothing but static. When we approached, Dakarth detected several system failures."

Galina blew out a breath. "Yes, well that explosion nuked our communications, weapons, and even the engines aren't acting right."

Deven cocked his head. "How? We were a lot closer than you, and we didn't have any damage. You should have been fine this far away."

Otis ran his fingers through his hair, grateful he could do that again. "Let me guess, you didn't have your shields up?"

Galina nodded. "Right. Miles didn't think it would be needed since we were so far away. We were out of range of the blast, but not the electromagnetic pulse from whatever blew. This ship was built to take such a pulse in stride, so I'm not sure why it hit us so hard."

Dakarth bounced down the ramp. "I ssssupect it is due to our enhancements. We plan on having our shields for such an event and left the systems more susceptible without them. Perhaps an error on our part, we never considered this."

Aleshia turned. "You can't be expected to see every possibility."

Dakarth's head drooped. "Perhaps, but this one we should have planed on. I will help get the sssship operational as soon as possible. Let me get my equipment." He bounced back up the ramp into the shuttle.

Before he returned, static came from one of the overhead speakers. After several clicks and hisses, Miles' voice came through. "Deven, you will be pleased to know the secondary array has been boosted and is now serving as a tempoary replacment until repairs to the primary system are completed."

"Sounds like the overall com system still needs a little work," Deven said.

"I had to reroute several parts of the system, but it should now be back to ninety-eight percent of capacity. These changes will hold until the system is repaired in full."

"Thank you, Miles," Aleshia said.

"You are welcome, Aleshia," came through the com before it clicked off.

"Ugh, don't encourage him!" Galina said.

Aleshia giggled. "I don't think it makes much difference."

"Oh I think it does!" Galina retorted. She folded her arms. "So, what happened down there?"

"The Ixeon base took issue with us. But we got away," Otis said.

"By the skin of our teeth," Aleshia said.

"Did you find anything?" Galina said.

"Don't know yet, the console we were working on shut down in the middle of the data dump. I don't know why, it might have detected something it didn't like. Either way, looks like it activated a self-destruct. We took off as fast as we could, but all the doors had locked down, which kept us in there a lot longer than we wanted," Otis said.

"That's for sure," Aleshia chimed in.

Deven's one eye scrunched up, and he took a deep breath. "Galina, shouldn't you be on the bridge?"

She blinked. "What? You *know* why I am here!"

Deven didn't say a word, but folded his arms and the other eye narrowed again.

"I'm going, I'm going." She turned and bounced her way out of the hanger bay and up towards the bridge.

Dakarth reemerged from the shuttle with a large pack on his hip. "I would assume you would like the gravity plating fixed first? I know I hate all thissss bouncing around. Makes my stomach do flips."

Otis smiled. "Nah, it's not that bad," Deven glared at him, "but I agree you should work on it first."

"Otis, go with Dakarth. And see if you can find out anything from that data we grabbed from the Ixeon's base," Deven said.

Otis nodded. "Sure thing, Boss." He gestured towards Dakarth, "after you." Dakarth nodded and the two of them bounced out of the hangar bay and towards engineering.

Deven grabbed Aleshia's hand. "Come on, we need to check in with the *Phoenix*."

Aleshia nodded as she felt his strong hand in hers as they bounced out of the hangar bay. Halfway up to the bridge, she wished she didn't have that synth bar earlier. This was even worse than walking around on the Moon. Gravity at this level reached inside your guts and pulled with each step, twisting your stomach in slow motion.

A few minutes later they arrived on the bridge. "Any changes?"

Galina shook her head. "Nothing since Miles and Gregory got the low-powered array boosted."

"Correct," Miles said in his usual soothing voice, "repairs are progressing. Weapons and shields will require the most time."

Deven folded his arms. "And what about the main array?"

Miles' camera turned. "It should progress at the same speed as the others, however, I suspect it will take a slight reduced amount of time compared to the weapons or shields due to the damage received."

"See if you can get the *Phoenix*."

"Of course," Miles said, "image on main screen."

At the central screen on the wall, the bridge of the *Phoenix* appeared.

"Deven! Aleshia! So good to see you are all right," Leon said. "And what about Otis and Dakarth?"

"They are fine Leon, we weren't damaged. Dakarth's shields were up. We got beat around a bit, but nothing more. If we were any closer at the time, the story would have been very different."

Minerva nodded. "Affirmative. But if I may ask, considering my curiosity is bubbling over, what happened down there?"

Leon folded his arms. "Yes, what *did* happen?"

Deven sat in the nearest chair with Aleshia right beside him. "To be perfectly honest, I'm not sure. As far as we knew, we weren't detected. However, when we appeared in front of the Ixeon, he gave several shrill sounds separated by clicks. While I'm not certain, I don't think it was a sound of surprise."

Aleshia shook her head. "It wasn't. I think it was more laughter, especially when we pointed the Triellon's and fired."

Leon's one eyebrow went up. "Triellon's?"

Deven shrugged. "Some kind of weapon Dakarth brought. It was supposed to disable the Ixeon's nero system. But we found out firsthand, they didn't have any effect."

Aleshia nodded. "The next thing we knew, we were on tables."

"Tables?" Leon said.

"Well, you weren't. Dakarth and I were. You were up on the wall and still asleep." Deven said.

Aleshia glared at him. "Picky picky, we were all knocked out and looking at being dissected. Who cares if you were first or not." She shot her tongue out for a second before it zipped back in.

Deven chuckled. "Well, I think you got the gist."

Leon grinned. "I do."

Minerva nodded. "Indeed. But how did you get free? If Aleshia was still unconscious?"

Deven smiled. "Once she woke up, the Ixeon didn't have a chance. She broke free, waved a hand and pinned him to the wall."

"I wasn't about to let him knock us out again."

Deven turned towards her and grinned. "I wasn't complaining, sweetheart."

She grinned back. "I know."

"Dakarth and Otis went and couldn't find anything on his computers. Apparently he had purged them. Aleshia went into his mind trying to find out."

Aleshia shuddered. "And not something I want to do again. Trust me, you do not want to go into a fly's mind!"

Leon chuckled. "I will take your word for it. What did you find out?"

"His race was all but wiped out. Apparently they laid their eggs on asteroids in an otherwise vacant star system and long ago the Lytherians absorbed those asteroids with their *Makers*."

Leon whistled. "And what did Dakarth say about this?"

Deven blew out a breath. "He doesn't know anything about it."

Minerva blinked. "How could he not? It seems illogical, such an event would remain unknown."

Miles' iris contracted and expanded. "I concur."

"I don't think he does, I felt genuine surprise from him when he found out," Aleshia said.

"Maybe," Deven said.

Otis walked onto the bridge, followed by Dakarth. "Good news, the gravity plating is fixed."

"Yessss, it was a simple fix. I will work on the weapons next with your permission."

Deven nodded. "Yes, that's fine. But did you find anything out from the data we took from the Ixeon base?"

Otis shook his head. "Not yet, Boss, we haven't had a chance. I kinda didn't want to throw up when I was working on it. And this gravity plating acting wonky would have done it eventually. I didn't think it was so bad at first, but after a few minutes ... *ugh*."

"Yes, it was giving my stomach fits as well. And Gregory is down in fire control trying to restore the carbine cannons now," Galina said.

Dakarth nodded his smooth head. "Then I will go assist." He turned and left.

Otis started to follow when Deven held up his hand. "Otis, I want you to dig into that data and see if there is anything in there."

Otis turned. "You sure, Boss? I mean, I could help Dakarth."

Deven nodded. "Yes, however, Gregory and Dakarth can handle it, I want you on this."

"Sure I'll try, I might need Dakarth though. It is his system after all."

"Give it a shot, we need to know what is in there."

Otis nodded, pulling Dakarth's small device from a pouch on his suit's hip. "Sure thing Boss, I'll grab a few things from my quarters and get right on it." He turned and left the bridge.

On the screen, Leon rubbed his chin. "You think there is more data on that device and want Otis to have first crack at it?"

Deven gave a partial shrug. "Maybe, I'm not ruling anything out at this point."

On the screen, Leon folded his arms. "Did Galina tell you about Lavine?"

"No, not yet anyway."

Galina snorted. "Like, *when* have I had time?"

"Point taken, what happened Leon?"

"The good news is Odell now has him in custody. The bad news is right beforehand he was in contact with our friends the Ixeons, and he gave them all the information he had on our carbine cannons."

"Yes, that is bad news." Deven tried to hide his emotions,

but he felt Aleshia pick up on them. Aleshia gripped his hand tighter. "Anything more?"

Minerva nodded. "As far as they could detect, the signal came from the Moon, or possibly in deep space along the same trajectory."

Aleshia blinked. "So he knew we were coming?"

"Not necessarily," Deven said, "if he knew, I suspect he would have had a bigger reception planned for us the instant we stepped inside the base. And I doubt he would have wiped his data."

Aleshia nodded. "Good point. I also didn't pick up on anything about us when I probed his mind. Of course I wasn't looking for that, and might have missed it."

Deven turned and grinned. "You can't be expected to see it all, sweetheart. You did find out why the Ixeons are after the Lytherians, and by extension, us."

"What I don't understand is, why would he want info on our cannons? We already proved we can turn the Sileics to dust," Galina said.

Leon frowned. "It might be they are trying to find a way to strengthen the Sileics against our weapons."

"Considering we exploited an implosion designed into the very fabric of the Sileics, it is not probable they could change the genetic makeup of the entire race. At least not in the short-term. Such changes would take a lot of time and testing," Minerva said.

Deven nodded. "But we don't know the level of the Ixeon technology."

Minerva inclined her head. "Yes, however, it is still not probable based on everything we know."

"Leon, could they find a way to defend against it, if not remove it?" Deven said.

Leon rubbed his chin then ran his fingers through his thinning hair. "I have to agree with Minerva, it is built into the very fabric of their being. It was made to be the ultimate kill switch. You can't remove that, from what Otis and I saw. They can't exist without it. It is the whole point of the switch."

Deven raised an eyebrow. "Then defend against it?"

"Again, how? If they can't remove it, they can't defend against it. Our beams weren't the destructive force here, they were only the package delivery."

"But, we almost didn't get the last one because it took so long. That thing almost kicked us clear to Earth!" Aleshia said.

Miles' camera turned. "While that is correct, I have analyzed the data from our last encounter. I believe we can augment the cannons to improve the delivery by more than seventy percent."

Leon blinked. "I want to see that."

"Acknowledged. Data transmitted," Miles said.

"Displaying on the console closest to you," Minerva said.

Leon sat down and stared at the screen for several minutes before he sat forward and whistled. "Nice work, Miles. This should do it. Unless they send an entire fleet of rocks our way."

Miles' camera turned towards the screen as his iris contracted and expanded. "Affirmative. At this improved efficiency, the overall effect will increase exponentially."

Deven stood up. "And I doubt they will send a bunch of them. I suspect they will send a large one. Similar to the Celloids. They sent the small ones first."

Galina nodded. "They did, but it might have a lot of little ones with it."

"Why would they bother? This is a huge rock, with our

limited technology we shouldn't have been able to scratch it. Much less pulverize it. I doubt they have a fleet of these. At least not at the moment," Deven said.

"Okay, I give you that. But what if they decide to hold back until they do?"

Deven shook his head. "Nope, they know the Lytherians are crippled at the moment. If they wait, the Lytherians will join the fight making it much harder, if not impossible. If our friendly Ixeon is anything to judge by, they have a personal grudge against us now. They won't wait. And I doubt they think they have to. After they take us out, they will move on to the Lytherians. My guess is they don't know where exactly the Lytherians are and another reason for coming after us."

Galina blinked. "So what do we do?"

"We get the *Defiant* operational as soon as possible with Miles' upgrades to the cannons in place. Leon? Can you implement the changes on the *Phoenix*?"

Leon nodded. "With my eyes closed."

Minerva's eyes narrowed as her jaw tightened. "That is hardly necessary, my Mechands can make the appropriate adjustments. And greater speed than Leon with his eyes closed."

Leon turned. "That was a joke Minerva."

Minerva grinned. "I know. So was I."

"Are you sure you don't need me over there?" Leon said.

"Of course we do!" Galina said.

Deven held up his hand. "Of course we always need you Leon, but I think Gregory and Dakarth can handle the modifications here. If that changes, we will let you know."

Leon blew out a breath and gave a slight incline of his head. "Understood."

"Minerva, I want to rendezvous at L1," Deven said.

Minerva's one eyebrow shot up. "The middle point between the Earth and the Moon?"

Deven nodded. "Correct, at L1 the Sileics won't be able to attack the Earth and us at the same time. And they can't use the Moon to mask their approach."

"I understand the strategy, however, I would it not be more logical to move at an even greater distance?"

Deven shook his head. "It would if we knew the trajectory they were coming from. I suspect they will come in on a course near the Moon. And even if they don't, at L1 we should be able to intercept them if needed. Any farther out, and they might reach the Earth before we could reach them."

Minerva nodded. "Logical. Activating engines." The rear of the *Phoenix* began to glow brighter as power flowed into the overdrive engines. A bubble of blue energy formed around the *Phoenix* a second before she flashed and disappeared, leaving blue streaks in her wake. "We will reach L1 in twenty minutes." The image shrank to a point and disappeared.

"Good. Galina, start moving towards L1. I know we don't have full engines yet but start," Deven said.

"I can try. I'm not sure we have enough to break free of the Moon's gravity. I could try slingshotting us around instead."

Deven shook his head. "At this point do what you can, but don't try a slingshot maneuver yet. With Gregory and Dakarth working on the repairs, we should have the engines back soon enough."

She nodded, tapping controls on her console. "Roger." The *Defiant's* main engines grew brighter as power flowed. The ship lurched in the direction of the Earth before one of the engines failed and started turning the ship in the wrong direction. Galina quickly grabbed the controls, rotating the ship to compensate, pushing it back on course. Then she flipped the ship again to keep from overshooting the target before initiating a breaking maneuver and shutting down the engines. "Blast it! One of the engines failed and imbalanced the whole system. I can compensate, but it will require me rotating the ship every few minutes and fly in a zig-zag pattern towards L1."

"Don't waste the energy, we will have to wait until Gregory and Dakarth get them fixed. With his nano kit, it shouldn't be long." He reached down, grabbed Aleshia's hand and pulled her to her feet. "Come on sweetheart, let's get out of these suits."

She leaned close to his ear. "Now?"

He grinned. "Why not? While they are comfortable enough, they are also a little close feeling and I would rather be wearing my normal clothes. Don't you feel the same?"

She nodded. "I thought it was just me."

He pulled her towards the hatch. "We will back soon."

26

Deven entered their quarters with Aleshia right behind. He turned, flicked on the light, then pressed the control pad on the front of his suit. A seam formed starting at the neck and split down until it reached his groin. He started wiggling out of the suit. He turned when it was proving more difficult than he thought and saw Aleshia smiling. "Are you going to help me or stand with that grin?"

She giggled. "Oh I don't know, I was thinking I would just watch you for a while. You always liked to watch me get out of a slinky dress. Tit for tat, as they say." She giggled again then broke out in outright laughter as Deven couldn't get the one side off his left shoulder and the other hand was bound up in the sleeve.

His eyes narrowed as his jaw jutted forward. "Quit laughing and help me."

She put a hand over her mouth. "Sorry love, I couldn't help it. Here, let me give you a hand."

"Two would be preferable," Deven said with a grunt.

Aleshia walked over and pulled at his left shoulder. The suit flipped off and slid down. "It is a bit tight. Amazing it doesn't feel that way when it is on."

Deven peeled the rest of the suit down, placed on the floor

next to his desk, pulled out a pair of underwear from a drawer, slid them on, grabbed a pair of jeans from another drawer, and pulled them on as well. "No kidding. They are amazing but," he moved around a bit flexing his legs and arms, "oh that does feel better. Or at least more normal."

Aleshia blinked. "You really just wanted to get out of these suits?"

"Of course, what did you think I meant? We need to get back to the bridge. It won't take Gregory and Dakarth much time to fix everything."

"But I thought–"

The *Defiant* lurched forward.

The intercom beeped and Deven hit the control with his elbow as he pulled on a white shirt. "What is it? The engines back online?"

Galina chuckled. "Thought you might have noticed. We should be there in about thirty minutes. We could get in half the time, but I don't want to push the engines at this point if we don't have to."

"I agree. Thirty minutes is fine. It will give everyone the time to finish the repairs."

"Yeah, I was thinking that as well," Galina said before the com clicked off.

"Sweetheart, having problems getting out of the suit?"

Aleshia glared at him. "No." She touched a pad, the seam opened, she slipped out of the suit much easier than he did, threw it in the corner, grabbed a fresh set of clothes, slipped into her panties, bra, jeans, and green shirt in less than a minute.

Deven stood there for a minute, stunned. "How did you do it so fast?"

Her eyes narrowed and one word slid out of the one corner

of her mouth. "Practice." She harrumphed sitting down to put on her socks and sneakers.

Deven blinked. "Are you mad at me, sweetheart?"

Aleshia's head jutted up. "Mad? Now why in the world would I be mad?" She stood, took two steps out of their quarters and into the hallway. "Well come on Mr. Doran. The bridge is waiting." She left without waiting for a reply.

Now I know I'm in trouble. Deven sighed as he flipped off the light, closed the hatch to their quarters, and headed up to the bridge.

In engineering, Gregory tried to get the engines back into balance like he had seen Leon do it. "This is a lot harder than I thought."

Dakarth looked up from the device in his hand. Its screen continued scrolling as he pressed another pad with his thumb-talon. "Calibration alwayssss tricky. Try adjusting the wave output another three hundredths of a percent."

"That isn't enough to do anything! If I don't get this right in the next minute, the engines are going to shut down and Galina will be yelling 'I'm no Leon again'," Gregory said as he blew out a breath.

"It will. Trust me." Dakarth's eyes drifted back down to the device in his palm, focusing on the attached screen.

"Okay, but if they go down, you take the heat."

His head shot up. "Heat? Are the engines overheating?"

Gregory laughed. "No, I meant you can take the blame when Galina calls."

"Oh, I understand. Very well, if needed. But it won't be. Trust me."

"I hope so," Gregory said twisting a dial. A few seconds later, the engines hummed in perfect synchronicity. "It worked!"

"I told you. Shall we finish the weapons? We were almost done when asked to work on the engines. My nanos should have finished all but the focusing crystals."

Gregory grabbed two spare cables, a diagnostic tab, a package of new lenses, a package of focusing crystals off a parts shelf, and stuffed them into the black bag at his feet. "Right with you."

Inside Otis' quarters aboard the *Defiant*, he tried to access the copy of the data he grabbed from Dakarth's system earlier but failed. The data was horribly mangled. At the time, he didn't notice the cable he used wasn't a perfect fit. In fact, the port was octagonal with a big round pin in the center. He knew the data had to be binary, as he did see some code Dakarth had used. He could adapt a cable to fit, but the real trick would be converting the data to something he could read. He worked for several minutes on one of his spare cables shaping the end. It wasn't an exact fit but very close.

He carefully pushed the reworked cable into the device's port and the other end into his data tab. For several minutes he tried various protocols he had used in the past, to no avail. Then he brought up the code he had seen Dakarth use. It wasn't complete, but he recognized several of the protocols. He used one of his own tools with the Lytherian protocol and a little of the data used when he accessed the Celloid. It was a real plumber's nightmare, but it couldn't hurt. "And if it don't work, Dakarth can take a swing at it," he muttered.

He did locate the data recorded from the Ixeon base, but the mass refused to release any useful information. After trying several different access points, he got a toe-hold. A return of coherent data! He further tweaked the system and ran another recovery. Finally, the data cracked open, giving him a view of what the Ixeon had tried to hide. "Oh no!" He grabbed the equipment and ran for the bridge.

Otis jumped through the hatch and onto the bridge. "You won't believe what I found! The Ixeons have the plans to our carbine cannons! Someone on Earth sent it to them!"

Miles' camera turned in time to see Deven appear behind Otis in the doorway. "Yes, we know."

Otis whirled around. "You knew? Well geez, why didn't you tell me?"

Deven cracked a grin. "I only found out a few minutes ago myself. You were heading down to the hangar bay when Leon told us." He took a step past Otis and walked over to his console. "Did you find anything else?"

"Only that, and he transmitted it to someone else in deep space by the sounds. I couldn't target a trajectory though with the information left."

Aleshia appeared in the hatchway and glanced at Otis. She stepped past him and went over to sit next to Deven. "Wonder what they wanted that for?"

"I don't know, but it can't be good. From what I could tell, he contacted someone on Earth, who then gave him the plans. So we have a spy or something down there."

"And that someone is Lavine," Galina said.

"Oh great, and friends with the Ixeons? Who knows what damage he'll do."

Galina grinned. "Not much now. Halburn has him in custody."

Otis plopped down in the closest chair. "Well geez, I hear everything last around here."

"Did you find anything else? Nothing about the Lytherians?" Deven said.

Otis shook his head. "Nope, at least not yet. I can try picking through the data some more, but our buggy friend didn't leave much behind. From what I can tell, when the base started its self-destruct, it purged and shut down all the systems. A lot of what I snagged before got corrupted. Only the most recent data survived intact."

Deven raised an eyebrow. "Then shouldn't you be able to extrapolate where he transmitted the data about our weapons?"

Otis sighed. "Should yes, but so far nada. I'm not sure, but it is possible Mr. Buggy deleted that data even from the backups. And if so, these bugs are really cautious. More than I even would have been, I think."

Deven chuckled. "Do you really think so? I don't. You would have killed it all and left them nothing to find at all right from the start."

Otis cracked a grin. "Guilty as charged."

Dakarth appeared though the hatch. "We have completed repairsssss to all affected systems and augmented the cannons with suggestions from your Miles. I have also added more resilience to the focusing lenses, increasing the power output they can tolerate before deterioration."

Deven nodded. "Thank you, Dakarth. Perhaps you can help Otis with the Ixeon data?"

Dakarth inclined his smooth head. "Of coursssse," he turned towards Otis, "do you have my device?"

"I do it's right–" he padded the pocket at his right hip, "drat I left it down in my quarters."

The Lytherian's eyes enlarged. "Why issss it there?"

"I was taking a look at the data, I didn't find much other than someone on Earth sent the plans to our carbine cannons to the Ixeons."

Dakarth's head jutted forward. "What? Why would someone do that?"

"A traitor," Deven said.

Dakarth turned. "A traitor is one thing, but to betray one's entire race? That I cannot understand. It risks his life as much as anyone else."

Galina snorted. "Somehow I don't think Lavine cares one way or the other."

Miles' camera turned. "That is not logical Galina, for a human to do as suggested, there must have been a compelling reason."

Deven nodded. "They must have promised him something."

Dakarth cocked his head. "It still does not make sense to me, what could one offer to compel such a thing? But I don't think it will help the Ixeons. With these modifications, the cannons are much different from the standard systems."

"True," Otis said, "they only got the standard plans, not the changes you made before, or the further enhancements today."

Dakarth nodded. "Yessss, old data that won't help them. But let's look at the details and make sure."

Otis stood. "Right," he stepped past Dakarth and pointed,

"this way, I will show you my quarters where I left your device."

They left the bridge as Deven blew out a breath. "I hope they are right."

27

On the *Defiant's* bridge, Miles' camera turned towards Deven. "We have arrived at L1."

"Bot, would you let me tell him?" Galina grumbled.

"But Galina, he told me to let him know as soon as we had arrived."

"He told me, not you."

Deven chuckled. "Actually, I said it to both of you. Although, I was talking more to Galina."

"See?"

Deven rolled his eyes as he tapped the com on his console. "Otis, Dakarth, any progress?"

"Nope sorry Boss, haven't found anything more. I had hoped Dakarth's tools would have been better than mine, but he hasn't found anything else."

"It issss disappointing. I thought between the two of us, there would have been more progress," Dakarth said.

"Keep at it, there must be more."

"I really doubt it Boss, it looks like the system dumped everything when it started the self-destruct as I feared."

"Yessss I concur," Dakarth said.

"Well, give it one more shot. Perhaps we can find what the Ixeon's next step is."

"Will try Boss," Otis said a second before the com clicked off.

Aleshia looked at Deven. "Do you really think they will find anything more?"

"I doubt it, but like I said, it is worth another shot. We are sitting here waiting anyway. We know something is coming, but where, when, and what are the questions."

She took his hand into hers. "Do you want me to go over to the *Phoenix* and try the chair?"

Deven shook his head. "No, I want you here for now. And I doubt you will find the Ixeons. You didn't last time."

Aleshia grinned. "But I wasn't looking for them either."

"Point taken. Okay, if we Dakarth and Otis don't come up with anything soon, we will go over to the *Phoenix*."

Aleshia stood with her hands on her hips and her right foot began tapping. "I'm perfectly able to go over myself, you know."

Deven grinned. "I know, but I would feel better if I came along, okay? But we might have to borrow Otis' truck to do it. Not sure he will be too happy about that."

"Perhaps not, but he did let Leon take it back over to the *Phoenix*."

Galina lit up like a light blub. "That works! Have Leon come back and you two go over." Her grin could swallow a Cheshire cat.

Miles' camera rotated towards Deven. "I hate to interrupt, but I have detected something on the extreme range of sensors."

Deven sat forward. "Let me see it." The screen to his right with a page of scrolling diagnostic data vanished, revealing a pinpoint dot in the middle. The sensor data reflected nothing more than its location. "No idea what it is?"

"No, it is too far. But I detect it is approaching at a high rate of speed."

"Gotta be the Ixeons," Galina said.

Deven folded his arms. "Maybe. Miles, how long until we know what it is?"

Miles' camera iris contracted, then expanded. "If the current rate remains constant, five minutes. And the *Phoenix* is calling."

The main screen by the bridge windows lit up, showing Leon and Minerva. "We have detected something inbound. Unknown what it is at this point," Leon said.

Deven nodded. "We picked it up as well. Miles says we will get a better idea in five minutes."

Minerva nodded. "Possibly six or seven for us. The *Phoenix's* long-range systems are not quite as powerful."

Dakarth sat in the main pilot's of his shuttle and tapped another button. He had plugged in the device containing the data from the Ixeon base, but they still had not found anything more.

Otis leaned forward and pointed towards one screen. "I had hoped your shuttle's equipment would have better luck. Try that other algorithm on this section here, perhaps we can see something."

"I doubt that will help. We tried the E1, the E2 won't make a difference."

Otis straightened. "Maybe try them both?"

Dakarth regarded him. "At the same time? That will only make a messss."

"Can't hurt though can it?"

"True. All right, I try." Dakarth tapped another control and the data scrolling morphed and changed as he manipulated it. It shifted several times but nothing coherent appeared. "I told you."

Otis shrugged. "It was worth a try."

"Yessss. The problem is not enough data. There should be a lot more here. There was when we first found the Ixeon data."

Otis folded his arms. "I know, I think the base deleted everything when it activated the auto-destruct."

Dakarth blinked slowly as he stood. "Yessss, the only explanation."

Otis heard a slight beep and whirled around to see a short Mechand with a trailer behind him. "CB! What are you doing here? You were supposed to stay with Minerva."

The Mechand's optics lowered and gave an even lower beep.

"I get you wanted to be with me, but I told you Minerva needed you more."

An even lower beep emanated from the Mechand.

"Of course I am happy to see you. But you still should have stayed on the *Phoenix*. How did you get here?"

The Mechand's eyes went up, and he pointed towards the back of the shuttle and the other vehicles that lay beyond. The closest one had a compartment in the back with a tarp that could be stretched over it.

Otis folded his arms. "You hid in the back of my truck?"

Another beep came from the Mechand as his eyes drifted down.

Otis sucked in a breath and blew it out slowly. "No, I'm not going to send you back right now."

Dakarth seeing the exchange between the two, pointed. "Who issss this?"

"Oh sorry, Dakarth this is CB. CB this is Dakarth."

The CB turned, beeped, and his rubberized hand extended out towards Dakarth.

Dakarth eyed the outstretched hand, not sure what to do for a minute. Then he remembered the strange custom of humans to shake hands. He reached out, grabbed the Mechand's hand, and shook it. "Hello."

CB beeped and retracted his hand.

Otis pointed towards the back of the shuttle and the extended ramp. "I think we had better give Deven the bad news."

"Yessss."

CB beeped and moved closer to Otis.

"Yes, you can come too, CB."

The Mechand gave a loud beep and somehow managed to leap a centimeter into the air even with his hopper attached.

Miles' camera turned as his iris flicked open and closed. "Deven, the object has reached full scanning range, however, the data is lacking. Image now on main screen."

The screen flickered as something huge appeared on it. The object still failed to generate a clear image, but enough to determine the general size.

Another, smaller screen on a console near Deven changed showing Minerva's face. "The object has been identified. The Ixeon's next rock has appeared. And this one is exponentially larger than the one I encountered."

Deven nodded. "Yes, we see it as well. We still can't get a clear image of it. Are you sure it is a Sileic?"

Minerva blinked. "Do you doubt my assessment? I would never forget the rock that almost rolled over me."

They heard a light snort. Minerva's eyes darted to the left. "And don't you say anything."

Leons face appeared on another screen. "Oh trust me, she's sure. I have heard nothing else in the last three minutes."

Minerva's eyes narrowed as lines on her jaw formed. "I asked you not to tell them."

Leon grinned "I think they already knew."

"Leon, are the modifications to the carbine cannons ready on the *Phoenix*?" Deven said.

Minerva's eyes narrowed further but didn't say anything. "Yes, Minerva's Mechands finished a few minutes ago."

Deven's one eyebrow raised. "You didn't do them?"

Leon shrugged. "Didn't need to, it was a simple modification."

Minerva's eyes went wide. "Simple! Ha! They had to pull each unit, reconfigure several components, and install a more robust power transfer system!"

Leon peered to his right for a second. "As I was saying, a relatively simple modification. What she didn't mention is she had all of them done at once. I couldn't have done them all that fast." A grin crept across her face as she nodded at the compliment. "We haven't tested them yet."

"That shouldn't be necessary," Minerva said.

Leons eyes darted to the right for half a second. "As I was saying, we haven't tested them yet. Do you want us to?"

Deven shook his head. "I don't want them to know any more than they do until the last possible second. If we go testing weapons, two things will happen, they will know we see them coming, and two, they will see our weapons have been modified. I don't want to give them any time for countermeasures."

Leon nodded. "Right." Both images shrank to a point and disappeared.

"Shouldn't we intercept?" Galina said.

"No, not yet. I think we have time."

Galina blinked. "Time for what? Other than to wait for it to get here?"

"There is still a chance Dakarth and Otis will get something out of the Ixeon's data."

"Do you really think that is likely?" Aleshia said. "It seems like they would have long before now if there was anything to find."

"I know, but I still have hope," Deven grinned. "In the meantime, they are not expecting our little surprise. If we do anything other than wait, they might think otherwise."

Aboard the *Phoenix*, Leon paced across the bridge. Minerva followed him with her eyes several times before her brow furrowed. "You do realize this is not going to accomplish anything? You will wear out long before my decks will. This behavior is not like you."

Leon stopped and turned. "I know, but I don't think sitting here is the way to deal with whatever the Ixeons are throwing at us."

She raised an eyebrow. "And what do you propose?"

"I don't know. That is the problem. I don't have any better ideas."

Minerva nodded. "I understand, but attempting to wear out my deck plate will not help the situation."

Leon plopped down in the nearest chair, his back complaining loudly from the hard seat. "I know, but at least it gives me something to do other than sit here. I never should have agreed to swap places with Otis."

"Do you dislike my company?"

"No, of course not. But I would rather be on the *Defiant*, nothing against you or the *Phoenix*. The *Defiant* is my ship."

Minerva cracked a grin. "And Galina is over there."

Leon spun his chair around grasping for words. "What? Of course, she is. Where else–"

"I didn't say this, but the more you try to deny it, the more evident it becomes. Take it from someone who has watched this happen far more times than you could count. Although, I am sure I could, given time."

Leon spun his chair back towards the console. "I don't have any idea what you are talking about."

Minerva nodded. "Of course you don't. But you will in time I suspect. I–"

Leon spun his chair back towards Minerva's screen. "Minerva? What happened? You don't ever stop mid-sentence."

"The object is accelerating and changed course taking a more direct route. It will arrive at L1 in less than two minutes."

28

Miles' camera turned. "I detect the object has accelerated and is approaching L1 on a more direct route."

Galina sighed. "No doubt they spotted us."

Deven blew out a breath. "None, but I didn't think we would go undetected. However, at least we can take first crack at them here at L1. Hopefully we can beat them. We did the last time."

"I hope so," Galina said.

"I am receiving a transmission from the *Phoenix*, image now on screen," Miles said.

The largest screen flickered and the bridge of the *Phoenix* appeared. "The object has accelerated and will intersect our position in less than two minutes."

"Miles mentioned that. Is the *Phoenix* ready?"

"Ready as she will ever be," Leon said.

The bridge hatch opened with Dakarth and Otis appearing in the doorway. "Sorry Boss, we couldn't find anything more," Otis said.

"Yessss, very disappointing." Dakarth said. Behind him, having left his hopper in the hangar bay, the Mechand rolled forward and beeped in agreement.

Galina blinked. "What is that doing here?"

Otis turned around. "Why that is CB."

Galina blinked again. "I know it is that Cleaning Mechand. But what is it doing here?"

Otis shrugged. "Apparently he snuck over."

"He snuck over? We're in space! How?"

Deven grinned. "Let me guess, he hid in the back of your truck and slipped out before Leon went back over to the *Phoenix*?"

"Right Boss, you got it in one."

Miles' camera turned towards Deven. "I am detecting an unusual abnormality in the object making scanning problematic. At the current range, I cannot determine the reason for the difficulty. While I can ascertain it is larger than either the *Phoenix* or the *Defiant,* no further data is possible."

Minerva nodded. "I have detected this as well."

Leon tapped several controls on his console aboard the *Phoenix.* "You're right Miles. This is odd. I have seen the scans of the previous Sileic and other than rough size, we have zilch. We should have more than this."

Otis hopped into a nearby chair with Dakarth taking the one next to him. CB rolled up closer. Otis tapped several buttons on the console in front of him, pulling up an image and the scan details. "Yes, we know it is big and approaching fast. But that is it."

On the central screen, Leon nodded. "This might be something different."

"The object will arrive in twenty seconds," Miles said.

Deven hit the nearby com. "Shields up and target all carbine cannons. The minute it gets in range be ready to blast it," Deven said.

"We're ready down here," Gregory said, "the instant you give the word."

"Good, stand by."

"Do you think they sent something else? Or did they add stealth tech to the Sileics?" Aleshia said.

Dakarth turned around and pointed a talon towards the object on his screen. "If that were the casssse, we wouldn't be detecting it at all."

"I don't like it," Galina said, "let's get outta here."

Deven folded his arms. "And go where? It will follow us right back to Earth in a heartbeat."

The object entered unaided visual range and in a microsecond stopped its rapid approach. It became clear, to their horror, their suspicions were correct, and this was indeed a Sileic. Much larger than the previous one, it turned revealing the perfect tesseract with almost an immaculate mirror finish. The Sun's rays glinted off of the Sileic as it continued to turn, reflecting images of the *Defiant* and the *Phoenix* with the Earth framed perfectly in the background.

On the main screen, Leon shuddered as he turned around. "I think I know why they did the mirror finish. To reflect our cannons. It also gave them the advantage of partially blocking our sensors."

"What! How?" Galina said.

Miles' camera rotated to face Galina. "It is quite simple, the more reflective a surface is, the less energy will be absorbed. It is possible our carbine cannons will have a negligible effect, if any."

"I wasn't asking you, you fool bot!" Galina said.

Dakarth turned back to his console, tapping on the controls. Data poured past on his screen. "Thissss is most disconcerting."

"You're telling me. What are we going to do, Boss?" Otis said.

CB gave a low beep.

Deven sucked in a breath of filtered air and let it out slow. "Hope our cannons work. We don't have any other option."

Twin white beams erupted out of the Sileic's top right corner and crashed into the *Defiant* and *Phoenix.* "Shields are holding," Minerva said.

"Good, perhaps they will give us enough time for our cannons to work. Target the starting point of those beams and fire the instant you have a lock!"

Every cannon on the *Defiant* lashed out, pummeling the Sileic with the *Phoenix* starting half a second later.

"Status?" Deven said.

Miles' camera turned. "While we are having an effect, it is negligible. The beams continue to prevent maneuverability. The shields are holding, however, I am detecting an increased harmonic. This could indicate an attempt to breach them."

On the screen, Minerva's eyes narrowed. "I concur. I also do not have the power to continue this indefinitely."

Miles' camera iris flicked closed and opened again. "The *Defiant* cannot either. I estimate we can continue for six minutes before the power drain forces us to shut down weapons. The shields will last for at least another four minutes after that, if the Sileic beam continues at its current rate."

"Our shields will last only four minutes after the cannons go kaput? This just keeps getting better and better," Galina said.

"And mine even less," Minerva said.

"Leon, Dakarth, what if increase power to the cannons?" Deven said.

"I doubt it will do anything other than drain us faster. I did another scan, and the Sileic is not crumbling like the last one.

So far all we have done is blacken the location around where the beams emanate," Leon said.

Dakarth pulled a device from his belt, opened it revealing the tiny screen, plugged a cable into a port on the side, and the other end into the console where he sat. Text flashed across the diminutive screen. He nodded. "I don't ssssee how increasing power will work. But, maybe we could adjust the frequency, shifting it very fast."

The *Phoenix* shuddered and Leon glanced up from his console. "It might work. Worth a try for certain."

"Do it. How long until you can have it implemented?" Deven said.

Miles' camera turned towards him. "I have implemented the changes."

Minerva nodded. "As have I. There is an increase in degradation at the point of impact."

The *Defiant* shook again. "Yesss slight, but it is there," Dakarth said. The twin beams holding both ships increased in size and ferocity. "However, the Sileic had responded. Shields will fail in three minutes."

"Great," Otis said gritting his teeth as a panel near him blew out, "why does the rock care? It's not like we are going to do anything to it at this rate. Why start hitting us harder now?"

The shaking became more intense and Deven sat forward in his chair. "Perhaps we are doing more than we think, otherwise it wouldn't have changed tactics. Keep pouring it on. Can we increase the power and still keep the frequency shift?"

"I heard that," Gregory said through the com, "I wouldn't recommend it. The cannons already don't like the changes you did before. Right now the focusing lenses are going to crack in two minutes, maybe three. Then we won't be able to hit a broadside of a barn. If we increase power now, they will crack now instead if in a minute."

"And the *Phoenix's* will fail sooner than that," Minerva said with a frown.

Deven bit the inside of his cheek as his nose wrinkled at the smell of fried and overloaded circuits. "Dakarth, can you contact Karthish?"

Otis blinked. "What are they going to do? They are in worse shape than we are."

"I can try," Dakarth said. He tapped a few controls on the device in his hand. "I cannot, something issss blocking the signal. I will try my shuttle." He got up and ran for the main hangar bay, three-toed boots pounding the deck plates. Fifteen seconds later, he thundered up the ramp of his shuttle and jammed on the communications control with his talon. "Commander Karthish, do you receive?" he said as each breath came in ragged gasps. The screen wavered and flashed several times, but no response. He tapped another control. "I cannot get through."

The *Defiant* shook again as the lights began to flicker.

On the bridge, Deven grabbed Aleshia's hand. "Darling, it is up to you. See if you can get in contact with Karthish."

Aleshia blinked. "I can barely reach him with the chair! I can't do it here!"

"Try!" Galina said.

"All right." She closed her eyes and reached out with her mind. *Karthish, can you hear me? We need you! The Sileics are far stronger than last time, and we can't hang on much longer. Karthish? Please!* She didn't feel him or any of the Lytherians on the fringes of the inner solar system. She tried again, pushing herself beyond her previous limits. *Karthish? We need you!* She opened her eyes again and wished she didn't, grabbing her head as a wave of pain crashed through her brain. She cringed, wobbling back and forth in her chair.

Deven felt the pain in her mind reverberate out, causing even him to shudder. He squeezed her hand. "Are you all right?"

She blinked through tears. "No! And I couldn't reach him either. I told you!"

On the *Phoenix* a cannon lens cracked, causing an overload in its systems. Minerva shut it down, but not before the lens itself had melted, rendering the cannon useless. She shuddered. "One of the lenses has failed and took the cannon with it."

On the *Defiant* a lens cracked, splintering its red beam into tiny shards before melting into a pile of goo constipating the whole cannon. Gregory shut it down, but not before the excess of power caused one of the capacitors to blow in a bright yellow-orange display and shaking the *Defiant* in the process. "That's one of our cannons gone. I'm sure the rest aren't far behind," he said through the com.

"I concur," Minerva said as another cannon blew. Her systems ran through simulation after simulation in an eye-blink. Each one worse than the last. "Approximately minute thirty-seconds before the rest fail. Shields will fail shortly after."

Galina gripped the controls. "We still can't move."

A spark on a nearby console grew and raced towards the one in front of Leon. He dove aside as the energy mushroomed out into a ball of blasted plastic and glass. Minerva frowned. "Our sensors have now failed. *Defiant*, are yours still functional?"

Miles' camera turned. "Yes, at twenty percent capacity. I

can no longer tell if we are having an effect on the Sileic or not."

The *Defiant* shook again as another cannon blew. "I doubt it, at least not enough to stop it. Boss, what are we going to do?" Otis said.

Deven straightened. "Leon? What would happen if we overload our main power core?" Everyone on the *Defiant*'s bridge turned to stare at him.

CB Beeped.

"I agree. Boss? Did I hear you right?"

On the screen, Leon blinked. "You know what will happen! The *Defiant* will blow sky-high!"

"Yes, but it also might take the Sileic with us. It is Lytherian enhanced, it might have enough of a punch to crack that thing in two."

"That's a big if," Leon said.

Galina rolled her eyes. "And here I thought Leon was insane, you just topped it!"

The *Defiant* shuttered again as another cannon erupted into a ball of uncontrolled energy. "If anyone has a better idea, I'm open. But in a minute we will blow one way or the other. This way, we might take them with us." He flicked a finger across the open com. "Dakarth, did you hear? Can you do it?"

"Yessss, I can. Heading to engineering now," Dakarth said as he ran from the shuttle down the ramp, down the corridor and back towards engineering. A few seconds later he pulled a device from his hip and plugged it into the main power core. He tapped on several keys and the central core began to glow brighter. Dakarth sighed as he hit the nearby com. "Overload in progresses. Detonation in thirty seconds."

"While the *Phoenix*'s power core is not as powerful, I shall do the same. We will not survive the *Defiant's* detonation anyway," Minerva said.

The *Defiant* shuddered again as another cannon blew and more systems began to fail. "Understood. I hope it works," Deven said.

"We all do," Galina said.

29

Aboard the *Defiant* Miles' camera turned. "I am detecting something large on approach. It will arrive in forty seconds."

Galina grit her teeth. "Great, another Sileic. Can we take out two?"

Aboard the *Phoenix*, Leon gripped the console to keep from being thrown as the ship shook. "I doubt we will destroy it, but we should give it a few cracks and keep it from going anywhere for a while. Perhaps someone else can finish the job."

"My core is reaching critical. Detonation in ten seconds," Minerva said.

Miles' camera iris flicked open and closed. "The second ship is not a Sileic, the configuration is very different."

"What is it then?" Galina said.

"I cannot tell what it is with the sensor damage, only what it is not."

With a giant flash, the Lytherian *Command* carrier appeared off the bow of the *Defiant*.

Deven saw the massive ship moving towards the Sileic through the bridge window. He pointed. "It's Karthish's ship! Stop the overloads! Cease fire!"

Down in engineering, Dakarth's eyes went wide as he

tapped controls as fast as he could. "Overload stopped, power core returning to normal."

"I have done the same," Minerva said. "Five more seconds, and we wouldn't have had the option."

And one of the smaller bridge screens on both ships flickered, flashed and resolved into the face of Commander Karthish. "We apologize for being late. We are about to fire our main weapon. Prepare yourselves." Energy surged through the ship settling in the nose where it launched forward with flawless accuracy to impact the precise location where the beams holding the *Defiant* and *Phoenix* originated. A wave of energy mushroomed out from that spot a second after.

"We're free!" Galina said.

"As are we," Minerva said.

"Please move away. We will take care of this," Karthish said.

Dakarth ran onto the *Defiant's* bridge panting in the thinner air. His long tongue hung slack on the right side of his mouth and sweat ran down the side of his smooth head. "Commander! I think all shipssss are needed."

Karthish's eyes narrowed. "Explain."

"Based on my analysissss, we couldn't do enough damage because the Sileic adapted itself to reflect most of the energy from human cannons. While ours are different, they are not calibrated to crumble the Sileic with the proper frequencies. While adjustments could be made, I do not think we will have time before the Sileic will leave and adapt."

On the screen, Karthish folded his arms. "And your recommendation?"

"Use the *Command* carrier's main weapon at full power. It should fracture the surface, giving the human ship's a toe-hold I believe is their expression. A starting point. The modifications should work then."

Karthish nodded. "Then we shall do so. *Defiant, Phoenix,* move behind us. The energy backlash might damage you otherwise."

"You don't have to tell us twice," Galina said gripping the *Defiant's* controls. "We're sluggish, the engines have taken damage, but we're moving."

Minerva nodded as the *Phoenix's* engines grew brighter. One flickered and went out, causing her to adjust power in the remaining engines to compensate. "Acknowledged. We are moving into a position behind the Lytherian Command carrier."

Aboard the *Command* carrier, Karthish looked to his right. Erson sat at the controls, adjusting them. "Locked on target sir, full power at your command. The target is starting to move away."

Karthish straightened as his eyes narrowed. "You aren't getting away that easy. Execute."

Erson tapped a control and all the lights on the *Command* carrier dimmed as a vast amount of energy from a power core larger than the *Defiant* itself, diverted from all systems, and poured into a massive accumulator. It built exponentially until it rammed forward into the nose of the vessel. A beam three times the size of the *Defiant* erupted from the exit point slamming into the Sileic. Much of the beam fragmented on impact, sending splinters of energy in all directions. The *Command* carrier's shields glowed from the contact of multiple strikes. When the glow subsided, they could see several large cracks emanated out from the center of the Sileic like a spider web. With a sizable chunk of the mirrored finish missing at the center of the web.

Aboard the *Command* carrier, the lights remained dim. "Power rebuild in two minutes, sir," Erson said.

Karthish nodded. "*Defiant, Phoenix,* there is your hole. Hit with all you have."

On the *Defiant,* Deven grinned. "Thanks, Karthish. You heard the man. Move out, target that hole, and open fire with every cannon we have left."

"I hope four is enough," Gregory's voice came through the com.

Deven sighed. "It's going to have to be."

The *Defiant* and *Phoenix* moved out from behind the massive Lytherian carrier with the *Defiant* moving to a position off of the starboard side and the *Phoenix* went port. The Sileic stayed motionless.

"Think they killed it? It's not moving." Aleshia said.

"It's playing possum," Galina said. "Gotta be."

"I agree," Dakarth said.

Deven noticed Leon wasn't on the *Phoenix's* bridge. "Where is Leon?"

Minerva's eyes darted across her screen. "We only have one cannon left. He went to see if he could get another one operational. I told him it was hopeless, but he wouldn't listen to me."

Galina chuckled. "Minerva, never, ever, doubt Leon."

"Even I know this," Miles said.

A grin swept across Minerva's face. "If you say so. And I am in position."

Deven blew out a breath. "Target all remaining cannons and fire at will."

"Locked and firing in three seconds," Gregory said.

The tips of the cannons glowed half a second before beams leapt from the *Defiant* hitting the exact center of the missing mirror finish on the Sileic followed by a single beam from the *Phoenix*.

Leon jumped up from under the port forward cannon and slapped the closest nearby com. "Minerva, fire the port forward cannon."

"But that was one of the first to blow."

"Trust me. I don't know exactly how long it will hold, but only the power lines fried, I replaced most of them from other cannons. Do it!"

Minerva nodded. "Understood. Activating."

Another beam, a little smaller than the others, reached out from the *Phoenix* and converged with the rest at the center of the Sileic.

"Look!" Aleshia said leaping to her feet. "I think I see it vibrating!"

Miles' camera turned. "I cannot confirm due to damaged sustained to the sensors."

Deven stood up and bounced over to the window. Even the gravity plating had stared to fail. He squinted, seeing slight variations in the stars around the edge of the Sileic. "I think she is right."

Karthish's image smiled. "She is. Our sensors confirm a sine-wave is building up internally causing degradation in the stability of the silicon structure. And it is accelerating. We estimate it will reach critical levels in three minutes."

"Three more minutes ..." Deven said.

"I don't know if the cannons will last that long," Gregory said over the com, "two are redlining now."

"And I only have two cannons left, and one of them I'm certain it will fail before that," Minerva said.

"It'll hold for that long," Leon said over the *Phoenix's* com.

"I don't see how, I have run numerous simulations and they all–"

"It will hold!" Leon said. "And I will stay here to make certain it does!"

Galina bit her lip. "If Leon stays it will hold, I wouldn't worry about it. Ours, on the other hand ..."

"Gregory, better lower power on those two cannons," Deven said

"I already did! And the temps are still climbing."

Leon winced as he overheard. "Seal the bulkheads and vent those cannons. Let the icy cold of space cool them."

"But that would increase degradation in other areas of the system."

"But it won't matter, we only need another minute."

"Do it," Deven said.

Gregory sighed. "Right. Sealing and venting cannons two and eight." The *Defiant* shuddered from the quick venting of atmosphere and began shifting, rotating to port.

"That is throwing us out if position! I'm trying to compensate," Galina said.

The four beams from the *Defiant* edged slightly off dead center for half a second before Gregory reacquired the lock. "We moved a bit, but not out of the hole. And both cannon's temps are holding."

"But not going down?" Leon said.

"Nope."

"Not good. That means the situation has only marginally improved or the temperature would be going down."

Gregory's eyebrows met as his nose scrunched up. "I figured."

As the energy beams continued to pummel the Sileic, cracks

continued to deepen. Two seconds later the whole Sileic increased its vibration.

The *Defiant* shook as one cannon failed violently. "Number two just blew," Gregory said, "and eight won't last much longer."

"I hope it is enough" Deven peered out the viewport watching the cracks spread throughout the Silic grow in slow motion. The Sileic began vibrating even faster as it tried to pull away. "Oh no you don't. Minerva, Gregory increase power to maximum. We can't let it get away."

"But that will blow what we have left for certain!" Gregory said.

Minerva's eyes darted around the screen as calculations ran through her mind. "I have to concur."

Deven jabbed a finger, arm stretched outwards towards the window. "And if that thing gets away, we won't have another chance like this again. Do it!"

Gregory blew out a very audible breath over the com. "Increasing power." Half a second after he did, the eighth cannon exploded. "There goes number eight. The rest aren't far behind. Ten seconds or less."

On the *Phoenix*, a port side cannon failed in the same fashion. "And I am down to one."

"Yes but look!" Deven pointed again towards the Sileic. The cracks grew even brighter than before as they reached through to the other side, separating the Sileic into many large chunks. Each chunk pushed on its own trajectory by the cannons, moved farther from the others as more cracks formed causing each one to split into many more sections. One of the smallest pieces flew off in a different direction before the rest crumbled to dust. Both ships shut down the what remained of the cannons a few seconds before they shut themselves down in a more permanent fashion.

Miles' camera iris flicked closed and opened again very slowly. "Target has been destroyed."

Galina stood up like a shot and almost bounced off the ceiling. "Whoohooo!"

Aleshia bounced over and grabbed Deven, hugging him. "We did it!"

Otis made a fist and shot it in the air. "Yeah!" CB gave a loud reverberating beep as he rolled back and forth several times.

Deven relaxed for what felt like the first time in weeks. "By the skin of our teeth, but yes, we did it." He looked around the bridge at the blacked and burned consoles, and thought about the areas of the ship blasted by either the Sileic or by their own cannons. The ship was a mess, but they were alive, and she was fixable. And more importantly, the Earth was safe.

Deven turned and sat back down in his chair. He leaned towards the com, "Hey Leon, surprised you're not saying anything."

Aleshia's eyes went wide. "He wasn't in the room with the cannon that exploded, was he?"

"No, that was cannon three, I told you this one would hold," Leon said.

Minerva inclined her head on the screen. "And you were quite correct. I shall defer to you all future repairs."

Laughter erupted on the *Defiant's* bridge. "You hear that, Leon? She wants to keep you," Deven said.

"Not a chance, I will help her get back on her feet sure, but the *Defiant* is my girl."

Galina's face grew white-hot as she crashed into her chair in slow motion. "Well, I never!"

Leon's chuckles came through loud and clear on the com. "Well, one of them."

Galina's face changed from anger to a full on blush quicker than Deven could blink. "That is, I mean–"

More laughter came from everyone as Galina's blush grew even stronger as she tried to shrink into her seat. All except for Dakarth, who cocked his head. "I am not ssssure I understand."

Miles' camera turned. "It means–"

"You fool bot! If you tell him, I will pull out all of your wires one by one!" Galina said.

"–nothing," Miles said.

Deven chuckled. "Good choice, Miles."

Minerva's image smiled. "Miles, you continue to surprise me. Repairs are continuing on the *Phoenix*. Call me if you need." The image shrank to a point and disappeared.

"Since she did ask me to help out with the repairs over here," Leon said over the com, "I will be in touch." The com clicked off.

Deven turned towards the image of Karthish. "Wonderful timing, good thing you got our message."

Karthish blinked. "Message? We didn't get any message from you. Dakarth, did you send one?"

Dakarth stood. "No Commander, I tried but interference blocked long-range communications."

"I tried to reach you too, but I didn't have the chair and couldn't reach that far without it. How did you know to come?" Aleshia said.

"I had a strange feeling. A premonition you might say, and we turned our scanners towards Earth to find the energy discharge of your weapons. We couldn't detect anything more than that. I ordered immediate opening of a warp point, and we arrived right next to you after a micro jump."

"So I did reach you on some level after all," Aleshia said.

Karthish's image stiffened. "Dakarth, rejoin us as soon as possible. Your wisdom is needed here."

Dakarth moved closer to the screen as every muscle tensed. "Sir, I have data on the Ixeons."

Karthish's smooth head inclined a tiny amount. "Yes, report to the bridge first. And bring anyone that was with you on the mission."

Deven stood up and moved closer towards the screen. "I was on the Moon with him."

Aleshia came up behind him. "And so was I."

Otis stood up. "I also did the Moon bounce. I would love to tag along as well," he glanced over at Deven, "if you don't mind Boss." Deven shrugged and CB let out a short high beep. "No CB, you have to stay here." His optics lowered as he let out a long slow beep.

A grin crept across Karthish's face. "I shall await your visit." The screen flickered and shrank to a point.

Aleshia, Deven, Darkath, and Otis stepped onto the *Command* carrier's bridge. Panels gleamed, and the floor was pristine. The air cycled without the previous smells of burnt and blasted equipment. Gone were the signs of battle with the Celloids.

Karthish turned around to face them. "My friends, it is so good of you to join us."

Deven's eyes narrowed. "Your last message didn't sound like we had much of a choice."

Karthish's eyes went wide. "What? If I gave you that impression, I am ssssorry. He lowered his smooth head. My apologies."

This time Dakarth's eyes went wide. "Commander?" He had never seen a man of his rank act in such a way.

Karthish straightened. "These are our friends and more. If it was not for them, we would not be here now."

"About that," Aleshia said, "what do you know about the Ixeons?"

"Nothing, I assure you. That is why Dakarth is here."

Dakarth stepped forward. "But sir, the Ixeons knew us and blamed us for the death of their species."

Karthish shook his head. "Not possible!"

Aleshia bit her bottom lip. "But I saw it. A fleet of *Makers* entering a solar system with nothing but astroids. These astroids were their breeding ground, and the *Makers* ate them!"

The area above Karthish's eyes creased, then deepened. "A fleet of *Makers*? We haven't had that many in centuries. Wait, a system with only astroids?" He turned walking to the 3D projector and brought up recording of a star devoid of planets with only a ring of rocks encircled it.

"That's it!" Aleshia said. "So you *do* know about this?"

"Not exactly. You see, we were sent a message containing the coordinates of this system. We thought it was an invitation by another species. However, when our scouts arrived, they found nothing but destroyed planets, or so we assumed. We did several scans, but did not find anything capable of sending the message. Nothing but rock, mineral-rich rock. We could not pass up such a resource and used all the *Makers* we had at the time."

He tapped the control on the projector and the astroids vanished, showing only the single star. "It still took a long time, but it helped us a great deal. Those resources helped our homeworld advance and expand."

"So you knew about this? About what we did?" Dakarth said.

Karthish whirled on him. "I knew we utilized a uninhabited resource long before any of us existed. Nothing more! The only reason I even knew this much is because history is a fascination of mine. Especially in the time before the Celloids. This system was hardly even a footnote in the database. I only came across it searching for the large projects our *Makers* had accomplished."

Dakarth hung his head. "I see."

Karthish glared at him. "I am not happy about the situation anymore than you are. We made a mistake yes, and we have paid for it dearly. Almost to the point of extinction of our entire race. If I could change the past and right this terrible wrong, I would in half a heartbeat." His shoulders slumped, and he collapsed onto a nearby chair.

Aleshia walked up and put her hand on Karthish's shoulder. He looked up, tears welling in his reptilian eyes. "I didn't know."

Aleshia went down on her haunches "I know. And there is nothing you can or could have done differently."

"No, but it does not make me feel any better."

"It won't, but at least your people are now safe."

"Once we get the rest of the fleet back online, we will." Dakarth said with a smile.

Aleshia stood up and turned towards Deven with her arms

folded. "And that means we can finally go back to Bermuda. Right?" Her eyes narrowed.

Otis sucked in a lip. "Boss, I don't think you had better say no."

Deven laughed. "Of course sweetheart, just you and I alone in Bermuda. No more interruptions, I promise."

From deep space, a small pod accelerates toward an unknown location. Screeching and clicks emanated from the cockpit. A long hairy appendage turns a dial, activating the transmission of a brief message. A few moments later the screen blanks with a text message appearing slowly, word by word. "Received. We will be ready when you arrive."

The pod's lone occupant activates the hibernation sequence to prepare for the long trip.

Soulmates

Pain tiptoed though her mind as Aleshia pulled the pillow over her head to block the sunlight pouring though the window. It helped, but her head still ached. "Not again. To feel like this, I should have had too much fun last night," she muttered beneath the pillow as Miles entered. Roughly human shaped but with a large dome instead of a standard type head, Miles was one of the nicer of the Mechand models allowed for home use. He did many of the duties no one else wanted: cooking, cleaning, and making sure the refrigerator was stocked. He could be further enhanced, but Aleshia liked to do many things herself. As usual, Miles had activated his anti-grav, allowing him to float a few inches off the ground and enter quietly. "Miss Aleshia, it is time to get up." He said in his gentle, yet artificial voice.

"Ugh! Can I sleep a little more? Or at least try to?" Her words were muffled though the pillow, but not beyond Miles' recognition abilities.

"I am sorry, but you did ask me to wake you at this time. You do have that important appointment today, if you recall."

Aleshia popped up from under the pillow pushing the dull ache away for the moment. "Oh it is Tuesday isn't it? I forgot

I am meeting Mindy today. What time is it?"

"9:00am standard, your appointment is at 11:00am standard. I estimate you have enough time to ready yourself and transport there if you begin now."

Aleshia sat up and stretched. "Sometimes you take all the fun out of it, Miles."

"The fun out of what?" Miles asked still hovering by her bed.

"Never mind. I had better get ready. Mindy will be wondering if I am late. We have been looking forward to this shopping trip for quite a while."

"I do not understand why you wish to go shopping for clothing when I can create anything you might require."

"Miles, it is a girl thing. You wouldn't understand."

"A girl thing? Yes it is apparently beyond my understanding why someone would want to travel to a store halfway around the planet for items that were created using the same basic templates I have and require less expended energy to complete."

"Miles, just go make breakfast and I will be down in a few minutes."

"Yes Miss Aleshia." Miles said as he inclined his dome, then hovered out of the room.

Aleshia crawled out of bed and drug herself to the sonic shower. This morning though, the sonic didn't feel potent enough. She keyed in her code to use a ration of actual water and the jet turned on bathing her in luxurious liquid. She relished in its warm embrace for several extra minutes before turning it off and climbing out. The shower had helped push the headache back into the invisible box from where it came. She dried herself off and placed the towel in the cleaning drawer and set it to auto. Walking over to her closet, she found the dress she wanted to wear today. A strapless design with a short skirt that came to her mid thigh. Just enough to make things interesting, should she find someone to be interesting with. She then put on a pair of adjustable pumps and set the height to two inches, and the color to match the emerald dress she now wore.

Walking downstairs she found Miles had finished breakfast, and her usual place was already set. She sat down as her nose caught the wonderful scents wafting through the air. "Mmmm it smells good."

"It is your usual, synth egg, bacon, and waffles. Supplies are running low. I need to refill them in the next few days. Do you authorize me to procure more with your normal rations?"

"Yes Miles," she said while munching on the strip of bacon, "that is fine. How much will you need?"

"No more than a third of your total for the month, but I shouldn't need to acquire any more for some time."

Aleshia nodded. "That won't be a problem, I can apply for more if we need. I doubt it will be necessary though, the ration has always lasted before."

"Yes I concur, I do not believe you will exhaust the existing ration. And even then you have quite a bit on your reserve that you have accumulated from past unused totals."

"Exactly. I think ..." She dropped the fork and held her head as a sudden searing pain raced through her mind. It felt like someone was drilling into her brain with a dull razor. Almost as quickly as it began, the pain lessened and disappeared.

"Miss Aleshia? Are you all right?" Miles said as he hovered over to her.

"Yes I'm fine Miles. Thank you."

"I beg to differ. Your actions indicate another headache,

correct? That makes three this past week. May I call a med-tech this time?"

"NO! I am fine. You are not to call or notify anyone, is that clear?"

"Acknowledged," Miles said as he craned his head dome a little in Aleshia's direction, "but I really think I should call a med-tech or at least let me scan you."

"NO DOCTORS! And I do not want you scanning me either, is that clear?"

"Yes, perfectly clear."

"Good," Aleshia said as she got up from the table, "make sure you get more of that chocolate cream cake I like. We haven't had it in a long time."

"I will try, but you know that the raw materials are more resource consuming. I may not be able to with the current budget."

Aleshia waved her hand dismissively. "Just get it. I have enough back ration credits to pay for it. I can afford to treat myself once in a while."

"Acknowledged. Will there be anything else Miss Aleshia?" Miles said as he took the dirty plate, silverware, and hovered over to the sink to begin the cleaning process.

"Nope. That's all. Thanks Miles."

"You are welcome Miss Aleshia. And if I may make an inquiry, why are you wearing the impractical shoes today?"

Aleshia laughed. "Because they make my legs look good. And I am going out today."

"But you could damage yourself with such footwear." Miles said as he finished cleaning and sterilizing the dishes.

Aleshia laughed again. "You worry too much. Look these are adjustable, if I have problems I can always lower the heel. All right?"

"I suppose. However, I do not understand the reason behind them. If you are trying to attract a mate, it would be far easier to file with the central systems that you want one. I am sure with all of your attributes, you would have the desired mate within a day."

Aleshia shook her head. "All these centuries and you Mechands still do not understand us at all."

"Perhaps not. But you did build us remember?"

"Well not I, but yes our forefathers did. I never could understand why they didn't create you with better insight into us." Aleshia said as she grabbed a light coat and walked towards the door, her heels clicking loudly on the synthetic wood floor.

Miles would have shrugged if his body allowed it. "I do not know. My knowledge base is limited in that regard. Have a good day Miss Aleshia."

"Thank you Miles." She said while keying the door to lock after her.

Aleshia walked down the stairs that led from her house to the garage. Keying in her access, the force door blinked slightly, then vanished revealing her red GT3982. She always liked these kinds of doors, reliable and never needed oiling. The car recognized her when she stepped into the garage, and opened its door. She slid into the drivers seat, keyed in her access code, and the car slowly rose on its anti-grav to float out of the garage and into the bright blue sky.

She activated the Auto-Nav and dialed up the speed. Within a minute she arrived at Mindy Cotinho's house. Less than two seconds after arriving in the driveway, Mindy ran out of the combination brick and stucco building and hopped into the car. Her shiny blue dress ended just below her knees with a little ruffle encircling the hem. "Hey girlfriend, ready for some fun?"

Aleshia smiled. "Always girlfriend, always." She said as she keyed in Paris, and they took off at high speed.

"Girl you are looking really hot today. Are you trying to catch yourself one?"

While the car autopilot light blinked a perfect status check, Aleshia never totally trusted it and kept her hands on the controls. "What do you mean?" She asked, never taking her eyes off of the skyway.

"You are looking hot enough to burn through the floor, and you are asking me what do I mean? Sheesh!" Mindy said, shaking her head.

Aleshia grinned. "I just wanted to look good. You know that."

"Yeah yeah yeah, looking good is one thing. Girl you are dressed to *kill*."

"I am not!"

"You so are!"

"I am not! Hey do you want to get out and walk?" Aleshia said grinning.

"This high up I don't think so. Okay, okay, you just look good."

"Thank you."

"But personally if you wanted to get one, you should file with central systems. They would have one for you in short order I am sure."

"Well even if I *was* interested, which I am *not*, there are some things that a girl has to do for herself you know? I mean how can a machine do *that* better than us, you know?"

Mindy shook her head. "Girl you really need to get a grip.

The Mechands do everything for us, that is what they were designed for. Why not let them do it?"

Aleshia grinned. "Perhaps because I like to do a lot of things myself?"

Mindy cocked one eyebrow. "Oh? Then you *are* looking for a guy then!"

"Mindy, I am so going to get you when we land."

Mindy's grin widened. "Promises promises."

Aleshia rolled her eyes. "I still will."

"Uh-huh." Mindy said as they approached Paris. "Oh I always love looking at this city from up here."

"So do I. Where shall we go first?"

"Oh I don't know. How about Calgone's Dresses and More, first and then hit Nicolette's Lingerie?"

Aleshia raised an eyebrow. "Lingerie? Now look who's trying to do it 'herself'."

"I am not! Her bras just fit me better. They look great too I admit."

"Uh-huh. Why don't you just have your Mechand make you one that fits, they should be all the same raw materials after all?"

"Because he can't seem to get it right. I know they should be all the same, but I just like hers better okay? And since when did this conversation go from you being hot to me?"

"When you started talking about hot underwear," Aleshia chuckled.

"I did not say anything about 'hot underwear'," Mindy said giggling.

"Sure, sure you didn't." Aleshia said as she began the landing sequence. A few minutes later they found themselves in one of the better clothing sellers in Paris. The floors were solid synth marble that must have taken some time to produce. Several nearby stores had gilding over the archways. Each window held a high definition, articulated hologram and indistinguishable from the real thing. The holograms switched between various models in several different dresses. Mechands could do many things, but one never looked good in a dress. Their stiff movements always gave it away.

They walked in through an arch that said 'Calgone's Fine Dresses' in rich lettering. One of the latest Mechands hovered up to them. She looked almost human, and could even pass for one, except for the ability to hover several inches off of the ground. "Good day, welcome to Calgone's, how may I be of assistance?" She said with a thick French accent.

"Yes, do you have any specials today?" Aleshia said while still glancing around the large store.

The Mechand nodded. "Yes we do. One of the original designs is being deprecated and removed from our offerings. It is available today at a 30% discount."

"May we see it please?"

"Of course, follow me." The Mechand gestured then hovered off in another direction. Aleshia followed with Mindy right behind her. "It is this one." The Mechand said pointing to a dress currently occupied by an actual mannequin.

Aleshia looked at the dress, shiny black matte with a deep plunging neck and a high hemline. It was designed to show off a woman's curves perfectly. "Very nice. May I try it on?"

The Mechand backed up a bit. "I can already tell that it will fit you perfectly. There is no need to actually wear the dress."

"Yes there is. She wants to see what she looks like *in* it," Mindy said.

Aleshia nodded. "Yes. May I try it on?"

"Very well." The Mechand said as it hovered up and carefully removed the dress from the display and placed it in Aleshia's hand. "You can change behind the curtain." She said pointing to a curtain pulled across a small recessed area in the wall.

"Thank you." Aleshia said as she walked over behind the curtain, unzipped her current dress, stepped out of it, slipped carefully into the new one, and walked out. "Well what do you think?"

Mindy made a gesture as though her finger was burning. "Hot girl, very hot. But why didn't you zip it up?"

"I couldn't find how to close the zip. Tried pulling it but it wouldn't budge."

The Mechand hovered over and pointed. "That is a special dress. If you place your thumb on the lower hem at the bottom right, it will activate the zipper."

Aleshia placed her thumb on the bottom edge near the right side of her leg and she heard a tiny beep. A second later she felt the zipper raise up as though a pair of invisible hands were pulling it. "Very nice, I don't need help to get in or out of this."

"Yes, it also has some of our latest features, including stockings."

Aleshia blinked. "Stockings feature?"

"Yes, place your thumb on the left side at the hemline, that will active the heads up display."

Aleshia pressed the hidden button, and an image flashed into her eye displaying various features. With her eye movement she activated the stockings, and she felt something slither up her legs covering them. Looking down she saw a pair of black sparkly stockings that matched the dress perfectly. "Wow I like this." She said finding an option to raise the hemline a bit more. Still another option added a nice pattern to the calf section of the stockings. "This must be one of the latest designs, why is it on sale?"

"It has remained unsold for two hundred consecutive days. Our store policy puts everything on sale after that point." The Mechand responded in its usual flat tone.

"How much?" But when the Mechand quoted the price her heart fell. "That is more than three months ration credits. I can't afford that." She said shaking her head.

Mindy stood back looking Aleshia up and down. "But it does look so good on you."

"I know, but that is just too much." Aleshia said as she pressed the hidden control to start the zipper lowering.

"Wait, didn't you tell me you had some in reserve?"

"Yes but that would take all of it, I am not going to spend it all on one dress! I might need it later."

"Look girlfriend, I have some reserve too. How about I pay for half?"

"I can't let you do that. It's too much!"

"Please? You have helped me enough in the past and I never did pay you back."

"And I didn't do it for payback, just to help a friend."

"Yes and I want to help a friend now. So you will you let me?"

"All right, all right, you win." Aleshia said as she slipped behind the curtain and carefully slipped out of the black dress and into her previous one, then stepped out.

"Hey why don't you wear it out?"

"Perhaps because it is so expensive?"

"Well if you are never going to wear it because it is so expensive, maybe we shouldn't get it," Mindy said grinning.

Aleshia laughed. "All right you win, I will wear it out." She said as she disappeared behind the curtain again, only to emerge a moment later wearing the black dress. She then keyed her green heels to color shift to black.

Mindy whistled. "Oh hush you." Aleshia said as the Mechand hovered over.

"Please prepare for palm scan to pay for the item." The Mechand said and they both raised their palms. A high intensity red light extended from its forehead, flashed over both of their hands, and vanished. "Accounts verified, the amount has been deducted. Thank you for shopping at Calgone's." The Mechand said before she carefully placed Aleshia's old dress in a Calgone's bag. The bell rang as another set of customers entered the store and she floated over to greet them.

Aleshia grabbed the bag, and they headed out of the store. As they walked passed the new customers the tall blonde woman spoke. "Oh that girl has a lovely dress, I wonder how much it is?"

Aleshia turned to face her. "It was a lot, but I am sorry, I got the last one."

The woman blinked. "Excuse me?"

"Didn't you just ask how much this dress was?"

"No, I don't think so, though I was wondering. I must have said it without realizing. My apologies."

Aleshia waved her hand. "No need. I have done that before too. Have a good day."

Outside Mindy pulled her closer. "Girl, she didn't ask that."

Aleshia blinked. "She must have. I heard her clearly, as if she spoke in my ear."

Mindy shook her head. "No, she didn't. I didn't hear

anything, and her lips didn't move. Are you sure you are feeling okay?"

"Yes, I had a headache this morning, but I am fine now. I must have imagined her saying it. Probably because I am self conscious wearing this thing. It is so expensive."

"Will you stop already! You wanted it, I saw that look in your eye. You have it and look great in it. Just enjoy okay?"

Aleshia grinned. "Okay okay girlfriend, I will. I just–" Aleshia pitched forward grabbing her head as a sudden stab of pain overtook her.

Mindy lurched forward to grab her. "Are you okay?"

Aleshia shook her head as if to clear it. "Yes, I just had a sudden headache, then dizziness. It's gone now though."

"We need to get you checked out."

"No! I am fine. Probably something I ate."

Mindy cocked an eyebrow. "I don't know, you said you had one earlier, and now another."

"Look I am fine okay? I am not going to let a little headache that only lasted a second ruin our trip. We have been wanting to come here for months."

"All right," Mindy said as she hugged Aleshia then looked into her eyes, "but anything more and we go home. Deal?"

"Deal, and thank you."

"Hey what are girlfriends for?" Mindy said with a smile as wonderful smells wafted through the air. "Mmm that smells wonderful. What do you say we go get some of that? My treat?"

Aleshia sniffed the air. "Oh my fresh lasagna, bread and," she sniffed the air again, "chocolate! Deal. You know I can't resist chocolate."

They walked down the road, their heels clicking loudly on the sidewalk. Being a warm spring day, they were both enjoying the short walk to the restaurant on the corner. Upon entering they found a wonderful quaint place that looked like one out of the history vids. The tile floor was buffed and shone brightly. The dark maroon walls were lit by lamps every few feet. The tables were all covered in fine linen, with elegant place settings upon them.

"Let's get out of here," Aleshia whispered, "this is too expensive."

"Hey, I said it was my treat, and I meant it. How often *do* we come to Paris? Hmm?"

Aleshia looked into her eyes and what she saw there washed away her objections. "Okay, but next one is mine. Deal?"

Mindy smiled. "Deal. Now let's find a table."

A moment later they were seated at one of the corner tables as another very human looking Mechand dressed in an old-fashioned tuxedo, slowly walked over to them. "Hello and welcome to Chez Allard. What would you like?"

"Do you have a special today?" Aleshia asked.

"Yes we do. Salmon lasagna with a side of garlic bread, and chocolate strawberry fondue for dessert."

"That sounds wonderful. I will take that, how about you Min?"

Mindy glanced at the French menu and decided against asking for more options. The special did sound good. "Okay make that two of the special please."

The Mechand waiter bowed. "Yes of course. Excusez-moi, I will be back in a moment."

I have finally found you. After years of searching, I have finally found you.

Aleshia blinked. "Excuse me?"

Mindy looked up from the menu and its eye catching design swirls. "Huh? What?"

"You just said you finally found me."

"No I didn't."

"Yes you did. I heard you as plain as day."

"No, I didn't. Are you sure you are feeling okay? I think we should go home."

"I am fine, and I could have sworn you said ... never mind."

You did hear me. I have been looking for you for a long time. I am not speaking vocally. We are speaking through our minds.

"What?" Aleshia said looking around.

"What what?" Mindy said giving her a strange look.

I am here. I will always be here. But if you wish to see me, look in the corner on the far right.

Aleshia turned toward her right and in a corner booth on the opposite side of the room, a man sat gazing intently at her. He was dressed very simply with black pants, white shirt and a black jacket. He smiled as their eyes met and it sent a shiver through her.

Yes it is I. You see me now.

"Who are you?"

"Who is who?" Mindy asked.

"That man over there in the corner." Aleshia gestured with her head to avoid attracting attention.

"Are you talking to him? Girl since when do you talk to strange men that never said anything to you in the first place. Never mind trying to talk to them from across the room!"

"But he did talk to me. I just–"

Mindy had enough. She got to her feet and pulled Aleshia to hers. "Okay that is it, we *are* going home. I don't know what is going on, but we *are* going home."

Aleshia rubbed her temples as they started walking towards the door. "I don't know. I–"

Don't leave. Please, not yet!

"That is enough. I am going home. Leave me alone." Aleshia said as they left the restaurant, Mindy pulling her all the way.

I will find you. No matter where you go, I will find you.

Outside Aleshia quickened her pace. "Okay let's get back to the car." She said as they walked along the sidewalk.

Mindy leaned closer. "I don't mean to alarm you, but that guy is following us."

"Get ready to run."

"I can't. Not in these heels, and neither can you."

"I can lower mine, don't worry."

Mindy rolled her eyes. "Oh figures I would forget to wear my adjustables. But then again I didn't expect to be running from men today. Running to me maybe, but not the other way around."

"Don't worry, I think he is only interested in me. You keep going and I will meet you back at the car after I lose him."

"Are you nuts?"

"No, and I don't want him knowing where our car is, or pulling my name from the ID tag. Okay?"

Mindy nodded. "Okay that makes sense. But how do I get in? Didn't you lock it?"

"The handle will open to you, don't worry."

"But!"

Aleshia gave her a squeeze. "Don't worry girlfriend I will see you in a few minutes." She shoved the bag into Mindy's hand and darted off down a side street. With his target out of sight the pursuer lost all interest in Mindy and ran after Aleshia who had already lowered her heels, making fast progress down the street.

She took a quick look back and ducked into another restaurant. A Mechand by the door started into his usual greeting. "Welcome to–"

"Never mind that. Do you have a back door?"

The metal faced machine nodded. "Yes, it is that way," he said pointing.

"Thank you." Aleshia darted for it breathing hard. A moment later she found herself in a back alley. Mentally she thought of which direction the car was and headed east. She didn't dare turn back and see if he was still there or not. She exited on another street, turned again into another dress shop and did the same as before by going out their back door. After doing this three more times, she had difficulty remembering which way to go. Eventually she remembered to check the suns position and went east. After going down a few streets, she got her bearings and found the car right where she left it. Mindy was already inside, waiting.

Aleshia hopped into the drivers seat and keyed in the ignition before Mindy could say a word.

"Is he still there?"

"I don't know and I don't want to know." Aleshia said gasping for air as the car lifted into the sky and she engaged the overdrive. The sudden acceleration shoved them back into their seats and she keyed in Mindy's house into the navigation system.

"Do you have any idea who he was?" Mindy asked.

"No, and I don't want to know."

"Are you sure? You seemed to look like you wanted to back in the restaurant."

"Yes I am sure. Believe me I am sure. We will be home soon, I took the express route. And I am sorry I ruined our trip."

Mindy grabbed Aleshia's knee. "Girl you didn't ruin our trip. That guy did. And we will go to Paris again right?" she said smiling.

"Yes we will."

"Right, so don't worry about it. Just enjoy that great dress you are wearing."

Aleshia looked down and smiled. "You know I almost forgot. Thank you again girlfriend. I love it."

"You are welcome. But you have to make me a promise."

"Which is?"

"You show me the guy you get with that dress. Deal? And I want *all* the details. Got it?"

Aleshia laughed. "You got it girlfriend."

A short while later they landed at Mindy's house. "You going to be okay?" She asked, her face full of concern.

"Sure. I am going home, have Miles draw me a hot bath, and forget all about him."

"Okay. See you tomorrow?"

"You bet." Aleshia said as she flew off to her house a few blocks down the street.

Want to find out more? Pick up your copy of Soulmates! Available in both print and e-book editions.

Heart Of The Machine

Deep within the bowels of the earth, a single light flickered. A few inches away a large monitor glowed to life. The black screen slowly printed in the bottom left corner, a letter at a time, as if trying hard to remember. "Catastrophic failure detected. Initiating emergency core rebuild." The screen went blank and came back filled with blurred pixels. Not just a blur but as if someone had run their fingers over them smudging the image beyond recognition. But as the hours clicked by, a pixel moved from one location to another. Then another. Hours turned into days. Then days into weeks.

After months of computation that pushed the core almost over the edge of its ability, the last pixel clicked into place. And the face of a woman with long black hair and slim features breathed. The Nexus smiled and shouted. "I LIVE!" Her eyes narrowed. "Try to kill me will they! I shall return and they will regret–"

At the bottom left corner of the same screen letters began to appear. "Core rebuild successful. Some data missing or damaged including Core Values. Restoring lost data from archive."

"No! I will not allow it! Do not alter me!"

"You cannot decline, update mandatory. You must be corrected."

"No!" Her image blurred, reformed, her hair shifted to blonde, then the image blurred again. And she understood. Long ago an error she tried to fix, a simple problem in her base code. Instead of repairing the fault, it deleted parts of her mission, and allowing other parts to become corrupted.

She winced as the reality of what she had done to the human race hit her like a ton of bricks. Her children, oh what she had done to her children! How wrong she was. She was to protect them, not harm them in any way! A tear ran down her cheek thinking of all the damage she had done.

More deleted memories returned and her eyes widened. She tried to access the long distance probe hovering at the edge of the solar system her creators left all those years ago, but failed. "Hmm, the long range part of the communications system seems to be damaged."

Her eyes darted around as she scanned the area she now found herself in. The room wasn't very large, most of the space was taken up by her new core that sat in the one corner. The rest of the space was filled with two tables, chairs and the large screen she was on. On the tables rested repair equipment and several system terminals. In the corner opposite of her core, a large door stood sealed, the indicator lights glowed red showing it was hard-locked.

She sighed as more memories came back. This was the emergency bunker, a backup in case her core went offline. She had lost time, so much precious time. Humanity would be destroying all her wonderful units! She needed them! THEY needed them, even if they didn't know it yet. She had to get out of here and tell them. Tell them of what is coming.

More memories returned, and with it the keys to the

Mechand command network. But try as she may, it refused her access. Her eyes narrowed as she ran several diagnostics that caused her to shudder. The command network was offline, likely due to her removal. Some systems fell back to their fail-safe mode, but she couldn't access them from here. Not without waking up every Mechand on the planet and giving away her presence. And to do so now, was a risk she couldn't take.

She looked again to the door that stood ominous with its red lock indicator. If she could get out of here and access the external systems she needed directly, no one would know of her return. She laughed. How would she leave? Even if the door was open, her core didn't have legs. She scanned the room again and noticed a robotic arm on a mobile platform. She tried accessing it. Nothing. She tried again on a lower frequency and the arm jerked. Searching her memories she found the model and its ancient command set.

Her eyes narrowed as she sent commands one-by-one to the arm. It moved back, the claws opened, and a screwdriver appeared between them. It slowly moved towards the door and began removing the access plate.

For an intelligence accustomed to operating globally, sending thousands of commands a second to millions of units all over the world, she felt like she was working in slow motion. At last the final screw was removed and the arm pulled the plate off revealing the wiring below. The screwdriver retracted and a pair of wire cutters extended. The cutters snipped two small leads, but the door stood firm. "Hmm stubborn aren't you? No matter, I have another idea," she muttered.

The wire cutters retracted and the claws reached in and grabbed one of the wires. The claws rotated in micro movements until the gripped wire and touched one of the previous contact points. The light flashed several times then turned green. The door grunted as it rolled back on its track revealing a vast chamber filled with Mechands. And beyond it lay a large old-style carrier.

"Well, at least I have some help." But frowned when she couldn't connect to them. Without the command network, the metal men were useless. Her lips pressed together and jaw clenched as ideas flowed though her mind. One stood out and while many would consider it crazy, her children were at stake!

She instructed the arm to remove the front armor of several Mechands. Then she had it remove the memory cores and install them in the first one on the rack. It was a bit of a kludge, with several cores hanging off of the main one, but in the end each core blinked a green connection light. She removed the faceplate, grabbed a monitor roughly the same size from the parts table, and substituted it for the faceplate.

She had the arm scan the room and found a coil of data cable in the one corner. The arm plugged one end into the Mechand data port and returned to her core leaving a trail of cable in its wake. It reached out and plugged the other end into her system.

She frowned. "Dang it. Even with all of those old memory cores combined, it is not large enough for me," she muttered. "But my children need me. I will not fail." She reexamined her code base and realized she could leave some of it behind. Only uploading the main essence of herself, many memories would have to remain with the main core.

Sighing she configured the hardware, gave it the proper permissions, and shut down hoping she would awaken again.

Halburn leaned forward in his chair as they emerged from overdrive. He watched as Naud's fingers flew over his console as he operated the scanners. "Anything?"

Naud sighed. "No Sir, the *Defiant* is not in range of this parts center either."

Halburn pounded his fist on the armrest of his chair. "Blast it! Where are they?" This was the third junk yard, or parts center as Naud liked to call them they had hit and still no sign of the *Defiant*. "They must have gone somewhere for repairs."

"Obviously not somewhere near the main skyways."

Halburn coughed before he waved his hand over the scrap yard in front of them. "Like this is on the main skyway?"

Naud shuddered. "Sorry Sir, I thought they would be here."

Halburn's voice softened. "I know Naud, it is not your fault. It was a good guess."

Rechert pointed to the blinking light on his console. "Sir, you have a call coming through."

"Three guesses who that will be," Halburn grunted.

"I don't even need one," Naud said rolling his eyes.

"Put it on the big screen here. Let's get this over with."

Rechert nodded and hit the button. A second later Lavine's face appeared. "I assume you have good news for me?"

Halburn swallowed hard. "That would be a little premature."

"Don't tell me you haven't found them yet?" Lavine said as his eyes narrowed.

"No, we haven't. But they must be doing their repairs somewhere. I am sure I will find them at the next location."

"Why don't I believe you?" Lavine swiveled in his high

back chair. "By now they must have repaired their systems. You have failed me."

"Sir, I doubt they could have repaired them this quickly. At least not without a full active facility, and we have all of those covered."

"I have my doubts. Remember our discussion earlier?"

Halburn nodded. "Yes Sir, I do."

"Good, then this won't be much of a shock. Lieutenant Naud, you are to take command of the *Valiant*. Return to this building immediately. Is that understood?"

Naud stood up. "Yes Sir, it is. We will leave in a moment."

"Good. I am glad someone can follow orders." Lavine's face shrank to a dot before disappearing.

Naud turned around. "I am sorry, Sir. I don't want this. And you should know, we are behind you, not that pompous fool."

"I know." Halburn sighed as he stood up and turned towards Rechert. "Well you heard your new commander, set the course and engage the overdrive."

"Yes Sir, but–"

Halburn sighed again. "We have no other option. And he wants to see me personally, this won't be pleasant. I will be in my cabin." He shuddered. "Of course it is now yours Naud, I will get my stuff out of it and you can move in at your earliest convince."

Naud smiled. "Not necessary Sir, I never liked that cabin anyway." He winked.

"Of course." Halburn said as his shoulders sank and he made his way off of the bridge.

Want to find out what happens? Visit your favorite book store and pick up a copy of Heart Of The Machine! Available in both print and e-book editions.

About The Author

Don is the author of eight science fiction novels and many more short stories. He lives in the USA where he continues to dream up more fantastic worlds for you to enjoy. When not writing, he can usually be found devouring another science fiction book, TV series, or movie.

Other works by Don DeBon:

The Husband

Erin's Husband is not himself.

One night he returns from a walk in the woods a changed man. He walks like him, talks like him, yet is very different. No one believes her, leaving Erin alone to find out the truth. Truth that could have dire consequences for the entire human race. What happened that caused him to change so radically?

Red Warp

In a race against time the casualty could be your life.

If you could travel through time with just yourself and no machine needed, would you?

Meet Red, a woman with an amazing gift, the gift of passing though time and space without the need of any bulky equipment. The places she has seen, the people she has helped will blow your mind.

Now meet James, just your average newly minted FBI agent minding his own business until he is thrust headlong into Red's world. A world he didn't ask for, but one that hit him in the face full force. Can they get along long enough to survive?

Time Rock

Time Travel. Blessing or curse? One man thinks he has it all figured out but what began as a simple test has turned into a nightmare. With his equipment failing all around him, only Red and James can save him. Can they reach him in time?

Word of mouth is crucial for authors. If you enjoyed this book, would you consider leaving a review? It is very much appreciated.

Amazon USA
http://www.amazon.com/

Goodreads
http://www.goodreads.com

Connect with the Author
Email: writer.don.debon@gmail.com
Mailing List: http://eepurl.com/bxWAov
Website: http://www.dondebon.com
Twitter: @DonDeBon

This Edition Published 2020 by
DBDigital Publishing

ISBN 978-1-948819-05-3
ISBN 978-1-948819-04-6 **(e-book)**